Sebastian
Faulks

Snow
Country

HUTCHINSON
HEINEMANN

1 3 5 7 9 10 8 6 4 2

Hutchinson Heinemann
20 Vauxhall Bridge Road
London SW1V 2SA

Hutchinson Heinemann is part of the Penguin Random House group of companies
whose addresses can be found at global.penguinrandomhouse.com

First published in the United Kingdom by Hutchinson Heinemann in 2021

www.penguin.co.uk

A CIP catalogue record for this book is available from
the British Library.

ISBN 9781786330185 (hardback)
ISBN 9781786330192 (trade paperback)

Typeset in 13/16.5 pt Fournier MT
by Integra Software Services Pvt. Ltd, Pondicherry

Printed and bound in Great Britain by Clays Ltd, Elcograf S.p.A.

The authorised representative in the EEA is Penguin Random House Ireland,
Morrison Chambers, 32 Nassau Street, Dublin D02 YH68.

Penguin Random House is committed to a sustainable future for
our business, our readers and our planet. This book is made from
Forest Stewardship Council® certified paper.

For Veronica,
with love

The present contains nothing more than the past; and what is found in the effect was already in the cause.

Henri Bergson

Author's Note

This is the second book in a planned Austrian trilogy, the first being *Human Traces* (2005). Each novel can be read on its own, however, without reference to the others.

Lena is pronounced 'Layna', rather than 'Leena'.

PART ONE

1

From his height only a hundred feet above the trees, the pilot could see two people running over the ground below – one coming out of a wood, another through a gate in the lane, clinging on to his hat as he ran. Their goal was a long brown tent, set against a hedgerow that marked the border of a field.

Under the canvas, by the light of two kerosene lamps hung from a wooden pole, the surgeon raised a man's arm above his head. 'Hold this here.' A nurse gripped the wrist in position.

'Name?'

'Heideck,' she said, lifting a tag with her free hand. 'Initial, A.'

The surgeon's fingers numbered the ribs. 'Four ... Five. If in doubt, go high.'

'What?'

'Let's go in here.'

A scalpel cut downwards, through a thin layer of fat and into the flesh. 'Where's the sister? I need someone to hold back the muscle.'

'She hasn't come. But I can do it,' said the nurse. 'I can tie his arm like this, look. Then my hands are free.'

She attached the wrist to a tent pole with her belt and put her fingers in the intercostal space. 'Is that all right?'

'If in doubt, aim posterior,' the surgeon said.

'What?'

'I'm talking to myself. My old instructor in Graz. Don't pull, don't pull. Just lift. Keep it out of my way. I'm going to put my finger under here, into the pleural cavity.'

There was a popping of air as the tissue parted. The man on the trestle remained unmoving, his eyes closed, his arm tethered behind his head. Blood came from his chest, first bubbling, then spurting up and falling over the nurse's shoes and onto the grass round her feet.

In the darkening sky, the biplane banked and turned into the wind, making a long circle over the woods. The pilot could see a vehicle pull up on the farm track. Another man and a woman climbed out and started to run across the field.

'More light,' said the surgeon. 'I must have more light. We need to put a tube in to see if I can drain any fluid.'

He pushed back the left lung with his finger. 'There's a fragment of something here. We're going to have to extend the incision.'

'What?'

'Anterior. A long way. I need to get at what's in there. Is he still out?'

The nurse lifted the man's eyelid with her bloodied fingers. 'Yes.'

'Is there a better scalpel? This one's not very sharp."

Breathing in, the surgeon slid the blade through flesh, making an incision round the ribcage, halfway across the back, the skin recoiling either side of the purple wound.

The tent flap banged open and the man and the woman came in, breathing hard.

'You can wash in that bucket. And there's disinfectant in the bowl,' said the surgeon.

While the others got ready, he swept between the ribs with his fingers. 'Are you all right?' he said to the nurse. 'You look pale.'

'It's the lamplight. I'm fine.'

'We need something to spread the ribs. Otherwise—'

'There's no equipment like that here. It's just a tent where—'

'It's so dark. I can hardly see ...'

With the help of the orderly, he pulled the ribs apart enough to reveal the indifferent heart, twitching in its bony cage.

'He's lucky,' said the surgeon. 'I can see something now. Move him onto his side. Give me the forceps. Don't twist his arm. Untie it now. You: hold his elbow up.'

Dusk was falling on the field as the pilot, his observations made, banked his plane one more time, gained height and set his course for home, fifteen minutes over the blackened landscape, along the river, using the spire of the church to guide him back to the raised landing strip.

'I've got it,' said the surgeon. He dropped a piece of metal into an enamelled tray. 'Help me close the wound. You, stop this bleeding here. Nurse, give me whatever needles you have.'

'We haven't got the kind of thread you need.'

'Just do the best you can. You do know how to sew?'

'We used to make our own dresses at home.'

'Do your best.'

'Is he going to survive?'

'Of course he is. Poor soul.'

2

Anton Heideck had arrived in Vienna at the age of nineteen in the wet autumn of 1906. The fallen leaves stuck to the pavements of the narrow street in Spittelberg in which, after a demoralising search, he'd found a room to rent. He was one of the few students not to press into the cafés after lectures in the hope of catching a glimpse of some literary hero; what he admired were the newspaper dispatches from Viennese correspondents in Paris and Moscow. This could be a life, he dared to think one day, when he was buying a late edition of *Die Presse*. Writing reports from a foreign country might be a way of engaging with the world – not as the protagonist, but as the recorder of other men's actions.

The Styrian town in which he had been brought up was known as a centre of Catholicism and the old ways; to Anton as a boy it had seemed simply disconnected from anything that was urgent, or desirable, or worth striving for. His brother Gerhard was seven years older and did everything that was asked of him by their father: he was the victor ludorum at the school athletics and took his First Communion with shining hair and a pious look; he was the subject of admiring reports from his teachers at the end of the year. His parents hardly seemed to notice Anton, who sometimes wondered if his arrival in the world had come as a surprise to them. Gerhard meanwhile treated him with maddening tolerance, even when Anton brought his best friend Friedrich home from school and used his elder brother's bedroom for a wrestling match.

Their father ran a sausage business, successful enough for Anton to follow Gerhard in due course to the Gymnasium and sit with the other little scholars, their backs aching, their eyes strained by the dim light. Friedrich's family was also in trade, but their timber business was a hundred years old and carried the air of noble forests – unlike the sausage factory, with its daily deliveries from the slaughterhouse. Friedrich, who was fair-haired and taller than Anton, seemed to glide over the surface of the world, knowing the right way to greet a friend of his parents in the street or what to tip a porter. Anton hoped that by walking with him, invariably half a step behind, he might catch something of the grace he lacked.

There was not much in the school curriculum to hold their attention. The days were long, the teaching uninspired; there was no understanding of the need for activity or adventure. A ten-minute break in a corridor was all that was on offer before they resumed their places, two by two, on the wooden benches in the schoolroom. In winter, the hours were extended by the blue light of gas jets; in summer the windows were covered so that the sunlit outdoor life could not distract them from learning.

After lessons, Anton and Friedrich would walk home down the Bahnhofstrasse, talking furiously as they looped through the smarter districts where families had lived in the same houses for three generations. They had laughed at the lack of intellectual curiosity they imagined behind the high railings and double front doors, from where they could hear the sound of piano scales, practised by the daughter of the house in the dying light of a winter afternoon. They swore to one another that they would never descend to such an existence.

Throughout the eight years of school, Anton assumed he would go on to the university in Vienna, then make his life there. To settle anywhere else, he and Friedrich agreed, would make it seem as though they were in some way joking; and, as he discovered within a day of his arrival, Vienna was nothing if not serious. Almost every building was a palace or a concert hall or a ministry. He wondered where the poor people lived; there seemed to be no simple lodgings, no slums or tenements to break up the imperial vistas, with the archduke processing each morning between palaces in his horse-drawn carriage.

The city saw itself as the centre of civilisation. From the excitement with which people spoke about them, it was as though they still expected Beethoven or Haydn to show up any day at the Esterhazys' town house for an impromptu performance. People boasted about how, when the old Burgtheater was to be dismantled and rebuilt, they had been among the audience who refused to leave until they could take away a splinter of the stage in their pockets. Not himself much interested in music, Anton found it hard not to laugh when even the fishmonger offered a critique of the brass band as he strolled in the Prater with his wife on a Sunday afternoon.

After a time, he discovered that there were in fact poor areas of the city, that the grandeur could abruptly stop and the cobbled streets become winding and narrow. His Spittelberg lodging was in a house that belonged to a Polish widow. A commercial traveller and two other students were his fellow lodgers and the house had a distinctive smell, as if hundreds of dead mice had been boiled in strong tea then left to rot behind the plaster. The landlady's daughter, who was said to be a prostitute, lived with her mother on the ground floor. She came and went through a back door that opened onto a courtyard with a low gallery. In the evening, men would walk through from Sigmundsgasse and buy white wine from a stall.

Gerhard, who had studied medicine at his father's insistence, told Anton that if he chose philosophy he could avoid all contact with the university until his final year, when he would have to present a thesis and sit a single exam. The rest of the time could be spent in the bars and concert halls, riding horses and chasing women. He warned Anton that he might never have such a chance again and it was his responsibility – his duty, almost – to make the most of it. This uncharacteristic advice made Anton wonder if his brother wanted him out of the way, so that he would not emerge later as some sort of rival. Gerhard needn't have worried, Anton thought: medicine held no appeal for him.

The main problem for Anton was that he had no money. His mother had wanted him to go straight into the family business; his father could see the advantages of the university, but only if he studied medicine or, at a stretch, law. If he insisted on philosophy, then he would have to fund his own studies – by teaching and whatever odd jobs he could find. Chiefly because he wanted some breathing space after the Gymnasium, Anton agreed; but it was a second-rate experience of the capital. The Opera was beyond his means and he found he was allergic to horses. When it came to women, he was deterred not by shortage of cash but by a lack of confidence. His moustache was an embarrassment; the coarse hairs grew round the rim of his nostrils and out of the lip membrane itself. His eyebrows were thick, his hair wiry and his nose rather hooked. He tried to befriend the landlady's daughter, but she seemed to have sniffed out his poverty. When he suggested an evening together, she laughed. He told himself that women held no interest for him, but it was not easy when the glance of a dark eye that happened to meet his on the street caused him an ache in some space behind the lungs.

After he had graduated with an unremarkable degree, he continued to live in much the same way. His aim was to make a living as a journalist. His first article had been published in the student paper in his second year at the university and he had gone on to write on politics and foreign affairs with a fluency that seemed almost suspicious – as if he somehow didn't mean it. His output was checked when he graduated. Student magazines were happy to take long articles on anything from German naval policy to where you could find the best strudel, but established papers were less keen. Anton lacked gravity and age. One or two of them allowed him a filler in the social or financial pages, but he was unable to persuade them to send him to Paris or New York.

His mother wrote to say that Anton's father despaired of the boy ever making something of himself and she was beginning to feel the same way herself. He put the letter aside.

'I am a superfluous man,' he told Friedrich, as they drank white wine at a table in the courtyard.

'Have you been reading Pushkin again?'

'No, I came to that conclusion all by myself. I've always found it hard to believe that there was any space for me in this world. Anything with my name on it.'

Meanwhile at night in his small room, Anton tried to map out a life that didn't include blood-sausage or the opposite sex. While he waited for another magazine commission, he paid his rent by tutoring the children of rich families in mathematics, French or English; the work enabled him to leave Spittelberg and travel to more pleasant parts of the city.

Among his pupils was a boy called Erich, whose family occupied the entire first floor of a building in Döbling, a wealthy area that backed onto woods and vineyards. Once a week, long after Anton had graduated from the university, he caught a tram there and was let in by the porter. He ran past the doors of the lift, up the curved stone steps two at a time, his feet soundless on the crimson runner, rang the bell and waited for the maid to open it.

On one visit, in the spring of 1913, Anton was waiting in the drawing room, breathing a little heavily from his sprint upstairs, when he heard a piano. At this time of the afternoon, he would have expected the tinkle of an exercise or bagatelle – something

10

built on a pattern with a little flourish at the end, when the variation was complete. What he heard was a piece in which the chord changes seemed to follow no pattern. It was only after two or three minutes' listening that they seemed to make sense. He went to the door of the music room and peered in to see who was producing these mournful sounds.

Behind the vase of cut flowers on the piano, he could see the head of a young woman, tilted downwards as she played. The light from the tall windows fell across the lid of the piano, but the player remained in shadow. It was neither Katrin, the elder sister, nor Birgit, the little one. The music gathered speed, then seemed to run out of steam – to drift away and meander. Anton ventured further into the room, but the pianist was concentrating too hard to look up. As he took a pace or two closer, he could see that she was not following a score and wondered if she might be improvising.

It occurred to him that he should avoid giving her a shock; the last thing this woman in her reverie would want was the sight of him staring at her. He began to retreat over the Turkish rug, but when his shoe touched the parquet, the wood let out a small creak and she looked up.

'I'm so sorry,' said Anton. 'I was intrigued, and I . . . I'm sorry to disturb you.'

'That's all right. I'd almost finished.' She spoke with a foreign accent. He crossed the room to shake hands.

'My name's Anton Heideck. I'm here to give Erich his lesson.'

He didn't catch all she said in return, but gathered her first name was Delphine and that she was there as a companion for Katrin.

'A "companion"?'

'She's supposed to learn French from me.'

'I see. How long have you been here?'

'Three weeks.'

'I haven't seen you before.'

'I try to keep out of the way.'

'And ... do you like Vienna?' It was a feeble thing to say.

Delphine was a little older than he was, perhaps thirty-two or three. Her eyes were expressionless, like the surface of a deep pond; a thin shadow of dark hair ran along her upper lip.

'I do. I have seen very little of it. Katrin's father likes us to be accompanied when we go out. But, yes. I like it.'

'It's ... large, isn't it?'

'I've lived in Paris so I don't mind that.'

'You're a Parisian?'

'My family come from Rouen. Most of them are still there. Have you been to France?'

'No,' said Anton. 'Not yet,' he added, as though his ticket was in the post.

'Are you a teacher by profession?'

'No. I'm ... I don't have a profession. I studied philosophy at the university, travelled a little and now I'm trying to make my way as a writer. Or a journalist, to be more precise. And you, Mademoiselle? Are you a professional musician?'

'Good heavens, no. I would ... At least only in my daydreams. I'm from a family of four daughters in Normandy. One of us is married, the others wait for husbands. Or so my father thinks.'

'Have you been to concerts in Vienna?'

'Only one. A piece by Richard Strauss. I didn't like it.'

'Oh. Would you prefer to hear some ... Beethoven, perhaps? Or Haydn?'

'Or perhaps Mussorgsky. Do you know him? But I doubt that Katrin's father would allow it.'

'Suppose Katrin came too?' He had lost control over the words escaping him. He could never afford three tickets.

'I can ask. Excuse me, I must go and talk some French to her now.'

She left the room with a rustle of silk and Anton heard her footsteps disappear down the corridor, purposefully, as though she couldn't wait.

The last few minutes had disturbed him. It was partly a matter of surprise, encountering this woman from another country who seemed trapped in the stuffy nineteenth district. How many more people lived in that huge apartment, he wondered – an old nurse, or a blind composer toiling over his great symphony … On the other hand, there seemed something inexplicably familiar about Delphine, as though he had known her as a child, or had seen a photograph of her in someone's house.

He met Friedrich for dinner in a cheap restaurant in the Landstrasse district where the waiters would bring second helpings to their favourite customers.

'I'm so tired of being young,' said Friedrich. 'No one takes me seriously. I'm going to grow a beard and a large belly.'

'That's your fault for working in the ministry.'

'In my department no one gets his own office till he's fifty. But don't tell me it's not a problem for you, too.'

'The only two editors who give me any work have no idea how old I am,' said Anton. 'I put on a grave voice on the telephone. I make my prose sound like an old man's.'

'What about your tutoring?'

'Erich's father was reluctant to hire me at first. But I was very cheap. Rich people like a bargain.'

As the waiter brought beer and schnitzel, they agreed that their upbringing had not prepared them for life in the city. Childhood had been enjoyable if dull; then the Gymnasium had crushed them. And while they had laboured in the schoolroom the only virtue praised by their parents at home was 'solidity' – a compound, it seemed, of age and decorum. They wondered what they were meant to do with the next two decades, how they were supposed to spend their reserves of energy and humour until society was ready for them.

Friedrich had decided to live a double life. Having studied law, he had not alienated his parents; three years after graduation, he still received an allowance from his father, on top of his salary. He had somehow got to know the sort of people he had been warned against – actresses and painters' models. Anton wanted to tell Friedrich about the French 'companion' he had met that day, but what was there to say? A pianist who seemed original yet familiar ... Someone he had asked to a concert he couldn't afford ... It was hardly the sort of drama to detain his old friend.

When Anton was a child, neither his mother nor his father, nor for that matter Gerhard, had ever spoken to him about sex. At the Gymnasium there had been a lecture that explained how amphibians reproduced. There were some suggestions in the Bible – including the story of Potiphar's wife, which had made him feel sympathy for Joseph, the object of her advances. At the age of sixteen, when he and Friedrich were on their way home from school one afternoon, they were stopped by a man in the park who offered to sell them postcards of naked women with ankle boots and body hair so abundant he thought they must be from a circus.

Anton concluded that something powerful was being withheld from him and his friends. It still felt unresolved when he arrived in Vienna, where women flaunted themselves on the street. At first he wasn't sure what they were offering; but something in their manner, cooing yet hard, soon made it clear. He discovered they were known as 'line girls' because of an agreement with the police that they would stay close to the buildings, behind an imaginary line drawn down the pavement. They were found not only near old plague pits and cemeteries, but in the best streets off the Ringstrasse. Anton was once tempted enough to fall into conversation with a girl, but only because she looked so forlorn. She quickly made it clear that she could look after herself.

In the books he had read, both in medieval poems and in novels set in run-down passages of Paris, the lovers were obsessed yet pure. If there was physical lovemaking between them it must have taken place on some higher plane, where such things were allowed.

A part of him aspired to this kind of life, but the trouble was that it seemed entirely literary: he had seen no examples of it in his home town – in the husbands and wives, whose marriages seemed like a business partnership, or among young people, whose schools had kept the sexes apart. At the opposite extreme, the street girls of Vienna seemed to be offering the kind of coupling he had glimpsed only once, when his father had taken him to see a supplier at a pig farm. Some natural arrangement, he felt, was being made elusive by a society that had found no way of accommodating it; and it was puzzling that the capital of the greatest empire in the world should have come up so short on the simplest principle of life – like a horse that had thrown its rider at the first fence and whose subsequent run was therefore of little interest.

Friedrich warned him off the line girls with stories of syphilis and the treatments that followed. 'They coat your body in mercury and all your teeth fall out. Bits of your nose drop off.'

'My nose? I wouldn't mind that.'

'And in old age you go mad. You imagine you're the king of Spain.'

The combination of ignorance and fear had crushed Anton's instincts, but in his second year at the university he had spent three months in Berlin and, on the night he was due to leave, managed a fumbling connection with his landlady's daughter. He was quite sure there was no chance of disease because Gudrun was a good girl, as her mother often said, though for some months he dreaded a letter informing him that he was the father of a little German. After his return to Vienna he decided that, having at last joined the ranks of authentic men and – unlike everyone else he had ever heard of – without recourse to a prostitute, he would not be bothered by such things again.

Yet at the age of twenty-six, there was still that lung-stabbing ache that could be brought on by a single glance; and there was still Delphine at Erich's house. In the days after their first meeting, her face seemed to be all he could see. He focused his thoughts on the thin line of hair on her upper lip in the hope that it might put him off; but it seemed to have the opposite effect. He wanted to run his tongue along it. He was fascinated by the fact that she was older, with all the experience that implied – Paris, music and late nights in the Latin Quarter. 'One of us is married, the others wait for husbands. Or so my father thinks.' How playful had that remark been? At night he fell asleep to the sound of her chord changes.

Having borrowed money from Friedrich, he left a note for 'Mlle Delphine' on his next visit to Döbling. He was anxious about what concert to book because he knew so little about music; he remembered her dismissal of Richard Strauss, whom he personally, until then, had rather admired. There seemed to be nothing on offer by Mussorgsky, but in a small theatre he found a programme that featured works by Mahler and Schoenberg and felt confident she couldn't dislike both. Mahler was a god of Vienna, once its youngest prodigy, and as for Schoenberg ... Anton hadn't heard his work performed, but in the window of a gallery had seen his self-portrait in green and thought his music must at least be better than his painting.

'Dear Herr Heideck,' came the reply to his lodgings, 'it is kind of you to invite Katrin and me to the concert. Katrin's father has given his permission and will accompany us to the concert hall, where we can meet in the foyer ten minutes before the performance begins. With kind regards, Delphine Fourmentier.'

Anton scribbled back, 'Dear Mademoiselle, I should be honoured if you and Katrin would join me for dinner afterwards. I would of course arrange for a cab to take you home immediately afterwards.' He had sealed and addressed it before it struck him that both sentences ended with the same word.

Delphine replied in French: 'Cher Monsieur, On serait ravi de diner avec vous après et de profiter du fiacre après ... DF'. 'We would be delighted to dine with you afterwards and to take the cab home afterwards.'

Through gritted teeth, Anton persuaded himself that the teasing was not dismissive but playful – perhaps even flirtatious. When the day arrived he dressed in his best suit, his only suit, and made his way to the concert hall near the hospital in the ninth district. It seated only 300 people, though the stage was large enough to accommodate a full orchestra. The early arrivals in the foyer were different from the crowd he'd seen on the steps of the Opera House; there were not so many furs or top hats and most of them had the look of people who had had to rush from work.

Katrin's father appeared in the swing doors and delivered his two charges to Anton with a threatening smile. Anton adopted the voice he used to editors on the telephone, blasé yet reliable, as he confirmed the arrangements for 'afterwards' and escorted Katrin and Delphine up the carpeted stairs, running his fingers up the dustless handrail.

As he settled himself between the two young women in their cheap seats, it occurred to Anton that he barely knew either of them. Yet here they were, Delphine in a dark green dress with black brocade and black shoes peeping out from underneath, Katrin in a white frock with a yellow ribbon in her hair, their knees an inch or so away from his, their arms sharing a rest with his, their breath warm on his cheek as they chatted about how the orchestra would manage to squeeze onto the stage and what little Erich had said yesterday ... Here they all were at his bidding.

Waiting for the auditorium to fill, Anton sat back and gazed up at the rococo ceiling. He was grateful for the women's talk because it gave him time to calm his nerves. Katrin seemed excited by the new experience, though, as a child of privilege, immediately at ease with it. Delphine was still being a professional companion, prompting responses from Katrin, even slipping into French at one point. And he, Anton, what was he? Alive, he thought: alive, at least. Drenched in the moment. He brought a sort of middle-class wariness. He was confident that he could rely on his good manners, but he was watchful, taking nothing as his due.

Schoenberg came up first. It was a string quartet – a strict form, Anton thought, that it would be hard to turn into an atonal mess. The players assembled downstage, in front of the space set up for the orchestra; the first violin raised his bow and they began. It seemed to Anton that the instruments were all playing a different piece. It was hard to settle into it; there were none of the repetitions of Mozart or Haydn that formed a reassuring progress with a conclusive ripple at the end of each section. In later movements, the cello groaned while the violins plinked and pirouetted; he had an image of a skylark, high up in the clouds, while on the ground beneath some low sounds were prophesying war.

He closed his eyes to concentrate better, but opened them again when to his amazement he heard a woman's voice. A singer had joined the players and stood with her hands folded at the waist. This was not what he'd expected in a string quartet. Was it allowed? The soprano trilled indignantly, as if someone had made her an indecent proposal. It was hard to distinguish the words. Then she took on a religious air and Anton gathered that her character had been spared from death by some sexual or holy rapture.

The applause in the hall was polite.

Delphine was smiling. 'At least no one's walked out,' she said. 'That's what normally happens with Schoenberg.'

'Is it?'

'Some places ask in advance if you're a walker-out by nature, then they seat you in the aisle so as not to put off the performers.'

'I hated it,' said Katrin. 'Especially the singer.'

Trying not to think how much the evening had cost him, Anton said, 'I'm sure you'll like the symphony more.'

The players had found their cramped places behind the music stands, whispering and smiling to one another as they shuffled in and sat. The conductor rapped his baton on the rail of the podium, raised his arms ... and ... well, the symphony was certainly much easier to lose oneself in, Anton thought. Was that a woodwind cuckoo, for instance, calling above the strings? Mahler liked to keep you on your toes, but, unlike Schoenberg, he didn't try to knock you off your feet. He clearly had in mind a pattern whose shape would be revealed if you were prepared to go along with him. In the final movement, there was a teasing return to earlier themes, which then seemed to be left hanging; but underneath it all there was an architecture, whose grandeur was revealed at last.

Anton dared to look at Delphine as the final notes faded and saw her eyes shining. He felt a sense of vindication, almost as though he himself had had a hand in writing the music.

The applause was unambiguous and the audience left the hall with animated faces.

'Yes, I liked it,' said Katrin as they went downstairs, 'especially the bit that sounded like "Frère Jacques".'

Anton had reserved a table in a restaurant he had scouted with Friedrich the week before. It was good value for such a solid-looking place, with wooden booths and chandeliers, though the service was erratic and the food tasted as though it had been kept warm. He was not in a mood to care, because he was too fascinated by Mlle Fourmentier. He could hardly bear the wait while she and Katrin were in the powder room; he passed the time by ordering a carafe of Grüner Veltliner and downing the first glass himself.

Katrin settled herself on the plush-covered bench and Delphine slid in beside her, leaving Anton to face them, badly placed to catch the attention of the waiters. Katrin might in other circumstances have interested him, being arguably closer to his own age, with wide eyes and a ready laugh. But he could sense no character in her; she was a page on which no one had yet written and it was possible, he thought, that she might stay like that for ever in her

19

father's muffled rooms. Delphine was the opposite – shaped by experience, with cloudy contours and jagged, possibly painful, edges. He pressed her for details of her life and every answer suggested five further questions there would be no time to ask.

'No, I wasn't classically trained, but I spent some time learning from a soloist who'd fallen on hard times.' 'My uncle had lost an arm in the Franco-Prussian War.' 'Isabelle was the beauty of the family, then she married a man who … Never mind.' 'A financial difficulty meant we had to move in a hurry.' 'This dress? It was made for me in Rouen. I knew a seamstress who owed my father money for some reason.' 'The convent was strict. But we sometimes found our way into town.' 'We used to visit the garden at Giverny, but we never saw the great man.' 'She called herself a cook, but she was barely capable of stoking the range.'

When Delphine asked him the odd question in return, Anton answered as briefly as possible so that he could resume his interrogation. To start with, Katrin made the occasional remark, offering opinions in which he could hear the influence of her parents, but after a while she fell silent and began to glance about the restaurant.

The waiters, for some reason, stopped avoiding Anton's eye and became prompt. The plates were cleared, dessert was brought and a bill was presented in the space of a few minutes. Suggestions of coffee were declined and Delphine consulted her watch.

Outside, on the street, it was raining. Anton found a cab and gestured to Katrin and Delphine to come over from the shelter of the restaurant porch. Before leaving home, he had counted out the money for the fare back to Döbling and put the coins in his waistcoat pocket so he wouldn't spend them by mistake on a tip at the cloakroom. It had meant no lunch for three days, but it seemed worth it as he pressed the money into the hands of the driver. Delphine had her back to him as she climbed into the cab. He stood in the rain, watching. The cab was already under way when he saw her – as an afterthought it seemed – turn and lift her hand. It was too dark to see if she was smiling.

To pass the idle hours, of which there were many, Anton imagined the life he would have with Delphine. Theirs would be an unconventional ménage, of course. They would live in a hunting lodge, somewhere he pictured at first as a sort of dacha not far from Moscow – before settling on a sleepy part of Bavaria, in a forest clearing with a river nearby. Sometimes he pictured them both naked, children of the woods. At other times, Delphine was dressed in her green dress, at the piano for hours while he chopped logs and prepared dinner – with a previously unsuspected talent that went well beyond 'stoking the range'. There was sex in his fantasies, though it drew little on his night in Berlin and not at all on the circus postcards. For this, he and Delphine both seemed to be naked again, he asleep on a huge couch at the fireside, she bending over and guiltily waking him with hands and lips, being, against her better judgement, unable to resist. In what happened next, the failure of Viennese society to deal with the passions of its people was quite thrillingly resolved. When they lay together afterwards, under a bearskin rug while she told him more about her sisters and he kissed her upper lip, the shortcomings of the world – unhappiness itself – seemed to exist only as a remote and rather comic hypothesis.

In reality, the lady companion stayed fully dressed in the nineteenth district, while Anton was stuck in the narrow streets of Spittelberg. Although he made enough money to pay the rent and feed himself, his imagined apartment off the Ringstrasse seemed as remote as when he had first arrived in Vienna.

Anton's career as a journalist was fitful, but not hopeless. It was easier for established newspapers to keep one or two correspondents in the big capitals than to send reporters from Vienna on expensive and time-consuming journeys. One day in 1911, two years before he met Delphine, he read that the *Mona Lisa* had been stolen from the Louvre. The editors he approached dismissed it as 'another French scandal', probably instigated by the government itself. So, in the end, he had borrowed some money from Friedrich and paid for his own train ticket, arriving in Paris just in time to see the poet Guillaume Apollinaire arrested for the theft. To Anton's delight, Apollinaire tried to palm the blame off on his friend Picasso.

The longer Anton stayed in Paris, the better the story became. More than twenty-four hours, it seemed, had passed before anyone noticed that the painting had gone: the museum was simply too big to police. Glass panels previously erected in front of the *Mona Lisa* to stop vandals had inspired derision in the public because their reflections obscured the view. Some Parisians thought the Germans had stolen the painting to demoralise them; the German press claimed that the French had staged an act of self-sabotage to distract attention from their disastrous foreign policy. The wounding of French national pride was an easy target for the foreign press and Anton tried to find a better angle. The Spanish name of Pablo Picasso led him to investigate the extraordinary number of artists who had come from abroad to live in Paris and to ask them what made Montmartre, a semi-urban village on a slope, preferable to Málaga or Livorno.

He was able to sell these pieces to magazines in Vienna, where they were well received. As a result, one of them dispatched him later that month to Moscow to report on the assassination of the premier, Peter Stolypin, at the Kiev opera. What the two stories had in common was the gratifying sense of Austria's enemies in turmoil: in Vienna there was a real hunger to hear how the tsar had been sitting in a box overlooking the stage when a man had walked down the aisle and shot Stolypin at close range with a revolver – a Browning, Anton specified, knowing his editor's passion for detail. The assassin was a lawyer, a socialist and a police informer. He was also Jewish, and in the days that followed there were rumours of a pogrom against all Jews in retaliation.

The editor was pleased, but Anton remained sceptical about the value of what he did. He found it satisfying to build a picture, piece by piece, of what had happened. At first, he wrote down everything, his hand aching to keep up; but after some days the people he was questioning could tell him nothing new. By then, the flow of information was reversed and he was able tell them what he'd discovered from previous interviews. If the page in his notebook was still blank at the end of the meeting he knew he had finished his research. The trouble was that when he spoke to painters in Paris or civil servants in Moscow, he imagined their lives and felt something close to envy. However poor the artist, however constrained the official, they seemed to have a purpose and an identity: they would have careers, a life with shape and purpose. Whereas he ... As much as he enjoyed his truth-discovering, he felt inessential. No one at home needed to know every nuance or corrugation of a story. It was only entertainment for them, he thought – which in turn made him not much more than a parasite.

He tried not to think about it too much. In the morning, he could spin out a cup of coffee beneath the electric chandeliers of the Griensteidl while he read the French and English newspapers. The play of European current affairs seemed entertainment enough, albeit of a rather menacing kind. Lunch was often sausage and beer from a stand in the Prater before he headed off to do some tutoring in the afternoon. Poverty was relative, he thought. Magazine commissions would come again one day, and the habit of living cheaply didn't diminish him if the alternative was a return to the family chitterlings.

He always arrived early at Erich's apartment, exchanging pleasantries with a maid or governess while hoping to catch a glimpse of Delphine. More often than not, he was successful. There was a footstep in the corridor, a rustle of fabric. 'Ah, Monsieur. I didn't know you were coming today. I'll fetch Erich for you.' Then a non-committal smile and she was gone.

One afternoon, he arrived a full half-hour early and was in time to catch her playing in the music room. He stood in the doorway and watched. She nodded her head when she saw him, but carried on playing.

'How long will you be staying in Vienna?' he dared to ask when she had finished.

'The arrangement is for two more months.'

Anton shifted his weight. 'Perhaps you could come to another concert one day.'

Delphine looked out of the window, unspeaking.

'I read an article by you,' she said eventually. 'In a magazine. About the diplomacy between London and Paris.'

'Ah, yes. It was a bit dry, I'm afraid.'

'It was interesting. I had no idea how much conversation was carried on informally.'

'It isn't meant to be. A government has a policy and the foreign department's supposed to put it into practice.'

'But if the officials on either side develop things in private, isn't that against the rules?'

'It's ... unusual. Because it ignores the will of the government.'

'I hate to think what the English are plotting with the French.'

'Yes,' said Anton. 'I think they're making private treaties through the British embassy in Paris. Their Parliament knows nothing of it.'

'It sounds dangerous. I mean ... If there's a war.'

There was a pause. Anton wondered if he had bored her.

'Do you play the piano?' said Delphine.

'No. I had lessons when I was at the Gymnasium. It was compulsory up to a certain age. But I was never any good. And I was allowed to give up after two years.'

24

'Come and sit here.' She pulled a chair up beside the piano stool. 'Show me.'

Anton, after a moment's hesitation, sat down and played a schoolboy exercise, the first that he and Friedrich had been taught.

'Can you do this?' She played a variation.

'Probably.'

'It's the same as what you've just played, but you use these black notes as well. It sounds better.'

'Yes.'

'Keep doing that.'

While he did as he was told, Delphine began to play a melody in a higher register. Anton concentrated on his repetition, trying not to look at Delphine. She struck a chord between his two hands before returning to her end of the keyboard. Eventually, Anton relaxed enough to listen to the sound they were making, her descant on his schoolboy repetition. He began to smile.

Delphine began to laugh. 'The look on your face!'

'It's just that it seems . . . like magic to me. I'm so bad at it.'

'Never mind. You like Mahler and you hate Strauss. That's a start.'

'Where shall we go next, then? You must choose a concert. Look at the newspaper and tell me the one you would most like to go to. I'll buy the tickets.'

Delphine stood up. 'You're very kind, Monsieur.'

She looked out of the window, in silence again, and Anton felt his life hang on her decision.

At last she turned to him and said, 'Perhaps we should try the theatre for a change.'

Standing next to her, Anton put his hand on her forearm and kissed her cheek.

Then he turned and made his way quickly to the door. 'You must let me know,' he said. 'On Tuesday, when I come again.'

'Are you leaving?'

25

'Yes. Yes, I have to go now.'
'What about Erich's lesson?'

Anton never afterwards remembered the details of the first time he made love to Delphine. He was too startled by the fact it was happening to be able to record each element. In retrospect, years later, he often wished his memory had mentally photographed her skin as it emerged from the layers of clothes. He ought really to have been able to carry a clear picture of the woman he had come to love, naked in front of him for the first time.

After yet another concert – fifth, sixth, seventh – he had spirited her upstairs to his room on the pretext of lending her a book. 'Rilke,' he lied. 'I've just bought his *New Poems*.'

'Anton, I am rather overwhelmed by you,' was all she said, standing in his room, her arms spread wide, in stockinged feet, her shoes in one hand so as not to alert the landlady.

'I can't find the book.'

She put down the shoes and took the pins from her hair, so it rested on her shoulders. He kissed her upper lip, then licked it. She touched his tongue with hers.

'Undo these hooks on my dress. That's the best way.'

He swallowed and took off his jacket.

She ran her hands over the small of his back and pulled him against her.

'Shall I turn off the light?'

'No. Stay here.'

She told him then how much she had thought about him. Night and day, apparently. They sat on the edge of the bed. Delphine took his hand while she explained something.

Then she spoke for a long time, patting his hand occasionally, her freed hair falling down over her cheek, like a small girl's. His presence had surprised her that first day, she said … as if she had been caught swimming naked in a lake. She had been embarrassed, defensive, but in some way – she stumbled on the word – aroused. His sincerity, his lack of money, his politeness to Katrin, which had made her, Delphine, laugh inside … Obviously he had wanted the girl to go home and leave them alone that first evening after the Mahler symphony in that awful restaurant …

She laughed, then grew serious again and squeezed his hand.

'And then the articles of yours I've read. Do you know how remarkable they are?'

'What?'

'I've read them all. So clear, so calm. And a kind of stubborn fairness that shines through everything.'

Anton couldn't take in what she said, because he was too confused with thoughts of his fumble in Berlin and the rumours he had heard of how much more was now expected of him.

He tried again to concentrate because he could see that what Delphine was saying was important to her. She was now talking about a man. A different man, not Anton, but a man she had known at home or perhaps in Paris – and then some long and painful disappointment.

'… So you see why I have to be careful. I have to be sure.'

He was looking at the moles beneath her breasts that he could now see for the first time. He was not concentrating on her story.

'Of course,' he said.

She was clearly wanting to lay out some important truth before him. It was as though she wanted him never to have grounds for some future recrimination. He wished now he'd followed what she said more closely. He wanted to ask, 'And *are* you sure?', but was worried it might stall the momentum. He couldn't believe this woman was about to grant his most passionate wish. Better to be silent.

He was still sitting on the bed when Delphine stepped out of the last of her underclothes and stood in front of him. 'Anton, you won't … betray me, will you? For all I'm giving you.'

He knelt down and rested his cheek against her. She stroked his hair.

'Never.'

'Now take your clothes off, too.'

When they lay down together on the bed, she began to talk in French to him, whispering instructions in his ear. He liked the change of language, into her own. It was as though she had taken him to her heart.

'*Oui. Comme ça. Doucement. Et je peux? Comme ça? Tu aimes?*'

Anton felt the silent disapproval of his parents, the teacher at the Gymnasium looking on in disgust. Then she was touching him in a way that made all thought impossible, and then it was too late.

A few minutes later, Delphine said, 'You're an excellent man, Anton. Look at this.' She touched the part that had disgraced him. 'Let's be patient. Swear to me that you'll be patient with me, too.'

She seemed to be forgiving him. Perhaps she too had fears, he thought – fears of not being what she was supposed to be – but which of us really is? Then he sighed, and sank into the arms of her forgiveness, where she could now take care of everything, including him.

After a short time, he went outside and boiled some water on the landing. With some effort of will, he remained naked as he poured the boiling water and brought the tea back to the room.

'Won't they miss you?' he said.

'There's a night porter. And I have an indoor key. The apartment is so huge they hardly know if I'm there or not.'

They talked for hours, but in a different way, as if there could be no pretence. Anton began to feel he had to invent more secrets, to betray confidences he had never taken on, so as not to disappoint Delphine's curiosity. She was older and more worldly than he was; but she was also like a child who in some way now belonged to him.

He had the sensation of being on a toboggan going down a hill, unstoppably, into the life and being of another. Was it too fast? He found himself smiling. There was no snow in summer, no hill and no sledge. But the sense of hurtling remained.

His top-floor room was hot, even in the small hours of the morning. When Delphine had said all she needed to say and he was making love to her, he remembered a drop of sweat he had seen on her forehead the first day when she was playing, because now her breasts were slippery as they rolled against his chest and a strand of hair stuck to her temple, from which he pushed it back with his finger.

A few days later, Anton returned to his home town in Styria for his father's funeral. The whitewashed church was full and the coffin handles gleamed. He tried not to look at the box at the head of the nave or to imagine his father inside, because it raised too many questions about washing and fixing and decomposition. The congregation was there to mourn or mark the end of something abstract – a life – and the presence of the body, as matter-of-fact as one of the dead pigs delivered to the door of the sausage factory, seemed an intrusion.

His father when alive had never shown much affection towards Anton, behaving instead as a kind of route supervisor: infant school, Gymnasium, Bible study; social duties, politeness to your mother, the university if you must and, above all, respectability. Anton felt little more for him than he would towards a tram conductor who had pointed out the stops along the way. He cast his mind back to his youngest days and thought he could remember his father playing with him once in the garden of their house when Gerhard had been at school. And there had been a picnic, perhaps, on a hot day, a walk in a wood, when for a moment his father had thrown off his years and himself behaved like a child. It seemed in retrospect to have been an empty game, when the end was written all along: the dead weight on the rickety bier.

At times during the service, for instance when Gerhard was reading from the Bible, he had to force himself to concentrate. If he was not careful, he found himself in a Delphine reverie. It was not that he was picturing anything sacrilegious; it was only that he felt insulated from normal life, because he had discovered something more urgent. At the gathering afterwards in his parents' house, several old people asked him if he would now come home to run the business. His life in Vienna and his work as a journalist appeared to them a self-indulgence that would last only until the start of the real work, in sausages. He slid out of these conversations, saying that he needed to help Gerhard pour the drinks.

The next day he sat down and talked to his mother. Since Gerhard was now settled at a hospital in Vienna, with a fine salary and every chance of promotion, she said, it would make sense for Anton to come home. He explained that he had no interest in the sausage works or in ever coming back. The obvious solution, surely, was for her to sell her late husband's interest to his brother, Anton's uncle, who was the joint owner of the company. They would need an outside valuation, but it wasn't complicated; the profits were steady and it would provide enough for her to live on.

'I've been asked to go to the United States,' he said. 'To report on the opening of the Panama Canal for a magazine. I'm leaving next week on a steamship from Southampton. In England.'

'Why do you want to go to America?'

'Every journalist would like to. I'm very lucky to be asked. I've been in the cold for more than a year, since I turned down a trip to the Balkans. This is a big chance to get going again. All the great newspapers of the world are sending reporters.'

'What's wrong with our country?'

'Nothing at all. Though I'm fed up with writing about the Treaty of Bucharest. All writers want to visit other places. It's what first drew me to the idea of newspapers when I was a student. Do you remember when I went to Moscow? And to Paris? They thought I did well. I was mentioned for some state prize. I didn't win it, of course. But that's not the point.'

'Isn't it time you thought about getting married?'

'I'm far too young. Who should I marry anyway? And why?'

When he returned to Vienna, he felt that his life was taking shape at last. Delphine had extended her stay with Erich's family and, with the help of a loan from the bank, Anton took three rooms in a building in the third district. It was a modest area, dominated by gasometers, but he had his own bathroom as well as a small sitting room and no Polish landlady. To his delight, Delphine kept some clothes in a battered Biedermeier chest and helped him to arrange his possessions in a way that made the place seem more habitable. She brought candles and coloured shades for the electric lamps that cast a pleasing glow on the cushions of the sofa and the books on the shelf behind.

Anton saw no suggestion of permanence in these rooms, though he was aware of the happiness they brought him. He valued it and thought he should try to hold on to it, whatever that might mean. How should he keep the days from going by?

And then he had to make his way to Paris, to Calais and across the Channel for a crossing to the New World.

3

Balancing a pad of paper on his knee, Anton wrote:

My dearest Delphine,

I am sitting on a wooden veranda in a jungle. I'm surrounded by snakes and monkeys, parrots and spiders. The cries of birds and insects quite unknown to me. It's raining (it's always raining in Panama). I have just had an early dinner – rice, peas and what may have been chicken, and am now drinking some cognac left by the previous occupant.

The villa was built for a French engineer. It's on the Atlantic side, up on a hill, supposed to be safe from the landslides.

There's an English journalist here as well, a man called Maxwell whom I met on the ship coming over. I had to have someone to talk to. Five weeks it took! Also, it's good to have an English-speaker with me because although my English may be all right for tutoring Erich, it's nothing like good enough for all the technical talk.

We have a West Indian maid, who is the sister of one of the labourers. Her name is Emerald and she's devout. She prays for her brother day and night. She sleeps in a small back room and when not praying is sweeping the floor and muttering about the rain.

I'm going on the railway as soon as I can to meet her brother because I want to hear from him what his life's been like. He's been here for five years. It's hard to get across to where he's working, near the Pacific side, because the railway is still being used to carry away the 'spoil' – the rocks and earth they've dug out of the infamous Culebra Cut (known as 'Hell's Gorge'), which is a passage through the mountains they've enlarged by blowing out the rocks with dynamite.

From where I sit, the hillsides are entirely covered in trees, plants, creepers, undergrowth: green, breeding, dripping. When the French began their attempt at a canal more than thirty years ago, they sent in Chinese and West Indians with machetes and shovels. They died in their thousands from yellow fever and malaria. The river Chagres is in flood for half the year (it rains nine months out of twelve here). It buried the little paths they cut through the jungle under its mudslides. So many died that they had to put on special trains to take the bodies back up to the cemetery at Mount Hope, not far from here. Others were just rolled off the hillsides where they fell – down into the sodden undergrowth where the mud became their grave.

All right, my dear Delphine. I have a few moments of daylight left. Night falls at six ten. It takes no more than a couple of minutes – there's no dusk to speak of. Eleven hours later, the dawn comes up like a thunderclap.

Now at this very moment in the wicker chair on my veranda, glass in hand, I'm looking down at a huge lake. It looks as though, like the jungle and the immense crocodiles, it's been here since the world began. You can picture ptero-dactyls skimming above the water as the light fades.

But in truth it's only a few years old. Some clever American engineer called Stevens had an idea. Instead of fighting the monstrous river with its constant floods, let's make the river work for us. So they dammed the Chagres and let it flood an area of the central isthmus large enough to reach almost to Culebra. So most of the 'canal' is in fact a man-made lake! I won't bore you with the engineering wonder of the locks at either end (though believe me they <u>are</u> a wonder). They will, when it opens next year, lift huge ships up in three steps to the height of the lake, then down again at the other end. In transit, the ships will float above the American watershed that runs from Alaska to Tierra del Fuego – what they call the 'continental divide'.

As I sip the cognac, hearing the patter of the rain on the tin roof, I feel smaller than the tiniest cell in the giant organism of this earth. The mountain and jungle so magnificent, the animals so prehistoric, the diseases so deadly to a young species like us . . . And yet what we've done here! To tame the teeming, untouched land, to join two oceans and bring all nature under our command . . .

I think of you very often and of our rooms in Vienna, though I sometimes find it hard to believe that it all still exists. Did you find the material you wanted for the curtains? I miss you with all my body and soul and I hope that you are real, not the figment of a white man's imagination here in fever country. Will you be there when I return? Will your hair be the same dark brown, tied with my favourite bow? Will your hands still slide across the keys and release the music hiding there? Will you still be my uncompromising teacher?

You can write to me at the poste restante at Colón. They seem quite efficient there and I enjoy meeting people in the saloon next to the telegraph office.

Je t'embrasse très fort.

A

To begin with, he had hated Colón. At first sight, from the deck of the New York steamer, it seemed to float on the bay, its white houses and their red roofs hanging against the overpowering green backdrop of the jungle. Most of the population of Colón was now West Indian, men on their way to or from the Culebra Cut. The military engineers from West Point and Annapolis had gone home, their work accomplished, though there were still some Americans who had found in humid Colón a refuge that Cincinnati or Wyoming had denied them. There were pay clerks, remittance men and recent college graduates who were the worry of their families and churches back home. The Americans were paid in gold dollars, the West Indians in silver; and the length of the canal, the 'Silvermen' had their own inferior bathrooms, canteens and drinking fountains.

Colón had been much worse in the French era, Maxwell told Anton. 'Shiploads of wine arrived every week. The French said they couldn't drink the water. They had girls shipped in from all over the world. When a new consignment came in they used to send a message down the telegraph line. "Langoustes arrivées." "Lobsters arrived."' Maxwell laughed. 'Half the girls were on the company payroll. Of course the Americans tried to clean it up, but old habits die hard.'

Nothing took Maxwell by surprise, Anton soon discovered. He had reported from South Africa, India and the Sudan and was convinced that there was nothing new under the British Empire sun. The most perverse twist of events was met by the response: 'Typical'. Anton found him a useful companion because he understood the common feeling. The Americans, to Maxwell, were childlike, bullying and without moral scruple, particularly in the way they had avoided paying Colombia, of which Panama had been a province, for the land required for the canal. This had been achieved by telling a restless Panamanian faction that if they declared independence from Colombia the US would support them. The coup had passed off peacefully, with an American warship in the harbour at Colón firing a single shell for form's sake.

The French, in Maxwell's account of things, could never have got the job done. Ferdinand de Lesseps, a hero in France, had overseen the digging of a ditch through the flat sands at Suez; but Panama was jungle, river, granite, floods, basalt, plague, mud, mountain and tropical downpour. De Lesseps was not a mathematician, not an engineer, not even a surveyor; he was a retired diplomat of no great distinction, a seventy-eight-year-old show pony who 'couldn't keep his whatnot in his pantaloons'. He came to the isthmus and had himself photographed at parties and riding up a hillside on his horse, then went back to his several mistresses in Paris.

It amused Maxwell that the financial collapse of the French effort had brought down the government in Paris. Most of the deputies in the chamber had taken bribes to vote more money to the failing enterprise; de Lesseps' son was in prison and the old man excused jail only on sentimental grounds. There had been suicide, cover-up and a scandal that had involved even Gustave Eiffel, architect of the recent tower. Typical French, was Maxwell's conclusion.

The only thing that lowered Maxwell's spirits or caused him doubt was the thought of someone back in London he referred to as 'Pop'. Anton discovered that this person, whose real name was Dawson, was the managing editor of Maxwell's paper, for ever demanding that he send over stories that showed they were keeping up with the opposition. '"*Times* reports dynamite accident in Cut,"' he read out loud to Anton one evening after a visit to the cable office. '"Many dead. Require your matcher soonest." How in God's name am I supposed to know? I can't get across to the bloody Cut and anyway the Yanks would just deny it. In any case I happen to know their man's sitting on his arse in the best bloody hotel in Panama City. Typical.'

Along the lines of Maxwell's simplifications, Anton could make out where public opinion lay. The president, Theodore Roosevelt, contemptuous of the French, had been determined to get the thing done the American way, and at any cost. The price had turned out to be the lives of thousands of workers from Barbados and Jamaica, dead from plague and mudslide; and the betrayal of Colombia. On the other hand, the United States had purged the isthmus of yellow fever and spanned it with a piece of engineering whose ingenuity was as dazzling in execution as it had been simple in Stevens's lake-and-lock brainwave. The willpower to build a canal through the most difficult place on earth could perhaps only have come from a young country eager to prove something to the world.

Yet Anton could not quite accept that Europe – and France in particular – was as corrupt or as doomed as the Americans and Maxwell maintained. Something in him rebelled and made him think the truth might be both more complicated and more interesting (and Delphine's native country was not to be written off so easily). He took the story of American competence triumphing over Old World decadence and set out to undermine it. He had always found this a good principle: to acknowledge the received ideas before destroying them with accumulated facts.

He thought constantly of Delphine, though for reasons of self-protection he sometimes tried to think about her less. Being with her had made him feel a more capacious, multifaceted character; it made him feel interesting, even to himself. It would not be going too far, he thought, to admit that she had changed his understanding of what his life could be. And that was to say nothing of the sybaritic pleasure of her skin, the scent of her and all they did to one another – their own solution to Vienna's failure to find a proper way for men and women to be close. He sometimes wondered if he should ask her to marry him, but didn't want to risk upsetting an equilibrium that he didn't understand.

After two weeks, he was compelled to think of something other than Delphine when he managed to find a place on a train heading down through the isthmus towards the Culebra Cut.

'You going to let me come, old man?' said Maxwell, holding on to Anton's elbow.

'You can come to the station if you like. I can't guarantee anything. What about you, Emerald? Do you want to see your brother?'

'To see Amos? Of course I do.'

'That does it,' said Maxwell. 'If she goes, I go. Who the hell else is going to look after me here?'

They went by mule up to the station at Colón, which was little more than a platform built up on the side of Main Street. There was some wrangling with the guard, who was unwilling to take Emerald on board the caboose attached to the back of the train.

'It's no place for a ...' He seemed to struggle for the word.

'For a lady?' said Emerald. 'I'm no lady. I've ridden worse than this pile of rust. I'm getting on.'

Maxwell fished two silver dollars out of his waistcoat pocket, pressed them on the guard, and the deal was done.

'You saw that, Heideck. I'm claiming those two dollars back from Pop Dawson when I get home.'

'As God is our witness,' said Anton. 'All aboard.'

The train took them through the jungle on a recently completed line, just north of the man-made lake. The rain had eased off and the sun was shining on the wet green of the jungle, though to Anton's surprise Maxwell seldom lifted his eyes from his book, *The Return of Sherlock Holmes*.

'You don't know what you're missing,' he said.

'What?' said Maxwell, looking up. 'It's good, this, you know. I'll lend it to you when I've finished.' He took a bottle of brandy from his bag and handed it round.

On the open platform at the rear of the caboose, Anton could see where the undergrowth and rocks had been scraped out by giant slides; it was a mud glacier in whose terminal moraine lay the bones of men. Eventually they came to the nine-mile stretch of the Culebra Cut itself and the guard had the train stopped so they could look down.

Hundreds of feet below they could make out the tiny figures of the labourers on the floor of the Cut, from whose bed rose clouds of sulphur and boiling steam. Small engines puffed and shunted like overwound toys. Unworldly sounds drifted upwards – the rumble of the dirt trains, the metallic ring of drill on rock and the boom of dynamite that reached them only after the smoke had begun to rise.

That evening they found Amos in a settlement on the outskirts of Panama City. His lodging was divided by a curtain into parlour and sleeping area, though the whole thing was only the size of a maid's room in Vienna. The walls were papered with pages torn from illustrated magazines. There was a cooker on the veranda out front, on which Amos began to make dinner while Maxwell went in search of liquor.

Amos declined the offer of beer when Maxwell returned, but told Anton about his life in the locks where he was now working. His job was driving rivets into the concrete wall; with four other men he stood on a plank held up by chains. This makeshift scaffold covered the face of the empty lock to a depth of eighty feet in a series of platforms, like a giant and unstable rope ladder suspended from the rim. If one plank fell, it would take others with it. Amos said he preferred the risk of falling to working on a steam shovel in the Cut where he was for ever being told to dive into the slime to free the suction pumps.

Amos's voice kept rumbling on in the humid little room. He wore a red neckerchief above his collarless but clean white shirt. It was knotted so tight it seemed to make his eyeballs bulge, as though he had just stopped someone on the point of throttling him. His eyes were red round the rims from the cement dust that came out of walls they drilled. Yet his tone hardly varied, even when he described a man spiralling off a plank to his death on the lock floor, 'where the blood run deep as the waters when they let 'em in to carry the big ships up'.

Emerald sat gazing at her brother, while Anton's hand struggled to keep up in his notebook. The rain, the sweat, the church services on Sunday, the heatstroke, the riding of the steam shovels in the belly of hell ... That was the story he would dedicate himself to telling.

Anton carried Delphine's most recent letter with him and reread it at idle moments.

My dearest Anton,

Thank you for your letters from the tropics. They are not like your magazine articles at all. They show the passionate side of you that perhaps only I have seen here in Vienna. Will your professional even-handedness return when you come to write your account for the magazine?

I like the sound of this Emerald, but I wouldn't want you to be become too attached to her. May her God watch over both of you.

Perhaps by the time this reaches you, you'll have made your way across the isthmus, found out all you need and will be thinking of your journey back. I don't know how I can wait that long, but I suppose I'll have to find a way.

Katrin is making such good progress with her French that I'm afraid her father will soon think my work is done. I have to make sure we never speak French in front of him. Erich has asked after you and I told him you'd write if you had a moment. I have taken over some of your tutoring duties. He's a dull child, isn't he?

In answer to your question, yes, I am still playing the piano every day, looking for what lies beneath the keys. Sometimes

it rises up to greet me, sometimes it hides its head. And sometimes it turns into the 'afternoon bagatelle' you despise. I
haven't been to a concert or a play once since you were gone,
though a business friend of Erich's father did invite me. I
gave him what you call my headmistress look.

I have visited your rooms and dusted them. I've also left
money with the landlord as we agreed. He gives me a curious
look and clearly doesn't believe I'm just your music teacher.
But he makes no fuss and pockets the money at once. I take
off my shoes and lie on the bed and imagine you there.
Speaking of which, I've thought of some new lessons you can
be taught. I hope you will find them instructive.

As a treat, I had lunch yesterday at that place at the top of
Schottengasse that you like, with boiled beef and horseradish
and the spinach purée with so much nutmeg and salt. It made
me think of you when you wolf it down.

The newspapers continue to talk only about unrest in
Serbia and other staples of life in the Balkans. I know you are
utterly tired of all that. I've also read of exchanges between
Moscow and Berlin. Statesmen do like to trumpet, don't they,
like elephants in a jungle.

And talking of jungles ... please be careful of the mosqui-
toes. Sleep beneath a net, or do whatever the Americans do to
stay healthy. I don't want you in some terrible hospital with
all the men moaning and feverish.

Hurry home to me. Send me news soon. Tell me you're on
the ship home. Please.

Je t'embrasse même plus fort,
Ta Delphine

From the cable office in Panama City, Anton sent an article to
the magazine at home. It was the simple update – news of what
had been going on – that the editor had requested. To make it

worth the expense of having sent him there, he added descriptions of the terrain and opinions taken from interviews he'd done. His main work, it was agreed, would be undertaken on his return; this would include a new perspective on the French failures.

The seas at either end had meanwhile been allowed to press against the lock gates. In October it was decided to flood the Cut; the rest of the clearance could be done by dredges underwater. So the steam shovels and the rail tracks were lifted out of Hell's Gorge for the last time; thousands gathered to watch a triumphant explosion, to be triggered by President Roosevelt down a telegraph wire from Washington. It was intended to be the moment at which the great oceans met, but a mudslide in the Cut had the last word, its debris obstructing the connection. No amount of explosive could shift the mess, and the tourists went home.

A short time afterwards, the river Chagres flooded. Anton was on his way back to Colón when he noticed gangs of men working to divert the flow. The driver stopped the train and they watched from above as the stream became a torrent and began to sweep the stubborn mud and rocks from its path. In the end, it was not the touch of the president's finger that joined the Atlantic to the Pacific, but the invincible local river, channelled at the last moment into a cut made, after all these years, by an old French dredge.

4

On his arrival back in Vienna, Anton noticed a change of atmosphere. For the first time he saw schoolgirls walking without governesses and young women without chaperones; there were also fewer line girls on the streets. The parks were fuller and the people, for some reason, looked as if they had become more healthy. Some were returning from the ski resorts, which explained their glowing skin; others seemed to have benefited from exercise regimes or an improvement to the posture. And in the newspapers he skimmed in order to catch up, there were reports from Paris, London and Berlin of new museums and theatres, broader boulevards and more luxurious shops; there were production figures that showed shipyards and steelworks at full stretch.

At the offices of the magazine, the editor was clear. 'I want the readers to feel they've been at the bottom of this Cut,' he said. 'I want them to sweat with fear and tropical fever. Spare us nothing. I'm getting the pictures in tomorrow. We can sell a lot of copies on this.'

For the first time in his life, Anton had enough money. He decided to rent a small house in Baden, a spa town less than an hour by train from Vienna. It was not his dream dacha near Moscow nor the lodge in a Bavarian forest, but a small white house up a lane with a garden that gave on to the Kurpark, from which there was a trail into the Vienna Woods. It had a thatched roof and was two minutes' walk from the next house; it would provide him with all the quiet he needed for his work while being near enough to the life of the town.

The other important thing about the Baden house was that Delphine would be there.

'I've saved up all my pay from the last six months,' she told Anton, lying fully clothed on the bed in his Vienna rooms, smoking a cigarette. 'Is there a piano in the house?'

'I've arranged for one to be brought in.'

'Good. I won't play when you're working.'

'How did you save all your money?'

'By not spending it! I bought no new clothes, I took all my meals in the apartment, as I'm allowed to, even if it meant putting up with Erich's conversation. I suppose I bought some stamps to write to you, some soap and things like that. Nothing else.'

'No cafés, no theatres?'

'Well, my love, I must confess I did allow that friend of Erich's father to take me to the Opera one day. And to a couple of concerts.'

'Were they any good?'

'The opera was *Don Giovanni*, so it was good. The concerts … less so.'

'And did you allow him anything else, this music lover?'

'I allowed him to buy me dinner once. And to pay for my cab home.'

'Afterwards.'

'Afterwards. Exactly.'

Anton sat down next to her. 'I thought that some of your underwear … What you had on the night I got back … That was new, wasn't it?'

'In honour of your return I bought some new stockings, yes. All the old pairs had holes in them. I was so frugal. There are one or two other things I think you'll like which I've already packed for Baden.'

'And what will you do all day while I'm working?'

'Read books. Write letters to my sisters, walk in the park. Ride the bicycle. There is a bicycle?'

'There are two.'

'... Prepare your dinner. Make myself ready for the evening. Every night a recital. Or a new adventure.'

'Did you leave Erich's parents on good terms?'

'Yes. They'd extended my stay there so many times it was beginning to be absurd. I believe Katrin now speaks better French than I do.'

What they could never discuss was how long Delphine would remain in Austria. She could have found work in any household or office, being fluent in three languages; but she never looked at the job columns in the newspapers or asked for advice. Anton wondered if in addition to what she had saved she had some allowance sent by her father in France. He must have been a proud and doting parent because – however much she praised Jeanne's kindness and Isabelle's beauty – Delphine would surely be his favourite child. Beyond this Anton didn't like to ask; it was as though there were a kind of spell – a suspension of the normal rules of time – that his questioning might break.

So Delphine took a train the day ahead of him to make everything ready. She collected keys from the letting agent and stopped to buy flowers at the market. Then she took a cab to the house to be ready for the grocer's delivery that afternoon and spent a day in preparations, moving lamps and chairs, putting candles in their holders and, after the vintner had called, unloading wine into the small cellar.

Everything seemed normal yet exciting to her, as she busied herself in the house. Her only anxiety was that she had not been able to tell Anton that she had been married before. The first night in his room, she had tried to explain that she was not the innocent

45

French teacher and chaperone he seemed to think. She held his hand tight and repeated herself; but he had been too transfixed by her nakedness to take in what she said. Then she hadn't wanted to break the spell he was under because it was too exhilarating to be the object of such awe.

One day she would spell out the unremarkable truth about Georges Duvivier, how she had been pushed towards him by her father, how much he drank and the arguments in their small apartment near the Place des Ternes. For the time being, it didn't seem to matter. Anton had at least registered that her past had been eventful. One day she would also tell him that she was unable to have children. For the time being, for the life they expected to lead, it was of no relevance.

When Anton arrived the following day, he found that Delphine had set up a work table for him at the window looking over the park.

Having never lived with a woman before, still less with one who fascinated him so much, he found it difficult to settle down to work. Panama seemed more than remote, it seemed unreal. Emerald and her devotions, Maxwell and his brandy bottle, the giant wheel that turned the lock gates lying flat in its braced iron bed ... Perhaps he had in truth caught yellow fever and hallucinated all these things.

What was real was the smell of coffee from the kitchen next door, the sound of Delphine singing to herself as she tidied, her footstep on the wooden floor. He went in, stood behind her and put his arms round her waist, then pressed himself against her. She turned and let her fingers trail across his shirt front and kissed him on the lips.

'This won't do, Anton,' she said. 'Work for two hours, then I'll bring you more coffee.'

He took her hand and kissed it, then went back sulkily to his desk and began to type.

If she felt her presence was distracting him, Delphine took one of the bicycles and went into town. There was often a quiet smile on her face as she left, which Anton took as confirmation that she enjoyed her power over him — and was content in their life of suspended time.

Their bedroom looked over some rhododendrons and out onto a cobbled lane. The brass bedstead had been painted in a shade of magnolia pink that Delphine tried not to notice. The straw mattress was thin; no amount of pummelling could make the brick-like pillows yield. Over the whole room the scent of mothballs mingled with something damper and more vegetable, like boiled asparagus. After a few days Delphine said the bed was making her back hurt and suggested they move to the second, smaller, room at the rear of the house. Here the bedhead was made of polished cherry and the mattress was deep; at the market, she bought two soft pillows and some old linen cases to go on them.

What the new bedroom had was charm, Delphine explained. It lay in the white-painted floorboards and the faded rose pattern of the curtains; in the casement window with bubbles in its original glass, the narrow glazing bars and the way it could be adjusted to let in just the right amount of summer air. Such things made the difference between a mouldy boarding house (the first room) and a pure enchantment. And a magnolia that wasn't white was an abomination. Anton nodded his head, as though he understood.

After her bath each morning, Delphine spent at least an hour sitting on the bed, reading in German and French while Anton worked in the living room below. In the evening, sometimes she served dinner on a low table in front of the large chimney breast, where it was still cold enough to have a fire; if it was warmer, she called him out to the veranda. She had a horror of the freshwater fish admired by the locals and spared Anton the sight of sausages. She tried instead to make Norman dishes from what she could find in the market; butter, mushrooms and cider went into the sauces and once she ordered an ox cheek that she marinated for two days in red wine.

When Anton found it hard to work, he urged himself on by remembering Amos and his friends, and the thought of them was enough to bend him to the typewriter once more. From upstairs, Delphine heard the clack of keys, the pauses and the rattling surges, looking up for a moment from her book, taking in a patch of morning sunlight on the distempered wall.

During the silences, as he organised his thoughts, Anton leaned back in his chair with his hands behind his head. He tried to think about French national pride and yellow fever, but found himself picturing the curve of Delphine's lower back, which he had massaged when she complained about the hardness of the bed. There was something touching about the softness of her skin over the firm, athletic flesh. He liked the trust she showed in him, lying naked, as though he were a doctor. She chatted about music and the shops in town while he kneaded and stroked; then she sprang from the bed and put on her clothes again, before he had finished admiring the base of her spine.

Sometimes he felt wary of Delphine. She had read everything he had, and more in her own language. He ought really to have taken his studies more seriously, he thought. Kant, for instance. He had found him wonderful, inspiring, but so difficult to read that he had given up halfway. Delphine was older, of course: she had had more time. And she seemed more worldly, too, in the way she could organise the house or sum up visiting tradesmen at a glance. 'He's been in prison. You can tell from his shaking hand … The other one's reliable, but he'll overcharge.' Her clothes were not old-fashioned, but they were proper, with skirts and laced boots and petticoats and pins in her hair, even if they were alone with no visitors all day.

Yet in other ways she was like a young girl. She ate when she was hungry, apple tarts and roast chickens and litres of coffee. She might drink no wine for days, then a whole bottle at lunch. It was hard for her to hide it if she was bored, though she did her best, for the sake of his work. And when she wanted to make love to him, she made it clear that now would be a good time, Culebra Cut or no. She had a green hat that she wore with a long, pearl-headed pin. It made her look formidable when they went out into the town together, she like a governess, he like an overgrown charge who, if he behaved himself, would be granted liberties on their return.

Anton had had friends at school and at the university and found it easy to get on with people quite different from himself, like Maxwell or Emerald; with Friedrich he had a bond based on the way they laughed at their confessed inadequacies. But with Gerhard so much older and seldom at home and Friedrich going back to his own family after school then working elsewhere when they were older, he had never had the thrill of a confidante who was there all the time. It was only now he could see what he had been missing all these years – someone who understood his point, even before he made it, then might add a twist of her own.

His weaknesses – feelings he had never seen as weaknesses, merely aspects of the way he was, everyday irritants – seemed less shameful once they were admitted. He invented names to indulge her, as though she were a favourite child; he had never known before that he had a paternal bent. She appeared also to reawaken some impetuous aspect of him that he'd been forced, by the gloom of the papered-over windows of the Gymnasium, to shut away before its time. There seemed no end to the versions of himself that Delphine brought to life, and no need to settle on a particular one. Sometimes it was agreed that if they were going into town she might pretend to be a prudish friend of his mother's whom he was obliged to show the sights – before inveigling home; at others she was a second cousin in her first summer after leaving school, abandoned by her parents for a weekend in his care.

It didn't occur to Anton that he was laying himself open in a way he might come to regret, because the process felt both natural and predestined. He was aware that, for the time being at least, he no longer felt superfluous. In disclosure there was an intimacy that all his life up to this point had lacked; and in each new intimacy there were discoveries.

As the weather grew warmer, it seemed a pity to return to Vienna, so Anton extended the lease for the months of June and July. Once a week he took the train back to Vienna, delivered his copy to the magazine and did a round of other papers to see if there was anything on offer. The Panama Canal was due to open in August, and the first of his long articles ran in mid-June.

The response was what the editor had hoped. 'Nothing could have been achieved by the Americans at Panama without the vision of the Frenchman, Ferdinand de Lesseps,' Anton's article concluded.

The French attempts ended in scandal and disaster, but this was not due to arrogance. The tragedy of de Lesseps was that he trusted the scientific advances of the last century too much. He viewed engineering not as a process, but as a kind of miracle – and believed that those more qualified than he would 'find a way'. His was a nineteenth-century life: he was a man from an era when all things seemed possible – even the Canal, which represents the greatest liberty ever taken by mankind with nature. And in the end he was proved right. Without his self-belief and his ability to inspire others to complete what he had started, the oceans would never have been joined.

With a series of dizzying photographs taken from above the Cut and some from inside the West Indian quarters of Panama City, the articles helped the magazine to sell out and reprint. Readers, it seemed, liked to hear about yellow fever and mudslides from the comfort of their armchairs. At the tables of the buzzing cafés, they disagreed with Anton's exoneration of de Lesseps and wrote to the magazine in their scores to say so. Anton was disappointed by this deluge, but the editor was delighted. 'They don't have to agree with us,' he said, 'they just need to buy the magazine to see what's coming next.'

Friedrich took him out to lunch to congratulate him. 'And your French governess. She must be pleased by your devotion to her countryman.'

'I'm sure Delphine appreciates the force of my argument. And the facts on which it's based.'

'And I expect she'll find a way of showing her appreciation ...'

'Are you a little jealous, Friedrich? Are you still spending your evenings with the chorus girls?'

'No, I have a proper girlfriend of my own. Not in a love-nest in the Vienna Woods. She lives with her parents and two sisters in a fine apartment. Time didn't stand still while you were away.'

'Ilse? I met her. She was charming, but I thought she seemed out of your—'

'Enough! Your Panama piece has really irritated a lot of people, you know, Heideck. Having been away so long you may not be aware how much feeling has hardened against the French. Most people think they're in league with the English. Privately.'

'League for what? I don't believe these noises about war. According to the Berlin papers, the Germans have stopped building battleships in any case. And what possible point could a war serve? When the whole continent's flourishing.'

'Control of the seas, I suppose,' said Friedrich. 'But mostly, I think, the problem is that everyone expects a war, but they don't want to be the one to declare it. As that French fool Poincaré said, "It's difficult to declare a defensive war without appearing aggressive."'

'Let's not talk about "enemies",' said Anton. 'What makes a country that's so long been your neighbour suddenly try to kill all your friends? Instead of serving you breakfast in your *pension*, they turn a rifle on you. Didn't you leave a big enough tip for the waiter? I'll never think of France as an "enemy". It's an absurd way of looking at the world. Or take Italy. Would they side with us, or with England, or whichever of us buys more ham from Parma? There's no point of principle. None at all.'

'Are you a pacifist, Anton?'

'Maybe. Perhaps my French "governess" has made me one.'

'Wouldn't you fight if some foreign power sent their troops into our streets? If the Russians occupied the Opera?'

'If it meant an end to evenings of Tchaikovsky, then ...'

'You're such an original philistine,' said Friedrich. 'A Viennese who hates music ... Like an artistic Englishman. Or a Frenchman who admires another country.'

'I don't dislike all music. I like what Delphine plays. Parts of Brahms. Most of Beethoven. It's just that some of Mozart sounds so dry to me – like a mathematical proof.'

'So you want to have your heart wrenched?'

'No, I hate that. Those songs of Schubert that make you look into some icy region of death. Or worse. Who would want to go there?'

The next day, the magazine asked Anton to join the world's press in Paris at the trial of Henriette Caillaux, which was due to start on 20 July. Madame Caillaux, the wife of the finance minister Joseph Caillaux, had gone into the offices of Gaston Calmette, the editor of *Le Figaro*, and shot him dead with a revolver. The newspaper had printed articles and private letters that suggested Caillaux had behaved dishonourably; they had further letters, said to be 'intimate', that they would not rule out publishing. The gunshots were the revenge of an insulted woman defending her husband's honour, as though in a duel. The late Gaston Calmette had become editor twenty years earlier when still in his thirties; he was admired for his tactful intelligence and had recently been the dedicatee of a book by a young writer named Marcel Proust. Madame Caillaux had made no attempt to escape the scene of the crime, though had insisted on being driven to the police station by her own chauffeur.

'I don't want to go,' said Anton.

'But you must,' said Delphine. 'It's an honour to be sent.'

'It's just another French scandal. Sex and corruption and—'

'You're the victim of your success, my love. When you went to Paris and you wrote so beautifully about it . . .'

'No, I was trying to prove they were in league with the English. Illegally.'

'Yes, but you wrote another article, too, about how the new boulevards had destroyed the old neighbourhoods of Paris. When you went to write about the *Mona Lisa*.'

'I didn't think anyone had read that.'

'I looked up the back numbers.'

'But I'm happy here. For the first time in my life.'

Delphine touched his hand. 'But it's not a very long life, is it? Not yet.'

'You think I'm being dramatic.'

'You have a tendency. But listen. Two weeks in Paris. Then you come home. Most people would love that.'

'I have a fear . . .'

'What?'

'That you won't be here when I get back.'

'I'm not going anywhere. Well, perhaps I'll go to the rooms in Vienna for a few days. That's all.'

'What if my country declares war on yours?'

53

She leaned up to kiss him on the cheek. 'Everything will be fine.'

They were standing face to face on the veranda in the summer evening. He was gripping her by the wrists as he stared into the brown eyes in whose light, for some reason, all his future seemed to lie – glittering, it was fair to say, yet unbiddable.

She smiled at him again, an eyebrow raised.

There was a pause.

'I wish I'd never met you,' he said.

'Oh, really!'

'I do. I thought loving someone would make me feel safe. Not precarious. Not balanced on a precipice.'

Delphine looked down. It was the first time he had seen her abashed.

When she raised her head at last and looked at him, she said, 'Well now you know.'

'Do you mean ...' He stopped, unwilling to believe himself. 'No. What *do* you mean?'

'That's why I was careful, why I took my time. I didn't want to be standing on that precipice alone.'

'So ... So you love me in the same way.'

'You're starting to understand.'

'But I have so little to offer you.'

'Let me tell you a few of the things you offer. Respectability to a woman with a slightly ... compromised past.'

'Respectability! In our unmarried household in the middle of—'

'Ssh. Let me finish. Not some neat petit bourgeois version of respectability. I lost that years ago. But you represent something fair-minded, something that won't be rocked or swayed by fashion or events. I could live a life with you and be neither bored nor betrayed.'

'It doesn't sound very exciting.'

'Will you stop interrupting! And then there's all the joy. The sound of your voice, the feel of your skin. The laughter and the way my heart lifts when I hear your footstep coming to the door. The sight of your doubtful smile.'

'I never knew.'

'I didn't want you to become big-headed.'

'I don't think I—'

'No. But one day you may become well known. Or rich. Or something else annoying. And then there'll be a danger.'

'But you'll be here to save me.'

'If you want me to be here.'

'I could no longer choose another woman than I could choose a different mother – or another name.'

'How fortunate, then, that you found me.' Delphine had begun to smile again. 'In the music room.'

Anton packed his suitcase as though every shirt he put in, every sock and every book was a thrust to his heart. It didn't feel like the prospect of a visit to one of the world's great cities; it felt as if he was preparing his own funeral. The hours ground by, slower than the hands of the old Gymnasium clock. He went with heavy foot-steps in a world that had grown cold; Delphine waved from the door, her left hand making high circular motions in the evening light, as the cab took him away.

The magazine had found him a hotel near Notre Dame de Lorette, north of the Bourse, in the foothills of Pigalle. The room had floral wallpaper that was coming unstuck near the cornice. It smelled like most of the cheap hotels his life as a reporter had sent him to, of failed plumbing and cigars. The window over-looked a courtyard where some cab horses whickered and stamped on the cobbles.

From a stand on the rue des Martyrs, Anton bought an armful of newspapers and flicked through them to see if Monsieur Poincaré had yet returned from Moscow – and if so what alliance with the Russians he had built to go with his undertakings to the

British. But he found little about the looming war; almost all the space was given over to Henriette Caillaux's state of mind and to the details of how her relationship with her husband, the imposing Joseph, minister of finance, had begun when both were married to other people.

The court of assizes met in the Palais de Justice on the Île de la Cîté. The courtroom held around 300 men, including the press, which made a peculiarity of the female defendant, whose mauve blouse was almost the only flash of colour among the black morning coats and legal gowns. It was a cavernous room, in which many oak trees had gone to benches and to panels that reached up to the ceiling, from which hung glass-globed chandeliers. Anton's seat was in a back row, among the other reporters, and he had to fight for a place between two Italians.

Henriette Caillaux, under questioning, described herself as 'bourgeoise', and, apart from a fancy feather in the band of her hat, there was little to suggest otherwise. With her narrow mouth and slightly hooked nose, she looked more like a housekeeper than a femme fatale. Her victim's paper, *Le Figaro*, described her as having the 'banality of a shop girl'. Most of the Paris press thought Caillaux had been about to drop her, as suddenly as he had left his first wife, and that her desperate act had been her way of forestalling him. If she was found not guilty, she would be shackled to a marriage in which love had died. One columnist declared she would be better off going to the guillotine.

Looking at her impassive face and sober clothes, Anton wondered what control she had once wielded over Caillaux, himself a known womaniser. Why had he forsaken his first wife, Berthe, a society beauty, for this woman with the pursed lips? Henriette had carried the pistol, a Browning automatic, hidden inside a large fur muff; but what other powers, fatal not to Calmette but to her husband Joseph, had she concealed beneath her clothes?

The inner lives of others were unknowable; and in that mystery lay the interesting part of the drama. The complexity of what they must have felt was at odds with the vulgar entertainment of which they had become the cast, Anton thought. The newspapers' language of scandal and outrage could barely hint at the murkiness of the desires experienced by the participants in their stuffy apartments.

'Heideck! Heideck!'

As he crossed the forecourt of the Palais de Justice, Anton heard his name called by a familiar voice, one that took him back at once to a jungle and the rasp of Emerald's broom.

'I saw you on the other side of the court, but I couldn't catch your eye,' said Maxwell, shaking Anton's hand, puffing, beaming.

'An unexpected pleasure. How are you?'

'What a circus. Dear God. Where are you dining tonight?'

'I'm not sure. I've only been here a couple of days.'

'Come with us. With me and Thompson, the man from Reuters. We're going to a place in the rue Victor-Massé.'

'All right.'

'Thompson swears by it. Do you like French food?'

Anton pictured Delphine's *noisettes de veau aux champignons* in cream and cider sauce. 'Yes, I do.'

First, they crossed the river and went to a bar on the rue des Halles, where a handful of reporters had taken to gathering after the day's proceedings and comparing notes.

'Don't bother with the man from *Le Figaro*,' said Maxwell, 'the fellow over there with the long face. We know what they're going to say. Cold-blooded murder. Guilty as charged.'

He handed Anton a glass of white wine. 'They keep their own barrels in the cellar. It never makes it into a bottle. The patron has a share of a vineyard in Macon. Cheers, old man. Very good to see you.'

'*Santé.*'

'You speak French?'

'Yes. Don't you?'

'Hmm ... Not really. Stick close to me, Heideck.'

The noise in the bar began to increase, as regular customers on their way home from work joined the journalists from the trial.

'This would never happen in England, of course,' said Maxwell. 'We have something called "contempt of court". It means the press can't pass any comment on proceedings.'

'None at all?'

'Not while it's going on. Because what you say might prejudice the outcome if it's read by a juror. You can only give a verbatim account of what's said in court. But the French press had run their own trial before the poor woman even took to the witness box. Half the papers calling for her head, half of them screaming for her to be acquitted.'

'It's certainly outspoken,' said Anton.

'It's typical,' said Maxwell. 'The defence is trying to get her off on the old *crime passionnel*. Prove she wasn't in her right mind. Plus some newfangled stuff about her unconscious urges taking over her conscious willpower. So it wasn't really our Henriette who pulled the trigger, but some force from outside. Or inside. I'm not quite clear which. But you'd understand all this guff. Being Austrian.'

'Oh yes. Psychology is a Viennese speciality. Like schnitzel and prostitution. We've discovered the existence of "the unconscious", which, they say, makes up nine-tenths of our mind.'

Maxwell laughed uneasily. 'The other thing that's on trial is French manhood. They want their men to be warriors and their women to stay at home in nice dresses. Trouble is, Napoleon was defeated by Wellington and then they were trounced by the Prussians at Sedan. Then another revolution in Paris, the Commune and more bloodletting. So they're feeling emasculated. Ungovernable. Like perennial losers. They hate the idea of women

58

taking over. They don't want to give them a vote. They want our Henriette to be a girl with a fit of the vapours. What they're terrified of is what they call an "*hommesse*" – a woman with a whatnot.'

'How have you worked all that out?' said Anton.

'Pop Dawson gets the French press translated and wires the best bits over.'

Thompson from Reuters turned out to speak, or at least understand, French and was circumspect in his judgements. He also seemed fond of snails, of which he ordered two dozen in the restaurant where they had gone for dinner, in a side street off the rue des Martyrs. The tables were close together and Anton felt anxious about being overheard, but calmed himself with the thought that no unguarded speculation of his could be wilder than those already printed.

'This'll interest you, Heideck,' Maxwell was saying, as he spread some foie gras over his toast. 'Calmette made his name as a junior reporter in Panama! Oh yes, he was there at the same time as de Lesseps. And they say that's what accounts for his extraordinary wealth. He comes from a modest family and he was only ever a journalist like you and me. But, like half the Chamber of Deputies, he took the de Lesseps shilling, or franc I should say, urging his readers to vote more money to the French scheme. He ended up worth millions apparently. More wine, Thompson? I think it's Reuters' turn tonight, isn't it? You look distracted, Heideck.'

'Yes, I had a telegram at my hotel. My country has sent Serbia a diplomatic note. We've as good as declared war.'

'Dear God.'

'The rest of Europe will follow.'

'Can't it be confined to the Balkans?' said Thompson.

'Not when Germany joins in.'

Maxwell and Thompson looked down at the fillets of sole on their plates while Anton waited for their response. It was as though they resented time away from their favourite topic.

59

'It won't last long,' said Thompson with a sigh. 'If the French drag us into it we'll soon put the kaiser back in his box. And don't forget, Europe's been at war off and on since 1618.'

'Exactly,' said Maxwell. '*Plus ça change.*'

'I thought you didn't speak French, you old fraud,' said Thompson.

'God, I've been found out! And by the way, one of the reasons they don't like Caillaux is that when he and Poincaré went on holiday to Italy, Poincaré kept his mistress hidden, but Caillaux flaunted his in public.'

'I thought they were all allowed to have mistresses,' said Thompson.

'They are. But showing her off at a reception is considered poor form. The belle époque has strict rules about these things. Etiquette …'

And so the question of the coming war faded from sight. Squeezing between the tables and the wooden partitions with their glass panels, the waiters brought sweetbreads in mushroom sauce and *pommes vapeur*. They drank more wine, a red from Bordeaux on the Reuters account, and for the first time since he had been in Paris, Anton stopped thinking about his house in Baden and about what Delphine would be doing. He even managed for a short time to put aside thoughts of a war between his country and hers as he sank into the hot noise of the room.

The following day, after the court proceedings were over, he didn't go to the bar in the rue des Halles, but back to his small hotel, where he wrote a letter.

My dearest Delphine,
    You were right. I had to come. I've seen nothing like it in my life. It's like watching two children fighting over a toy while their house, with all their family inside, burns down

behind them. A windy comparison, I'm sorry. I mean the coming war will put this nonsense in perspective.

The courtroom is immense and often rowdy. The calmest person is Joseph Caillaux himself. From the other side of the court all you see is his perfectly hairless head and smooth, impassive face. He looks like a boiled egg. Hard to believe he is one of the most feared and hated men in France. When he was prime minister, a few years ago, he did a private deal with the Germans. You probably remember. He let them have part of the Congo in return for their leaving French interests alone in Morocco. The Germans withdrew their gunboats from Agadir, after which many in his own party, who are worried about the waning of French virility, accused the pacifist Caillaux of depriving them of the war they 'needed' to prove themselves a warrior nation once more.

Today I got a closer look and could see his stiff collar and stud, his beautiful silk tie with its pearl pin and dove-grey waistcoat. A boiled egg maybe, but a dressy one. There's something about him that seems wound up wrong. He's out of step with the times. France wants a warrior, not a fixer. Also, he exudes a powerful self-interest. He refers to his wife as 'my poor child', but you feel he already has replacements in mind, that he'll make a decision about her future in the same way he dealt with Agadir and income tax, swiftly and without looking back.

I've run into Maxwell, the Englishman from Panama. He's quite unchanged. He sees the world in simple terms, but those terms are helpful to me. We smack each other on the back and buy more drinks. He tells me about his plans to retire one day to a town on the coast of Suffolk, a house overlooking the sea.

The trial turns on whether Mme C was really herself when she pulled the trigger. We've heard a lot about the weakness

61

of the female mind. There have been quotations from a psychologist, a disciple of the famous Pierre Janet, about how women's passions overrun their meagre resources of character. One paper even claimed that on the day of the crime Mme C was undergoing her monthly period. So that explains a murder! To her supporters, she's described as frail and either weeping or on the verge of tears. The prosecution presents her as an accomplished marksman who practised pistol shooting on an indoor range at the gunsmiths Gastinne-Renette – a killer, emotionless and calculating. According to the papers that support this view, she has shed not a single tear, but has remained frighteningly detached. I don't think both reports – constantly in tears, utterly dry-eyed – can be accurate.

But, my dearest D, no one seems to care what's really going on. All of Russia was fixed on the visit of Poincaré and what it meant for an alliance. In Paris, you need to get through eight pages of gossip and sex before you reach even a short account of it.

What are your plans? Please consult Erich's father about what he thinks will happen to 'enemy nationals' in the event of war. I will try to find out more from my editor when I cable my report this evening. There is talk here of camps in which foreigners will be made to work.

It may be best for you to leave by train while you still can. It might also be an idea for me to stay in Paris and wait for you, though of course I don't know what arrangements the French will make for people like me. I like Paris well enough, but I don't want to be locked up (though I suppose it might be better that way than actually fighting against your coun-trymen and killing them).

Keep buying the newspapers and see what advice you can find. Should you also visit your embassy and see what they say?

The timing is awful. If only I could get away, but I have to wait for the verdict of this insane trial. Cable me if necessary at the hotel.

Je t'embrasse très fort, ma minouche.

A

It was easy for Anton to maintain a journalistic detachment. The conduct of the trial was lax, the reporting scandalous and the participants hard to like. It made him laugh, it made him angry, but, like Maxwell, he couldn't take it seriously.

However, on the sixth day there was a change of atmosphere when the lawyers at last agreed which of the 'intimate letters' could be read out. The defence had argued that Le Figaro's apparent intention to print these letters was what had placed Madame Caillaux in an impossible position; they thus had no choice but to agree that their contents must, to some extent, be revealed. The exchange came from a time when the correspondents were both married to other people, and much of Caillaux's first lengthy letter was about the deception of his then wife and his reassurances to Henriette.

Having arrived two hours early, Anton had found a seat as near the witness stand as possible. Henriette Caillaux, wearing the same mauve blouse as on the first day, held on to the rail of the stand as her inner life was laid bare.

The lawyer's voice was soft, apologetic for the intimacy it betrayed, but in the silence of the courtroom it was loud enough.

Madame Caillaux's complexion, never healthy, grew paler as the lawyer's voice went on. While the contents of letters were thus made public, Le Figaro became at liberty to print what it had previously only threatened to disclose. Was it the thought of millions reading it that made Henriette grip the wooden rail so hard, Anton wondered. Or was it the knowledge that everyone in the courtroom was picturing her in the act of lovemaking, wondering what

noise she made, about the softness of her skin or what little prefer-
ences she had revealed to her bald lover.

Anton looked away from the poor woman's face for a moment;
when his eyes returned to her, it seemed that all the blood had
gone from her cheeks.

The lawyer's quiet voice resumed: 'A thousand million kisses all
over your adored little body . . .' But he got no further, as Henriette
Caillaux collapsed and fell to the floor.

'What a piece of acting,' said Maxwell. 'They must have rehearsed it.'

'I was sitting quite close,' said Anton. 'She couldn't have faked
the pallor of her skin.'

'It was the perfect drama for the defence. It showed her as the
feeble woman with no self-control – which has been their argument all along.'

'It could be both. Genuine and helpful. It can't be easy to know
that everyone in court's imagining you in bed with your husband.
Or someone else's husband, as he then was.'

'Well, personally I tried not to think of old Caillaux poking her
all round the moon. Can you imagine?'

They were in a bar on the rue des Écoles, having decided to
venture into the Left Bank for a change.

Anton drank some beer. 'Do you know what your government
plans to do with Germans and Austrians on British soil when war
breaks out?' he said.

'There was a question asked in Parliament. Someone mentioned
a camp at Newbury racecourse. But I think the government's still
hoping to find a solution. So it wasn't very forthcoming.'

'It's too late,' said Anton.

'I know. But the truth is there are a lot of people at home who
want a war. There's terrible unemployment in the big cities –
Liverpool, Manchester, Glasgow. Strikes. TB and rickets in the
slums. Do them good to get some fresh air and three meals a day.'

'Don't you feel this whole trial is a bit of a sideshow?'

'Yes, but look at the space it's getting. I'm on the front page every day, even in London. Pop Dawson loves nothing more than a Frenchman making an arse of himself. But a whole country! It's a godsend. Don't be a prig, Heideck. You can make your name on this. This is your big chance.'

'Will you volunteer to report on the war?'

'I'll go if they send me. I'm too old to fight, thank God. What about you?'

'I'll have to fight.'

'Will you be conscripted?'

'If I have to go, I'd rather volunteer.'

'Dear God, Heideck, you know how to spoil an evening.'

'I'm sorry. It's just that I'm worried. About someone I know. She's French. In Vienna.'

'Let me get you another drink.'

While Maxwell was gone, Anton looked round the bar, whose clientele was younger than that of the café in the rue des Halles. Many were students at the nearby faculties of law or medicine, crowded close at the tables, smoking, interrupting, laughing in a way that seemed forced. The gilded mirrors on the wall doubled their number on reflection, spinning back a vision of enthusiastic health into the lamplit room. Soon their glossy hair would be shaved, Anton thought, their jackets and cotton scarves replaced by greatcoats and marching boots. Did the French infantry have wine delivered with their rations? Perhaps they did. These budding advocates and doctors would become old men – those who survived, at any rate – their darting eyes replaced by the stare of those struggling to forget what they have seen.

On the eighth day, when the verdict was due, Anton made a deal with Maxwell that they would share details of what happened, one operating inside the court building and one outside. Together they first mingled with the crowds in the morning, where armed municipal guards were trying to separate rival supporters. An hour was long enough to gather that those who passionately backed Caillaux believed he and his Socialist ally Jean Jaurès could still save the country from war, even at this late hour, by revealing how Poincaré had entered into illegal agreements with Russia as well as with Britain. The other side, more belligerent, believed Caillaux was depriving them of the war they craved, as he had once before, at Agadir; that he epitomised everything that was rotten in France and that both he and Jaurès should be shot. It was rumoured that a man had been found to do the deed and issued with two pistols, one bearing the letter 'C' and one the letter 'J' on the handle.

'I'm going inside now,' said Anton. 'If I can't find you afterwards, we'll meet in that bar on the *quai*.'

'All right,' said Maxwell. 'At least Paris has stopped thinking about sex for a moment.'

The lawyers' summings-up came to an end and the jury retired at eight in the evening. They were back within the hour. They found that Henriette Caillaux had not been clear-headed or self-reliant enough to be responsible for the murder of Gaston Calmette. At the foreman's second enunciation of the word '*Non*', the defendant fell into the arms of her lawyer, though during this collapse she remained conscious. The room broke up into furious shouting, '*Vive Caillaux*' and '*Ass-ass-in!*' The judge pronounced the defendant free to go, his voice straining to be heard, then shrugged and left his court through a door in the panelling behind his seat.

Anton ran outside, where in the melee he was able to push his way over to Maxwell.

'Half of these people are here to make trouble,' puffed Maxwell. 'They're mercenaries. You know what we should do? We should go with Caillaux and see if we can have a word with him. He'll be feeling pretty pleased.'

'How do you know where he lives?'

'He's going to his best friend's house. Thompson told me. Come with me, Heideck. The champagne'll be flowing. Let's see if we can bluff our way in.'

They ran over the bridge and found a cab near the little garden of the Tour Saint Jacques. Ten minutes later they were at an *hôtel particulier* in a quiet street; but they were not the first. Scores of hostile people had gathered on the pavement and were chanting outside the house.

'So much for the Reuters plan,' said Maxwell.

When a cab delivered Joseph and Henriette Caillaux, they had to be all but carried up the steps by police wielding batons to keep the mob at arm's length. Eventually the guards managed to secure a passage for friends and supporters to make their way up to the first floor, where the lights glowed in triumph.

As the protesters grew more numerous, however, the flow of guests began to dry up.

'Word's got out,' said Maxwell. 'I think they'll make a run for it. It's not safe for them here. Let's go round the back.'

The rear of the house gave onto a cobbled mews where a row of cabs was waiting and some horses were being fed from iron mangers on the walls. There was also a motor car with a rear section enclosed by a metal roof, alongside which stood a chauffeur in uniform.

They waited for half an hour in a doorway.

'Maybe it's all dying down,' said Anton, looking at his watch.

'Let's give it another few minutes. They won't get far in that contraption anyway.'

'I've got a train from the Gare de l'Est,' said Anton. 'To Vienna.'

'Where are your bags?'

'At the left luggage office.'

'Wait. There's someone coming out.'

A back door opened and a maid appeared, carrying two suitcases. She went over to the car and handed them to the driver.

'When they appear, you're going to have to translate' said Maxwell. 'I know what to say, but you'll have to put it into French for me.'

The maid went back into the house and shortly afterwards Joseph and Henriette Caillaux appeared in hats and coats despite the warmth of the evening. Showing a turn of speed that surprised Anton, Maxwell crossed the cobbles and stopped them.

'Tell him who we work for and that we'd like to talk to him.'

Anton, catching up, did as he was told. Caillaux eyed them both in silence.

'Tell him we want to give him a chance to explain how France can stay out of the war. Him and Jaurès. Say our papers are dead against war.'

Elaborating a little on what Maxwell suggested, Anton threw in some flattery towards Madame Caillaux, using idioms he'd learned from Delphine.

Caillaux said nothing, but began to walk towards the motor car, where the chauffeur was cranking the engine.

'Ask him if he's going to his country retreat,' said Maxwell.

Caillaux held the door open for his wife as she climbed into the back of the car. He looked Anton slowly up and down, then let his gaze travel over Maxwell. This was not a man, Anton thought, with warm feelings towards the press. But perhaps the fact that they were not from Paris, still less *Le Figaro*, might help.

Caillaux spoke briefly before climbing into the car and slamming the door.

Anton translated. 'He said, "Tell your English friend I will make a statement at twelve if he wants to be there. But tell him it will be in French."'

'Dear God, Heideck, you're a wonder. Let's go. Gare Montparnasse, I think. He'll switch to the train once he's out of Paris. He won't risk that contraption.'

'I'm not coming.'

'Don't be a bloody fool, Heideck. This is the chance of a lifetime!'

They followed the car out of the mews and back onto the main street, where a newsboy was selling the evening paper. 'Austria Declares War' was the headline. Anton ran across the street and bought a copy.

'You can't go back now, can you?' said Maxwell, laughing.

'I can if I hurry.'

'If Austria's declared war, then Germany's in as well. The game's up.'

'I've got to try.'

'The trains won't be running. Come with me. I need your French. Let's get this Caillaux thing done. Then in a couple of days, things will be clearer and you can go back to your little sweetheart. Come on, Heideck! Two days won't make any difference. It's your big chance!'

Maxwell hailed another taxi and asked for the Gare Montparnasse. Anton climbed in beside him, his head full of misgivings.

Near Le Mans, they stayed at a small inn on the edge of the village in which Caillaux had his country house. Maxwell was able to get his story over to London, where it appeared on the front page, with Caillaux's comments on the trial translated for English readers by an uncredited interpreter. Anton's magazine worked on a longer deadline, so he offered what he had to the daily newspapers. They either had their own correspondents or were more interested in the fact that their country was at war. *Die Presse* took two paragraphs of quotation from Caillaux for an inside page. It was hardly the career-changing moment Maxwell had promised.

On the third day, they returned to Paris. Anton was in his hotel at Notre Dame de Lorette when he heard from the hall porter that Jean Jaurès had been murdered in a restaurant a short way down the road, in the rue Montmartre. Someone had fired two shots through the window into his back. Jaurès was dead within minutes.

Finding himself among the first people at the scene, Le Croissant, Anton felt obliged to telephone his magazine and let them know. It appeared that the murderer was a young nationalist who was hot for war and determined to stop Jaurès attending an international peace conference. There was blood and broken crockery on the floor, but the significance of what had happened, Anton suspected, lay beyond imagining.

It was two weeks into August before he was at last able to return to Vienna, by way of Lyons and Geneva. As the train pulled in, he noticed in the newspaper he was reading that the Panama Canal had officially opened, with the first commercial crossing from one ocean to another made by a steamer called *Ancon*. The report was on page fourteen.

There was no sign of Delphine in their rooms and he could find no one else in the building to ask for information. When his telephone call to Baden went unanswered, he returned to the station and took a train.

The thatched house was locked and the ground-floor windows were shuttered, as they always left them when they went back to Vienna. Both bicycles were propped up against the wall of the veranda. Inside, everything was tidy. There was no note for him on the writing table in the window, and nothing in the small kitchen, where all the dishes and pans had been washed and put away.

Upstairs, the brass bed was stripped down to its uncomfortable mattress. In the wardrobe were the clothes they kept there, country things and a little spare linen, everything folded as it would normally be.

In the smaller room, the bed with the cherry-wood frame was made up with clean sheets; the windows with the bubbles in the original glass were closed, though a dead fly lay on the sill.

PART TWO

1

'War,' said Lena, who was eight years old. 'What does it mean?'

'How should I know?' said her mother, Carina, who, before Lena, had had five children by five different men. The only time she felt happy was when she was pregnant; with a child growing inside her it was impossible to worry about the small things of life. She had no interest in her children once they were born; they had all been taken into orphanages. Carina was unable to read or write; her favourite days were the ones when she could drink schnapps until she fell down. She was a familiar figure in the neighbourhood, and easy to avoid.

'Will men kill each other?' said Lena.

'Yes.'

'Will they kill us?'

'I don't think so.'

They lived in a two-room lodging in the sawmill district of a town in Carinthia, only four hours by train from Vienna, but seeming to belong to a different world. The narrow streets where they lived had small brick houses and goods depositories used by a dwindling river trade.

Lena often asked about her father. 'I've told you. His name was Stefan,' was all that Carina would say.

'Was? Is he still alive?'

'I don't know. Stop asking questions.'

'How can you not know?'

Born in the poor wing of the hospital, Lena was named after a character in a song her mother had once liked. The doctor made his rounds two days later. 'And will this child be given up to the orphanage at St Spyridon's?' he said, looking at her as she lay in bed, feeding the baby. 'Like the others?'

'No,' said Carina. 'I've decided to keep her.'

She had had no such thought until that moment.

'And how will you feed and clothe her?'

'I'll find work. At the mills. Or maybe here at the hospital. I can scrub the floors.'

'I know the people at the clinic on the Wilhelmskogel. They might be able to offer you some work.'

'The madhouse?'

'Yes, they have a very ... enlightened attitude. It's a big place and they always need housekeeping. Cleaning, laundry and so on.'

The doctor was no older than Carina, but had a sense of his own importance. He looked at her over his glasses and said, 'You can see the lady almoner on your way out and she can give you some clothes for the baby.'

'All right.'

He sat down on the edge of her bed. 'The child is a responsibility, you know. If you're going to look after her, you should make sure you have no more children. And you should be sober.'

Carina said nothing.

'Do you want the child to be baptised? The priest can do it here in the hospital if you like.'

She ought to go back to Trieste, where Stefan lived. If he still lived there and had not gone to sea again ...

'Well, would you like the child baptised or not?'

'Yes, I would.'

When she was allowed home with the baby, people noticed something different in Carina. It seemed that instead of avoiding

76

the neighbours, she was studying them. She looked surprised at the early hour at which they went to work, but she took in the way they dressed and talked to one another; she watched when they left home again in the evening to spend their money in cafés. The neighbours were amused to feel themselves inspected, even by a woman with bloodshot eyes.

The Wilhelmskogel clinic agreed to give Carina work as a cleaner, but it was an hour's walk from town and then a cable car up to the top. She had to take the baby with her. A blind woman called Mary, who did massages for the patients, would often look after Lena while Carina worked. She went only two days a week and had to make more money in other ways. At home, there was some passing trade from the dock workers and river pilots, but it wasn't easy to entertain men with her baby in a basket in the corner.

In one of the streets in the sawmill district there lived a man known as Herr Gustav, who was said to be a writer. When Lena was about two years old, he gave her some old books with pictures in them. For want of other toys, she became familiar with the illustrations. Unable to read the rudimentary text, she invented stories of her own about the monkeys in red breeches and the lions in top hats.

When she was old enough to go with her mother to the market, she looked at the faces of the men who sold the vegetables and wondered if one of them was her father. It might be the man in the green apron who sometimes gave her an apple. He would be a good person to have on your side. Or it could have been the man who sold the woollen waistcoats with brass buttons in the cobbled street behind the square. He might be richer than the apple man and might live in an apartment in one of the old buildings with open courtyards. He would teach her how to make money for herself and what to say in church. Most of all she hoped her father was Herr Gustav. He seemed lonely, walking in his heavy coat, with his gold glasses and the books held under his arm. She could quite easily have looked after him in his brick house and made him food at night.

Lena viewed all society as hostile because her mother did. The town hall and the shops, the schools and court buildings were frightening to her, inhabited by the ones who understood – people of a different kind. On rare occasions, Lena had a flash of hope, when she believed that not all these people were exceptional. Some of them might have started out like her, knowing nothing till someone handed them a key. But if she asked too many questions her mother sent her to play in the yard behind the wharf and told her not to speak to other children. Beyond the yard was the river, where Lena must never go for fear of drowning.

Rather than try to solve the mystery of her exclusion – or of how the world worked – it seemed easier to hope for luck. When she saw an institutional building, she hoped that it might at last be the one that admitted her, Lena, into the company of the elect. It was surely no more difficult than having a ticket in a raffle. And when she saw a young woman with a thoughtful face, she believed that she might be the one in a thousand who would explain things to her with a laugh and throw open a door.

One day when she was five, Lena was taken by her mother to the hospital where she'd been born. She had no memory of the building, which looked to her like a prison. Indoors, in the brick corridors, were printed signs with words she couldn't read. Men and women in white coats hurried past with long faces, pushing trolleys that rattled with a clank of twisted metal instruments half-concealed by cloths. The dim electric bulbs at intervals along the walls gave off the glow of winter twilight, but just enough to catch a fine moisture on the brickwork, a chemical sweat that caught

Lena's throat with a compound of iodine and what she thought of as the breath of illness.

They came to a hallway where four corridors met and a man in a glassed-in box directed them to a closed door.

'What are we doing here?' said Lena.

'We've come to see the lady almoner.'

'Why?'

'You have to go to school and I want to ask her how it works.'

'Why her?'

'She was kind to me once. And I don't know anyone else to ask.'

Fräulein Winkler seemed surprised to be consulted on a matter of education. 'Since the child is baptised, I presume you can send her to St Theresa's school,' she said, sitting at her desk with a picture of the hospital's patron behind her. 'They'll feed her at midday, too.'

'I have no money,' said Carina.

'The church provides.'

Lena squirmed in her chair. Other children didn't go to hospital to find the way to school. Her mother was like a child herself.

'Will she meet other children?'

'Of course.'

'I'm not sure I want that.'

'She can't be a hermit. She must make friends.'

Lena looked at Fräulein Winkler's pointed face and the grey hair drawn back from it. What did this woman know about children anyway?

They left the hospital and walked past St Thomas's church till they came to a building behind iron railings, a place Lena had often seen before, in a street that ran down to a bridge across the river. The man there asked Carina to sign a piece of paper. To Lena's relief, he didn't laugh when her mother told him she couldn't write, but signed her name himself. And a week later, Lena began her education.

It was the first time she had been in a room with more than two other people. She found a place on a bench at the back and looked straight ahead, wondering what on earth awaited her.

There were rows of these benches, with iron legs that came up and supported sloping tabletops. A wooden ridge at the base prevented books and pencils from sliding off. Most of the children seemed to know each other already; in a way that was extraordinary to Lena, they also seemed to know what to expect.

The teacher, Herr Kaufmann, held up pictures on large cards with a letter by each one. Lena was too fascinated by Kaufmann to concentrate on what he was saying. She looked at him as she might have looked at an entertainer in a circus. Did he live in a house? With a wife? Or in a teacher place? She pictured rows of Kaufmanns in a dormitory with iron beds. Herr Kaufmann's words and pictures – a zebra, a banana – flew past her eyes.

Lena looked at his suit with its silver watch chain. Everything about him was hard. She wondered if he had skin beneath his clothes or if he was coated in metal. He never smiled, though the chalk, when he ground it into the board, made a sound like a small creature laughing.

'Once you've learned all the letters and how they sound, you'll be able to read,' Kaufmann said.

The idea meant nothing to Lena. Looking down at her feet, she noticed that the floor was made of wood – not like the planks of the wharf where she lived, but small pieces fitted into patterns. Kaufmann's voice went on, unheard by her as she stared at the herringbone. She was never going to see the point of letters; but shapes and patterns ... Perhaps she could understand what lay behind them.

In a break between lessons, the children were allowed into the courtyard. Lena hung back against the wall beneath a high windowsill and watched. There were groups of boys, circles of skipping girls, calling to one another, playing with a ball or with stones they picked up from the ground. Presumably they had all been meeting in secret, practising games over the years, while she had done nothing but gaze at the riverboats unloading and tell stories to herself.

Without moving her head, she allowed her eyes to run over them. She wondered whether each girl and boy might be like her underneath – with feelings – but there seemed to be no evidence of it. Their large bodies and their shouting made it seem impossible that anything could be going on inside.

Sometimes Herr Kaufmann wrote numbers on the board. He seemed to be saying that, put together, these numbers could lead to other numbers; but why this mattered he didn't say. Lena was drawn to the look of eight, because it was shaped like two breakfast rolls, but she didn't really care how it differed from four with its hard crossbar. At lunchtime they went into a different room, where a grey-haired woman in a pinafore, Frau Schmidt, ladled out clear soup with bits of pancake in it. Afterwards there were cooked apples with honey and walnuts. Seeing that none of the other children seemed to like the nuts, Lena took some handfuls and put them in the pocket of her skirt to eat later. A boy called Lukas began to call her 'the Squirrel' and other children joined in the laughter. 'I bet she has a bushy tail as well,' said Emma, Lukas's sister.

Lena was pleased that someone had noticed her. She filled her cheeks with the walnuts, pretending to be a squirrel, but although Lukas and Emma and a couple of others laughed out loud there was something about the sound that wasn't humorous. 'Take some for your father,' Emma said.

Once the large hand on the clock had risen to the upright and the small one lay square, pointing to what she now knew was a three, she was gone, running over the courtyard and out onto the street as the handbell was rung by Frau Schmidt. For fear of being found out, she kept running until she had crossed the river.

*

81

Coming back from school one day, Lena found her mother sitting on the wooden deck outside her room, looking over the river and smoking a cigarette.

'I've had an idea,' she said. 'I think it's time you met your father.'

'What?' said Lena.

'Yes. He's called Stefan, as I told you. He comes from Villach. He's a sailor. On the sea. Who did you think your father was?'

'I ... I thought he was dead.'

'Did you?' Carina seemed surprised. 'Stefan lives in Trieste. We're going to take a train. When school stops for the winter holiday. I don't think he'll be at sea then because the weather's too bad. We'll visit him at home.'

'But how will you know how to find it?'

'I've been there before. I remember the name of the street and someone'll help us.'

Lena wanted to believe her. But the way Carina tossed her head and looked away, as though she was already thinking about something else, made Lena anxious.

'Why didn't you tell me before?'

'The time wasn't right.'

'Does he know we're coming?'

'No. He doesn't even know that you exist.'

'How can that be?'

Carina sighed. 'One day ... I had been in a bar near the railway station for a long time. And I was so ... tired. I saw a carriage that looked comfortable and I went through the fence and sat in it. And I fell asleep. It's a long story.'

'But you met my father?'

'Yes. In Trieste. He ... rescued me. I didn't know where I was. He let me stay with him.'

That night on her bed in the corner of the room, Lena tried to imagine what this man looked like. There was a picture of a sailor

82

in one of her books, standing on a deck with a knife between his teeth. He wouldn't be like that. She knew the men who worked on the river and they were sailors of a kind, but they didn't go to sea. She turned on her side. It didn't matter what he looked like because she already felt something towards him that was different from any feeling that she'd had before.

They went to the railway station in the best clothes they had and were told there was a train for Trieste in an hour. Lena had a boiled wool jacket in crimson with silver-coloured buttons that a river pilot had given her. Carina carried a canvas bag with some rye bread and smoked sausage and a few spare clothes in case they stayed. The third-class compartment of the train had wooden seats and dusty floors with cigarette ends and old newspapers.

Lena sat with her hands folded in her lap, opposite her mother. She was too excited to speak and was afraid that if she did say anything Carina would tell her to be quiet. She wondered why her father hadn't stayed with Carina – married her, like the fathers of the children at school. She couldn't help feeling that her mother had failed to appreciate him properly. She wouldn't make that mistake herself. Whatever he turned out to be like, old or young, with a beard, or with reading glasses like Herr Kaufmann, she wouldn't let him escape.

The engine stopped to take on water and Lena gazed at the countryside through the window. It was the first time she had seen farm animals, or fields and woods. They prompted questions that she knew Carina wouldn't want to answer. It was better to let her eyes linger on a cart with a dozen churns of milk, a dray horse tethered to a gatepost, a path running up into the hills past smoking cottages. She turned to her mother, her face alight with what she'd seen, but saw Carina staring at the man a few seats away from them.

At one point, as they were crossing into Italy, the guard asked to see their papers. The train didn't stop at the border; and when Carina told him she had no papers, he only shrugged his shoulders.

They ate some bread and sausage while the red-tile roofs of Udine were vanishing behind them; Lena fell asleep against Carina's shoulder and didn't wake until they were alongside the Bay of Trieste, which was sometimes open to their view, sometimes cut off by trees or by a high-sided motor lorry on the road.

For an hour, until they drew into the station, Lena's eyes never left the water, which glistened, catching the light at a thousand different points, then grew darker as the sun went down, still heaving against the shore.

On the platform, Carina held her hand tightly as they went through the crowd and out into the square. At six years old, Lena was strong and used to walking; she turned her head to watch the lights coming on in the buildings on either side. She smiled at the Italians, hearing occasional words of their language that made her want to laugh; she had to stop her feet from running on ahead.

They went into a bar, somewhere Carina thought she knew. They gave her a glass of water for Lena, while someone told her the way to the via dei Fabbri. A church bell was sounding seven when Carina finally recognised what she was looking for.

'This is it,' she said, stepping up into a dark porch where she rang a bell.

There was no answer and no sound in the tight little street except for a seagull's cry. She rang again.

'I don't think he'll be at sea,' said Carina. 'Perhaps he's gone to the bar. Or gone out somewhere to eat.'

They stood silently, waiting. A doubt entered Lena's mind. Her mother had invented the story. Or she had taken them to the wrong place.

Above their heads there was the sound of a window being pushed up, and then a man's voice.

'Is someone there?'

'Stefan? It's Carina. Do you remember me?'

'Carina? Of course I remember! Good God. Wait there. I'll come down.'

The door opened and they went inside, up stone steps to a landing and into a lighted room.

The man wore a white shirt with no collar, dirty old trousers and a waistcoat. He had no beard or eyeglasses; he was neither young nor old. His dark hair was curly and his face was lined.

'And who is this?' he said.

'This is ... my daughter,' said Carina.

'What's your name?' said Stefan.

He was holding out his hand. No sound seemed to come from Lena's mouth and she had to repeat the word as she placed her hand in his. 'Lena.'

'Come and sit down, Lena. You too, Carina. I can make some tea. Are you hungry?'

'No, sir,' said Lena, as though she were talking to Herr Kaufmann.

'Why not?'

'We had some sausage on the train.'

'Some sausage on the train? Don't tell me that! Wait here while I shave and change my shirt.'

When he came back into the room, he took a jacket from a chair and led the way downstairs. It was not far to a trattoria where the people seemed to know him. They called him Signor Fontana, which Lena thought was a good name. There were fishing nets draped over the walls and candles stuck into green bottles.

Stefan and Carina began to talk about things of no interest to Lena, who looked round the room at all the people. A grey-haired waiter came and spoke in Italian to Stefan, then brought them plates of spaghetti and clams with jugs of red wine and water to drink. Lena sucked up the spaghetti and asked Stefan if they could have some more. The same waiter brought a plate of fried fish and another jug of wine.

Afterwards, they went back to the rooms in via dei Fabbri, where Lena slept in the bed with her mother while Stefan took the couch. In the early hours she heard him snoring with a soft noise like one of the incoming boats when it sounded its horn at a bend in the river.

The next morning was cold, but Stefan made them hot milk and coffee and went out to buy bread.

'Would you like to come fishing on my boat?' he said as they ate. 'We won't go far because it's cold, but we could go just outside the harbour and catch something. My boat's up in that small dock where we first met.'

'No,' said Carina.

'I thought you liked the sea. That's what you said.'

'I only like to look at it.'

'I'll come,' said Lena. 'Can I come?'

Carina couldn't be persuaded to join in, so it was just two of them who set off to walk across the city, her hand in his as they went up the winter streets, Lena's body bulked out by wearing all the spare clothes she had brought. It took them half an hour to reach the dock, where they walked along a mole till they came to some steps. Stefan's boat was the last in the line. It was a good size, but had seen better days; the thin blue stripe painted round the hull had half peeled away and the woodwork looked dry and splintery. He grasped Lena under the arms and swung her aboard.

'Take this,' he said, handing her a canvas bag with a rope fastening. 'It's our lunch. Now sit down up there in the front. I'm the captain, so you have to do everything I say.'

The boat rocked as Stefan untied the mooring, gave it a shove with his foot and, just when Lena thought she might be going out to sea alone, jumped aboard. To begin with, he rowed, which was hard work for such a large boat; then when they were clear of obstacles, he pulled in the oars and hauled up a sail. Lena sat quite still where he had placed her, in the bows, watching the quick way he ran the ropes through his hands and tied them off. She could see the stones on the seabed in the shallow water.

Stefan sat at the other end of the boat, holding on to a long piece of wood attached to something under the surface that he moved from side to side.

'You all right?' he called out.

'Yes.'

'You can be the figurehead of my ship.'

Lena didn't know what he meant, but nodded.

When they were out of the small harbour into the bay, the sail picked up more wind and they began to travel smoothly over the water, which had turned a blue-black, so Lena could no longer see the bottom. The wind pinched her cheeks and the top of her ears. She watched as Stefan ducked his head when the heavy piece of wood that held the lower edge of the sail swung across the boat.

She thought she ought to say something, but she couldn't: she could only look with wide eyes at the water, the sail, the man in the stern and the city of Trieste, its streets and buildings losing their sharp edges as they blurred into the grey plateau that towered over it.

'Now we'll catch some dinner,' said Stefan, slackening the sail as he moved up the boat and opened his canvas bag.

Lena watched as he threaded four hooks on a piece of line, then wound them round a piece of bread. Words suddenly came to her.

'Is that all you do? To catch a fish?' she said. 'Don't you have nets?' She was thinking of a Bible illustration she had seen at school: the miraculous draught of fishes.

'Not for this sort of fish. When I've cast it, you're going to hold the line. Hold tight. Don't let it go. It's only good for a couple of casts and then the bread falls apart.'

He stood up in the boat and threw the bait out onto the water.

'It's a bit choppy,' he said. 'Let's see what happens. Come down here and sit next to me so you can hold on.'

The end of the line was attached to a small piece of driftwood, which Lena held as she sat on the bench next to Stefan. He sat to windward and put his arm round her.

'Can you feel anything? Any fish biting?'

'Yes, I can feel something.'

'It could just be the waves.'

Lena felt she had let him down. She was desperate to feel the tug of a real fish.

Stefan put his right hand over hers, the one that gripped the line, and said, 'Put your left hand up. Like this.'

She did as he asked, and he held his own hand up next to it. His was large, knotty and brown, hers small and pale. The low sun came through the webbing of their fingers.

'Like two peas in a pod,' he said.

Lena kept her hand up next to his for a moment longer, wondering what he wanted.

He put his hand back on his knee and kissed Lena's cheek.

'What?'

'I think ... Do you have a father at home?'

'No,' said Lena. 'You're my father.'

He laughed. 'Was she never going to tell me?'

'I think I've got a fish!'

'Let's have a look. Pull the line in gently and wind it round here. That's it.'

There were in fact two small fish, pinkish-gold, attached to the sodden bread. Stefan removed the hook from the first and held it up.

'What shall we do?' he said. 'Would you like fish for dinner? It's a bit small, but we can catch a few more, I expect. You don't look very sure about it.'

Lena flinched as she watched the un-hooking.

'Is it still alive?'

'I'll say. It's all I can do to hold on. Shall we put it back in the water?'

'Will he be all right?'

'Yes, he'll be fine.'

He dropped both fish into the sea. 'We'll go after some mackerel if you like.'

Stefan threw away the sodden bread and took a different line onto which he tied a small red piece of tin, shaped like a fish, with a hook at one end. They sat together in the stern, with Lena holding the line as the sail filled again. It wasn't long before she felt a wrench and was able to pull in a silver and blue fish that smacked the floor of the boat with its tail. This one they kept, and two others that followed. Stefan banged their heads on the deck to stop them thrashing, then put them in a basket while he and Lena ate their bread and cheese. After a couple of hours, Stefan turned the boat towards the harbour and Lena, tired out by the wind, rested her head against the oilskin of his shoulder.

On the way back to the via dei Fabbri, when it was starting to grow dark, they went into a café, where they drank tea and ate small, dry cakes. A few minutes later, they stopped outside the window of a fishing shop and Stefan pointed out the seashells on display amid the wooden models of sailing boats.

'I need to buy a few things in here,' he said. 'Come and have a look inside.'

Stefan spoke to the shopkeeper, a man in brown overalls, who opened small boxes that he fetched from shelves behind the counter, while Lena looked at the models. It seemed to take Stefan a long time to find what he wanted. Eventually he came over to where Lena was peering at a lighthouse carved from wood and painted white.

'What do you think of that one?' he said, nodding towards an old galleon.

'It's nice.'

'Is it your favourite?'

'No, this one is,' said Lena, pointing at a single-sail fishing boat.

'A bit small. What about this one?' said Stefan, holding up a steamship with a funnel.

'No, I like the small boat best.'

'All right, let's see if we can get the sail up.'

Lena watched the line of cotton between Stefan's huge fingers as he pulled the sail into position and tied off the thread round a miniature cleat.

'There you are. Under full sail now. Well. Just about.'

Stefan took the model over to the man at the counter and paid for it, then handed Lena the parcel as they left the shop.

'Keep it in this wooden box, to stop it getting knocked on the train.'

'Is it ... for me?' she asked.

'So you'll remember your day at sea.'

2

When they were home, back in their room in the sawmill district, Lena asked when they might see Stefan again. Carina told her she didn't know.

A year went by.

'Perhaps he'll come in time for the summer,' said Lena.

'I don't think so.'

'When will he come? He said he'd come one day.'

'Don't keep asking questions.'

A few weeks before her seventh birthday, Lena saw Herr Gustav in the street and crossed the road to speak to him.

'Could you help me, please? I want to write a letter.'

Gustav took a pace back. 'You go to school, don't you? Haven't they taught you to write yet?'

Lena had no excuses. This tall man with the gold glasses was the only person who had shown an interest in her; and now, at the first hurdle, she had let him down. And why could she still not write? The letters made no words for her. Her hand couldn't make the chalk move the right way on the slate. She was stupid and she had no father. She couldn't tell Herr Gustav any of this, but she opened her eyes wide, then took his hand.

Gustav puffed, but relented. They went into a café where some workers were having lunch and sat down at a table. 'Dear Father,' he began to write on a piece of paper he had taken from his bag. Lena told him the address in Trieste.

'Write "Signor Fontana". That's his name.'

'What day is your birthday?'

'In March. The twelfth. We don't know for sure, but that's the day I've chosen.'

'Why?'

'I like the number twelve because of the twelve men in the Bible.'

'The apostles?'

'Jesus's men.'

'I've got an envelope at home. You'll owe me for a stamp.'

'I'll pay you back. How long will it take to get there?'

'Three or four days, I should think. I'll post it tonight. What's the name of the building where you live? So he can write back.'

Lena told him. Then there was nothing more to say. She looked at Gustav's lined and disappointed face.

'You should learn to read,' he said. 'We need readers. My life depends on it.'

Lena felt that for the first time in her life she had found a way round her failings: something had turned out right for her. To express her surprise, she reached up and kissed Gustav on the cheek.

At school, Emma kept talking about her First Communion, which was due to take place at St Thomas's. Lena asked Carina if she could go. She had been baptised after all, so it was only right. 'And perhaps Herr Gustav could be my godfather.' Carina was not interested, but Lena discovered the day and time of the service and presented herself at the church. The other girls had white dresses, as if they were brides, and the boys wore velvet suits and ties. The church was crowded with their parents and supporters.

Lena went to a pew at the back and watched what the other children did. When the time came to take the sacrament, she followed the others to the altar rail and knelt. Looking from the corner of her eye, she crossed her hands and held them out in front of her.

The body of Jesus was placed in her palm, which was damp with excitement. When she touched it with her lips, she felt a charge go through her spine. A second priest came with a silver cup, wiping the rim with a white napkin as he tilted it towards her. Lena had to restrain her hands from grasping, but managed to take in some of the sweet liquid with her lips. She closed her eyes.

She felt the hand of a priest on her head. 'Bless you, child, you may return to your seat now. Go in peace.' She opened her eyes and saw that she was the only one left at the rail. She made her way quickly back to her place.

In the days that followed she tried not to think too much about Stefan. He had seemed pleased to meet her when he held his hand up against hers on the boat and let the sun shine through; he had appeared to like her when he put his arm round her shoulder. Yet some twitch of self-preservation made her tell herself he wouldn't come. He'd get the letter ... but only when he returned from a long time away at sea. It would be too late. And he might not have enough money for the train.

And he probably had other children. In Ancona or Dubrovnik or one of those funny-sounding places he'd mentioned.

She'd never paused to think about this properly before, but now it seemed obvious: she was not his only child – much as she might have liked to be.

The letters that came through their door were most often from a workplace with a note of how much Carina had been paid, or from the school, to tell them when the new term began and that Lena's work continued to be disappointing. Lena watched to see if the postman would climb to their front door, but he never did, hauling his heavy sack onwards to the wharf offices, then uphill to the parts of town where the houses sat behind high railings.

The February fogs gave way at last to the winds of March. Lena could see the days pass on the calendar at school and worked out that the twelfth would be a Wednesday. It didn't matter how often she told herself that her father might not come because by now she was expecting him. Every strange figure who crossed the school-yard could be him. Was he that tall? She couldn't remember. Did he walk with a limp like that man? She didn't think so. But one thing she did know. Stefan would come.

At midday she was too excited to eat the soup, though she filled her pockets with nuts as usual because Carina liked to roast them in the evening.

'Look. The Squirrel's taking extra nuts,' said Emma.

'Perhaps her mother's expecting a caller,' said Lukas.

'As a matter of fact,' said Lena, 'my father's coming. It's my birthday, you see.'

'I didn't think you had a father,' Lukas said.

'Of course I do! He lives in Trieste. But he'll be there when I get home.'

Lukas and Emma were silenced.

When she left school after lessons, she walked calmly, imagining what she would say to the newly arrived Stefan, who would probably be casting round the room, looking for somewhere to put down his suitcase. She'd have to ask him about his journey, but in truth she was more interested in what present he might have brought her. She'd liked the model boat, and it still sat above the fireplace; but what she wanted most of all was a doll, a creature that, unlike the animals in her book, was three-dimensional. Stefan would have understood that, and Trieste, because it was so big, was sure to have toy shops.

Lena climbed the steps outside their building, the muscles of her freckled legs tensing and sliding below the hem of her cotton dress. She pushed back her uncombed hair as she let herself in, smiling.

There was no one there. The kitchen-cum-scullery in the corner of the room had a couple of dirty plates, but she recognised them as the ones from which she and Carina had eaten the night before. Her mother's bed was unmade and the low divan held only the imprint of her own body. She checked the washroom behind the curtain before going onto the wooden balcony and looking over the wharf towards the bend in the river, wondering if Stefan might have surprised them in choosing to come by water.

No. But it was still all right, she thought. Her father's train was late and her mother had gone to meet him. Carina had said nothing of this because she wanted to surprise her. He was going to come.

Lena sat on the balcony for two hours, watching a boat unload. Its cargo was wheeled down a gangplank in barrows, then carried off through the double doors of the warehouse. Did the men who worked in the wharf have parents, she wondered. That young man, there, the one she liked with the dark blue shirt and the cap pushed back on his head, the one who sometimes whistled, did he have a father and mother or was he now too old for parents? Was the young one related to the old one with curly grey hair and the cigarette, the one she imagined was the boss? It was fascinating in a way to watch and think.

And yet. This world, she thought, outside my reach ... I can't be someone looking on, all my life. I can't forever stand the way I do at school, peering through the iron gate while the others play their games. I can't wait for a man who never comes.

Carina arrived home shortly before midnight, unsteady on her feet. She found her daughter lying on the balcony outside, her eyes so swollen that even through the mists of alcohol Carina couldn't help but notice.

'Have you been bitten by an insect?'

Lena shook her head.

'Did one of the children hit you at school?'

She lifted the light body and carried it inside, putting her down on her own bed.

'There. You can sleep with me tonight.'

The girl curled herself away.

'Here,' said Carina, 'have some of this.' She mixed some schnapps in a glass with a little sugar and water. It was the best she could offer and it cost her something to dip into her own supply. Lena refused to take it, but climbed under the blanket, which she pulled up to hide her face.

Carina drained the glass. 'You'll feel better in the morning,' she said, lying down beside her daughter and falling asleep.

When she was thirteen, Lena left school. In that time, she had received three postcards from Stefan and two promises to visit, but had had no sight of him. Sometimes she wondered if he had drowned at sea. His fishing boat had drifted beyond the bar to be swept up by ocean currents, blown and buffeted till it capsized, leaving him trapped beneath the upturned hull with its thin blue stripe … It seemed to her that the best course of action was to save some money and take a train to Trieste. She had made the journey before, after all; the only difference was that this time she would be alone.

First, she had to find work. She was too young to clean at the clinic with her mother, to be a waitress or even a washer-up in a café; but Frau Winkler, the lady almoner at the hospital where she had been born, said when Lena reached the age of fifteen she could come and work in the laundry there.

The money from the hospital, it turned out, was barely enough to buy food to keep her going. One day, after she had spent the morning folding sheets, she saw a young man on crutches with a leg in plaster, coming down the corridor. He had curly hair and a reddish face that to Lena suggested kindliness – like the man in the wharf with the blue shirt, but less intimidating. It was not the type of colouring she'd seen often in the streets, where the people were dark-haired; it was almost a girlish face.

The young man smiled at her and, for all the caution she'd been taught by her mother, Lena smiled back.

A few days later, she saw him again, this time hopping round the small courtyard at the back of the hospital. She waved. He put his cigarette between his lips, stuck one crutch next to the other and waved back with his free hand, almost toppling over. Lena laughed as he regained his balance, and he laughed back.

His name, she discovered from a girl in the office, was Rudolf Plischke, and he was nineteen years old. When the surgeon had taken off his plaster and he had strengthened the leg with some exercises, the notes said, he would return to his father's house in a village above the Worthersee.

By postponing her break from work, Lena found herself in the courtyard two days later when Rudolf was taking his exercise.

'Hello, little girl. I'm not falling over today. Not to please anyone. What's your name?'

'Lena.'

'I won't shake your hand, for obvious reasons. My name is Rudolf.'

'I know.'

'Well, do you now? And how come? Have you been in the ward at night, looking at my fever chart?'

'No. A girl in the office told me.'

Rudolf laughed. 'I'm pleased to meet you, Lena. Aren't you rather young to be working in a hospital? Shouldn't you be at school?'

'I'm fifteen. I left school because I was no good at lessons.'

'Education doesn't stop when you leave school. I'm going to sit down on this bench now and have a cigarette. As you noticed, I need another hand to manage if I'm standing up. A third hand.'

He was very jolly, Lena thought. No one had spoken to her like this before. He sat down and pulled a cigarette from his pocket. He struggled with the matchbox and the crutches.

'Let me.' She lit it for him, and he sat back and puffed.

'I'll be off soon. Back to my parents' house. I broke my leg working on a farm. My father thinks I spend too much time reading so he makes me do outdoor work in the summer. He'll think twice about that now.'

'What sort of work?'

'Cleaning out pigsties. Making hay. Feeding cattle. Anything the farmer asks.'

'I've never seen a farm. Well, I saw one once, from a train window. On my way to Trieste.'

'What were you doing there?'

'We went to see my father.'

'Is he Italian?'

'Partly. Is yours?'

'No, my father is as Austrian as they come. He's a lawyer in Klagenfurt. He draws up agreements for landlords and drives poor tenants out onto the street.'

'He sounds—'

'I'm exaggerating. Most of what he does is making wills for old ladies. I'm studying to be a lawyer myself. In Vienna. But I don't really like it.'

'So why do you do it?'

'So I can make money one day. And ... God knows, Lena. Why do I do it? I'm only interested in politics, really.'

Rudolf pulled his good leg up onto the bench beneath him and stuck the broken one straight in front of him, the plaster heel in the gravel.

'Tell me about your family.'

Lena looked away. 'My father ... My father is the captain of a ship. He sails the Adriatic Sea. To foreign countries.' She wondered where the word 'Adriatic' had come from.

'And your mother?'

'My mother ... is a dressmaker.'

'Where does she work?'

'She has a shop. Just off the main square.'

'I must pay her a visit one day.'

'Don't do that. She doesn't like visitors.'

'Then how does she—'

'Except ladies. To buy dresses, of course.'

'Of course.' He laughed.

They talked for another half-hour, after which Rudolf levered himself up from the bench.

'Don't be late back,' he said.

Lena turned to go, then stopped. 'I won't work in the hospital all my life. It's just till I'm sixteen.'

'And then what?'

'I expect I'll go to Trieste. And then I'll go to Vienna.'

'You could open a dress shop for your mother.'

'Yes. Or maybe I'll work on a farm.'

'I think you're too ... small. The milkmaids have strong hands.'

'I can still grow.'

'Take this,' said Rudolf, handing her a card. 'This is my father's name and his office address. If you write to him when you're older he'll send it on to me. I might be able to help you find some work.'

Lena felt her mother's hand restraining her, but forced herself to take the card.

'Why don't you put down your own address?' she said.

'Because I don't know where I'll be in two years. Another student lodging, probably. But my father isn't going anywhere. Don't worry, he doesn't mind being used as a poste restante.'

'Why do you want to help me?'

Rudolf chuckled again, a sound that was beginning to worry Lena, as if everything she said was laughable.

'Shouldn't people always help each other? In our next life, I'll be the one who needs assistance. And I hope I'll meet you. You

99

might be a wealthy landowner. And some instinct will stir in you. A vestigial memory.'

'Do you think we live again? After we've died?'

'I expect so, yes. At least, no other theory of existence makes any more sense. You'd better get going or you'll be in trouble.'

Lena felt there were other things to say, but the thoughts wouldn't find a shape in her mind.

There was a worker in the laundry called Sophia, a little older than Lena, who seemed to think it was her duty to educate the younger girl. Sophia had been brought up in an orphanage near Villach, but with boys as well as girls. Following complaints of bad behaviour, she had been moved to St Spyridon's, where two of Lena's half-sisters had also been, though Lena herself knew nothing of their existence. Sophia had tried a few jobs before ending up at the hospital, sent there because Frau Winkler had a reputation for taking on the most hopeless cases.

'You remind me of someone,' Sophia said one day. 'A girl at St S. She had fair hair and brown eyes, like you. The boys liked her.'

Lena was not sure whether to feel flattered. Sophia, with her large bust and loud voice, intimidated her. She said nothing.

'Do you like boys?'

Lena looked down at the tiled floor, puddled in places from the dripping laundry.

'What's that on your hand?' said Sophia. 'Is it measles?'

'I don't think so. My hands itch when I've touched the wet sheets.'

'You're in the wrong job. Do you have your period yet?'

'What?'

'You know. Bleeding.'

'Yes. Yes. My mother gave me some of her old ...' It was one of the few things Carina had done for her.

'Her old what?'

'Nothing. How old are you, Sophia?'

'Seventeen.'

'What will you do next?'

'Next? God knows. Find a job better than this place. Find a husband one day. A rich man so I don't have to wash dirty sheets.'

Lena thought of Stefan in his room in Trieste. It would be good to be married to someone like him.

'You'll be all right,' said Sophia. 'When you're older.' She laughed. 'I don't suppose you've been with a boy yet.'

'I don't know what you mean.'

'When I was in the first orphanage there was a boy used to come to our dormitory at night. He had this ...' She leaned and whispered in Lena's ear. 'We used to take turns touching it.'

Lena barely understood.

'Don't be a fool,' said Sophia. 'It's all quite natural, you know. How do you think you came into the world?'

'I was ... I was born in the hospital. But my father lived a long way away.'

'Got no brothers, have you?'

'No.'

'Did you know boys at school?'

'Not really.' Lukas.

'There must have been some!'

'Yes, but we weren't friends.'

'Ever met any men?'

'Yes ... Yes, of course.' Herr Gustav. The apple seller in the market. Stefan, her father. The wharf worker with the blue shirt. Rudolf Plischke.

'It's all they think about. Men. When they see you. Maybe not you, not yet. But when you get to my age. Know what they want to do?'

Lena shook her head and turned away, but Sophia held her tight round the shoulders and whispered in her ear.

101

'That's all they think about. Day and night.'

'I don't believe you,' said Lena.

'You'll see. With your own eyes. You will.'

Lena pictured what Sophia had described and began to laugh. It was too ridiculous. It was impossible to believe that sober grown-up people would do these things. But some remembered moments from her early childhood – heavy footsteps, a second glass on the table, her mother's startled face – took the edge off the humour.

In her work in the laundry and in the course of her walk to and from the hospital, Lena began to see a world beyond her home and the schoolroom. Her mother had told her to distrust and, if possible, avoid other people, and this was the basis from which she began. By the time she was sixteen, however, she had begun to think that the lessons of her own experience counted as much as her mother's advice.

'Now that I'm sixteen, I'm going to work in a café,' she told Sophia one day.

'Where?'

'Maybe I'll go to Villach. Or Vienna.'

'Don't go to Vienna. You'll get eaten alive.'

'What do you mean?'

Sophia dropped an armful of wet sheets into a basket. 'You say things young girls shouldn't say. You say the first thing that comes into your head.'

'What's wrong with that?'

'You need to be more careful. Half the girls in Vienna are on the game.'

'I still don't know what you mean.'

'I saw you kiss that young doctor.'

'I wanted to say thank you. He'd given me some ointment for my hands.'

'People get the wrong idea. If you go round kissing men.'

'I don't "go round" kissing anyone.'

'Go to your stupid café in Vienna, then. Come back pregnant.'

Carina became ill that winter and was taken into the poor wing of the hospital. The years of alcohol had damaged her organs, though the doctors seemed to think she could survive if she gave up drinking. Carina was happy to be in a warm bed with no worries about food or money. When she became delirious, seeing creatures on the wall, they gave her medicine to make her sleep.

Soon after her seventeenth birthday, Lena found work with one of the men she had once hoped might be her father – in the shop that sold woollen waistcoats. He also stocked leather trousers, dirndls, jackets and shoes. His name was Herr Thaller and he was paternal enough. He paid her very little, but he had given her the job without asking for any references and it was better than working in the laundry. The rash on her hands improved once she was no longer in contact with detergent.

To begin with, she was kept busy at the back of the shop, stock-taking and sweeping up while Herr Thaller dealt with the clients himself. He went out to lunch every day to a brewery where they served fried chicken and potatoes at long tables; and during his absence Lena was allowed to look after the customers. She was worried that she wouldn't be able to work out the right change, but she found that just enough of Herr Kaufmann's arithmetic had stuck in her head.

Talking to the women was the part of the job that interested her, discussing what best suited them, or if there was something not in stock that she could order in. It appealed to the part of her that had liked staring at the schoolroom floor: a sense that something worthwhile could be found in patterns, beyond the logic of numbers and the giggling chalk. She made drawings on the back of paper bags to show the women customers what she meant and they told her the names for the things she drew, pleats, darts, hems and gathers. When she had been working six months she had saved up enough to buy a dress she liked, cream with damson-coloured embroidery. She managed to get her hair under control with a ribbon of the same colour and one of the customers complimented her. Lena persuaded Herr Thaller they should offer at least a small selection of dresses that she'd seen in catalogues from Vienna. He secured some good terms from the manufacturers and let her go ahead with her own rail, though he told her it would never replace his traditional lines.

Lena kissed him on the cheek. 'You'll see.'

Herr Thaller went back into the stockroom.

The shop did good business, some of the items on Lena's rail were sold, and after a year Herr Thaller, who had taken to staying out even longer over his fried chicken, allowed her to buy in some men's clothes as well.

Carina was back from the hospital and Lena took charge of the upkeep of their two rooms. Herr Thaller gave her a small pay rise and Carina was well enough to resume her cleaning work at the clinic, which was moving back from the mountain to its old home by the lake, the Schloss Seeblick.

The bell on the shop door rang one afternoon and Rudolf Plischke walked in.

'Do you remember me?' he said.

'Of course. How's your leg?'

'It healed. A long time ago.'

'And how's Vienna?'

'I finished at the university. Now I have to work at a law firm to complete my training. It's very dull. Who did this drawing?' He held up a paper bag with the outline of a dress.

'I did it. For a customer.'

'It's ... elegant. Is this your mother's shop? The one you told me about?'

'It's ... She sold it. This is a different shop.'

Lena looked hard at Rudolf. His eyes were sky blue, the colour of honesty. He was still thin, like a boy, but his manner suggested a man who had lived in the city and knew how life worked.

'I looked for your mother's shop,' he said. 'But I couldn't find it. I wanted to see if you were all right. You didn't write to my father.'

'I didn't need to. I had a job.' She had been too ashamed of her spelling to risk writing. 'Shall I show you some of our jackets?'

'Yes.' Rudolf seemed amused, in just the way she remembered.

He stayed for a long time, trying on jackets and waistcoats until Herr Thaller returned, smelling of hops and tobacco.

'I'll take this,' said Rudolf, holding up a flannel shirt he had previously shown no interest in.

'I'll wrap it for you.'

'Do you do other drawings? For fun. I mean landscapes. Or people.'

'No, just these, for the customers. I couldn't do those things.'

'But perhaps you could,' said Rudolf. 'You could go to a class in the evening. An old friend of mine teaches one. Near St Thomas's.'

'I couldn't afford it.'

'Oh, he wouldn't charge much. If anything.'

She looked at him. Everything in Rudolf's face seemed reliable. His eyes, his smoothly shaved face, the curly hair almost as out of control as her own had been, before the ribbon: a boy not far from her own age, and yet a man. She couldn't be a spectator, staring through the iron gate while the others lived their lives.

Rudolf enrolled her in the class and she began by going once a week. The teacher, whose name was Tomas, said she showed promise and he wouldn't charge her for a second class on Fridays.

After her first Friday, Rudolf was waiting for her outside.

'I'm taking you to dinner,' he said.

'I have to get back to my mother.'

'I won't keep you long. I promise. Just this once. What do you like to eat?'

'Cakes. And fruit.'

'Which fruit?'

'Blackcurrants are my favourite.'

'What about the first course?'

'Schnitzel. Spinach.'

'Do you like wine?'

'I've never had it.'

'All right. I know the place to go. It's five minutes' walk.' He took her arm. 'Come on. I'll explain to your mother. I'll walk you home afterwards.'

Lena found she liked wine.

'Don't drink any more,' said Rudolf. 'It might give you a headache.'

'I like the taste. And it makes me feel … blurred.'

The restaurant was full of noisy students. It seemed to Lena that each table was in a competition to be seen to be enjoying themselves more than the others, by talking louder.

She felt Rudolf's eye on her, and collected herself. 'When will you go back to Vienna?' she said.

'I'm staying here for a time, working for my father's firm. I'll soon complete my training.'

'I'd like to go to Vienna one day.'

'I could see if I can find you a job there. If you like.'

'That's very kind of you. But my mother … Maybe when she's better.'

Rudolf took her out to dinner every Friday after the art class and began to talk to her about politics.

'You're grown up now, Lena,' he said. 'You should know about these things.'

Lena, who was starting to feel more confident with him, said, 'Why?'

'Because you'll have a vote soon. And for the world to get better everyone alive must play a part. You can't live a life of isolation.'

He explained how Austria had lost half its young men dead or wounded in the war. And the world's greatest empire, Austria-Hungary ... gone to dust, like Carthage or Rome. Now was the time for the people of the factories and the farms to have their say. They had given their young men to the slaughter; they were owed something in return.

Lena was distracted by the flush of his cheeks and the light in his eyes, which at one point seemed to fill with tears.

'The group I belong to,' he said, 'has socialist principles. But the difference is, we have a spiritual belief as well. We believe in a god, very like the Christian god you know from school. The New Testament.'

'Jesus. Yes. And his apostles.'

'I also believe there is a universal economy of good and evil, so that what you mete out in one life will return to your ledger in the next.'

'I see,' said Lena.

'Think of a great lake that's drained and refilled over many years. The water evaporates and the rain falls, but the level of the lake remains the same.'

'I see. Though the river we live near is sometimes in flood and sometimes it's so low that a man stands in the bow with a long stick shouting out to the pilot behind him.'

Rudolf laughed. 'I think there's a metaphor there, my dear Lena. Let me work on it for a few days.'

Passing over the word 'metaphor', Lena said, 'This group of yours, does it meet here?'

'God, no. We meet in Vienna.'

'Does it have a name?'

'They've tried lots of names. Now it's simply called Rebirth.'

'So should I vote for your party?'

'Of course you should. This is a dangerous time. The Heimwehr, the private army of the Right, killed ninety people who were demonstrating. They opened fire in a place called Schattendorf. The Palace of Justice in Vienna was set on fire.'

'Do you have any candidates?'

'Not yet. But soon.'

After dinner, Rudolf walked her home, as he had promised. Lena grew anxious when they crossed the river and came into the sawmill district.

'You don't have to come any further,' she said. 'I can see my house from here. There's a light, so my mother must be home.'

'No, that's all right. It's no trouble. And I'd like to see where you live.'

They went down a narrow street and into the open area towards the river and the wharf.

'It looks like a warehouse,' said Rudolf. 'It's ... romantic.'

'It's damp,' said Lena. 'Leave me here, please.'

But Rudolf had already run up the outside wooden steps and was standing at Carina's door. Lena moved quickly. To soften the abruptness of the farewell, she kissed him on the cheek as she slipped behind him and shut the door after her.

The following week at the Friday art lesson there was a life model, a middle-aged man Lena recognised as a porter in the vegetable market. The dozen students stood behind their easels in a half-circle, while Tomas explained some simple rules with the help of a skeleton, hung by a hook through the skull: the femur is always longer than the tibia, he pointed out; the eyes are lower in the head than you imagine, almost halfway down. Hands he advised them to ignore for the time being.

The model stood holding a long staff of wood. His belly hung low and the veins of his legs stuck out in knots. Lena noticed between his legs the thing Sophia had told her about, though this man seemed to have three of them. Slowly, glancing back and forth from her paper, she worked out it was the third bit, the middle one, that Sophia had been referring to. It seemed insignificant to have been the cause of such excitement. By the end of the hour, however, she was reconciled. She wouldn't have minded prodding it with her finger, to see how it reacted.

When she looked at Rudolf at dinner, she wondered what his would look like. Not like the market porter's. But it was impossible to look at his face, his eyes full of thoughts, and think of the other thing at the same time.

'There is a ladder of perfection that we climb all our lives,' Rudolf was saying. 'Through contemplating God, coming closer to Him and allowing his spirit into our thoughts.'

'I see,' said Lena. 'So in your last life you must have been better than I was. Because now you're handsome and going to be rich and I'm just ...' Heaven knows what sort of life her mother must have lived last time around.

'No, no! It's not that simple. Anyway, you have beauty of spirit, Lena.'

'I think I'd rather have beauty of face.'

'It's your soul that matters.'

Lena became quiet as dinner went on, but Rudolf's voice was beautiful and so were the things he said. They sounded just and uplifting.

'I wish I hadn't left school so young,' she said at last. 'I'll never really understand all the things you talk about.'

'That's not true. Your education begins the day you leave that dusty building. I've learned ten times more since I left the Gymnasium than I ever learned while I was there. All you need is a book. Then you read another book. And the ideas that once seemed so strange begin to sound familiar.'

Lena was won back a little by what Rudolf said. Then she remembered what Sophia had told her. Was his real intention something else? Perhaps he wasn't really thinking about the rights of workers at all.

In the course of their Friday dinners Lena learned to drink wine without the world spinning when she lay down later on her bed. She understood that the continent around them was in danger and that Germany could not be trusted. That the ordinary rules of 'democracy' might not apply for a time, as the ruined countries of Europe looked for ways to rebuild. That there was apparently a 'cult' of strong leadership, something real democracy shouldn't need, because the people, the *demos*, should be strong, *cratos*, enough in themselves ...

At the art classes, her life drawings always seemed to have awkward bits, as if the model were deformed. A woman sat for two weeks, but she was harder to draw than the market porter. Tomas told her it was difficult for Lena because she had had no teaching until then; but she was doing well, considering. Then they moved on to oil paints and Lena found the brush allowed her to suggest things the charcoal and the pencil had denied. She worked in a narrow range, not much concerned by how close her colours were to those of the real world. Figures and, in particular, faces were what she liked to do: girls with a haunted look, old men with knowledge in their eyes. She could make the clothes any colour she wanted – anything that heightened the feeling she was trying to find.

Rudolf returned to Vienna, but wrote to Lena often. He was dismissive of the existing political groups. 'The patriotic parties are not democratic and the democratic parties are not patriotic,' he wrote.

Lena read the sentence again and again, delighted by its clever turn. 'None of them has any spiritual life,' Rudolf went on. 'We recently killed 10 million European men for reasons of survival and national power. The result has been the opposite: impoverishment.

Now these politicians propose new alignments to the same ends: of empire and wealth. Have they learned nothing?'

The books he sent her had made her better at reading. She had no habit of concentration, but she could pick things up in spells of ten minutes or so, and remember most of them. In her replies to Rudolf, she never commented on what he had written, but she wanted him to know that she had understood, so she wrote back what amounted to a summary of what he'd told her.

The following spring, a postscript to one of Rudolf's letters took a different direction.

'You see, I've found you a job and a place to live. The work's not up to much – it's in a clothes shop much like Herr Thaller's, though the pay will be better. And the lodging is a maid's room at the top of an old hotel. It's a long climb up the stairs and it's very small. There's a bathroom at the end of the landing that you share. But you'll be able to afford it. And I can introduce you to some of the men at Rebirth. They're a fine bunch. If your writing and spelling keeps on improving I see no reason why you shouldn't take the minutes at our meetings.'

Lena had no qualms about leaving her mother. Carina was, after all these years, still almost unknown to her – as difficult in her way to understand as Lukas and Emma at school. She couldn't even tell if Carina was fond of her, because she was so reluctant to converse. Lena had been through a period of making sentimental advances to her, but had received so little in response that she had given up.

'I hope you'll be all right,' Lena said, standing by the door of their rooms, gripping a padded cotton bag into which her belongings had been crammed.

'Yes, I'll be all right,' said Carina, who was wondering if, with Lena away, she might go back to entertaining visitors. The money from cleaning at the clinic covered her rent, but not much more.

'I'll come back to visit,' said Lena. 'About the time of my birthday.'

From the station in Vienna, she was able to walk to the address Rudolf had given her. It was in a backstreet behind a church: a hotel in which the rooms had been turned into cheap lodgings until the new owners had the money to renovate the building. There was an envelope for her on a table in the hall. Inside was a key and a note from Rudolf with a map of how to get to the shop the next day.

Lena went up to the top floor and opened the door on a room with a bed, a chair and a small chest of drawers. Through a window beneath the slope of the ceiling, she could see people going into a park. She noticed that the sun was going down behind a distant building with a golden dome. She turned back into the room, sat on the bed and wept.

Every time she thought it was ending, it began again. She couldn't understand what had brought the crying on. She had wanted to come to Vienna. It was her idea, her chance. She stood up and puffed out her cheeks. The tears would make her feel better, probably. She rubbed her eyes with a towel she pulled from her bag and looked into a mirror on top of the chest. The skin of her forehead was clear where she pulled back her hair, the different strands of auburn and straw, pushed a comb into one side and re-tied it all with a new ribbon, a purple one. Her reflection smiled at her, holding her eye, and she turned to unpack.

The best part about life in Vienna was the friendship of Rudolf. They had dinner not just on Fridays but on Tuesdays as well. After a few weeks, he invited her to a meeting of Rebirth in an upstairs room near the Café Central. Lena sat on a chair at the back, one of the few women among the earnest young men; but because of all the time she had spent with Rudolf she understood what they were discussing.

112

It was the Social Democrats who, despite being close to them politically, were the biggest problem for Rebirth. Vienna had become a socialist island within the shrunken country of Austria; the Social Democrats who ran the city had built large and popular developments to house the workers. They were no longer expected to live six to a room in a damp basement in the middle of the city, but were offered space in modern blocks with laundries and kindergartens. The new dwellings were away from the centre, the largest being on the edge of Döbling, whose older, stucco-fronted streets now seemed to belong to another century. To Rebirth's irritation, the new housing with its dental clinics and lending libraries had given the Social Democrats a powerful grip on popular affection.

It was not that Rudolf and his colleagues disagreed with what the Democrats had done; it was just that it left so little room for Rebirth. All they could offer in addition was a religious element – an insistence that healthy living conditions were not merely a civic entitlement but part of a spiritual journey. Such ideas had been well received in the aftermath of the war, when people had looked for something radical to explain the trauma the world had been through; but it was becoming harder to sell. The division between Vienna and the rest of the country, which held to its old Catholic beliefs, meant that any talk of religion risked being associated with rural ignorance. It was atheism alone that had provided good water closets and on-site hairdressing.

Afterwards, Lena drank white wine with Rudolf and one or two of the others. There were vineyards in the city itself, she discovered, which was why the wine was so cheap. Carina would have liked Vienna, she thought. Within a few weeks, she knew her way round the city, even the lesser parts, beyond the Prater and across the Danube. Nowhere was too far to walk; and as she came to know the streets, her old home began to seem like another country. There was no point in writing to her mother because she couldn't read. The person she cared most about was sailing a foreign sea and she was resigned to never seeing him again.

At twenty-two years old, Lena was excited by her life in the capital. The shop where she worked was larger than Herr Thaller's and she had less responsibility, but the pay was enough for her to buy white wine and drink it in her room. The shop provided soup and rolls at lunch for the six girls who worked there and she bought cooked food from a stall to eat in the evening.

Twice a week there were dinners with Rudolf. He was her companion, her true friend; and as the weeks went by and she began to feel at home, she thought she saw in him the chance of a life that could be different. At the meetings of Rebirth, she noticed that the few young women present looked at him admiringly, while the men nodded agreement when he spoke. His enthusiasm never flagged; his devotion to the cause made his eyes shine as bright as the flames in the sconces outside the Opera. Lena wanted to be part of the world he was bent on creating; she wanted to be close to his vital force.

Rudolf's response to the admiration of the others was, to her, mysterious. He seemed modest to the point of not caring what anyone thought. He had no wife and no lover, so far as Lena knew, and on the nights he was not with her he attended further meetings or went home to read.

She herself was the only person in whom he seemed to confide. And so she came to believe that Rudolf loved her.

Her reflection gazed from the mirror. She lifted her glass of wine. It was hard to believe, yet there was no other way of looking at it ... Rudolf had not confessed his feelings because he was worried about the difference in their positions: he didn't want Lena to think that he was taking advantage of her. So it was her job to move their friendship on to a truer place.

She heard Sophia's dismissive voice: 'You say the first thing that comes into your head.' All right. So she would do exactly that.

After they had had dinner one Friday, she asked if he could come back to her room and help her move the chest of drawers.

'I see you've settled in all right,' he said, looking at the flowers she had bought at the market that day. Her clothes hung on a rail she had borrowed from the shop.

'Yes, I like it. I was lonely at first, but I like it now.'

They pulled out the three drawers and put them on the bed, Lena feeling ashamed of the underwear, which was mended in several places.

When they had manoeuvred the chest to its new place beneath the window and put back the drawers, Lena leaned up and kissed Rudolf on the cheek.

'Thank you,' she said.

He smiled. 'It was nothing.'

She held on to his forearms. 'I think I love you,' she said.

It had come out wrong. She had meant to say, 'I think you love me.'

'Thank you, dear Lena. You're a ... free spirit. I'm so fond of you, too.'

He hesitated, then, as though it was an afterthought, kissed her lips. Lena felt his energy enter her veins. For the first time in her life, she thought that someone might take the weight of her existence. She'd lose nothing by a division of herself; not if she could draw on his strength.

She took him by the hand and led him over to the narrow bed. She was not sure what ought to happen next.

'Should we be doing this?' said Rudolf.

Lena laughed, which felt better than answering. In what happened afterwards, she had to lead him, even though each step was unknown to her. At the very end, some instinct seemed to compel Rudolf's movements to a natural end. It was done quickly;

she felt no pain and little pleasure, only a desire to keep him there, close by her.

He lay beside her and stroked her hair, unspeaking.

She wanted him to tell the truth about his loving her. But for all that his body was still lying in her bed, she had little sense of Rudolf, her friend. That person seemed to have withdrawn.

Perhaps it was always like this, she thought, though surely it was now for him to speak or move. If she got off the bed, she would be shy about covering her breasts and letting him see her with no clothes.

Eventually, he stirred. 'You're more than I deserve, Lena. Such a dear girl.'

'Don't be silly, Rudi,' she said, relieved that he had spoken at last.

'I'm going to dress now,' he said. 'Have you got a dressing gown I can pass you?'

'No. Let me have that slip.'

She didn't watch while he picked up his clothes from the floor and put them on. She wriggled into the slip as she sat on the bed.

When she was sure he would be dressed, she looked across the room and caught his eye.

He looked down. 'I'm reading a paper to Rebirth on Friday,' he said.

Lena looked down at her bare knees. 'What's it about?'

'About what's happening in Germany.'

'That would be interesting.'

'I don't think you'd like it.'

Springing from the bed, Lena went and put her hands on Rudolf's arms. 'Are you all right, Rudolf? Have I done something wrong?'

'No, no, little girl. Not at all. I'm just a bit distracted, thinking about … You know, the paper and everything.'

'Was it all right, what we did? We don't have to do it again. You can forget it happened.' She kissed his cheek.

'I won't forget. It was ... lovely.'

'Are you sure?'

'Of course. We can talk about it all another time.'

'So is it all right if I come on Friday?'

'Yes. If you want to. I'd better go now.'

He hugged her briefly and Lena heard his steps on the landing, then going down the wooden stairs. Her legs folded beneath her and she sat down hard on the bed.

3

It was not the first time Rudolf Plischke had felt himself recoil from a woman he had slept with. It was as though he were the victim of some romantic judgement whose workings lay fathoms below what he could see, but whose decisions were final. One woman, one day, might be worshipped; but until then, others must be put aside. It was not a reflex he could control.

Sometimes he cursed the way it was. After all, he didn't enjoy seeing the look of disappointment in a lover's eyes. At other times, he thought his reactions were part of an idealism whose models of womanhood were as pure as his philosophical beliefs – and then he was more inclined to forgive himself.

He had always found it hard to conduct what other men thought of as a normal affair, but Lena had intrigued him for a long time. There was an innocence about her on the first day he saw her in the hospital corridor. She was like a morning in May, he thought, when the air was so fresh that it made you light-headed. The fact that she was uneducated was more intriguing than off-putting; their dinners together had encouraged him to believe he might help her.

When she threw herself at him, it had been hard to know what to do. He didn't think that someone of Lena's background could be a partner in his life's work; he didn't really believe that she embodied the feminine ideal he had imagined. But he was aroused;

and if the girl had made her wishes so clear, who was he to think he knew better?

Lena was pleased that Rudolf still asked her to have dinner with him on Fridays, though puzzled that Tuesdays were not mentioned again. He was polite and kissed her on the cheek when they met, but made no reference to what had happened in her room.

One day she saw him with another woman, walking towards the Belvedere Gardens. He was laughing in a way that she had never seen before; the woman, who was dressed in clothes Lena knew to be expensive, was clinging to his arm.

For days, Lena couldn't think clearly. She was late for work and there were dark smears beneath her eyes. Relying on her life's experience to that point, feeling that the circumstances, and the man, could not be better, she had pushed open a door to find – not the welcome she'd expected, but some sort of wilderness where she had no bearings. Then the door had closed behind her.

She couldn't confide in the women at work, though one of them seemed concerned and asked after her; nor could she consult her employer, Frau Haas, a genial but remote old woman, widow of the once owner, who spent her days in a back office, doing no one knew quite what.

A turmoil took over her mind, a panic that she was stranded in a lightless place. Living with her mother would have been preferable; or heaving the damp hospital sheets out onto the line, then scratching the skin from her hands on the rough waistband of her skirt.

On Sunday, she went to the church at the end of the street. It was quite homely, smaller than St Thomas's at home, and when she pushed open the door she saw that it was only half full. She found a place at the end of a pew, quite near the front, and knelt to pray.

'Remember you are coming into the presence of the Lord,' the religious teacher at school had always said. 'You must be humble in His presence. Bow your head. Gather your thoughts.'

She did as instructed, thinking about the Lord, in his white robes, and his long, soft hair. She also thought about St Peter, who she imagined to be older than Jesus, with a face lined by the wind, weather-beaten from casting nets on the Sea of Galilee. In her mind, Peter became one with another missing fisherman. Surely he would also hold up his hand to the sun so the light shone through. These absent men loved her.

And Thomas, James ... And John, the one whom Jesus loved. How odd that He had a favourite. Wasn't He supposed to care for all people equally? But it was not for her to question. She tried to feel more humble.

She liked the texture of the carved pew and roughness of the hassock's embroidery on her knees. And now the priest was chanting as he swung the censer. Her throat filled with the familiar smell. It was comforting in its way, a reminder of childhood, though it left her wanting more.

The services at home had little of the Bible, but this priest and his assistant both read from it. 'I will lift up mine eyes unto the hills, whence cometh my help.' The words made her picture a poor farmer trying to make his crops grow and looking up to a distant hill in desperation – looking for help to a god who was never visible, never there. But why? A test of faith, they had been told. But why had God submitted His people to this childish trial? He could much more easily have shown His will by being seen.

Lifting up her own eyes, she saw the vaulted ceiling above them. How on earth had they managed to shape and build it all, those primitive men hundreds of years ago? The flying stone arches were like the ribs of a bony cage. And she, down below, was Jonah in the belly of the whale.

After a sermon and many prayers, they were invited to Communion. Lena stood in a line of people in the nave until a place was available. She closed her eyes and held out her hands, waiting for the touch of the priest's hand and his murmuring words. Then her lips closed on the rim of the chalice and the blood ran into her mouth.

Lena felt she must try to find another Rudolf. She could not manage in this city, not in the desert in which she found herself, and certainly not on her own. There must be a man who, rather than hurry down the stairs when it was done, would stay in her room. A man whose love did not depend on his absence.

This aching for help existed alongside a conviction that she had by her impetuosity already lost Rudolf, the one who was meant to be her saviour.

At night, emboldened by the wine she drank in her room, she went into bars where there were singers and where men and women disappeared into back rooms. A young German offered her powder to sniff from a tabletop. She took him back to her own lodging, where she did as he instructed, stopping short of making love to him. He seemed pleased enough, and left some money. A friend of his, given her address, came and knocked on her door a few days later. She became known in a small circle as someone who was discreet and pleasant to be with, unlike the grasping line girls.

When she knew someone was coming, she washed and put on clean clothes. She prepared the room by placing candles at intervals around it and turning off the electric light. This made it seem romantic, she thought, and it helped preserve what modesty she had left, a diffidence about being seen.

One night she opened the door to a man with a thick moustache. He had clearly been drinking but was being careful to control himself. From the start, there was something in his manner that Lena warmed to. He had brought flowers and an envelope with money that he put on the chest of drawers before he took off his coat. He chatted about the effects of the war, the inflation that had taken hold in Austria but which now seemed to be over.

'The street lights are dim, though,' he said, taking off his jacket. He was wheezing a little from his climb to the top floor.

'Are they?'

'They're still saving coal. They used to be brighter before the war.'

'I've only been in Vienna . . . a short time.'

'They'll burn bright again one day. We all will.'

He smiled at her with dull eyes. His politeness seemed hard won, as though from a battle he was fighting with exhaustion. He sat on the bed.

'I don't want you to do anything that doesn't feel right,' he said, lifting his head as though it were a weight. 'You'll tell me if you don't want to. Do you promise?'

He was older than the students who had visited, but younger than the grey-haired ones who came hoping to regain some lost excitement.

'Will you take your clothes off?' he said. 'And put on these?' He handed her some stockings and underwear he had taken from a leather bag. 'And then this dress?'

He didn't watch as she took off her clothes, though she would have liked him to. The dress was good quality, but not a new one; it was a foreign style, she thought, French perhaps, a few years old. It fitted her quite well. She smiled at him as she smoothed it down over her hips.

She pushed back her hair. 'Now what?'

'I want you to pretend. You're middle-aged. A friend of my mother's. We've been to an opera together and now I've lured you back to my room on some false pretext. You must pretend to be affronted by the things I suggest, though secretly you're excited.'

He seemed to have difficulty breathing after such a long speech.

Lena understood what he meant and sat up straight like one of the customers come for a fitting at Herr Thaller's.

122

When in the course of the game he had taken off his shirt, she saw a raised white scar on his back. 'What's this?' she said, running her finger down it.

'Some butcher in a field hospital. He was trying to relieve the pressure on my lung. It's nothing.'

It was easy enough for Lena to play a role of false propriety. Beneath the guise of mother's friend or dress-shop customer she was beginning to be aroused by this polite man with his wound. She was almost naked, fondling him, when he took a final piece of costume from his bag: a green hat with a pearl-headed pin.

At another time, she might have laughed, but she was too far gone in the adventure and she knew then that she would let him make love to her and that she would like it. When he was settled inside her, he had one more demand to make. He whispered in her ear the words she must say. She said them as instructed; and many times more in the course of the next hour.

This man was not like Rudolf. He seemed desperate, yet he had control. When eventually it ended, she fell back on the pillow in a mixture of exhaustion and delight.

He thanked her and apologised for the odd things he had asked her to say and do.

'It doesn't matter,' said Lena. 'To be honest, I enjoyed it.'

'So it seemed.'

He laughed; and for the first time, he seemed happy.

'It's dark in here,' he said. 'With just the candles. I can hardly see your face.'

'I can turn on the light if you prefer.'

'No, it's all right. The flickering. It's exotic.'

'What's your name?'

'My name is ... Friedrich, if you like.'

Lena closed her eyes. Few men were willing to give her a name and she suspected that the ones they offered belonged to someone else, in a joke to be shared later with a friend. It was to be expected.

The sense of health and well-being that had washed over her when they had finished making love was starting to fade.

'I can make you some tea,' she said. 'Would you like that? Or some wine?'

'You must think me very strange,' he said. 'I'm not really. In every other way I'm normal. It's just something I have to work through. It's as if ... One more time, and I'll be over it.'

'How long have you been like this?'

'About ... I don't know. Many years, I suppose. But it's better now. After the war, I was too shocked to think about women or the past. But then the war feelings, the shock, receded, and my other life, before the war, came back. The grief. I suppose in the last three or four years it's haunted me. I've tried to purge the longing. To burn it away. It's as if there were a number of women – a score, a tally that I needed to reach. And then I'd be normal again.'

'You've seen ... Other girls.'

'Yes. I'm afraid so. I don't know their names, most of them.'

'You can see me again if you like.'

'That's not the point. I don't want a—'

'You wouldn't have to pay.'

He laughed, then raised his hand to her cheek and stroked it, 'You're a funny girl,' he said.

'People always tell me that.'

Lena got off the bed and put on her slip. She poured some white wine for them both. The man was still naked under the sheet as she handed him the glass.

'What happened to her?' said Lena. 'Did she die?'

'I don't know. I imagine she's alive somewhere. It was the war.'

'Did you love her?'

'Oh yes. She was ... There was only her.' He coughed and caught himself, as though remembering his manners. 'Have you known someone like that?'

124

'I think so,' said Lena. 'I think so. But perhaps I'm too young to be sure.'

They talked for another hour, after which he said he had to go.

'Please come and see me again. I meant what I said about not paying, I think we ... we could fit together well.'

But she could see from his eyes that he had already left, and was adrift again on some private sea. He was gathering up the women's clothes from the floor and from the bed, stuffing them back into the leather bag.

'It wouldn't be fair on you,' he said. 'I'm a hopeless case. I'll burn out the disease one day. Cauterise the last of it. Until then ...'

He kissed her, gently – fondly, she thought – and then she heard his footsteps on the landing, more reluctant than Rudolf's, yet still leaving with no intention of return. She turned back into the room and saw that he had left another banknote on the chest of drawers, a tip.

A week later, as she was returning from work, she saw on a table in the hallway of her building that there was a letter for her.

Dear Lena

I'm afraid I have bad news. I am writing because I am the only one who has your address. Your mother died on Wednesday. I believe she did not suffer. There is to be a funeral on Saturday.

I trust that life is treating you well in Vienna. We miss you at the shop.

Yours sincerely

Ludwig Thaller

The problem was that she had no money for the train.

She walked in the alleys of the Stadtpark, wondering how it had ended for Carina. Never having seen someone die, she had little sense of what it entailed, but in her imagination Carina had been kneeling on the balcony, looking out towards the river, confessing her sins to God when her soul was taken up to heaven, leaving her outer body, the shell, to collapse.

Lena felt aggrieved that Carina hadn't somehow warned her. She must have sensed that an end was near; she could have asked Herr Gustav or Herr Thaller to write.

A man was playing an accordion, standing in front of a dry flower bed as Lena walked past, dashing tears of frustration from her eyes. Judged by the standards of the world, Carina had not been a good mother, yet she had at least made sure Lena was fed and sent to school. The fact that she herself was now penniless and betrayed could not be blamed on her mother. It was her own fault.

Yet what a waste Carina's life appeared now it was over – more like the life of an insect under a stone than of a woman in a free country. She had had the occasional moment of lightness, but not many. Lena wouldn't make the same mistakes. She would lift her gaze from the ground. As she strode on down the dry walkways she told herself that she must see Carina's death as a liberation. She was at last free from her mother's influence. She decided to feel invigorated, and she walked swiftly, swinging her arms.

But what she really felt was alone. Carina had been all she had known: not much, but everything. It was this absence that slowed her steps and robbed her of energy, compelling her to sit down on a bench and lower her head. She stayed still, with no ability to move at all.

When some vitality eventually came back, she knew that a plan, any plan, was better than none. She would go home: she would concentrate all her energy on that one thing.

The next day she went to see her employer.

'So, let me be quite clear,' Frau Haas said when Lena had finished. 'You're not only resigning your position without notice, but also requesting a loan for a train fare home.'

126

'Yes,' said Lena. 'I promise to repay the money as soon as I can.'

'I've never known anything like it,' said Frau Haas, her glasses catching the light as she looked up. 'And I've been running this business since my husband died twenty years ago.'

Lena said nothing. She had tidied her clothes carefully and secured her hair with the purple ribbon before knocking on the door.

'... And for that reason, I'm going to say yes.' She opened her desk drawer and took out some money. 'Think of it as a reward for your impertinence. It's not so very much to risk after all. And this is for you to buy something to eat on the journey.' She held out her hand.

Rising suddenly from her chair, Lena went to kiss Frau Haas on the cheek, but stopped herself. Kissing didn't seem to work.

'I will repay you,' she said. 'I promise.'

'Come back to Vienna one day.'

Carina was buried in a corner of the local churchyard. Herr Thaller had organised a subscription for a headstone from among his clients, for 'the mother of the nice girl who used to work here'. Enough of them remembered and donated; the poor wing of the hospital, in whose women's ward Carina had died, gave one of their coffins from the sawmill, made from pulp with a paper-thin veneer of pine.

A young priest from St Thomas's said a prayer at the graveside, where the mourners were Lena, Herr Thaller, Herr Gustav, a worker from the wharf who had been on friendly terms with the deceased and two men nobody recognised. From the corner of her eye, as the earth was thrown onto the coffin, Lena kept a watch on the gate in the churchyard wall in case it might swing open to admit a sailor from Trieste.

Then she gazed up to the sky, in which high clouds were moving on the wind, as if there might be a shaft of light, or a voice, to help her make sense of what her mother's life had signified. There was only the sound of rooks in the top of the trees that ran along the churchyard wall, then the sense of her heart beating rather heavily beneath her thin coat. The priest said his last prayer and crossed himself; the mourners dispersed and the two men no one knew left together, walking in the direction of a street with several bars. Lena watched them go and wondered if they were sharing stories of how they had made love to her mother, paid her money, then clattered down the outer staircase into the night. Or maybe one of them had loved Carina, drunk deep with her and begged her to marry him. Maybe.

At home, there was a letter from the landlord, giving her notice to quit. The lease arrangement, an unorthodox one, had been peculiar to Carina and was not transferable. There was a further letter for her: from Schloss Seeblick, signed by someone called Martha Midwinter, who, Lena thought from the name, might be French, or English.

Dear Lena

I was sorry to hear about the death of your mother. As you know, she worked for the clinic for several years as a cleaner. Some of my colleagues remember looking after you as a baby when she brought you to work.

I wonder if you need work yourself. We are quite a large place these days and always in need of keen and loyal staff. My father, Thomas Midwinter, was one of the founders of the sanatorium and my sister and I were born here. As you may know, we recently moved back from another home, on top of a mountain, the Wilhelmskogel, which had fine views but was quite cold ...

Lena didn't reply at once. She wondered if she should return to work in Herr Thaller's shop and resume her art classes. But without Rudolf it seemed pointless; and perhaps he had been paying Tomas for her lessons anyway.

One phrase in the letter kept coming back to her: 'We are quite a large place these days'. Carina had told her little of what went on at the clinic, but she had gained the impression that there were dozens of people working there. She might make friends, she thought, and live a more normal life, with people of her own age.

She wrote to the landlord, saying she would leave at the end of December, then to Martha Midwinter, saying she could start work in the first week of January, provided they could give her lodging.

4

The train came out of a long tunnel into snowfields, whose pallor glowed under the night sky. There had been a blizzard when they entered the tunnel, but on this side no snow was falling. The country lay silent under its covering.

Lena looked through the window. The train slowed, then stopped at a halt. There was no sound. An old man sitting a few seats away from her stood up and pulled down the window, letting the cold rush in. There was no one else in the carriage.

On the platform she saw a man with a lantern. He wore a railwayman's cap, but his face was covered by a scarf, his chin tucked down into the layers. Only his eyes were uncovered. Flakes of snow were caught by the furred glow of the platform light. The man with the lantern walked the length of the train. No one boarded and no one left. The buildings of the halt were unlit and closed up.

'It's getting worse,' the old man said, speaking as though to someone far away.

'The soldiers can't help clear it,' the railwayman called back. 'This is the last train tonight.'

'Need a fire inside.'

'There's no more coal.'

The old man raised the window. The railwayman was disappearing into the night, rolling as he walked.

Lena's breath made fleeting statues in the air as she wrapped her coat round her. On the rack above her head was a bag of her belongings, tied with a cord.

The train heaved and jerked back, twice, then began to move. She smelled coal from the steam and smoke that drifted past. She dragged her sleeve down the window and touched the cold glass with her finger as the snowfields began again.

At the next halt, she climbed down from the train, crossed the platform and went through a gate. She looked into the darkness.

'Are you Lena?' It was a man whose face she couldn't see beneath his hood and scarf. 'For the Schloss?'

'Yes.'

'Come on. Get in.'

He helped her into a carriage, threw her bag in after her and shut the door. He climbed onto a seat outside and called out to the horse. It was an old trap and the seat was hard, but she was under cover.

After a short drive they pulled off the road through some iron gates and Lena became aware of a large building with irregular lights in brackets on the outside walls and the occasional candle flickering in a higher window.

The man opened the door and took her bag. 'Follow me.'

It was hard to see clearly by the light of the lamp ahead of her, but they seemed to be in some sort of cloister and then in a courtyard from which opened a smaller flagged area, a gate in a corner, bare wooden stairs, three flights, and then a door onto a room with a single bed and a washstand with an enamelled jug. There was a fire just alight in the grate and a half-full coal scuttle beside it. The man, who had still not told her his name, lit a candle on the bedside table.

'I think you need to be downstairs at seven,' he said. 'Daisy will come and get you.'

The prospect of the night and day ahead might once have been a trial, but since her time in Vienna she felt indifferent to such things. She put some more coals on the fire and pulled a wooden chair up in front of it. When she felt warmer, she went to the window under the eaves, opened it and for a moment looked out at the snow tumbling in the darkness.

She awoke as it was beginning to grow light, dressed and crept downstairs. She crossed the small courtyard and entered a larger one, from which she found her way into the cloister, through a gate in the wall and out into the gardens. In front of her was the lake view promised by the name of the sanatorium.

There was no water visible, only the wide stillness, with a dusting of snow from which the sun was reflected through crystals sparkling in the air. Lena had once seen the river freeze at home, but never had she seen such an expanse of ice; it was a chance of nature, she thought, a snow lake. On the far shore there was a line of fir trees and a few ochre-painted houses, bold against the white hills behind. How long might it take to walk across, she wondered, moving easily, like Jesus on the Sea of Galilee.

A sense of joy filled her, as she slapped her cold hands together. She went down the slope of the gardens, out over a path and between some shivering birches to the lake. The reeds at the edge were a frosted green; she went to snap off a stem in her fingers, but hesitated, as though this world was not hers to touch. She let her eyes move over the horizon. There was smoke coming from a distant chimney, but she could see no living thing and it seemed from the silence that no bird had braved the morning. She put one foot on the solid surface, then placed the other one beside it; she jumped up and down, twice, but it was harder than a road. Pushing her boots through the white dusting, she began to skate away from the edge out towards a floating wooden platform that had tilted at an angle into the ice. When she reached it, she sat on the raised rim and looked back over the path, through the birches, at the facade of the Schloss Seeblick, where the low sun was catching the windowpanes.

She didn't know if she'd be mopping floors or clearing the mess of mad people's beds, whether there'd be young women, girls of her age, or if they would all be men telling her what to do. But if Rudolf Plischke came to call, she would be kind to him. There must be reasons for the way he was, she thought, and he had meant no harm; it was even possible that in his head he was as lost as she was, albeit in a way she didn't understand. She laughed as she remembered Lukas and Emma at school and how they'd made her wonder if other children had feelings, or if it was only her.

Meanwhile there was the snow lake, where she would presumably be allowed to come and sit in her time off. She walked and slid her way back over the ice to the shore and then up towards the sanatorium. The whitewash of the outer walls was made to look dirty by the colour of the fresh snow piled against it, but there was a warmth in the timbers and the tiles, a sense that this place might be good to her ... But her future couldn't depend, she told herself, on lifeless stones or on the kindness of people she had yet to meet.

Lena's mood of confidence lasted until she was told by Frau Eckert, also known as Daisy, a red-faced old woman who spoke with a foreign accent, that she was more than an hour late for work. Before anything else, she would have to do some snow-clearing with Young Joseph. This turned out to be the man who had brought her up from the station; he was known as 'Young' to distinguish him from his father, who had been the lampman before him. He was in charge of the stables, guttering and other tasks in which he didn't seem to want Lena's help.

'After that, you can clean in the main house,' said Daisy. 'There's a lot of polishing to do.'

It was late morning by the time Lena was released from snow duties and given a slice of bread and butter with sugar sprinkled on it. This was served through a scullery window along with some coffee that had once been hot.

Daisy took her through a back door into the main house, down a passage and out into the main hall, an area of polished oak with a wide staircase at one end and a circular table with an empty vase. Half a dozen doors opened from either side, from one of which emerged a woman in an ankle-length green skirt with fair hair tied back in a bun, wearing small, silver-framed glasses.

She was hurrying across the hall with some papers, but stopped on seeing Daisy with the new maid.

'Are you Lena?' she said.

'Yes.'

The woman held out her hand. 'My name is Martha. I wrote you a letter.'

'Yes ... Yes, Fräulein. I ... I had the letter.'

Lena had never seen anyone like this before. She seemed so young, but she also seemed to be in charge; her skin was a girl's, but the glasses made her look like a professor.

'Is Daisy taking care of you?'

Lena stammered an answer.

'We'll get to know each other later,' said Martha. 'Maybe we'll have tea tomorrow. I have to take these papers into Dr Bernthaler now, or I shall be in trouble.'

She knocked on a door across the hall and disappeared.

The next afternoon, Lena found herself taken by the elbow and ushered into one of the rooms off the hall.

'Thank you, Daisy,' said Martha, looking up from behind the desk.

Daisy closed the door behind her.

'Sit down. There's some tea coming in a minute.'

Lena perched on a chair and looked round the room, which was lined with shelves. Only through the open door of the town library had she ever glimpsed so many books. Behind the desk was a window with a view over the lake.

'Is your room warm enough?' said Martha.

'Yes, thank you.'

'Does someone bring you coal?'

'No, but Daisy told me where to fetch it.'

'Good ... So. I like to have a word with people when they first arrive. Just so you know that if you have any problems you can come to me. Not that you will, I'm sure. Daisy runs everything pretty well.'

'She seems ...' Lena wasn't sure what word to use.

'Don't worry. She tries to be strict, but she's kind enough underneath. She had a difficult start in life.'

A maid brought a tray of tea. 'We have it in the English way,' said Martha. 'I hope that's all right. Strong, with cold milk. And today some cake, I see.'

Lena had hardly ever drunk tea. 'Are you English?' she said. 'You don't sound English.'

'My father was English and my mother is half English and half German. She was a patient here once herself. I was brought up speaking both languages. With a bit of a local accent, people say. And French. My cousin was half French. Daniel. That's a photograph of him there.'

It was all rather confusing, Lena thought. 'What's wrong with the people here?' she said.

'They are all ... unhappy. That's perhaps the simplest way of looking at it.'

'And was your mother, was she ... a lunatic?'

'Not at all. One of the least lunatic people you could meet. We don't use that word here, by the way. We call them patients.'

Lena was thinking of Carina and couldn't let the subject go. 'But your mother, was she—'

'It's a long story,' said Martha. 'It nearly caused the whole place to close down. I only found out the truth myself quite recently when I came across some old papers. She came here with certain symptoms. One doctor thought they were caused by unhappiness – by sadness and desires she hadn't been able to face. Another doctor found she had cysts growing in her womb and was still suffering from a childhood illness called rheumatic fever.'

'So one of the doctors was right and one was wrong?'

'Yes. But the one who was wrong was wrong for good reasons. His intentions were ... for the benefit of all.'

'And who was the right doctor?'

'He was my father. His name was Thomas Midwinter. He later married his patient. My mother.'

'Is he dead now?'

'I'm afraid so. He died quite young. From one of the many diseases that fascinated him. Dementia.'

Lena drank some of the English tea. 'What was he like, your father?'

'How can I describe him? I would say that he was ... He was like a knight on a quest. And he killed himself searching. It was as if he wore out every cell in his brain in his attempt to find some holy grail.'

'And the patients here. Are they dangerous?'

'No. I'll tell you a little bit about them, Lena. You went to school, didn't you?'

'Yes, but I was no good at it. I didn't stay long.'

Martha sighed. 'Well, some people have illnesses that are caused by things which have happened to them. They're quite well until things in their lives cause them to become sad or very anxious. Or they can't sleep. They can become really quite unwell. These people need to rest and they need to talk to someone who understands. That's what I try to do. To understand. To help them untie the knots.'

'I see.'

'And some people have something wrong deep down. In the blood, if you like. It's something they've inherited from their

136

parents, like brown hair or blue eyes. It means their minds don't work properly. And this can make them seem very strange and behave in frightening ways. They suffer a great deal. And there is very little we can do to help them. At the moment. Though we're always hoping, and trying out new things.'

'There are both sorts of people here?'

'There are hundreds of sorts of people, I'm afraid. But yes, you could say most of them come under those two headings. To begin with, my father and his partner, Jacques, liked to have a mixture. Sometimes the ones who were just tired or nervous were also rich. They could be charged quite a lot of money, which meant we could treat the poor ones for nothing. Also, they got better with rest and diet and the right therapist. So the cures made everyone happier and helped the atmosphere.'

Lena felt her head furring up, as it had when she first drank wine with Rudolf. 'But,' she said. 'Your mother. How could someone think that sadness could give you lumps in—'

'Cysts.'

'Yes. In your belly. Or give you that fever you said.'

'The mind and body are related in strange ways. When did you last cry?'

'When I first arrived in Vienna. I was lonely.'

'Did you cry much?'

'Yes, I sat down on the bed. By the time I stopped my dress was soaking.' She attempted a laugh.

'There you are,' said Martha. 'A thought turned into water.'

'What?'

'A thought has no colour, or shape or weight, does it?'

'No.'

'But your mind told your brain you were lonely and a little bit of energy went out of your brain, travelled down a pathway of nerves and opened up the tear glands in your eyes. And suddenly your dress was soaked. By water which had started as a thought.'

Lena's second laugh was genuine. She took a piece of the cake, which looked Austrian, not English, and put it on a plate.

'I wish I'd spent longer at school,' she said.

'Don't worry,' said Martha, opening her arm towards the shelves behind. 'There are always books. Your education only starts when you've left school.'

'Someone else told me that once.'

'Who was that?'

'A young man I knew.'

'And what happened to him?'

Lena stopped laughing. 'I don't know. We don't ... We don't keep in touch.'

'You look sad, Lena. At the thought of this young man.'

Lena looked at Martha's hand. 'You're not married, are you, Fräulein?'

'No, I'm not. Nor is my twin sister. It seems we're not the marrying kind, though I think she was in love with a man once.'

'You have a twin?'

'Yes.'

'Does she look like you?'

'Identical. When we were young, Daniel, our cousin, was the only one who could tell us apart. We used to wear different colour hair ribbons at the start of the day, then swap them over secretly, for fun. I think even our own parents had trouble, but Daniel was never fooled.'

Lena said nothing. She had not done marvelling at this woman before being asked to imagine there was another one of her.

'Do you have brothers and sisters, Lena?'

'No. Well, I think I may do, but I've never met them.'

'So how do you know?'

'Something my mother let slip once. And the children at school. What they said. I think they were sent to orphanages.'

'But your mother kept you.'

138

'Yes.'

'That must make you feel ... something?'

'I've never thought about it. Not like that.'

'It can take you all your life to see yourself as what you are. Something that was in front of your face all along suddenly comes into focus for the first time.'

Lena looked doubtful.

'So,' said Martha. 'What do you like to do? Apart from work? Do you like the countryside? Walking? It's quite hilly here, but it's beautiful. Do you like wild flowers?'

'I don't know anything about the countryside. I've lived in a town all my life. And then in Vienna, for a bit.'

'How old are you, Lena?'

'I'm twenty-three. How old are you? If you don't mind me—'

'Thirty-two. Not that much older than you, really.'

Lena looked down. 'No.'

'We'll find things for you to do. I think Daisy wants you to work in the main house, here, to begin with. Mixing with the patients ... Well, you have to be tactful and it's something to get used to slowly. I think you should definitely do some outside work. You look pale. A couple of hours a day helping with the vegetables, perhaps. I work in the kitchen gardens myself sometimes. I like growing tomatoes in the greenhouse, the wonderful smell. And potatoes, when you pile up the earth as they get bigger.'

'I'll do anything I'm told.'

'And is there nothing else? Do you sing? Or play an instrument?'

Lena laughed. 'We were very poor, my mother and me.'

'But there was a piano at your school. There always is.'

'I didn't play. But I did like to draw. It was the only thing Herr Kaufmann said I was any good at.'

'Good. There are lots of things to draw here. There's a room where some of the patients go. You could use the paints there.'

'I only do people. Their faces. I can't do hands either.'

Martha leaned back in her chair. 'Well, you can do faces then. Did you bring any of your paintings with you?'

'Yes, I brought some. The others I left in the stockroom of a shop. Herr Thaller's shop. Where I used to work.'

'Show me your faces when we next meet, then. My father, when he was a young man – between your age and mine – worked in an English county asylum, a terrible place full of misery and filth. One of the things he did was to take photographs of the patients. It was an expensive process in those days and he used to sit up half the night in his darkroom. But when the prints were made, he used to show them to the patients, and they'd talk about them together. He said it helped them to see that they had a true existence outside the chaos of their own minds. That they could be seen and valued by others. They lived, they existed in the same world – in the same way – as anyone else.'

'Did it make them better? Seeing their pictures?'

'Who knows? It may have helped. The work we do is often about tiny differences. The one flake that makes the snowball roll downhill.'

The maid came back to remove the tray.

'I think I'd better get ready for my next appointment,' said Martha.

'Are you a doctor?' said Lena.

'No. To be a doctor, you have to pass medical exams, like Dr Bernthaler or Dr Andritsch. I trained to be a therapist. In many strange places with many strange people … Anyway, I talk to people and try to help them. But I don't write out prescriptions. I'm not allowed to.'

'But are you in charge of the house?'

'In a way, yes. The doctors are in charge of the patients. Frau Eckert – Daisy – runs the housekeeping. Then there is a matron for the nursing staff. I look after what we call the talking cures. We have two other therapists who come in every day. And I keep an eye on the place as a whole. It's quite a job. My aunt Sonia used to do it, my father's sister.'

'You must be busy all the time.'

'Yes, but I like that.'

Lena was reluctant to go.

'So, I'll bring you some pictures tomorrow, shall I?' she said.

'Yes. Daisy will introduce you to the other people. There are a couple of your age. Johanna and another girl. And you should meet Mary, who does the massage.'

'How will I know where to find you?'

'Here. This is my room. It used to be my father's. I'm always here, but if there's a wooden notice hanging from the doorknob you mustn't come in. It means I'm with a patient.'

'What does the notice say?'

'It says "Occupied". You ... you can read, can't you?'

'Of course I can,' said Lena.

'That's good. I didn't mean to suggest that—'

'It was only recently I got good at it. Reading letters from ... the young man.'

For some reason she had wanted to be honest with this woman and not to imply that she was better educated than she was. Not that Martha would really care, thought Lena, when she obviously had so many other things to deal with.

PART THREE

1

One morning in the summer of 1933, as he was sitting in his apartment in Vienna, smoking a cigar and staring out of the window with his boots up on the desk, Anton received a telephone call from the editor of a magazine he privately despised.

'I was wondering if I could interest you in writing for us. I saw a piece of yours in the *Neue Freie Presse* only a couple of weeks ago.'

'I'm trying to do less journalism.'

'I see,' said the editor after a pause. 'So what are your plans? Another book perhaps? It's been a while since your last.'

'My only.'

'Can I tell you what my idea is?'

'All right.' Anton settled back in his chair. The magazine had a large circulation and presumably paid accordingly.

'Have you heard of the Schloss Seeblick in Carinthia?'

'The madhouse? Yes. I remember some scandal years ago. They moved to the top of a mountain, didn't they?'

'That's right. But there were various … difficulties. Engineering problems with the cable car, I think. And then financial issues. The patients didn't like being so high up.'

'Didn't someone commit suicide? Throw himself off?'

'The superintendent's brother. There were other difficulties. Lectures that misfired … Anyway. The point is this. They were offered a large sum by a hotel company for the Wilhelmskogel, the place on the mountain, and they used some of it to buy a new lease from the owners of their old sanatorium on the lake. It's rather an intriguing place. Quite beautiful, I believe.'

'It belonged to two Frenchmen, didn't it?'

'A Frenchman and an Englishman.'

'Ah, yes. I remember.' The whole thing had had the air of a fable: two ambitious young men come from abroad to set up their practice in the closing years of the last century, with little acknow-ledgement of the Viennese School or Dr Freud; then the move to a purpose-built sanatorium on a mountaintop, as though they had scaled the peaks of human knowledge: the hubris and the fall.

'It's their fortieth anniversary,' the editor was saying. 'Near enough anyway. We can fudge it. We'd like to mark the occasion with an article about the place. And the question of where psycho-logical medicine stands today. There's a feeling that as a country we've rather lost our pre-eminence. To America perhaps.'

'I see.' Anton was envisaging train rides and the frontier prov-ince looking down over Italy; the mountains in their summer covering. The guts of the thing would reveal themselves as he went along.

'We all greatly admire your topographical writing, Herr Heideck. You'd have room to . . . spread your wings.'

'Topographical? It's only a train ride from Vienna. I went to the local town once before. A few years ago. It was . . . forlorn.'

'It's a blank canvas. We could carry up to eight thousand words.'

'That's a lot of—'

'Or as little as five.'

The editor mentioned a fee, which was many times what the *Neue Freie Presse* paid and said that all travel and living expenses for a month would be covered. While trying to make it sound as though he was doing Anton a favour, he was obviously desperate to get the article commissioned, to tick it off his list.

Anton took his feet off the desk. 'Leave me a number and I'll let you know this afternoon.'

After lunch, he went for a walk in the Stadtpark. He ought really to be doing something more worthwhile, he thought for the hundredth time as he crossed the street. Another book, for instance. But when he thought of the endeavour of holding 100,000 words and half a million thoughts in his head for however long it would take ... The spirit always seemed to fail him.

In the alleys of the Stadtpark, by the captive water, the mothers and governesses with their prams were 'taking the air'; the old people had done whatever it was they had done with their lives: they had no purpose now, any more than the drunks who slept on the benches.

Anton sighed. Many of his friends from school and university had died on the Eastern Front. Sometimes he felt it was absurd to make a living from simply asking questions and writing down the answers in a lucid way. At other times he felt he was lucky to have something he could still do and, more than that, fortunate to be alive at all.

The train journey from Vienna gave him a chance to read a file of newspaper cuttings about the Schloss Seeblick, borrowed from the library of the magazine. The clinic seemed to be a place haunted by misfortune, from the professional failings and disagreements of its founders, to the suicide of the owner's brother and the death of his young son, who had survived the Battle of Passchendaele, fighting on the Allied side, only to die in the Italian mountains at Asiago in 1918. Anton put down the folder on the empty seat beside him.

It was late in the afternoon when the track entered a deep wooded valley. So. 'Topographical', the editor had said ... Very well: there were shepherds' huts and wooden chalets with red geranium window boxes scattered between undistinguished towns on the river; there was a distant castle on a crag, giving the landscape a medieval air. The train idled at Kapfenberg while they changed engine driver; a few minutes later, when they had stopped for a moment in wooded country, he glimpsed a wild boar at the edge of the forest ...

When they finally arrived, he was met by an emissary from the sanatorium, who took his bag and, without speaking, threw it into the back of a motor van. He was shown to a room on the first floor of a building that overlooked a grass courtyard with a fountain. He wondered who had occupied it before him. There was a note on the table from Martha Midwinter, with whom he had already corresponded, inviting him to join her and others in the main house at half past seven.

Anton opened his case and hung up his clothes in the wardrobe. He had packed enough for a week and presumed that if he needed to stay longer they would at least do his laundry. In addition to the file of newspaper cuttings, he had some books by German and Austrian psychologists; a collection of essays on psychoanalysis that included contributions by one of the Seeblick's founders, Jacques Rebière; and an English volume called *Foundations of a Biological Psychiatry*, with a long piece by Dr Thomas Midwinter entitled 'The Worm in the Bud: Psychosis and the Price of Being Human'.

On top of these books he placed a framed photograph of Delphine, taken in the garden of the house in Baden, about a week before he had left for the Caillaux trial in Paris. It was not particularly flattering. She was wearing a straw hat and a cream dress with lace at the neck and cuffs. If you had known no better, you might have thought her a Salzburg choir mistress or a valued assistant to the chairman of a bank.

He had reconciled himself, he thought, to the fact that she was dead. Nothing else could explain her vanishing. Across Europe tens of thousands of civilians had disappeared into the soft margins of the slaughter. Jean Jaurès and Joseph Caillaux had been defeated in their attempt to persuade their countrymen that they needed no further test of their warrior mettle. And it was not only empires that had gone to dust; countries had ceased to exist and borders had been rubbed out. That was what history would record, he thought; and why should his life and Delphine's not be part of such an implacable tide?

There were quite a few reasons, he believed. Because he could smell the particular scent of her neck and taste her skin on the tip of his tongue. Second, because he had a permanent ache caused by the loss of the core part of his being that had been removed. And because he thought that if he had not been misled into staying in Paris, putting ambition before love, he could have got home to Vienna in time to save her.

After washing in the basin in his room, he went along the corridor, downstairs, through the cloister and towards the main house, picking his way by the light of gas lamps along the walls. His shadow loomed and hurried on ahead, then shrank behind him as he turned. A stick came tapping down the colonnade from out of the darkness and an old blind woman went past him. 'Good evening,' she said, with a strange accent, leaving him to question how she knew he had been there. He had read that there were patients with severe delusional illness as well as nervous aristocrats and he wondered how securely they were housed, and whether some modern ideas meant he would shortly be dining with them.

The hall of the main house smelled of floor polish; a wood fire burned beneath the stone chimney breast and a table was set with crystal decanters. A dozen people stood about, talking and drinking from small glasses.

A young woman detached herself from a group and came over to Anton, her hand extended.

'Herr Heideck? We corresponded. I'm Martha. Is your room all right?'

149

'Yes. It's … it's charming. Very comfortable.'

'We'll have dinner in a few moments and I've put you at our table, with the two doctors who run the place and a couple of others I hope you'll find interesting.'

'They don't mind my being here?'

'No. We have no secrets. I've told them all to say whatever they like to you.'

'That's … That's very helpful. You can tell them in return that I'm only on duty when I have a notebook in my hand. Nothing else will be quoted. Though I might store it in here.' He tapped the side of his head.

'That's perfectly all right. Would you like some schnapps? Or we have whisky from Scotland. It was a tradition started by my father. I don't think he ever drank it, but he wanted there to be some part of Britain here in Eastern Europe.'

'Thank you. I'd be happy to try some.'

'Well?' said Martha, when he had drunk from the proffered glass.

'It's … good. Very good,' said Anton, though he found the taste unpleasant – as if he had licked the sole of his boots after a mountain hike.

'I knew you'd like it. Men always do.'

A combination of the whisky and the wine that followed did nothing to alter his sense of having wandered into a place of strange unease. At his table sat the two superintendents, doctors Bernthaler and Andritsch, both near the end of their careers, the former of Swiss descent, he guessed, ascetic, drinking only half a glass of Moselle, the latter ursine, with a thick beard that retained a streak of black amongst the grey. Anton could picture Andritsch as a barber surgeon or a country doctor cheering up his patients on a village round, but not as a reader of the mind.

He turned to listen to a woman on his left, a widow whose husband had been a famous industrialist in Vienna. She talked as if paid not to stop, her tireless exposition containing no space in which he might have made a contribution; once when she paused momentarily for breath, he did squeeze in a question, but she closed her eyes and carried on as though he hadn't spoken. She must be a patient, he thought, too wounded to risk allowing the thoughts of others to brush against her nerves.

At the half-dozen other tables in the room sat some of the richer and less seriously ill residents, justifying the high price of their treatment by working their way through five courses and refilling their glasses from the decanters. The scene reminded Anton of one of the staider cafés near the Burgtheater, the Landtmann perhaps, though the mood was broken when a small woman in a seat near the window began to sob so loudly that she had to be escorted from the room by the man sitting next to her. Bernthaler pushed back his chair and followed them into the hall.

Later, in his bedroom, Anton lay awake, listening to the sound of a church bell that struck the half-hour remorselessly. In quieter moments he heard the wind coming up off the lake and the noise of some creature in anguish.

In the morning, there was breakfast in the dining room. He took a newspaper from a rack, poured some coffee and sat by the window. There were only half a dozen others, helping themselves to rolls and jam from the sideboard; the mentally unwell were late risers, it seemed.

A young woman had materialised by his side. She wore the staff uniform with a strip of purple ribbon visible beneath the lace cap.

'Would you like some eggs?' she said.

Anton looked up from an article by Engelbert Dollfuss, the diminutive chancellor, on why he had dissolved Parliament to assume absolute leadership of Austria.

'Yes, please. Some scrambled egg. Thank you.'

The girl blushed as she caught his eye and turned hurriedly away. How sensitive all the people in this place seemed to be, Anton thought; but perhaps that was hardly surprising in a nerve clinic.

He turned to foreign news. In Paris there was unrest on the streets, a fight to save the value of the franc as depression gripped; in Panama, it was reported, the Communist Party was making ground. There was only one word, he thought, to describe that. He hoped Pop Dawson was not making too many demands of his old friend. Twenty years had passed since they met in Colón, so it was possible Maxwell had by now retired to the seaside house he had always hoped to buy in a town called, if he remembered correctly, Southwold.

At nine thirty, as arranged, he knocked on Martha's door.

She asked him about his room and if he had passed a restful night; he thought it best not to mention the unpredictable wailing or the clock's all-too-regular clang.

'So where do we stand?' he said, sitting down opposite her. 'Is there hope?'

Martha smiled and sucked in her breath. 'Of course there's hope. Hope is what we live in. But this is not the great age of belief any more. We're a third of the way through the new century. But the great advance in medicine and science has stopped. Instead, we're trying to understand the death of ten million men.'

He saw her glance towards the framed photograph of a young soldier in British uniform and wondered for a second if he had fought against him.

'There are some advances?'

'Of course. In physics, for instance, and biology. But I was thinking of medicine. And our branch of it.'

'And did you ever believe, personally, that Dr Freud and his followers had discovered a panacea? A universal cure?'

'Are you teasing me, Herr Heideck?'

'No.'

'Regrettably, some doctors have tried to apply methods from one discipline to another.'

'Could you explain?' He knew what she meant, but wanted to hear her phrase it so that he could quote her words.

'Psychoanalysis was developed for the treatment of hysteria, an affliction of young women. It has little to offer people with illnesses whose basis is genetic.'

'That word . . .'

'Yes, a horrible word, I agree,' said Martha. 'Coined by a Dane, I think. There's an advance for you! "Inherited", shall we say?'

'And "hysteria"? A word coming from the Greek for womb, I think. So: a sort of womb fever.'

'You've done your homework.'

'It was a long train journey. But do we still think there is such a thing as hysteria? And if so, how can treatments for it be applied to men?'

'It's a difficult classification. Men were said to have something called "traumatic hysteria".'

'Or they may have fallen off a ladder and cracked their skull. Most of them had, hadn't they?'

'I think the intention was to describe a common process. In hysteria, the mind could separate the urges or emotions it didn't wish to deal with immediately, put them in a sort of mental side room — but unless they were given due consideration at some point, they risked becoming toxic and infecting the whole organism . . . That was the pathology of hysteria itself. But I think the under-lying idea, that things not properly dealt with at the time might eventually turn morbid . . . That was thought to be a process with a more . . . universal application.'

'But a man who was diagnosed with traumatic hysteria following an accident at work wasn't suffering from the repression of infant sexuality, was he? He'd more probably hurt his head.'

Martha smiled. 'I don't need to defend the last detail of the teachings of Freud – or Charcot before him. I don't belong to a school or a religion.'

'But that was the problem, wasn't it? Really? His terrible ambition, his "ego" as he might have termed it, would give him no peace until he'd done for the mind what Euclid had done for geometry or Newton for the laws of motion. And he bent the facts to fit his mission.'

'I think you're being a little hard.'

'He even tried to echo Newton's phrasing, to make it sound as if he had discovered a natural law. Think of Newton: "Every object attracts every object in inverse proportion to the square of the distance between them." Then Freud: "Every dream act embodies a desire in inverse proportion to the degree of the repression between them." Or words to that effect. It seems obvious what he was trying to do.'

Martha laughed. 'I do believe that behind the ambition – which I grant you was large – there was a genuine desire to do good. To heal the sick.'

'But they weren't healed, were they? Most of those early patients were epileptic, their spasms caused by some microscopic lesion in the brain. Talking can't heal that. And the pains of one poor girl were caused not by "hysteria' but by stomach cancer – of which she died, soon after having been discharged as "cured" of hysteria.'

'I didn't hear of that case. Poor woman.'

'Do you know what Freud's comment was on hearing of her death?'

'No.'

'He said, "It only goes to show what an adaptable disease hysteria is."'

Anton had discovered this case history the day before he left Vienna, in the papers of a psychological society, and had been shocked by it.

Martha looked out of the window. 'I'm glad I didn't follow too closely in that school, though there were times in Vienna when I came under its influence. People push you into one camp or another. They mock if you won't follow. They say you lack courage or conviction.'

'But you held out against the bullies?'

'What helped me was that I met one of Freud's early patients. In fact, she had been treated by Breuer, his colleague, but Freud concerned himself with the case. Her name was Bertha Pappenheim. This was when I was just starting my training. Bertha was in her sixties, I suppose. She was a wonderful old lady. She'd founded an orphanage and several women's charities. She didn't recover from her treatment while in Vienna, as Freud claimed, but eventually got better in a sanatorium in Switzerland. She'd been very ill with morphine addiction and some form of epilepsy. She'd seen many doctors, but from Vienna she remembered only a neurologist who smoked incessantly and tried to persuade her she had sexual feelings she'd never imagined.'

'That must have put you off the Viennese School.'

'It put me off all schools. I finished my training in a less ... doctrinaire place. In Salzburg.'

'You didn't want to go to your father's homeland? To London?'

'London was rather slow off the mark. There wasn't much on offer there. But by treating the British soldiers suffering from what they call "shell shock", they're starting to catch up. So my mother tells me. She lives there. It seems we can all learn a lot from shell shock.'

Anton felt Martha's gaze on him, deliberately unblinking, it seemed to him, as if implying that the term, and the condition, might be familiar to him. Since his time at the Gymnasium, he had disliked this form of silent suggestion, which had in those days come from a schoolmaster. At least Martha hadn't added a theatrical cough.

He looked down at his notebook. 'At the start you said something like, "doctors have tried to apply methods from one discipline to another". Could we go back to that?'

'Well, it's clear to me that talking to people is always helpful,' said Martha. 'By talking, you can help them to ask the right questions of themselves. But I've no doubt that some forms of acute mental distress are caused by an inheritance that leads to the brain being wrongly wired. When neurodevelopment is complete, the faulty circuit is joined. This in turn leads to delusions. Heard voices. And no amount of sympathetic talking can help the chemistry of the brain at that molecular level, I'm afraid. The voices will still deafen them.'

For Anton, any talk of 'molecules' brought back the smell of sulphur in the school laboratory, where he had always been distracted by Friedrich's muttered jokes; later, in the lecture hall, he had failed to distinguish himself in end-of-term papers.

'And that was a personal point of difference between the founding fathers of this clinic, wasn't it?' he asked, moving on to territory where he felt more secure.

'I was only a child at the time, but I know my father and my uncle did take different views, yes. To some extent it's a matter of temperament, I think, not just of intellectual approach. If you take the view that the most serious anguish is caused by the malfunction of particles we can't see or understand, then as a doctor you're resigning yourself to a life of ... of offering consolation at best. But if you tend to think that a mystery can be unfolded ... I mean, think of germ theory and how much progress we made there ... Then that search, that way of life, is likely to be more ... uplifting.'

'A cure for cancer.'

'One day. Why not?'

Anton put down his pen. 'I suppose you have quite a large archive here?'

'Yes, we have all the papers from the beginning of the clinic. Which, as you know, started life in this building. But everything came back safely from the Wilhelmskogel, I think.'

'Would I be able to see it?'

'Of course. It's in an old room upstairs. I'm not sure how well organised it is.'

Anton stood up. 'Perhaps in return I can leave it tidier than I find it.'

'Then we should have to pay you. And that wouldn't do.'

It always surprised Anton how trusting people were of him when, as a journalist, he asked them questions or favours. Martha had given him permission to talk to anyone at the clinic and to go into the archive unsupervised. As for herself, she seemed quite open in her views, not obedient to any dogma, and willing to let him have as much time as he wanted. She was a child of the Schloss, the daughter of a patient and a founder, but showed little sense of protectiveness, let alone secrecy. Perhaps parts of her youth had been spent in England or France, so her attachment was not continuous. She certainly seemed broad-minded, and he might ask her how she had managed to reach a state of equanimity that one would normally associate with someone older. She also made little of having met one of Freud's early patients, though he was fairly sure that Bertha Pappenheim was the real name of a subject of the most famous, or notorious, case study – that of Anna O, whose 'cure' was the cornerstone of the new treatment. The A for Anna came before B for Bertha in the alphabet, and O before P for Pappenheim – and by Freudian reasoning such a simple camouflage could only have been used by the doctors because they unconsciously 'wanted' their code to be uncovered and the identity of their patient to be revealed.

In preparation for his visit, he had read the early case histories of these girls with their aches and tics and stammerings and had been thrilled by the detective stories they contained. The patients were possessed of this invisible, protean malady called hysteria which could co-opt parts of the body to represent past emotion, as in a puppet play or charade. Sometimes the symbolism was direct, as when a pain in the finger stood for too much masturbation while fantasising the attentions of a forbidden lover. Sometimes hysteria came cloaked in paradox, presenting as its opposite. Only the magus could say for sure if a dreamed wolf on a branch represented the act of sexual congress or its pathological absence.

His enjoyment of the tales was as great as his relish of the Sherlock Holmes stories that Maxwell had lent him in Panama. In both, the great detective had to unriddle how the bizarre symptoms of a body in the library of a house in Esher had their origins in a steamy part of the tropical subconscious, or British Empire. And with the hysterical Viennese girls there was the happy ending of a cure, with no one dead.

Freud, in an unusually modest moment, had described himself as less a man of science than a short-story writer. What Anton hoped to do in his time at the Schloss Seeblick was to answer the question Martha had hinted at: why 'some doctors have tried to apply methods from one discipline to another'. Or, to put it more robustly for his magazine readers, why some doctors thought the permanently self-verifying basis of Freud's short stories could be used in the treatment of people whose brains had inherited defects. What on earth could have possessed them to believe that?

2

Like her mother before her, Lena had decided to be normal. By the time Anton arrived at the Schloss, she had been there almost three years and had found a rhythm in life that she had never known before. She remained nervous when she spoke to Martha, who was thirty-six now but still had the mixture of authority and youth that had daunted Lena on the day they met. She had secured herself in Lena's affections when, the previous autumn, she told her she must take a proper holiday.

'A week in the summer and the odd half-day is not enough. You must get away completely,' said Martha.

'All right,' said Lena. 'I'll go to Trieste.'

She set out from the same station as she had with Carina, on what she thought could well be the same train. If Stefan would not answer the letters she still occasionally sent him, he would have to acknowledge her in the flesh.

She looked at the farmland through the window, remembering her first sight of cows and horses. It had become clear from the few details Carina let slip that she had not actually got into a passenger coach after drinking herself to a standstill but had climbed onto a goods wagon to sleep it off, which explained why no ticket inspector had woken her before they arrived in Italy. Carina had at once gone into a bar, where else, and it was there she had met Stefan.

Lena had her own ideas of how things had developed from that moment. Once in the city, she imagined how it would have seemed to her mother . . .

The streets, with their squared-off junctions, were maddeningly similar to one another; sometimes a short flight of steps led up to another level, but Carina wasn't sure if these were the same steps she had seen a few minutes earlier.

The next day, Stefan found her in another bar and took her home. He let her sleep on the couch; but in the early hours Carina was cold and asked Stefan if she could get into his bed. In the morning, Stefan had to join a ship; he told Carina he would be back in a week. She went and sat in the port, on a harbour wall with her feet dangling, as she sipped schnapps from a bottle. Men occasionally accosted her, but she knew how to drive them away. Why would Stefan want to live in such a place? Because it was by the sea, so he could always be escaping. But if he was so fond of water, she could have shown him all the barges and narrowboats that still unloaded in the saw-mill district at home.

Carina lasted only two days, sleeping alone in Stefan's bed, before setting off for the railway station. Soon after she returned home, she knew that Stefan had left behind a souvenir of the night she had spent with him. Lena to be.

Laughing and crying as she pictured her mother's hapless life, Lena came to a street she remembered. The chandlery was still there, though the model ships in the window didn't look as well made as they had once been. Eventually, she came to the via dei Fabbri. A church tower was tolling seven when Lena recognised what she was looking for. She stepped up into a dark porch and pressed the button of a bell.

There was no answer and no sound in the tight little street except for a seagull's cry. She rang again. A window was pushed up on the first floor and Lena expected to see a man in a white shirt with no collar, dirty old trousers and a waistcoat – a man neither young nor old, with dark curly hair and a lined face.

A woman's voice asked in Italian what she wanted.

'Signor Fontana.'

Lena didn't understand the answer, but heard the word 'No' and the window slam.

At the end of the street was the restaurant where the three of them had had their one family dinner together. There were no longer fishing nets on the wall, but there were still candles stuck in empty wine bottles, and the place was doing good business. Lena sat at a table and asked for spaghetti with clams and red wine. The waiter didn't speak German, but her needs were clear enough. When he came back with a bowl piled high, she asked if he knew Signor Fontana.

He signalled to her to wait, then returned with the owner of the trattoria, who carried a jug. He told her he could speak some German. He pulled back a chair at Lena's table and poured them both some wine.

'My name is Lena.'

'Mario.' He shook her hand. 'Stefan has not been here for five years.'

'Did you know him well?'

'As well as anyone. He had many friends, but no one close. He was always away. At sea.'

'Was he a nice man?'

'Yes. He was decent. He liked women and the sea.'

'What else?'

Mario shrugged. 'Red wine.'

'What happened to him?'

'There was a rumour that he had moved to somewhere further down the coast. To Bari. Dubrovnik. Or even to Greece.'

'Is that what you believe?'

'No. A part of the hull of his fishing boat was found. With the blue stripe. Between here and Monfalcone. I think he drowned.'

Lena swallowed. 'Don't many boats have a blue stripe?'

'Not many, Lena, no. Have some more wine.'

For some weeks after her return to the Schloss, Lena was withdrawn and had trouble sleeping. It was not until Anton's arrival the following August that she seemed to come back to life.

Among the other maids, she had meanwhile made a friend in Johanna, whose parents had come from Hungary, and whose father had been killed in the war. Johanna worked mostly in the severe-patients' building because she wasn't frightened by their behaviour or cast down by their suffering. She told Lena awful stories, but with a smile. Lena had come close to confiding in Johanna some of the things she had done in Vienna – the bars, the white powder, the late-night callers – but always drew back.

She had also in the last year or so made friends with Mary, who sometimes came and sat with her by the lake. Lena felt proprietary about the view: she hadn't wanted to share it with Johanna, but with the blind woman it was different. Mary could remember looking after Lena when she was a child and had been brought to the Wilhelmskogel by Carina; she told her stories about the clinic when it had first started, here in the Schloss Seeblick, more than forty years before, of Thomas and Jacques, the founders. Mary had been in a county asylum in England, dumped there because there was no one to take care of her in the village where she had been born. Thomas Midwinter had been in charge of diagnosing her in the long line of new admissions to that awful place one Sunday evening.

'They shouted at him to hurry up and say what was wrong with me,' said Mary. 'They wanted to know which ward they should put me in, off the long corridor or down in the basement with the bad ones. But he said out loud, "This girl is blind." It didn't stop

162

them locking me away, but he kept an eye on me all the time I was in there and when he left he took me with him, me and Daisy.'

It was discovered, though Lena didn't follow how, that Mary was good at massage, as if her hands could see the knots beneath the skin. In the early days, this had been an essential part of the treatment, and Mary had been fully employed for almost forty years, at which point her fingers had become too weak. Now she was kept in modest retirement, deferred to by Martha as a connection to a bygone era. Lena was shocked by the bare little room where she lived, but Mary told her she was happy there, so long as Hans or Joseph brought her coal. She had no idea how old she was, because, like Lena, she had no record of a birthday, but thought she must be seventy at least.

Although Mary was hard to understand, with a strong English accent, her stories made Lena laugh, especially those about Daisy, Frau Eckert. It was clear that Daisy had been besotted by Thomas Midwinter, her saviour – a feeling that had grown, according to Mary, into an adoration that only marrying Hans Eckert, the odd-job man, had stopped from driving her mad.

On her afternoons off, Lena would sometimes borrow a bicycle and go into town with Johanna. She introduced her to Herr Thaller, who was on the point of retiring and handing over the shop to his son. Once they saw Herr Gustav in the street, in his long overcoat with a parcel of books in his hand.

'Any news from your father, Lena?' he asked.

'No ... Nothing yet.'

'Like Ulysses, still on his long wanderings? You must keep the suitors at bay.'

She smiled uncertainly and took Johanna's arm. Although they walked down as far as St Theresa's infant school, they never crossed the bridge or went near the wharf.

Lena wondered if she might see Rudolf – the young Rudolf with the broken leg. If she saw him here, on the street or on the steps of St Thomas's, he might be himself again and they could forget what had happened in Vienna. A small paragraph in the newspaper said that the Rebirth party was in talks about a merger with the Social Democrats, so presumably Rudolf was too busy to come back to his home town.

In her time at the Schloss, Lena had at first pretended to herself that the Vienna interlude had been a dream and that she had arrived at the Schloss Seeblick straight from Herr Thaller's shop. But the repetition of the routine and the sense that Martha was a reliable elder sister, available if needed, allowed her to feel less threatened and eventually to remember things in her own way.

It was not so terrible. According to a survey she had seen in a newspaper, three quarters of Austrian men had had their first experience of sex by paying for it; a few had done it with a maid or waitress and only a handful with a friend of the family or someone they would marry. The things she had done were natural and the men had paid for the pleasure voluntarily. She had enjoyed most of it. And Rudolf loved her, or so she had believed.

Since then, the period of chastity and a routine life had made her feel more like other people. Her parents were both dead, but unlike Daisy and Mary, she had not been confined to a lunatic asylum as a child, and her mother had at least tried to look after her. Lena was an adequate cleaner and waitress, according to Daisy, and she was now allowed to associate with patients, even those quite acutely ill. In the course of her day off she did some painting and was told by a patient (in a locked ward, admittedly) that it showed promise. On an average morning, when she rose at seven and breakfasted on rolls and coffee before going into the dining room, she looked forward to the day ahead. In bed at night, she let her mind go back to Trieste and to a fishing boat going over the water, the stones on the seabed clear through the shallows.

She had been content with this life, slowly growing used to the idea of being an orphan, until the morning she took an order for eggs from the man who had made love to her for an hour in her own bed in Vienna. And he had not recognised her. He had done such things with her, and for so long and still ... In the kitchen, as she waited, she pictured what would happen if her face were to register with him. He would push back his chair and storm across the hall to Martha's office. 'Your waitress took money for sex in a maid's room in Vienna. Send her away or I'll tell the world in my newspaper article.' When she brought the eggs to his table, she kept her eyes averted. The plate clattered as she put it down.

She learned that 'Friedrich' would be with them for a week while he researched his article. Since he took breakfast at the same time every day, she was able to swap shifts with Johanna to avoid him; at dinner there was so much commotion, so many people and chatter by candlelight, that she felt safer. If it came to a crisis, she would simply deny it. She had told no one of her time in Vienna, not even Johanna or Fräulein Midwinter, so she could forcibly claim he was mistaken.

Lena was made anxious by Anton's presence, but it also seemed to have a galvanising effect; it made her take an interest in her own life again. In her room, she stored bottles of wine behind the wardrobe. It was not difficult to keep the supply coming in from what was left over from dinner, to secrete a half-decanted bottle beneath her uniform when Norbert, the slow kitchen porter, was looking the other way. Frau Eberl, the cook, was always preoccupied with her pans and bubbling pots. Hans, Daisy's husband, was meant to keep an eye on the stock, but he seemed to have no real system. She had graduated from the white wine of the Vienna vineyards to whatever grape or colour was available. All of it helped to melt her edges and push her into sleep.

A few days later, Martha stopped her in the hall. 'Lena, please would you make sure the bedroom at the top of Lamp Court is made up? My sister's arriving this evening from London.'

'Your twin sister, Fräulein?'

'I have only one.'

'I can't wait to meet her.'

'Well. You must promise not to like her more than me.'

'I promise.'

'It's time we had another cup of tea, isn't it? Maybe tomorrow afternoon?'

'I'll come when I've finished sweeping up the leaves with Joseph.'

The teatime meetings happened roughly once a month and Lena no longer feared them. While Martha never confided personal feelings, she let Lena see that she was anxious about aspects of the Schloss.

'We need to find some new doctors,' she said, pouring tea from a brown pot. 'Dr Bernthaler's seventy next year.'

'That's the same as Mary,' said Lena.

'Yes. Franz used to do a lot of work with my father when he first came. It was before I was born, can you believe? As a young man, he'd studied in Frankfurt with two men called Nissl and Alzheimer. He was always a researcher at heart, I think. He taught my father quite a lot. They used to spend all evening in the cellars looking at bits of brain tissue under a microscope.'

Lena found the idea of taking bits of brain from dead people repulsive.

'Why don't you take over, Fräulein?'

'I'm not a doctor.'

'But you're a ... You know.'

'Therapist? Well ... Before all that, I taught for a time at a school in London. Young children. I enjoyed it, but I felt the pull of ... I don't know, I felt anyone could teach children their tables and spelling. Also, I wanted to come back here, where I had roots.'

'Was there a young man?' said Lena.

Martha laughed. 'Young men did come by occasionally. We lived in some rooms in Chelsea, a part of London near the river. I think Charlotte was always more interested than I was. I don't know. It was a bit ... unconventional, the life we lived. People in London called it "bohemian", though of course that means something rather different in this part of the world.'

'I've always liked the sound of it,' said Lena. 'Bohemia. I bet you had a lot of suitors, you and your sister.'

What she wanted to ask was whether they had slept with men, as she had, and if she had enjoyed it, that feeling of a man inside herself. She thought Martha would be attractive with her fair skin and her smart clothes, but perhaps men might not like her glasses or might think her manner too brisk.

'I was never sure about the idea of one man,' said Martha. 'When I was a child all the books I read seemed to suggest there was a prince for every girl. Then, when I grew up, the textbooks and the lectures seemed to talk about life in a very different way. About sex appetites and women being naturally in need of more than one man. There was a book by someone called Otto Weininger which said all women were designed to sleep with as many men as possible. It was very popular in its day.'

'Did you get all your feelings out of books?' Lena couldn't hide her surprise.

'Not my feelings. Not exactly. But an idea of ... society. Of how to behave and what other people think and feel. Most of that came from books.' Martha began to laugh, then checked herself. 'I suppose it does sound rather ridiculous, doesn't it? But if I hadn't read, shall we say, a novel by Jane Austen I might have felt I was the only one who struggled with these inner things. I might have felt alone.'

The names of Otto Weininger and Jane Austen were making Lena feel ill at ease.

'Tell me about that man who's been sitting at your table at dinner,' she said. 'With the moustache.'

'Herr Heideck? He wrote a book that was quite well known a few years ago.'

'Was that about sex, too? Like Herr ... the writer you just said?'

'No, it was more about his travels. And politics. He's here to write an article for a magazine in Vienna.'

'What's it about?'

'It's about us and what we do here at the clinic. And the world of psychological medicine. So he says. We'll have to wait and see. Why do you ask?'

'I just ... wondered. Do you like him?'

'Well, I hadn't really thought.'

'I mean, if he'd come to your rooms in London and asked you or your sister to go to the theatre or go for a walk by the river, would you have gone?'

'You are a funny girl, Lena. All right. Let me think. He's not really handsome, is he?'

'No.'

'But there's something about him that I find ... quite intriguing. I think he's been through some bad experiences.'

'I think so, too.' *I'm a hopeless case. I'll burn out the disease one day.*

'I suppose he must be forty or so. And that means he must have fought in the War. That usually left a mark.'

'Yes.' *Some butcher in a field hospital.*

'But I think my interest is professional. I always sit up when I sense something unresolved in people.' Martha was staring out of the window, her head towards the afternoon sun.

'How long is he staying?'

'It was meant to be a week, but it's nearly two already.' Martha turned back to face Lena. 'I'm going to have to start charging him soon.'

'Do you think it would be nice to go to bed with him?'

'Lena!'

'I'm sorry. I shouldn't have said that. It just came out. I'm sorry, Fräulein.'

'People have said worse things in here. Yes, really. But this room is like the confessional. Nothing escapes.'

'Sometimes I say things and they've gone before I can stop them. It's like when I kiss people. I don't mean anything by it, but–'

'Ssh, Lena. That's enough. Tell me. What do you think? Do you think it would be nice to go to bed with our guest? With Herr Heideck?'

Lena felt Martha's eyes, steady and amused, on her face.

'Yes,' she said. 'I think it would be rather nice.'

To her relief, Martha only smiled. 'You could be right, Lena. You might well be. But please try not to find out. Not until he's written his article anyway.'

There was a knock at the door and Johanna came in to take away the tea things. She looked from Lena to Martha and back to Lena. 'Well,' she said, putting a cup on the tray, 'is someone going to let me in on the joke?'

Allowed two hours off before she was needed at dinner, Lena went up to her room with a copy of the newspaper. She forced herself to read the news, and the comments on it. 'Vienna is a socialist island,' a columnist wrote, 'where Jewish atheists are in control. The working classes, voting for the first time ten years ago, procured themselves a standard of living higher than that in any other capital in Europe. Nothing better sums this up than the construction of the huge public housing estate, the Karl-Marx-Hof, one of a series of worker fortresses around the city.

'But all around this little red island is a great black ocean of rural Catholicism, where the people are poor and pious and tired of the privileges and pretensions of their big-headed capital. Traditional Austrians are prepared to make the best of their country's defeat in the War and of their empire's dissolution; but their patience with the self-important Viennese and their free medicines is not endless.'

Lena wished she had been aware of these entitlements. The city might have provided some ointment for the eczema brought on by the hospital laundry at home. She was not sure about this German, Karl Marx. She knew his work had inspired a revolution in Russia, her country's former enemy, but didn't know if it was considered successful, or if she wanted it to be. A part of her was drawn to the thought of pious farmworkers. Weren't they the soul of Carinthia? And what would Rudolf say? He was on the side of the Social Democrats and their low rents and free baby clothes, but he also wanted what he called a 'spiritual renewal'. Wouldn't that align him more with the shepherd and his family going to the village church on Sunday?

She put down the paper, washed her face and hands in the enamel bowl and changed from her day uniform into the dress she wore for waitress duties in the evening. She pinned back her hair, making it as tidy as she could, checking in the small mirror she had bought from her wages and wedged on the shelf above the chest. She often thought of her mother at this moment; it was the time of day when Carina would decide whether to stay at home with her schnapps or vanish without explanation into the night.

Entering the main house through the servants' area, Lena found herself in the hall, where drinks were already being served.

Herr Heideck was bravely sipping the whisky that Martha had told the girls to serve him because he had taken an instant fancy to it. He gave her a nod and a smile as she went past.

'Fräulein,' she said to Martha, 'would you like me to help with the drinks or go to the kitchen?'

'I think you should ask my sister. I'm not who you think I am.'

Confounded, Lena muttered an apology. This woman's sage-green dress was identical to one she had seen Martha wear. Her skin, her hair, the tenor of her voice ... Though now she looked, there were no silver-rimmed glasses to conceal the smiling eyes.

'I'm Charlotte. You must be Johanna – no. Lena!'

'Yes.'

'Martha told me about you. She said you were indispensable.'

Lena kept staring, trying to believe this was not Martha.

'Thank you.'

Herr Heideck was holding out his hand in introduction. 'Anton Heideck,' he said. 'You don't need to tell me who you are.'

Charlotte took his hand. 'I'm Charlotte. You know Lena, of course.' She graciously indicated with her other hand.

'Of course.' But his eyes stayed on Charlotte.

Lena stood where she was.

Turning to Anton, Charlotte said, 'Martha gave me a complete rundown on the new staff. Not that there are many since I was last here.'

'Perhaps we could have a talk some time,' said Anton. 'About the old days.'

'I'm not sure about that,' said Charlotte. 'I might say the wrong thing. I don't want to land anyone in trouble.'

'I would take every precaution. I guarantee there'd be no trouble.'

'I've heard that somewhere before.'

'Excuse me,' Lena said softly and backed away.

It was impossible to stand and watch. She didn't want Anton to talk to this woman, Charlotte, who was not quite who she ought to be – especially since Anton didn't seem to know quite who he was either.

She turned and walked quickly to the kitchen.

3

Anton was shown upstairs by Hans Eckert, Daisy's elderly husband. They crossed the landing of the second floor and walked down a corridor, where the oak parquet gave way to scrubbed pine, past the narrow doors of servants' rooms. At the end of a passage, behind a door that Hans opened, some iron steps led up into an attic. It was just possible to make out metal deed boxes piled round the walls; there were filing cabinets and shelves made from planks on brackets fixed to the brickwork on which were cardboard cartons, ranged ledgers and dated box files. It was like the public library of an old town that had been cut off by a natural disaster.

Hans lifted the bars on the shutters and folded them back, letting in the daylight. From the wall, he switched on an electric light bulb that hung over a deal table in the middle of the room. A hard, uninviting chair was tucked under it.

'You'll find that most of it's been labelled,' Hans said. 'Madame Rebière – Sonia – was quite careful about it all. But I expect some of it's got lost or mixed up. Or left behind in the move.'

'Thank you,' said Anton. 'Most of these are patient records, I suppose.'

'I'd say so. We can take two hundred people when we're full. So over the forty years, that's ... Well ...'

'That's a lot of notes.'

'How long will you be?'

'It depends what I find. An hour.' He looked round the walls. 'A year.'

'I'll send one of the girls up with a tray.'

'Don't bother. Maybe a glass of water at some point.'

'A glass of water? We can do better than that.' Hans backed out and went carefully downstairs.

The attic was surprisingly clean, Anton thought. There was not the airless or musty smell one might have expected, nor the impression that the roof had leaked at any point. Despite the size of what awaited him, he felt a sense of excitement as he began. It was important to understand the organising principle of the person who had been in charge, this Sonia Rebière, wife of one co-founder, Jacques, and sister of the other, Thomas Midwinter. Anton had already, in the three weeks he had been at the Schloss Seeblick, sensed the esteem in which Sonia was held. An oil portrait of her hung in the hall, an undistinguished thing by an ex-patient, but enough to give the sense of a worldly, humorous woman.

The deed boxes contained accounts, bills and legal documents; there were also architects' and engineers' drawings of fantastic intricacy concerning a cableway. These would be useful to him, he thought, in the part of his article that would describe the hubris of the clinic's ambition, when it had relocated itself on a mountaintop, from which to proclaim its revolutionary understanding of the human creature and what ailed it.

Meanwhile, the real drama lay in the patients' records, which were in the metal cabinets, organised by year and name. After a couple of hours, he could distinguish between the doctors' different hands and styles. Jacques was florid, wrote often in French and was for the most part speculative or psychological. Andritsch was an inexhaustible recorder of blood pressure and temperature in thick-nibbed black. Thomas was sometimes

173

illegible, in a mixture of English and German, with post-mortem and histological detail, interrupted by quotations from Shakespeare.

And this was what the agonies of those people had come down to. A name and a diagnosis with many outriding question marks; slight improvements, blank journal entries when ideas had run short, letters of discharge, death certificates. Water treatments, powders and sedatives; massage and the faradic brush, whatever that had been. Here, reduced to inky letters, were the Joan of Arcs and John the Baptists, their brain cells burned out by the last stages of syphilis. Alongside them were the ones so frightened of the air they could not risk moving a hand. In other records were the casualties of ordinary life, its turns and crashes, whose defences had run out of natural tears and sleep and had had to resort to removing the world from them, or them from the world, into a no man's land where nothing, so they reported, felt real to them.

And here, too, was the memory of those urged to kill themselves by voices louder and more commanding than any that ever issued from a human mouth. 'Is convinced that thoughts are placed in his head by the local priest, then reported in the national press'; 'Has been instructed by "the Scissor Man" to take his own life on numerous occasions. Says the Scissor Man is running out of patience.' There seemed to have been many suicide attempts, though the number of deaths that had occurred on the premises was small, to judge by Bernthaler's post-mortem notes.

At first, Anton was struck by the deformities of each mind, so distinctive in its perverse beliefs. But after a time, he could hear an echo between the old peasant man and the young city girl, between all of them in their varied forms, however grotesque, as if the same soul in torment lay behind each life; and it was as if this spirit passed like a conjuror's coin between the locked deed boxes to reappear with a flourish in the next one he opened.

Occasionally there were letters to the Schloss from former patients, stamped with the word 'Answered' and a date in Sonia's

hand. Some reported improvement, marriage or everlasting gratitude; others only gradual progress, exhaustion or a desire, despite
it all, to keep on living.

Anton sat down on the hard chair and rested his chin on his
hands. He tried to push away the babel of imagined voices
round his head, the excited storytellers from the past. It was
hard to accept that the existence of each one, its every second,
had been as real to them as his life was to him at that moment,
on a warm morning with the aftertaste of the Seeblick's breakfast coffee in his mouth. The weight of the idea was intolerable. Better to believe, like a child, that others were no more
than painted figures jigsawed from a hardboard sheet, who
ceased to exist once you had left the room or turned your gaze
away from them.

He was deep in some correspondence between Sonia and a
railway engineer when he heard a knock on the door. He turned
with a start to see one of the maids with a tray.

'I'm sorry it's rather late,' she said.

Anton looked at her uncomprehendingly.

'Frau Eckert sent me.'

'Of course. Thank you. You're ... you're ...'

'Johanna.'

'Yes, of course. The girl from Hungary.'

She had a humorous face with brown hair pulled back from a
high forehead. She put the tray down on the table and took off a
cloth to reveal some slices of sausage and cheese and an apple with
bread rolls and a jug of water.

'Do you like it here?' said Johanna, standing by the table.

'What? Yes. Yes ... it's interesting.'

'We thought you were only staying a few days, but it's been
three weeks.' Johanna looked a little like a horse when she smiled,
he thought, as her lips rolled back to show her healthy teeth.
Really, he should offer her the apple.

'Yes, yes, I know,' said Anton. 'There's so much here that fascinates me. So many mysteries to unfold.'

'And what do you make of us all?'

There was something suggestive in her manner, though he had no idea what she meant. Perhaps she was flirting with him.

'So many people,' he said blandly. 'The staff, the patients, the founders and their families. Their critics and admirers. Do you like working here?'

'Oh, yes,' said Johanna. 'It was hard for my mother when my father was killed. We lived in Budapest before the war. But my mother found work in Graz and I like it here. I have a nice room and I'm friends with Lena. It's very long hours, that's all.'

'You should join a trade union.'

'It's not Vienna.'

'What about the patients? Do you mix with them?'

'I see a lot of them. It doesn't bother me. I think I'll train to be a nurse one day.'

She stood staring at Anton, as though she expected more from him. He looked back to his papers.

'I'll come back for the tray.'

The following afternoon, after he had filled another notebook of his own, Anton came across a cardboard box that was unlike the others. Inside, tied up in string, were packets of letters, still in their original envelopes. All were addressed to Sonia, most from her husband, Jacques; some were from their son Daniel while a student at Cambridge and afterwards, when he was in the army, from Belgium and Italy; and a few were in the childish hands of their nieces, Martha and Charlotte.

Anton felt a quiver of unease at opening them, though the fact that they had been lodged in the archive presumably meant they were there to be read.

The run of letters that interested him most were from Jacques, who had crossed the United States by train in 1896 to visit Pasadena, where he was to inspect the scenic railway at Mount Lowe. The business of the trip was to report back on the feasibility of such a system for the lofty Wilhelmskogel, to whose summit the clinic was to move when its lease on the Schloss Seeblick ran out; but Jacques was also in some sort of emotional turmoil and there had been an element of compassionate leave or sabbatical about the venture.

The train went through frontier posts and one-horse towns that had clearly excited him, though not enough to overcome his anguish at his wife's absence.

We stopped at Sidney and my guidebook recommended a hotel called the Lockwood, where I had a breakfast of eggs and weak, boiling coffee.

I sleep some of the time, then wake as the train jerks to a halt at ... Dix, Antelope, Pine Bluffs ... wooden platforms built in the scrub by pioneers, named after the first thing they saw — creeks, forests, animals or in some cases (Archer, Atkins) presumably a brave surveyor. It is so grand, so redolent of human willpower even to the death, aching horses, covered wagons, children playing in the dust ...

And then Cheyenne. About twenty-five years ago, they took the railroad over Crow Creek and the town grew up around the bridge they built for it. They named the town itself after the tribe whose lands they'd taken. Now there's a big Railroad House with sixty guest beds and a huge dining room with heads of buffalo, antelope and even sheep. It's a wonder they didn't put an Indian scalp up there. I had dinner with a friendly local man who introduced himself as Casper Kingsley. He wore a cowboy hat and a pointed beard. He's an authority on local history and told me that in the early days there were gambling dens and 'cat houses' and drunken brawls, many of which led to death by knife or gun. Then a group of what he called 'law-abiding citizens' took matters into their own hands. Several of the worst drunks and murderers were found hanging one morning from the end of a rope. Others left the city and its 'law-abiding' people in a hurry.

We go on through mountain, desert, rock. Cooper's Lake, Aurora, Medicine Bow. There was even a stop called Separation . . .

Oh, Sonia, reading this back, I see how little I have conveyed what I have really felt in my travels – the utter loneliness, as though I knew not one soul in the wide world, had never seen your dear face; I sometimes wonder if you really still exist. The appalling strangeness of being entirely alone in this enormous world, a little collection of cells hurried west in clanking wagons. Above all this pointless sense of being alive, of being a soul – a self – perhaps for ever.

If the soul is not distinct enough to die, then what one wants is the utter extinction of all consciousness – because there is no rest in individual death . . . The belief of Buddhists that one's soul returns again and again on its climb to perfection is surely absurd. But what we can manifestly see is just as terrifying – as one is extinguished, another, near-identical, reaches self-awareness, and all the old intractable problems begin again. It is intolerable. The human mind has evolved in a way that makes it unable to deal with the pain of its own existence. No other creature is like this.

Anton put down the letter for a moment. It was as though this man could read his mind and was speaking his thoughts. He remembered sitting on the balcony of the wooden house in the jungle near Colón, writing to Delphine, and trying to express the same ideas. Jacques's letter ended:

Whether this thing I call myself is real or not, whether it is the flickering wave of some electromagnetic field, or exists only as a whirlpool – as a dynamic movement made of other particles – please, God, let it be real: because a self that does not exist cannot be extinguished.

And if my consciousness is not sufficiently differentiated from those of all mankind, then something so close to it as to be indistinguishable from it is born again each moment in some poor city or village on earth; and I, or a being so like me as to make no difference, is bound to live again, for ever, caught up in some loop of eternal return. Dear God, may my consciousness be real, so that it may die at last.

Anton was too disturbed to carry on reading. It would be one thing to have your mind read sympathetically by a priest or a lover; but to be understood – more than understood, anticipated to the extent that your own life was rendered otiose, as if it had been lived already by a complete stranger ...

He went downstairs, through the gardens and out towards the lake where there was a small boat moored to the jetty. He had never rowed before, but by imitating people he'd seen on the man-made pool in the Prater he found himself moving over the water easily enough.

Towards the middle of the lake was a floating wooden platform, designed for summer bathers. Anton tied the painter to an upright and sat back in the boat. The Schloss Seeblick on its raised slope was by far the largest building on the northern side, and from this distance and in the spring light could have passed for a grand hotel or a boarding school for the children of the Viennese gentry.

A female figure was coming down the through the silver birch trees towards the water's edge. Something in her walk caused him a pain in the space behind his lungs. He watched the swing of her arms and the slight locking of the opposite hip at the end of each pace, as though the joint were clicking, albeit painlessly, into place with every step. Yet overall the motion was, if not elegant, at least fluid and purposeful.

He knew that way of walking. He had seen it in the park at Baden, where the grassy trail went into the Vienna Woods; he had seen it going over the parquet of the music room and down the passage in a voluminous first-floor flat in Döbling. He had seen it come towards him in the rain after the Mahler and Schoenberg concert when he held the cab door open and checked his waistcoat pocket for her fare home.

Yet this woman wore the blue of the clinic's uniform. And there was something more girlish, younger, in her figure than in Delphine's.

He untied the rope, pushed the oars back through the rowlocks with a clatter and began to row. He needed to reassure himself that it was not Delphine. Or that, by some watery miracle, it was. He was facing the wrong way and had to strain his neck to see if she was still there. The blades splashed in the water and his shoulders ached.

The girl on the shore was moving out of sight, back through the trees, but he turned the boat around and stopped rowing so he could follow her with his eyes. As she disappeared, he saw a trail of purple ribbon from below the white cap. This, too, seemed familiar, though not from Delphine – from someone else's hair, another life.

4

One morning, when Lena was on her way back from the Emil Kraepelin Building, a place with locks on the doors but the best view of the lake, she was stopped by Daisy.

'There's someone come to see you. Says he's an old friend. I've told him you won't be free till two o'clock and he's to wait. He's in with Fräulein Midwinter at the moment.'

Lena couldn't bring any friends to mind. There was Johanna, of course, but she was not a 'he'. Herr Gustav had shown a passing interest. In her imagination she had once thought of the worker at the wharf with the blue shirt as a friend, but she had never actually spoken to him.

'Where am I supposed to meet this man?'

'You'd better wait at the back door.'

'What's he like?'

Daisy softened, as if for once not on duty. 'He seemed nice,' she said.

In retrospect, it was obvious who it would be – the man Lena saw coming up through the orchard and over the cobbles of the yard to where she was waiting ... How could she have blocked Rudolf Plischke from her mind? How could it have been anyone else, sweeping off his hat and opening his arms in welcome?

'How are you, little girl?'

'Not so little now.'

'You look well.' He bent as if to kiss her, but, receiving no encouragement, stepped back.

'What's brought you here?'

Rudolf sighed. 'The law. What else? I haven't been able to give it up yet. The Schloss needs advice about selling some more land. I've been advising Fräulein Midwinter. What a nice woman, by the way. But how have you been, dear Lena? Shall we go for a walk? Down to the lake, perhaps?'

'I've been all right.'

'Is that it? After, what is it, three years? Or more? "All right"?' He laughed and put his hand on her shoulder.

'I've made friends,' said Lena.

'That's good.'

They had gone through the cloister, out through the gates and onto the lawns, where a few patients were walking in the sun.

'I think I'd like to sit down,' said Lena, pointing to a bench beneath a chestnut tree.

'Don't you want to go down to the water?'

'No, this is fine.'

She sat with her back to the lake, looking at the Schloss.

'You disappeared from Vienna,' said Rudolf, sitting down beside her.

'I know.'

'You left no word.'

'My mother died.'

'I'm sorry. But you might have written. I thought we were friends.'

'I thought so, too.'

Rudolf pulled up a piece of grass from between his shoes. 'So much has happened in Vienna. We're drawing up a list of candidates. But there may never be another election.'

'I read something about that. Herr Dollfuss had cancelled the Parliament.'

'It's a rather magnificent place, isn't it?' said Rudolf after a pause.

'The Schloss?'

'It looks like an old college with lecture halls. Or a hotel in a medieval spa town, but with a country house attached. They've given me a room in what they call Clock Court. Do you know if that's nice?'

'It's the best. Are you staying?'

'Just for a few days. It's easier to stay than go back and forth.'

Trying not to look at Rudolf, Lena began to tell him how the Schloss worked, how the patients were divided and housed, how the staff were organised and who did what. He hadn't asked, but she thought it better to give him facts and figures than to risk answering questions about herself.

'I see,' said Rudolf, when she had come to a halt. 'So that all makes sense.' He paused. 'And tell me, do you—'

'Are you still living in Vienna?'

'Yes. Most of my work is there.'

'Of course.'

'But I wanted to come. When the chance came up. I said yes, not just for the work.'

'What else?'

'I wanted to see you again.'

Lena felt his eyes on her. Eventually, she said, 'You could always have written to me. It wouldn't have been hard to find out where I was.'

'It wasn't. I asked at Herr Thaller's shop. His son's shop now.'

'So why didn't you write?'

'I thought you were angry with me.'

'Why on earth did you think that?'

'I was ... confused.'

'You were confused! When you met me I was fifteen years old.'

'I remember! In the hospital laundry. With a rash on your hands.'

'I was a child.'

'I kept my distance.'

Lena looked away. Distance had been part of the problem.

Rudolf cleared his throat. 'I wanted to be kind to you. I thought perhaps you'd had a difficult start in life. Your mother was ... And your father ... But I didn't want to presume. So I tried to help. The art lessons. The job in Vienna.'

'That was kind.' Lena's voice was quiet.

Rudolf stood up and walked round the bench, as though in some physical discomfort.

'Look, Lena,' he said. 'I want to be honest with you. I feel I behaved badly. I can't quite explain why. Or how. But ...'

'It doesn't matter. It was a long time ago. I'm happy now.'

'But are you? Working here? As a cleaner in a madhouse?'

There were many things Lena could have said in reply. The unexpected humour of some patients; Johanna and Martha; the secret wine that made her sleep ... But all she could think of at that moment was the banknotes left on her chest of drawers in Vienna and the clatter of men's feet going downstairs. Without Rudolf she would not have known those things.

'Well?' said Rudolf.

Lena stared up at the leaves in the tree. 'It's nice to see you,' she said. 'But I don't know what you want.'

'Let me try to explain.'

'You're an important lawyer in Vienna. I'm just a maid here. That's all.'

Rudolf sat down next to her and put his hand on hers. 'All right. Let me tell you. I've always been a romantic. Oh, God, yes. I first fell in love when I was seven. It was a mortal agony.'

'Seven?' Lena bit her lip to hide a smile.

'Yes. I longed for her and worshipped her as much as I have any grown woman. When I was ten I fell in love again. A hopeless case! But don't think of me as one of those awful licentious men who lusts over photographs of women and—'

'I don't.'

'It's just that I'm a romantic. It's an illness, it's incurable.'

'And how many of these goddesses have there been?' Had the Belvedere Gardens woman been one of them – a goddess with a tight grip and an empty laugh.

'I don't know. Five, eight, ten, twelve. I think it's perhaps wrapped up in the spiritual side of me. A desire for purity. I first made that connection when I was lying in the hospital with the broken leg. You remember.'

Lena felt herself weaken a little. 'I remember.' He had shown such good humour despite his injury and was so friendly to her, for no reason.

'It's complicated,' said Rudolf. 'I'm not like other men. Some of them treat all women like ... like prostitutes. Or possessions. You should hear the way they talk in the bars. The descriptions. They describe them and leer over them. I'm not like that. Vienna is a cesspit in some ways. All those poor line girls.'

'Not so many now, I've heard.'

'My point is that there are two sorts of men. The sensualist and the romantic. I'm the latter. And I have a spiritual life, too. Perhaps that makes me harder to understand and if so, I apologise.'

Lena freed her hand. 'I expect there are more than two types of man.'

'You mean—'

'That's one thing I've learned here, in this place. Everyone's different. I think that's maybe why I like it. Everyone's accepted here, before they can be helped.'

Rudolf smiled. 'You've grown very wise.'

'No, I haven't.' She didn't want Rudolf's praise, especially when what she was thinking of was the hour she had spent with

185

Anton and whether the pleasure she had taken from it made him — and her — a 'sensualist', with no higher life.

Rudolf became more sombre. 'I think about the future all the time, of course. How we can rebuild a better world after all that was lost in the war. I sometimes wish I'd been old enough to fight. I could have found out what I was made of in that storm of steel. I might have been purified. Or killed, I suppose.'

Lena said nothing. She was picturing a raised white scar.

'But I also think a lot about the past,' Rudolf continued. 'And I question whether my behaviour has always been as good as it should be.'

He turned towards her on the bench. 'I have thought about you, Lena.'

'Have you?' said Lena. 'Have you really? It's been a long time.'

'Yes. On many long nights. I have lain there in bed, thinking. And I feel there is something unfinished. I feel as if I need to make amends for something.'

'There's no need.'

'Surely you believe in redemption?'

'I'm not sure I know what it means.'

Rudolf said, 'You are so ... pure. So uncompromising. I've never known anyone like you. You say and do exactly what your instinct tells you.'

'What?'

'I think in some ways you're already living on a higher plane. Enlightenment is not all about reasoning, or intellect. If you read any of the early mystic writers ... There was an English nun, a recluse, who—'

'What are you trying to tell me, Rudolf?'

For a long time, he looked at the ground, at the patches of bare earth where the grass had been worn away by the feet of those who had sat on the bench before them.

He stood up, as though he had shrugged off the burden of his thoughts. He smiled at her with the same expression she had seen on their first meeting, when he had waved and almost fallen off his crutches.

'Come back to Vienna,' he said. 'You wouldn't have to live in that little top-floor room any more. I've got a spare room in my apartment. It's in a nice part of town, three minutes off the Ringstrasse, behind the Imperial Hotel.'

Lena was too taken aback to speak. She stood up and began to walk towards the Schloss.

Hurrying after her, Rudolf took her elbow. 'You don't have to answer now. Take your time. Think what life could be like in Vienna, in a beautiful apartment.'

'I know what life is like in Vienna.'

'Can we just say that you'll think about it?'

'You can say anything you like. I'm going to my room.'

'Tell me you'll think about it.'

'Please don't let other people here see that we've met before,' she said.

'I won't embarrass you,' he called after her. 'I promise.'

That evening at dinner Lena found herself serving soup to her former lovers, who were seated at the same table, three places apart.

Rudolf met her eye with a look of exaggerated blankness, as if to say, I'm keeping my word.

Anton smiled and thanked her by name. Had she told him what she was called that time in Vienna? She couldn't remember, but since Lena was such a common name it would barely have registered in any case.

She had prepared herself for the evening by drinking a glass of wine from behind the wardrobe in her room. It had helped to stop her hand from trembling when she set the soup bowls down, but did nothing much to quell the fear she felt. It was hard to say what she dreaded most. Losing face, perhaps, losing the goodwill and trust of Martha, showing herself to be anything but 'indispensable'. More like a failed line girl, really, someone who took money for favours but had only made love properly twice.

Then, when it all came out, she would lose her job as well. Imagining the loss made her understand how embedded she was in the house, in its grounds, in its people. They had given her a chance to live. The madder some of them were, the better she liked it, feeling healthy and whole by comparison, not like the oddity that her mother and the children at school had long ago made her think she was.

And what if Rudolf and Anton should discover what they had in common? How did men deal with that? According to what Rudolf had said, they'd compare experiences, make comments on her skin or on her thighs and laugh at her – though he himself apparently deplored such things. And Anton. She couldn't picture him joining in the conversation for the simple reason that he hadn't really noticed her. For him, she had been someone else entirely – the stand-in or double of a woman he had loved. And his passion had burned so hard that it had consumed itself with a bellowing cry at the end.

She put down the plate of boiled beef and horseradish in front of him. He thanked her with the same good manners – with a warmth that was more than social form, that registered her as someone worth consideration: registered, but still failed to remember.

If the two men discovered what they had in common she would leave the Schloss and go ... Where? Not back to the treacherous parks and bars of Vienna. Perhaps to Bohemia. But she had no skills to offer, no way of making money, unless she took to painting portraits at the side of the street.

In the scullery, she drank some more wine from a bottle that had been partly decanted. When the kitchen porter was outside and the cook was bending over her pans, she drained another.

Back in the dining room, as she cleared the plates, she found a different mood had seized her. She felt desired. The fair man at Fräulein Midwinter's table with the bright blue eyes had begged her to go and live with him in a smart apartment in Vienna, to have her own room – though doubtless she was expected also to perform as his mistress, wear new dresses and entertain the thinkers of the Rebirth party. And the man with the unruly moustache and the big nose, though less handsome, had been so aroused by her naked body that he had made love to her furiously for an hour, doing such things as she had hardly imagined, then almost expired with joy, as had she, at the conclusion.

The world was not without its comic side, or its redeeming features. Lena began to smile, feeling lighter on her feet. Back in the kitchen, piling the cleared plates on the sideboard, she heard her name called by Daisy's husband, Hans, and turned to face him.

'We can let them sit for five minutes before dessert,' said Hans.

'A good idea,' said Lena, and kissed him on the cheek.

A crimson runner with brass rods went up the stone stairs that led to the floor where Lena had her room, but the passageway itself was of whitewashed brick. Over the years, she had grown to like the carved linen chest, touching it with her fingertips as she went past, and the painted wooden dresser that meant she had only twenty steps to go. Bric-a-brac not needed in the patients' quarters had been rehoused here: a drum with golden braids and a repaired blue vase, perhaps Chinese, watched over by a dark oil painting of a nobleman with a pointed chin that made her laugh.

Lena walked past, unsteady on her feet, having finished off more wine in the kitchen. In her bedroom, she splashed water on her face, took off her dress and fell asleep on top of the bed covers.

She awoke an hour later, thirsty and disorientated. As she was brushing her teeth, she heard the sound of laughter from beneath her window. The clock by her bed showed almost midnight. She put on her dress again and went down the passage to where a window gave a view of the cloister.

A man and a woman were talking as they went slowly down the colonnade. The man was Rudolf, his face visible between the pillars. He was gesturing in that carefree way of his, engaging the attention of his listener.

The woman, who was in the shadow, kept her distance. There was no contact between them, nothing irregular; they were merely two people enjoying a conversation. As the woman stepped out of the darkness, her face was caught by a gas light in the wall and Lena saw that it was Martha.

'Be careful, Fräulein, be careful!', she wanted to shout, though stopped herself in time: she was not that drunk.

Nevertheless, as she went back to her room, she felt troubled. Rudolf could have no innocent reason for a late walk with his client. Any discussion about selling land could be done by daylight, in her office. He needed no new friends, having colleagues and mistresses enough in Vienna. As for Martha, Lena felt an urge to protect her – which was absurd, when what she liked about Martha was her self-possession. On top of it all she felt that if anyone were to have more of Rudolf it should not be Martha, it should be her. With this thought, she closed her eyes on the spinning room and fell asleep again.

5

After a boiled egg brought by the Hungarian girl (the blushing maid from the first day never seemed to be on breakfast duty any more), Anton took a second pot of the strong Trieste coffee up to his room and sat at the writing table to make some plans.

He was ready to write. He had spoken at length to all the staff and had gathered anecdote and colourful detail to go with the narrative. He had a grasp of the medical background and could consult further in libraries or by letter (bearing in mind that it was a general magazine and the readers couldn't bear too much science). A day trip to the Wilhelmskogel could be undertaken at short notice and would help him develop his theme of what the history of the clinic represented: a well-intentioned but fatal over-reaching; or, if you were of a religious bent, a doomed attempt to see into the mind of God. He foresaw some good symbolic detail in the broken-down mountain railway that had aimed to take them to the summit. He could, if necessary, have knocked out a feasible article in two days.

Yet, he acknowledged to himself as he drained his coffee cup, he had no intention of leaving. Although the Schloss was a place of night cries, where shadows grew large on the walls, it held out possibilities for change. There was something in the air that had seduced him.

The shock of reading Jacques's letters home from America had begun to lessen. Europeans at the last frontier would always wonder at their own insignificance, like Cortez when from his mountaintop he first saw not the end of the world, as they had expected, but a boundless new ocean. In Panama, Anton had been one of a handful of people to see the subjection of nature to man's will. He should feel blessed, not disappointed because others had felt alone and overawed before him.

Going downstairs, he went into the main house and waited in the hall till he saw Martha's door open.

'Have you got a moment?'

Martha looked at the watch she kept pinned to her blouse. 'Ten minutes?'

Sitting in her office, he said, 'I wonder if it would be possible for me to stay on here. As a patient.'

'Why?' Martha stifled a laugh. 'What exactly is the matter?'

'I was hoping you'd tell me.'

'All right. Let me try again. What are your symptoms, Herr Heideck?'

Anton looked out of the window, over the sloping lawns. 'Fear.'

'Can you tell me more?'

'Of time passing. Before I can understand. The need to stare at something. At experience. Only to discover that it's meaningless. Living with that emptiness. And with the knowledge of what I've seen. Of what men are.'

'Perhaps you should be consulting a philosopher,' said Martha. 'Or a religious teacher.'

'I think not. I think that my ... intellectual difficulties are caused by an emotional impasse. Something I need help to clear. Like a Panamanian mudslide.'

'Well, it sounds interesting enough. A challenge, you could say.'

'So will you take me on?'

'We'd have to charge you, like any other patient. And in fact we charge a little more to well-dressed Viennese than to people from the villages who ... who have what we might call more medical symptoms.'

'I understand. I may need to buy some more clothes. Shirts and so on.'

'There are plenty of shops in town. Joseph can take you in.'

'I wonder if it would be possible for me to stay in the same room. I can pay whatever seems right. It's just that I find it conducive to work. And I sleep well there. Now that I've got used to that wretched bell clanging every ten minutes.'

'I'll speak to Daisy,' said Martha. 'And I'll have a word with Dr Bernthaler and see if we can find you someone to talk to.'

'I rather thought it might be you.'

'I don't have much spare time at the moment.'

'I've been impressed by our conversations.'

'Leave it to me for the time being.'

'Thank you.'

'We'll see you at dinner. It's Wiener schnitzel tonight, I believe. That should make you feel at home.'

'I already do, Fräulein. Thank you.'

The following afternoon, Anton saw Lena in different clothes, not the day uniform or the evening dress, but things of her own, with a blue ribbon in her hair. She was with Johanna, and they were on their way to the stables, from which they emerged on bicycles. Anton moved swiftly. He found Young Joseph with his head under the bonnet of the unreliable motor van that had first brought him up from the station.

'Can I borrow this?' he said, grabbing an old bicycle that was leaning against the wall.

'It needs air in the tyres.'

'That's all right. Thank you.'

He pedalled hard to the end of the drive and looked both ways. Two distant bicycles were heading in the direction of the town and he set off to follow them.

It was absurd, he knew, and perhaps distasteful, to shadow someone in this way. If they noticed him, he would have to pedal past, ignoring them or claiming some errand in town.

He wondered as he rode how many of Delphine's attributes had been essential to his passionate response to her, his sense that she was the irreplaceable other half of one being. If some parts of her body had differed in any respect, the whole might have been lost. The faint shadow on the upper lip, the triangle of moles beneath her breasts that he kissed in sequence. Perhaps there could be no negotiation there. On the other hand, it wouldn't have mattered if she had had a different name or had been a fraction taller; if she had read twice as much, or half as much ... if her laugh been pitched a semitone up or down; if her father had been German, not French. Perhaps Lena's differences from Delphine lay in inessential things like these and the essence of what he loved might turn out to have been preserved in a second woman. Shoulders, laugh, skin tone or a splinter of her soul ... And more than that, in fact; because however much he quantified and reasoned, he had no doubt that the woman he was following was Delphine. The uncertainty lay in exactly how, but he had no time to ponder such abstractions as the soft tyres bumped over the road.

Once in town, Lena and Johanna dismounted and left their bicycles against the wall of a shop. Anton was in time to see them disappear into the market square, where they lingered at a fruit stall. Lena talked to the old man behind the piles of apples and berries as he filled a paper bag for them. Their next stop was a clothes shop, selling traditional dresses he couldn't imagine were of interest to them, but again absorbing an inexplicable length of time. Anton was reminded of his childhood, when his mother had taken him on errands. The butcher's had been a particular ordeal, as they waited once, while he pushed the toe of his shoe round in the sawdust on the floor, to be served with the meat and then as long again to pay the woman behind the till before the bloody parcels were released.

Johanna and Lena emerged at last and walked arm in arm down the street. Anton was touched by their laughter as they turned to one another because he had never felt that either of them seemed happy when he saw them in the Schloss, heaving buckets or carrying laundry baskets. But what, really, did he know? What troubled him was that with her arm through Johanna's, Lena no longer had the swing to her walk that embodied Delphine. He wanted the Hungarian girl to visit a different shop, disappear on an errand of her own or, better still, head for the railway station and buy a ticket back to Budapest.

Instead, they walked down past St Theresa's school, where they paused for a moment as Lena pointed and explained, and over a bridge towards a gloomy area where the river looped back on itself and the streets were narrow. They were no longer arm in arm, but were almost touching, especially when they turned to share some joke. They seemed so absorbed in one another that Anton felt no fear of being seen.

He stopped for a moment on the bridge and rested his hand on the parapet. This pain was self-inflicted. No one was making him turn the knife in himself. It would have hurt less and been more seemly to leave them alone, to stop wishing.

Instead, he hurried on past a timber mill and was just in time to see Lena and Johanna go through the front door of a house in a back street. He would remember that door, he thought, and knock on it himself one day.

Then he dragged himself away from the dark street, crossed the bridge and made his way back, defeated, to where he had left his bicycle. He took his time pumping up the tyres.

*

195

Back at the small table in his room, Anton stared over the lawns, beginning to look bare at the end of a dry summer, past the horse chestnut and on through the silver birches where the ground fell away towards the lake. He wondered if the candles of the chestnut tree were white in spring. He hoped so, as the alternative, an icing-sugar pink, reminded him of cakes and long afternoons at Friedrich's house when he was young. He remembered Delphine's horror of pink magnolia.

Often, he had tried to draw reassurance from the natural world – with his eyes to dredge comfort from leaf and water. It had worked well enough when he was a boy. On walking holidays with Friedrich in the Alps he had gazed over the scenery when they had stopped beside a stream. He was no botanist and a poor painter in the art class, but the hard earth on which they sat, the grass and the spring flowers with the jagged mountains behind had made him feel part of something large and proper, to do with his grandparents and history and other things that were not his to question. He and Friedrich had had little enough to worry them anyway, when their worst enemy was the tedium of the school-room; but he liked the natural world to be there, in the back-ground, as it should be.

Now to him in early middle age, it seemed null. The slap of the water against the edge of the lake and the sound of an invisible breeze among leaves seemed less like a comfort than an absence that mocked his little brain and its conscious striving. Lying in the bloodied snow of Galicia, where the leaf mould was mingled with the flesh of men, had made it difficult to see the earth in the same light.

He walked round the room, tired of trying to solve his difficul-ties by thought alone. Why not push them to one side by focusing on something else? Perhaps when he returned they might have taken on a less intimidating shape.

He took out a pad of paper and a pen and began to write his article:

The town was once the subject of a painting by Egon Schiele, who, after a brief visit here before the war, showed its streets in overhanging tiers, the roofs of the buildings at angles, their tiles in umber and asylum green. The picture was not well received locally. True, the snow is often deep, the winters foggy, but not with the sense of apocalypse the artist scratched into his foaming sky. There is a slope in the south that rises towards the foothills of the Karawanken, but this doesn't mean the houses there are piled on top of one another, as if on the point of collapse.

In its guildhall, opera house and St Thomas's commanding church the town aspires to the dignity of a lesser Salzburg; but in the market square on Saturday, the Catholic women with their shopping baskets mingle with Muslim travellers from the East; there are Slovenes from across the border and peasant women from Moravia selling herbal cures.

An hour's brisk walk from the town is the Schloss Seeblick. With its tiled roofs, whitewashed walls and sunny courtyard where a fountain plays into a stone basin, it's a rather beautiful building, a visitor would have to concede. Yet within the long corridors, behind its closed doors, it has always been a place in turmoil.

Nominally in charge is Dr Franz Bernthaler, aged seventy this year; but the pulse of the clinic is to be found in the person of Fräulein Martha Midwinter, aged thirty-six, the part-English, part-German daughter of one of the founders, who moves about the premises with the lively but distracted air of the junior teacher who has unexpectedly been made headmistress.

It was a bit wordy, but he could thin it out later; and he felt the editor would like the way it hinted at graver things to come. All he had to do now was make sure to include all the most remarkable facts and quotations from his notebooks, stitching them together in a way that seemed natural. The main connective argument would with any luck reveal itself to him as he went along.

6

Lena was taking a basket full of sheets to the laundry when she saw Martha and Charlotte walking towards her, both dressed in dirndls with broderie anglaise blouses, though Martha wore a black jacket and Charlotte a grass-green cardigan.

'We're going into town this afternoon, Lena,' said Charlotte. 'Why don't you come?'

'It was my afternoon off yesterday.'

'I'm sure Martha wouldn't mind.'

'It's not for me to say,' said Martha. 'I'd have to ask Daisy.'

'I've only got a few more days here,' said Charlotte, 'and I promised I'd take some things back to our mother. But I need some help.'

'I don't think I could be much help. I've never met your—'

'I'll do a stint of cleaning for you instead, tomorrow. God knows, I used to do enough in the school holidays. Scrubbing the wretched floors. Do you remember, Martha?'

'I still have the scars on my knees.'

So it was decided. Daisy was informed (by Charlotte, who had been nursed by her as a child) that the cleaning rota would be changed. The three of them set off in the unreliable van with Martha at the wheel. She had never had a lesson, but had learned how to change gear by watching Joseph.

The shopping was quickly done, with twenty minutes in the confectioner's yielding four boxes of different chocolates and a short stop for a woollen skirt of a charcoal colour first stocked by Herr Thaller's father and now by his son.

Lena suggested shops that offered the kind of clothes that she had once sold from her single rail, but neither twin seemed interested. She tried to guide them towards a fruit stall in the market and the famous bookshop near St Thomas's, but sensed their enthusiasm for shopping was already starting to flag.

'Do you like cake?' said Charlotte.

'Yes, of course,' said Lena, remembering how Rudolf had once asked her what she liked for dinner. Cakes and fruit, she'd said, which had made him laugh.

'All right,' said Martha. 'That's really the only part of shopping Charlotte's ever liked. Let's go to the Café Mahler.'

This was a mock-Viennese building on the Bahnhofstrasse that Lena had never been inside before, though she had often eyed the confections in the window. They were shown to a round table near the back, where the lighting was strong and they had a view of the other customers.

Feeling self-conscious in the brightness, Lena excused herself to check her appearance in the lavatory. It was not much more than a cubicle, dark and primitive beside the gilded main room, but she could see her own face in the mirror above the sink. Did she look like a girl from the wrong side of the bridge? Did the twins want to be her friend? She wished she had had some powder or rouge in the handbag she carried: she looked pale. And her face was altering, she could see – as though the features of her parents were trying to push their way through her skin. She thought of Stefan and the way he had held his hand to the sun, next to hers, as they sat on his boat.

Back at the table, the twins were arguing about which cakes to order, but in the end agreed to a selection made by the waiter.

Martha wanted English tea, Charlotte ordered coffee and Lena asked for hot chocolate because she never had it at the Schloss. There was a boring conversation with the waiter about what made a genuine Sacher cake and then some chat about political things of no interest to Lena.

Lena began to feel uneasy as the sisters talked. Although they tried to involve her in the conversation, she felt that something was wrong. She looked hard into Martha's eyes as she was talking about the need to find a successor to Dr Bernthaler, but couldn't see the hint of a friendly conspiracy – of the two of them against the world – that had sometimes warmed her in the past. Reaching across for an éclair, Martha knocked her cup and spilt some tea in the saucer.

She burst into laughter. 'It's these wretched glasses. What on earth has happened to your eyes?'

'You're Charlotte, aren't you?' said Lena to her. 'I knew there was something wrong.'

'I'm sorry,' said the twin with the glasses, taking them off and handing them back to her sister. 'It's a silly game we used to play as children. When only our cousin Daniel could tell the difference.' She took off the black jacket and swapped it for her own green cardigan.

'You shouldn't have done that,' said Lena.

'I'm sorry,' said Martha, back in her own jacket and silver-framed glasses. 'You were gone such a long time ... And we thought ... We thought it would make you laugh.'

Lena said, 'I'm sorry if you were bored while you were waiting for me.'

The sisters looked uncomfortable – and strangely young. Lena found a hot pressure growing at the rim of her eyes and swallowed hard.

'Would you like some more chocolate?' said Charlotte.

Her eyes were quite different from Martha's, Lena thought: prettier, perhaps, but not as deep. She could see that now.

'No, thank you,' said Lena.

She turned to Martha. 'I knew there was something wrong.'

Martha looked down.

'People should be who they're meant to be,' said Lena. 'They should come when they say they will. On your birthday, if that's what you've agreed. I put everything on you, Fräulein. You were the first . . .'

'Dear Lena . . .' Martha reached a hand across the table.

'You were not like my mother.' She bit down hard. 'And not like my father. You were different.'

'I'm so sorry.'

Lena felt the heat leave her eyes, but she held Martha's gaze as she pushed back her chair and stood up.

'I was . . . I was absolute for you,' she said.

The following day, Lena was on her way back from the kitchen garden when she saw Rudolf with a suitcase, walking across the grass courtyard.

'There you are,' he said. 'I was looking for you.'

Lena glanced down at the clogs she was wearing and the mud on the thick stockings that went with the uniform.

'I can't talk to you,' she said.

'You can meet me before dinner. I know you have an hour off then.'

'But I don't want to talk to you.'

'Then I shall have to come to your room.'

'Are you leaving?'

'Yes. There's an evening coach. I'm taking my case over to Joseph now. He'll drive me to the stop later.'

'Then you're going back to Vienna?'

'Yes.' Rudolf was wearing a tweed suit with a navy blue tie that made him look like a sportsman on his way to a country house. His hair was slightly disarrayed, as though he'd dressed in a hurry.

Lena sighed. 'All right. Come to my room at six fifteen. For five minutes.'

'Thank you. Did you enjoy your outing yesterday?'

'No.'

'You looked in a very bad mood when you got out of the van.'

'How do you know? Have you been following me?'

'No, I just happened to be talking to Joseph, about arrangements for the coach tonight.'

'I didn't want to come back in the van. But I had no choice. Unless I walked. Have you finished your business?'

'A couple of days ago. I could find no excuse to prolong my time here. Fräulein Midwinter said she'd have to start charging me.'

'Which one?'

'Well, Martha. The one who runs it. The other one wouldn't . . .'

'No.'

When Rudolf came to her room, she was dressed for the dinner shift. They didn't have to wear their maids' caps in the evening and she had arranged her hair with a red ribbon. She envied Johanna, whose hair was long but always seemed to fall into place, however she wore it. Her own took so much work.

'I went to the wrong room first,' said Rudolf. 'It was the blind lady's.'

'She must have been surprised.'

'Very. I don't think she's had many visitors over the years.'

Lena stood back to allow him in.

'Well, this is a cosy little place, isn't it?' Rudolf walked round the small space. 'Oh, I like this,' he said, picking up a wooden model of a sailing boat. 'Where did you get this?'

'In Trieste.'

'Trieste?'

'It's a long story.'

'Oh. And who's this gentleman?' He picked up a half-finished drawing on the windowsill. 'Is it me by any chance?'

'No. No, it's ... no one.'

With a sigh, Rudolf sat down on the edge of the bed. The springs in the metal frame squeaked under his weight.

'I have to go back tonight.'

'You told me.'

'Lena, could you just ... relent a little. You seem quite hostile. But ...'

'But what?'

'We were friends. And then once we were lovers. I've done you no harm. I took you to meet all my friends, I found you a place to live, I took you to dinners and—'

'And I thanked you at the time.'

'Didn't I open up a world to you?'

'You did,' said Lena. 'And then you closed the door behind me.'

'I did what?'

'You took me to a place I didn't understand. Then left me there alone.'

Rudolf breathed out heavily again. 'You've no idea how much I've lain awake and agonised about this. I want you to know that. When we ... That night in your room ... You made as if ... I could tell it meant something to you, that you were offering something and ...'

'You felt sorry for me?'

'No, no. But I felt I could help you. And then it turned out that perhaps I couldn't after all.'

'But why now? It was years ago.'

'There was so much going on. This country. Heading towards civil war ...'

There was a silence in which the church bell clanged the half-hour.

Lena said, 'I thought you loved me.'

'You thought ...'

'I thought I was the one doing the favour.'

'What do you mean?' said Rudolf, pulling at his blue tie.

'I saw you with your friends from Rebirth and how they admired you, but you didn't seem to notice. And the girls, the women … they seemed to hang on your words. They used to stay on at the end of the meetings, pretending to rearrange the chairs, hoping you'd ask them out to dinner. But you never did. The only person you saw outside the meetings was me. And when you were with me you were like the man I'd first met, in the hospital. You were so … jolly. And you trusted me. You told me all about your plans and all about your father and how difficult that was. And your life on a higher plane, as you called it. All that politics I didn't really understand about the private armies of the left and the right. And your belief in God, but not just any god, some god you'd put together from all the other ones. I was … enchanted. And I just thought you were struggling to tell me that you loved me. So I thought I'd make it easier for you.'

'You imagined—'

'I didn't do it for myself. I gave myself to you because I thought it was what you wanted deep inside but were afraid to ask.'

'I see.'

'Of course, when I kissed you, then I did feel … then I thought there was something for me too. For a moment. It was like being drunk. I thought I could take some strength from you and that my life would change and become … light.' Lena looked down at her feet. 'It sounds ridiculous when I say it now.'

'I'm sorry, Lena. I think we were at different points. It can happen. I told you about the first girl I fell in love with when—'

'Don't compare me to a child! To a schoolgirl in a pinafore.'

Rudolf stood up from the bed. 'I understand that you're angry. But life is full of missed connections, of bad timing. I want to put things right with you. I have really thought so much about you and how much I want to make amends.'

'I don't believe you. I don't believe you've dreamed about me every night and woken up with tears on your face. I don't think you've looked in desperation at every woman on the street, imploring her to be me somehow, inside. I think I'm just a … project for you. Like a pamphlet. Like the new land you're advising the clinic about. I'm a way of passing the day.'

'Perhaps it's best if I leave you now, Lena. I won't give up, though. I can't. Because you're all I want. If you despise me now, I can bear it. I'm still young and so are you. But please believe that I acted in good faith, always. I believe these things will become clearer when we die. I know that you and I are bound to one another in a way more subtle and more true than I can explain.'

'I don't want to wait until I die before I understand. I just want not to be alone. While I'm living on this earth.'

Rudolf opened the door and twisted his head round to look at her a final time; then with what appeared to be an effort of will, he turned and walked away.

Lena stared at the wooden panels of the closed door as if she could set fire to them with the focus of her eyes.

7

'Thank you for finding time for me,' said Anton. 'Shall I sit here?'

'Yes, please,' said Martha. 'Or take the armchair. Most people do. Make yourself comfortable.'

Anton settled in and looked across at Martha, who remained behind the desk. He felt ashamed of the way he had described her in his article, though he could never quite rid himself of the feeling that she was too young for the role she had been given.

Putting appearances to one side, he reminded himself of their conversations in the past and of the quality of mind they had revealed in her; it was this seriousness, after all, that had led him to believe she could help.

She looked at him over the top of her glasses and smiled, but said nothing.

'Well,' said Anton. 'I liked your lawyer friend. Herr Plischke. Charming. Has he gone now?'

'Yes.'

'My father wanted me to be a lawyer.'

'Why?'

'He never thought I could make a living by my pen, as he put it.'

'Your book was a success, wasn't it?'

'To a point. Have you read it?'

'Not yet. Tell me about it.'

Anton breathed out. 'Where to begin? I'd travelled a fair amount before the war – to America, to Panama, to Paris, England, Germany. I'd even spent a week in Moscow. At first, the book was not much more than adding in the background to reports I'd sent. When you write for a newspaper, you have to put all the important bits in the first paragraph in case the reader gets off their train at that point. He needs to know at least the name of the new president or which horse won the race. With a magazine you can take a bit more time. But only a little. So a lot of subtlety gets lost.'

'And the book was made up of all the bits that went missing?'

'It started that way. But I began to see that most of the places I'd been to and most of the things I'd reported had something in common. I didn't see it at the time. It was only after the war and everything I experienced there that I saw a kind of pattern.'

Martha tilted her head, but said nothing.

'Of course, the war took time to digest. Was this what everything had all along been leading up to? The young men of the world's greatest nations dug into ditches a few paces apart firing metal into one another to see who would be the last man standing. Was this what Mozart and Montaigne had really had in mind?'

He looked round the room as he spoke, finding Martha's gaze too personal; it might be easier to remember if he focused not on a face but on some vague distance. Panama, he said, looking at a patch of sky through the window, had shown the worst and the best of human ambition, of men driving towards their goal at a heavy price. The aim, ostensibly, had been to help sea traffic, trade and the wealth of nations; but the men in the Culebra Cut had fought a war with nature and with their masters. The Caillaux trial had been a struggle of a different kind. The performers in front of the cloth enacted a comedy about sex; behind the curtain there was a drama about the need to avoid a war that would leave the world impoverished, in more senses than one.

'But war came, as we know,' said Anton. 'Men wanted it. The French needed it to prove themselves. Their warrior virility after a hundred years of political chaos. And humiliation by the Prussians at Sedan. The Germans wanted it, too. And our government provoked the Serbians, knowing what that would mean. But why? Why did we want to fight Russia? To make sure Austria-Hungary had its share of worldly goods? Or some idea of our people being better than their people. But who are "our people" anyway? The Vienna Parliament had thirty parties speaking ten different languages – with no translators. That wasn't even an entity, let alone one worth dying for. It was a Babel. With a crazy old emperor riding back and forth between his palaces in a horse-drawn carriage.'

He cast round again, feeling he had lost his way. 'Of course, if they'd known on the first day that it would last four years and cost ten million dead and twice that wounded, perhaps the men in charge might have thought again. But I don't think so.'

After a pause, Martha said, 'Your book must make rather gloomy reading.'

'No. I put in lots of stories and left out most of the speculation. I'm just going through that for your benefit.'

'How thoughtful.'

'But I came to have a low view of the human creature, the male in particular. He seems to be a deformed animal.'

'What do you mean?'

'We are obsessive,' Anton said. 'We appear to have bigger brains than other creatures, but we behave in a way that's contrary to our own interests. These harmful passions that drive us mad with love or with the need to slaughter one another. We don't seem very well ... evolved.'

'That's exactly what my father thought,' said Martha, sitting up suddenly. 'One in a hundred of us hears voices or becomes demented in some way because our mental machinery hasn't

209

settled in yet. It's too new. Some mutation made us much more aware than we had any need to be. But because the abrupt change made its possessors so successful, they outbred the others and it soon became standard in the population.'

'What did?'

'This freakishness you're talking about.'

For the first time since Anton had known her, Martha let her enthusiasm ride over her reserve. 'When Charlotte and I were small my father used to tell us a story about all the fish in the sea. The mackerels looked different from the herrings and the sardines, but they all lived the same fishy lives, really – for millions and millions of years. Then one day Poseidon gave a magic gift to a single sprat. The sprat could talk, though only the other sprats could understand him. He and his wife gave birth to lots of little fish, and soon all sprats in the ocean could talk. But they still lived in the sea. Talking didn't help. The whales still ate all the krill and the bottom feeders still lay on the seabed. This talking business was completely unnecessary for sprat life to prosper under the waves. All they really needed was a food supply, like the one they'd had for the last ten million years – and still had. Furthermore, it turned out Poseidon had been in a hurry and the gift was a bit dashed off. Not very secure. One in a hundred sprats was deafened by the sound of other sprats talking – even though there was not a sprat in sight! It's true some sprats composed fishy poems and nice sea shanties, but most of them just talked themselves into making armies to attack their fellow sprats. And the other fish – the bass and the brill and the octopus – just looked on in amazement. And then, as far as they could, they ignored the talking sprats altogether.'

'So what was wrong with Poseidon's gift?'

'My father was a bit unclear on the detail. Something about mutations taking time to settle. A pterodactyl didn't turn into a jackdaw overnight, he liked to say.'

Neither of them spoke for a while. Anton hoped, for once, to hear the church bell strike. Eventually, he coughed. 'I hadn't expected psychoanalysis to be like this.'

Martha looked down at her desk for a moment. 'I don't normally talk that much.'

'No.'

'I try not to talk at all if possible.'

'No, I enjoyed your story. I just thought the whole thing might be a bit less ... You know.'

'Piscine?'

'Exactly.'

'Of course. Let's go back to humans. You were saying ...'

'The book. *Adam's Lot*. Well ... I enjoyed giving descriptions of the places I'd visited in more detail. Evoking the life of the place by the habits of the people – what they eat and so on. Very few Austrians have been to New York, I think. So just an idea of the layout of the streets, the tarry smell, the separate occupations or nationality in each small neighbourhood and so on ... I felt I had to carry readers with me. Have you ever eaten Chinese food?'

'I've no idea what it consists of.'

'Nor had I, but there are plenty of Chinese there – in a couple of streets, anyway, mostly selling cigars, as far as I could see. But they have their little kitchen cafés. In the name of journalistic truth, I had to try it.'

'And?'

'It doesn't matter. Bean sprouts. What I wanted to get at was what was going on underneath. The gangs, the fighting, the cruelty. I began to wonder if there was just something in us. Something wrong.'

'Original sin?'

'Christians would say so. Karl Marx called it capitalism. That was what led to refugees. Poor people looking for work. Emigrating from hunger in their own country only to be used by other cruel capitalists when they reached their destination. It's Darwin as well. At any rate, it's Malthus. The struggle to survive.'

'I haven't read Malthus,' said Martha.

'Nor have I. But Darwin read him, and the idea of populations waxing or waning according to the survival of who was best able to adapt ... I think that was important.'

'How did you squeeze all this into your book?'

'I took a chance. I wondered whether all aspects of irrationality might be connected. Including sex and love. I do think Marx describes very well how an economy works to the benefit of the few. But it's an explanation of a system – one that works like a motor. It does give momentum. But the politics have never been able to solve the injustices that the motor generates.'

'Because politicians are wicked?'

'Some are. But I also wanted to suggest something else in the nature of human beings. In the Caillaux case, for instance. Maybe it was not a little sex comedy while a tragic war history waited in the wings. I wanted to see if the two follies were connected. Part of the same flaw.'

Martha sat back in the desk chair again. 'Eros and Thanatos. All that flurry in Vienna before the war. So many books!'

Anton coughed. 'I suppose I was influenced by what was coming out then. It was pretty interesting, after all. There was some suggestion that if you denied the sex instinct it would send you mad. I'm simplifying, of course.'

'Not much. Not according to Christian von Ehrenfels.'

'Who?'

'He made a splash at that time. I read it later. He thought that for young men the choice was neurosis if you didn't, syphilis if you did.'

'What was his solution?' said Anton.

'That all men should have many girlfriends. Though he had a long Greek word for it.'

'This was all going on when I arrived in Vienna to go to university,' said Anton. 'And very shocking it was. But the whole city was shocking to a boy from Styria. Girls were lined up on the street and the books we were reading suggested that women were naturally ... insatiable. That they embodied animal sexuality. Yet society told them they were supposed to marry as virgins and then be faithful. We had found no way at all of dealing with the central urge in nature. So what price Mahler's Fifth?'

Martha nodded. 'The denial of the sex instinct is even more harmful to women than to men. So Freud says. I don't see why it should be, but ...'

Finding a distant cloud beyond the lake to focus on, Anton said, 'And so, you see in my own life I was facing this turmoil. On the one side, all the writers in the Café Griensteidl insisting that being a whore was a natural thing for a woman – as natural as motherhood, according to Weininger. And on the other side, in my actual life, not wanting to sleep with line girls because I didn't want to use them like that, not even knowing their names ... Or to catch a disease, as your von Ehrenfels said. And then ...' He seemed to run out of impetus.

Martha looked interrogatively. 'Then what?' she said at last.

'Something happened that made me feel less ... superfluous. That gave me a stake in society. A foothold in the world. You must remember, I thought of myself as ugly, too. My nose, my skin, my—'

'Really? I wouldn't say—'

'Of course you wouldn't. You're polite. And in any case, that was a long time ago. My elder brother Gerhard tells me I've "grown into my face", whatever that means. And so ...'

'Tell me what happened.'

Anton breathed in. 'I met a woman who solved all these problems.'

'How very fortunate.'

'You mustn't laugh.'

'I'm sorry.'

'Well, it did come out a bit wrong ... You're forgiven. I'll keep the story of Delphine for another day.'

'As you like. Do you feel quite well? You seem to have a cough. I've noticed it often.'

'Don't worry, it's not an infection. It's from the war. I have slight damage in one lung. I'll tell you about that one day, too.'

'We have a lot to look forward to.'

'I feel obliged to entertain you. Or at least not to bore you.'

'Please don't feel obliged, Herr Heideck. I'm here to listen to whatever seems important to you.'

'How much more time do we have?'

'A few minutes yet. So you called your book *Adam's Lot*. Shouldn't it have been *Eve's Lot*?'

'I did consider that, but in the end I thought it seemed ungallant. And I thought a man's name could stand for mankind – *homo* not *vir*, as our Latin teachers used to say.'

'I see.'

'And I gave it a subtitle. *Travels with a Broken Heart*. And I hoped that could work for both sexes.'

'It sold well, didn't it?'

'Not as well as people think. Though more than Dr Freud.'

'Are you sure?'

'Everyone sold more than Freud. His *Interpretation of Dreams* took eight years to sell six hundred copies.'

'How do you know?'

'My publisher had previously worked at Franz Deuticke, Freud's publishers. He kept in touch. Publishers like to gossip.'

'So how come he's so well known?'

'Also a story for another day.'

'All right. Why did yours fare so much better?'

'I think most people hurried through the theoretical passages about the curse of self-awareness – your sprat story, as it were.

And they skipped the attempt to bind sexuality and aggression together as part of some ingrained malfunction.'

'So which parts did they read? What was left?'

'I think they liked my account of fighting the Russians in 1917. But to judge from the letters that were forwarded by the publisher, the thing they liked best was the bit about Chinese restaurants.'

Martha bit her lip. 'In New York?'

'Yes.'

'Well, I'd certainly like to go to America one day. Freud and Jung thought it was the new frontier. We could teach them something. And also learn, perhaps.'

Anton had a picture of Casper Kingsley with his cowboy hat and pointed beard explaining the law of the Wild West to a lonely French psychiatrist in a railroad house in Cheyenne, Wyoming in 1896.

'Maybe we could,' he said, smiling, as he rose to go.

Martha watched the door close behind him and put her feet up on the desk. She usually had five minutes before the next patient, but Anton was the last of the day.

She checked her notes. The first thing she had written was 'Lawyer manqué'. Ridiculous, she thought. She crossed it out. The notes went on:

Stress on missing subtlety, nuance. Feels has sold himself short in his career? Busy reporter but not great essayist? War as sex urge gone wrong: high libido? Lost love, 'Delphine'. French? 'Line girls': some history there? Presents self as man of his time: pushed by modern mores, what was he meant to do? Man without Qualities? Funny about writing. Dismissive of *Interp of Dreams*: Freud envy?

When she had thought for a minute or so, she wrote in a more measured hand:

I feel there is a sense of shame. He is knowledgeable about many things, but uses this to normalise himself. That seems to be his task: to be the unavoidable outcome of biology and the time in which he has lived. Oddly lacking in ego: v. few people <u>want</u> to be seen to be so hapless!

He was pretending to confess and was quite candid – shocking at times. But, despite the gazing into the middle distance, nothing cost him much today. Perhaps just winning my confidence. He hinted about revelations to come. But will they be cathartic when they do come? Or are they further screens to something he can't yet see – or face?

She took a new pen and concluded: 'Next step: To help him by not agreeing the weight <u>he</u> wants to give future revelations. To keep quiet and not talk about fish.'

After tidying her desk, Martha glanced at the photograph of her cousin Daniel in his oversize British Army uniform, which had made him look about fourteen years old. She remembered how much, when he had first learned to walk, Daniel had looked up to his girl cousins, trailing them round the Wilhelmskogel with a wicker basket of toys whose handle dug a pattern into the flesh of his bare arm. He had told Martha in a whisper so many times that she was his favourite, earnestly grasping her wrist as he did so; but somehow she was not surprised when, after his funeral, Charlotte revealed that he had frequently told her the same thing.

Martha worried that Daniel had been cold, lying up there in the mountains, with the life leaking out of him. She wished she had been there to cover him with a blanket. He had never been robust, though not sickly either and always the bursting delight of his mother Sonia's eye. What he had revealed in his short time in the army, in the slime at Ypres and on the plateau at Asiago, was an unexpected strength, expressed in soldier's humour. God knew what he might have become, what a man was lost.

She shut the door on the consulting room that had once been her father's; the latch bolt made a satisfying click as it sprang into the keep, exactly as it had closed on a thousand psychic dramas before.

It was her favourite time of the day, the lull before dinner, and she often heard her father's voice teasing her. 'Well, Martha-May, what have you done today to deserve a bowl of soup, let alone a glass of wine?' 'I don't drink wine, Daddy.' 'Why?' 'Because I'm only eight!' 'Oh, good, then I'll have yours.' She had learned that sentimentality, which might poison mature relationships, could sit next to pure and powerful emotion when it came to parent and child.

Quite often Thomas was late for dinner because he was shut in the cellar laboratory with Franz Bernthaler looking for lesions in sections of brain beneath the microscope. Then he'd come in smelling of the carbolic soap they used, and sometimes of wine as well, a glass of which he and Franz used to allow themselves after seven o'clock – Riesling from Franconia if they could get it.

Martha could hear Thomas's voice almost at will, not in the auditory sense that almost deafened some of the schizophrenic patients, but in the way that the eyes hear words on a page, with or without the tongue moving.

'Your Heideck is a typical Styrian, don't you think?' she heard Thomas say. 'When are you going to ask him about his god? I think you may be right about the shame. But I scent a Roman Catholic, don't you? *Cherchez la croix.*'

Crossing the hall, Martha climbed the main staircase, enjoying the spring of the oak steps, and made her way to her rooms, which had once been lived in by Jacques and Sonia. They were too large

217

for a woman on her own, but she drew only a small salary from the clinic and viewed them as her reward for working seven days a week. They were furnished with pieces left at the Wilhelmskogel by her parents when they returned to England and a few items of her own that she had had shipped from London. The living room was a little dark, but the bedroom had a double aspect, with one window giving over the front gardens and the other looking down towards the lake, on whose water the sun was now sinking.

The reason Martha had loved Thomas so much was the effect that she and Charlotte had on him. It seemed a matter of colossal amusement to him that he could have fathered not one but two creatures of the opposite sex, simultaneously. When they were still small, he would grasp one under each arm and pretend that they were sacks of coal that had to be delivered down a chute on the double bed. Whether he was bent over the accounts or writing up notes of someone critically ill, his bearing changed if either girl came into the room, as though nothing else now mattered. When you could produce this effect on someone by merely opening a door, it was hard not to love them.

After a bath, Martha put on a different dress for dinner and sat at the dressing table that overlooked the lake. She thought of her mother when she put on make-up. Every day she thought of her at this time for the simple reason it was Kitty who had shown her what to do. 'You've got my skin, so you don't need much.' 'Your astigmatism, too.' 'Yes, I'm sorry about that. Anyone's better for a little powder. You don't need lipstick, not that dark one anyway. You've got nice lashes, so you can ... up like that. Just a touch, that's all.'

Kitty, all at sea when she arrived, had found her own destiny in the Schloss Seeblick. Thomas's medical intervention had probably saved her life and his lasting love for her had made it a life worth saving. They had rescued something from the world's chaos and passed it on to their children in the shape of education and stability.

But the legacy was two-edged. Martha herself would probably never marry, she admitted, not for the first time, as she walked across the landing to the head of the staircase; and she would never have children. How many more dinners would she go down to as the young and still perhaps desirable daughter of the house; what was the number after which her independence would harden into unapproachability? There would be a day, a single day, when she would cease to be a girl of passion and would be seen only as the legatee of a previous generation's achievement.

She tried to smile as she felt the banister beneath her palm. Her dress rustled. It was her destiny to share the dividends of her fortunate upbringing and the range of her understanding. And God knows, she thought as she went down into the noise of the pre-dinner drinks, that ought to be enough for anyone.

PART FOUR

1

Rudolf was relieved to be back in Vienna, where his salary had enabled him to rent an apartment on the second floor of a building five minutes' walk from the Imperial Hotel. It was not the best flat in the building; any passer-by could tell from the external decoration that the first floor belonged to someone wealthier. But it was within walking distance of his office, the Opera and anywhere he was likely to go in the evening; it had a view of the Belvedere Gardens, glass-panelled doors off a parqueted corridor and a spare bedroom for when Lena changed her mind.

As an only child, he had been used to having his own way. The nurse who looked after him was easy to manipulate; his mother told him he was the teacher's favourite, and he believed her. His father was busy with his law practice and had little to do with his son from day to day. As he grew up, Rudolf believed he could live his life both ways: as a lawyer, nominally, to please his father, but a radical at heart; as a monogamous romantic with pretty mistresses at night. It enraged him when the world would not accommodate his needs. It was as if his father's unimaginative view of life had trumped his mother's ambitions for him. And his own response to women seemed so unpredictable. He wished he had been more like the junior clerk at his office, who simply went out chasing different girls every night.

Lena epitomised the frustrations he felt. He had recoiled from her in the little hotel room where she lived, but in the months and then the years that followed, he had thought often of her body and the way she'd offered it. He had come to believe that the warring parts of him, religious and material, could be unified in Lena. He could make amends; he could be redeemed. He could share his family's good fortune with her. And there was something about the way she lived – not quite an understanding, more a natural way of going about things – that he wanted to draw on whenever he might feel the need of it.

Lena meanwhile did not regret having been so firm with Rudolf when he came to her room. By offering to sleep with him that one night in Vienna, she had hoped to help him; she had sensed a conflict in him they might solve together. She wished now that she had thought more about her own feelings and less about his. In her dismay during the days that followed, she wondered if his erotic feelings were really stirred by women. He seemed to enjoy the company of men much more, barely noticing the female hangers-on at Rebirth meetings, but throwing his arm round the shoulders of the men as they went off to smoke and drink in noisy bars … But no. Rudolf had not been deterred by the fact that she was female, but by her inexperience, her lack of beauty or nice manners. These things, Lena told herself, were enough to make any man think again. Brief couplings happened all the time in Vienna and meant nothing. Yet still she found it difficult to relinquish finally the hope that had sprung up on the first day she met him at the hospital.

A few days after Rudolf had returned to Vienna, Lena found herself sitting on the floating wooden platform in the middle of the lake, to which she had rowed out with Mary.

When she had settled Mary on a wooden seat, she began to make a sketch of the Schloss. The place had a sinister atmosphere at night, there was no doubt about that, and she for one was scared to go down the cloister on her own after bedtime. She was not

224

frightened that one of the more unpredictable patients might accost her because the doors of the Emil Kraepelin building were barred at all times; it was more the suggestion of ghosts and shadows on the wall.

Yet in the morning, when Johanna came into the dining room in a clean white cap and Fräulein Midwinter appeared in the hall, it was a place of hope and order. How could she express these things in her drawing? With a face, you could show doubt in the eyes, but it was hard to imbue roofs and windows with a nameless fear.

'Mary,' she said, 'tell me what it was like when you first came here. Were you scared?'

'No. I was happy to be out of that awful place in England. The smell and the noise. I shared with Daisy to begin with. A little room in a building that's been knocked down now. Daisy used to say I woke up laughing every morning.'

'Did you understand what was going on here?'

'It was familiar to me,' said Mary, 'because I'd spent a lot of my life in an asylum, but of course I'm not a doctor so I don't know about all that. The difference here was that they cured people. In England it was like a warehouse. The staff used to do a lot of counting and roll calls, but no one saw a doctor. Here there are some people who can't leave for their own good, but they always had people getting better. Going home.'

'I heard there were terrible arguments, though. And people died.'

'That was Olivier. He was the brother of Dr Rebière, one of the founders. He'd been very ill since he was young. He was in torment, poor soul. He threw himself off the edge. When we were up on the mountaintop.'

Lena put down her charcoal. 'What did you do when you came?'

'I worked in the laundry. I could do that. Washing and putting things through a mangle.'

'That's what I used to do! That was my first job, too.'

'Dr Thomas said I didn't have to work at all if I didn't want to. He used to say, "Just sit in the sun, Mary, and imagine the view." Sometimes he'd come and join me for a few minutes and tell me about the lake and the Karawanken mountains. It was his idea that I should do some massage. He was watching me knead my hand-kerchief one day. He said my hands looked strong and they moved quick. I used to practise on Daisy in our room and it used to send her off in a trance. Then he took me to see someone in town who gave me some lessons. An elderly gentleman. And eventually I began to work on some patients. I was a bit uncertain at first. But they were all nice. And it made them feel more relaxed, I think, knowing I couldn't see them.'

'But how does it help them, being massaged?'

'Well, this wasn't the acute people, as we call them. This was the fashionable ladies and people who'd come for a rest. Some of them were overtired, that sort of thing.'

'So it was part of the treatment.'

'Yes, I think Dr Thomas thought it was all a nonsense. But his idea was that if we made them feel happy we could charge them a lot and we could use the money to look after the people who needed it. I used to argue with him and tell him it really did them good. We never did agree, but he was happy to let me carry on. Then he changed his mind when I massaged his wife. Kitty.'

'Oh, yes, I heard about her.'

'That's when they had their big falling-out, Jacques and Thomas. Anyway, she had a room over the cloister, number twenty-three it was. This was before they were married, when she'd come as a patient. She had lovely skin, very soft, I can still remember. She was always friendly when I went in, then she'd take off her dressing gown and lie there in silence. She was quite strong, you could feel the muscles, even though she was slim. She had ever such sharp little knees, I remember. But there was so much tension as well – and I had to use my elbow sometimes

226

between her shoulders and it made her cry out. But she used to be asleep at the end and I'd cover her with an eiderdown. Anyway, she told Thomas I was a miracle worker and that changed his mind. Though what made her better really was having an operation in the hospital.'

'And was the clinic a happy place back then or was it . . . strange?'

'Sonia and Kitty were the best thing. They were the sun in the morning, we used to say. Jacques was a very clever man and he wanted to help, but he could be moody. Thomas was more cheerful, you never heard him say an unkind word, but he worked too hard. When he'd finished for the day, he'd go underground into that laboratory and work some more.'

Lena looked over at the building, the whitewashed walls and tile roofs behind the birches and the chestnut tree. It looked too placid to contain that much passion, the mania and the arguments. She'd throw away the charcoal sketches and try to use paint: oils might be able to suggest the sun in the morning as well as the shadows at night.

'Mary, can I draw you now?'

'You can if you like,' said Mary.

'Just sit like that. Don't move.'

After a few minutes' silent work, using principles from her evening classes, Lena said, 'What's Charlotte like? The other twin? Is she nice?'

'Oh yes. I think she found it difficult making a life for herself away from the clinic. The clinic was family, a school, a whole world for those little girls. They were adored by all the patients and the staff. But they went back to London for a time, the family. The girls went to a college, then Martha was a schoolmistress for a bit and I think Charlotte worked in an office. And then Thomas fell ill with dementia. The Schloss didn't do so well after that, but Jacques was doing his own work in Paris and was finished with us. So it was decided that one of the girls should come back and one of

227

them should help look after Thomas. And they always say they just tossed a coin to see which one would come.'

'It's funny neither of them's married.'

'I know. And them nice-looking as well.'

'How can you tell?'

'Daisy told me. And I can hear it in their voices.'

'What do you mean?'

'They sound confident. As if they know they're admired. They speak quite softly, but they know what they're trying to get across. Miss Martha can be brisk, but she's mostly doing that for fun. It's an act.'

'Is that all? Sounding confident?'

'You can also tell from the way men talk to them. You know the man who comes each week to check on the pool and all the pipes in the hydro? If he's asking Daisy for something he takes no trouble. But when he speaks to Miss Martha, he speeds up and he says funny things to impress her.'

Lena smiled. 'I see. And what do you think they actually look like?'

'Like their mother. And don't forget I knew every muscle in her body.'

'All right. So do you think I'm pretty, Mary? What does my voice tell you about me?'

'It says you're poor. But you have ambitions.'

'You sound like a fortune teller! Ambitions for what?'

Mary licked her lips. 'To be happy.'

'But am I good-looking? Do men talk differently to me?'

'There's one man here, a visitor. His voice changes when he talks to you.'

'What's his name?'

'I don't know. I don't come into the dining room or anything. I don't know who he is or why he's here.'

'There's a lawyer called Herr Plischke, who's just left, and a journalist called Herr Heideck, who's older. How old is this man?'

'I couldn't say. Maybe forty. Shall I touch you? Then I can say if you're pretty.'

'Go on.'

Mary ran her hands over Lena's face, then through her hair and over her shoulders and down her arms.

'Now give me your hands. You've done a lot of work with these. Shut your eyes, I'm just going to touch your face once more. There. Finished.'

'Well?'

'Your hair's a bit of a mess, isn't it?'

'I do my best. And my face?'

'It'll have to do, won't it?'

'You're teasing me.'

'What colour is your hair?'

'Lots of different colours. Gold and brown and strawberry and—'

'All right. And your eyes?'

'Brown. Like a pale hazelnut. So someone told me. Of course, that doesn't mean anything to you, does it?'

'I can imagine. They're set deep, which is nice – and your skin's smooth, almost as smooth as Kitty's. Perhaps your nose is a little bit wide.'

'So, what do you think? Pretty or not?'

'Why don't you tell me what I look like first?'

Lena looked at the old woman's face with its chalky skin and staring white eyes as she sat with her head back in the sun.

'I bet you were a beauty.'

Mary laughed. 'Well, it doesn't matter now, does it?'

2

Anton spent the morning in the archive, where he found diaries and notes from a journey to Africa undertaken by Thomas as the medical officer to a cartographical expedition. They had come close to death, it seemed. There were also several drafts of a lecture on the origins of human consciousness and how the evolutionary change that enabled it (Anton thought about the sprat story as he read the notes) had simultaneously caused a structural weakness to enter humanity, with the result that one in a hundred people was the victim of severe delusions. Thomas had twice used the word 'schizophrenia' and twice crossed it out, the second time with the note 'badly formed, misleading term (E. Bleuler, who should know better!) for these chronic delusions'.

There were also some more letters and diaries from Jacques's time in America. He had ended up in California, where he seemed to have felt less like the last man alive. A bathing resort called Santa Monica had appealed to him before he went to Pasadena to inspect the cable railway at Mount Lowe.

The ambition of the two men was daunting, as they went through sickness, solitude and danger in America and Africa to satisfy their driving curiosity. Or perhaps they had been in competition with one another. Neither mentioned the other while on his travels; their concerns were with work, their own survival and the love of their wives.

There was a letter from Jacques that Anton had missed on the previous occasion but which he now held up to the light that came through the open shutters.

Thursday, we were in the mountains all day ... My heart melts when I think of the men and women and children who had to cross this terrible landscape. Legends of how some never made it, fell ill or died in the mountain passes, starved ... Ate one another ... Unimaginable – yet familiar.

And I somehow feel I know what it was to be a rider for the Pony Express, going on and on through all weathers, attacks from Indians, sunburned, snow-drenched, over prairie and mountain, terrible pain and lungs burning, but having to do it – no alternative or your wife and child will starve & at last seeing the light ahead of the station where you hand over the mail and fall exhausted into sleep. From coast to coast in nine days!

How do I know so much what it felt like? Is there some sort of universal human memory available to all? Or are our little minds just aspects of one consciousness?

I do not like these thoughts. They make our life seem perpetual, with no escape, even through death ...

There was a knock at the door and Martha appeared.

'I'm sorry to disturb you.'

'That's all right. I was just ... Wondering about things ...'

'You know you said you would need to buy some new clothes? I wondered if you'd like to go into town with Lena today. It's her afternoon off and I think she'd enjoy it. She knows all the shops. Joseph could take you.'

'Lena's the one who serves the drinks and waits at dinner?'

'Among other things, yes.'

'I'm not sure. She might feel awkward with just me.'

231

'Well, I can come too, if you prefer. There are always things I need for the house.'

At three o'clock, Anton presented himself at the stables, where Joseph was starting the van with a crank handle. Martha came down the drive from the main house with Lena hanging back a pace or two, looking at the ground.

There was not enough room for four, so Joseph had to stay behind while Martha took the wheel under his disapproving eye. Lena sat in the middle, gripping the edge of the bench seat, trying not to knock into either Martha or Anton when they went round a corner.

'Which is the best shop for men's clothes?' said Martha.

'There are three in the same street,' said Lena. 'I don't know which is the best. I could ask for advice at Herr Thaller's.'

Martha left the van in the market square and they began to walk. Anton found himself a few paces behind the two women, his mind still on the experiences of Jacques in America. It was odd that Jacques, out in the wilderness of Wyoming, had himself had strong feelings of having lived before. But there was an important difference between being able to imagine, or project sympathetically into the experience of others, and the conviction that you had actually undergone something yourself. Anton wondered if people under extreme stress as Jacques had clearly been – alone, exiled and in professional disgrace – lost the boundaries of themselves because they had nothing to rub up or measure against, no one whose habitual response would remind them of how they normally behaved or spoke. Thus undefined, they could inhabit the experience of others to an abnormal or even unnatural degree. It was quite easy to see how this faculty, if that was the word for it, would have conferred advantages on its possessors at some early stages of evolution. It would have made them more intuitive than others, less limited by self. And that usefulness would have led to sexual success and the spreading of the trait, so that it became widespread. That was a vaguely plausible explanation, though it did nothing to rebut the conviction he and Jacques had shared – that this was no useful delusion, but a fact: that they had in some way lived before. The difficulty lay in the harmless little phrase 'in some way' ...

Lost in these thoughts, Anton was distracted from the shopping expedition. When he looked up again from the pavement, he could see neither Martha nor Lena. He hurried along the street, looking into the windows of any shop that sold clothes. Something similar had often happened to him as a child when, unable to bear the tedium of his mother's half-hour visit to the china shop, he had wandered off alone.

After ten minutes, it was clear that he had lost them. Perhaps they were waiting at the outfitter's whose name Lena had mentioned earlier but which he had now forgotten.

He found himself near the bridge where he had stopped himself from following his obsession a few days earlier. Resigned to the fact that the purchase of new shirts would have to wait, he thought he could make his trip worthwhile by trying his luck at the house in the backstreet where he had seen Lena and Johanna call.

The door was opened by a tall, gaunt man in his sixties. Anton's life as a journalist had made him good at interrupting people and explaining himself rapidly. Herr Gustav stood back to let him in.

A narrow hall gave onto a low-ceilinged room whose walls were entirely covered by books, both upright and sideways on bowing shelves. There were rugs on the tiled floor and a desk with a lamp where Herr Gustav had obviously been working. Anton sat in an old armchair until his host returned with a coffee pot and cups.

'So, you want to know more about Lena?' Gustav's voice had the scratchy quality of an instrument not much used.

'It's just that she reminds me of someone I once knew. Very strongly.'

Gustav sighed. 'Her mother ... Her mother was a strange woman. I knew her quite well because they lived just nearby, down that way, overlooking the river wharf.'

'How well?'

'Please wait. I need to arrange the elements of the story. A writer's habit.'

Anton nodded.

'Very well. Let me assuage your curiosity at once. I was her lover.'

'The mother?'

'Yes. Carina was her name. She was an uneducated woman. Probably from Moravia originally. I never discovered. She was someone who lived only in the moment. I don't think she could read or write. She was like an animal that needs only warmth and sleep and some physical comfort. I became intrigued by her.'

'From a professional point of view?'

'At first. I thought if I created a character somewhat like her in a book it might help me see which habits of thought and sensation separate the human from the other animals. It might be interesting.'

'In an anthropological way.'

'Yes, but then I got to know her. And for one thing, I felt I couldn't use her like that. She had some privacy, some rights, even if she never read the book and even if it was well disguised ...' Gustav looked round the room and stopped speaking.

'And for another thing?'

'Yes.' Gustav met Anton's gaze. 'For another thing, I also saw that she was just as fully human as anyone else and that defining a human being as someone capable of rising above animal needs was a false trail.'

Restraining a desire to ask another question, Anton sipped from his coffee cup.

'She asked me to make love to her one day,' said Gustav. 'It was a casual invitation. You might think we made a strange couple and I suppose we did. But we were never ... together in that sense. I would just go to her house. I'd take some schnapps if I had some and leave the bottle. She was happy with the arrangement. I'd never had a lover like this before. She didn't want me to get to know her or make her feel safe and valued. She just wanted me to make love to her as much as I could. I became fond of her. She had no pride. If I didn't call for weeks, she didn't mind.'

'But wasn't that more like being with an animal, a pet?'

'No. There was friendship, of a simple kind. I liked her. Sometimes I thought she liked me, but what she really liked was sex. I think she had begun as a child with her brother and a neighbour. Perhaps her father as well. Then all the boys and the men in her building. The way she put it to me was that it was the great pleasure of her life. If people were willing to pay her, she liked that best. But she'd do it anyway. She had many lovers and many children.'

'And Lena?'

'I'm coming to her. Not surprisingly, Carina became pregnant. And she discovered that if there was one thing she liked even more than sex it was the sensation of carrying a child. She'd had five or six before I met her. She'd given them all up for adoption. When life was difficult she turned to drink and by the time I met her she had discovered one thing she liked as much as being pregnant, maybe more, and that was being drunk.'

'Poor woman.'

'She was not as unhappy as that makes her sound. She asked for little. Usually she was in good spirits.'

'And Lena was the child she decided to keep?'

'Yes. I don't know why. "There's something different about this one," she used to say. Perhaps it was just that she was getting

235

older and could see that it might be useful to have a girl who could help earn a living. She made sure she went to school.'

'So you watched Lena grow up?'

'Yes. I stopped visiting when she was born because ... You can't do that sort of thing with a child in the house. But I was fond of the little girl.'

'Why?'

'I assumed I was her father.'

Anton looked at Gustav, his yellowish face impassive in the light of the desk lamp. He didn't look much like Lena.

'Did Lena suspect?'

'No. Never. I was just the funny writer man who once gave her a book.'

'And when she came the other day?'

'She wanted me to know that she had made a friend at last. Johanna.'

'There must have been other candidates. To be the father.'

'Yes, though at the time when Lena was conceived maybe only three or four.'

Anton put down his cup, a little thrown by the possibilities. 'And what more can you tell me about Lena?'

'She was a child of nature. She ran wild, though her mother made her afraid of the river. I always felt she had intelligence, but there was no discipline. I think it didn't work out for her at school. Something didn't catch. You don't have much time as a child. And then the chance was lost. She was in a hurry to get out. I suspect the other children were cruel to her, because of her mother.'

As Herr Gustav spoke, Anton observed him with a reporter's eye, as though he would later have to write a description of the gold-rimmed glasses, the spidery lines on the skin of his cheeks and the voice so underused that it was already beginning to fail, requiring regular sips of water from the glass on his desk.

'Were you able to help?' said Anton.

'I paid their rent for two years. They didn't know that. But as you can see I have very little to spare. My own books sell in small numbers, I'm afraid. These three rooms, and these books, that's all I have.'

'But you remained friends with Carina?'

'Yes. We smiled at one another when we passed. We wished each other well. It was a very odd sort of friendship. But I did like her.'

'And did you ever model a character in a book on her?'

'No. But I felt I'd learned from knowing her. And I was protective of her right to live as she chose. I felt sad at her funeral. Hardly anyone came.'

As he walked back across the bridge, Anton felt disappointed. He had hoped for some clue to Lena, something that would explain how she embodied Delphine, but perhaps that had been an absurd thing to expect. Herr Gustav clearly didn't know Lena well; he had seen her from afar for the first dozen years of her life, but not much more.

What had been more revealing was Gustav's account of his relationship with Carina. He had clearly expected Anton to be surprised by it, and Anton had been careful not to reveal that he understood only too well. In the time when he was purging himself of the need for Delphine, he had slept with many women in Vienna whose names he had never asked. He had tried to be generous to them and gentle in his actions, but most of the women had been only a sensation, albeit pleasurable to both parties; they had been unaware of the function they performed for him by providing another foothold in a normality he had lost. Gustav, by contrast, had known Carina, returned to her, had anonymously paid her rent; to Anton, their friendship verged on the normal. He knew what Gustav meant when he tried to explain, somewhat shame-facedly, that even such an honestly carnal affair, with no thought of 'love', could have other qualities. For some years Anton had not only believed that such a thing was possible; he had in a phrase of Friedrich's that used to make him smile, 'bet the house on it'. One woman could stand for another, even if in the end it might take sixty to amount to one.

He had almost reached the market square, when he heard his name called and turned to see Martha waving from the Bahnhofstrasse.

'What happened to you?'

'I lost you,' said Anton. 'I was distracted and then ... I looked in all the clothes shops I could find, though there didn't seem to be many.'

'We waited in Herr Thaller's.'

'I'd forgotten that name. I'm sorry.'

'It doesn't matter. Lena and I went to the Mahler. We had hot chocolate.'

Anton looked at Lena, whose face remained averted.

'And,' said Martha, 'there's still time to get you what you need. We know the best place to go now. Unless you've gone off the idea.'

'No, no ... By all means let's ... go shopping.'

3

Lena had noticed that Anton had fallen behind them soon after they left the van. She had hurried Martha onwards, distracting her with gossip about the servants; when she saw Anton approaching the window of Herr Thaller's, where they were waiting, she stepped behind a tall display so as not to be seen. It was not long before she was able to persuade Martha to abandon the expedition.

She had enjoyed herself in the Café Mahler more than on her first visit and urged Martha to drive them both home afterwards. 'Now I know which are the good men's shops, I can just give him their names,' she said. They had almost reached the van in the market square when Martha, seeing Anton, put her hand on Lena's arm.

So they had retraced their steps, past the brewery where Herr Thaller had gone for his lunch every day, past the famous confectionery shop, through the courtyard of an old building and into the narrow street where the recommended men's outfitters stood almost next door to one another.

Lena hung back as far as she could. Yet her fear of being recognised and denounced by Anton was balanced by a passionate new wish: to be known. It was only when Mary had been unable to say which of the visitors to the Schloss was the one whose tone altered when he spoke to her that Lena understood the power of her desire

– beyond any doubt and whatever it might cost her: that the man with the changing voice should not be the handsome one who had loved her and then made a mess of showing it. No, not the one who was now trying to lure her back to his apartment in Vienna and who was the right age for her – not him. It must be, it had to be, the older one with the cough and the unruly moustache who seemed not to recognise her, though he had once tasted each part of her body as though it were the sacrament.

'Let us know if you need any advice,' Martha was saying to Anton, 'otherwise we can just wait here in the women's section while you make your choices.'

Presumably, Lena thought, he was, in addition to shirts, buying what was known in the laundry as 'linen'. Thinking of it, she had no recollection of what he had worn beneath his shirt that night; she remembered only the white scar on his back – and his gasps as the air was torn out of his wasted lung. It had been as though in those moments his life depended on her: on her alone of all people, on her – whom no one else had noticed. And she remembered, too, the fatigue that made it hard for him even to raise his head when he had sat on the edge of the bed afterwards.

Until that instant in the draper's, her life had been little more than a war with need: keeping herself alive while relying on the whim of others – those others who, since the days of Lukas and Emma at school, she had distrusted. And more than distrusted because she had had the childish, but persistent, suspicion that other people were not real in the inescapable way that she was, that their battles to survive were not as pressing as her own.

As a result, her innate compassion had had no outlet, any more than her affection; it had instead built up inside her for almost a quarter of a century. But now, hearing Anton's voice from the other room, polite yet weary, disengaged from what he was doing, she felt the swelling of an unstoppable emotion.

Rising from her chair, she went into the back room where the assistant was wrapping Anton's purchases.

'So that's all done,' the man was saying. 'For the last shirt, if you could choose between these two ... The thin stripe is more classic, but the cream you can wear with anything.'

Anton was fingering the material on the counter-top, but Lena could tell that he was not interested.

'I think you should have this one,' she said, pulling a blue shirt off the rail and holding it out to him.

He looked her deep in the eye as she stood with her arm outstretched. Was there a glint of recognition, she wondered, or was he merely surprised by her decisive movement?

'Do you have this in my size?' he said. 'I like the colour.'

'It would suit you,' said Lena.

'Let me see, yes, we do have it in your size. It's a very good quality cotton, a little more expensive than the others.'

'That's all right. I'll take it. Thank you ... Lena. I'm not very gifted when it comes to shopping, as you can probably see.'

'That shade of blue ... It was easy to choose.'

'I have very little sense of colour at all.'

'That's sad. I paint sometimes. Faces mostly, though I try to do landscapes with greens and browns. And white snow.'

'That must be hard,' said Anton. 'Getting a snow colour. I like looking at pictures. Dürer or Klimt. But I can hardly tell green from blue.'

He took the packages from the shop owner and paid him.

'What did you do while we were in the café?' said Lena. 'Did you go to the art gallery?'

'No. I went to see someone. On business.'

'Was it a good meeting?'

'Not particularly. But I think I may have learned something.'

'I can show you some of my paintings if you like. Back at the clinic.'

'Thank you, yes, I'd like that. I don't want you to think I'm an expert, though. I just ... admire the talent of others.'

'Don't expect too much.'

'Are we all done?' said Martha as they rejoined her.

'Yes. Thanks to ... Lena. I'm set up for another month now.'

'A month?'

'Will that be long enough?'

'Well,' said Martha, opening the door onto the street, 'it depends how much effort you put into it.'

Hauling laundry baskets down the cloister, digging carrots and potatoes in the garden, Lena felt as though her blood had been transfused. Outside, her eyes took in the surface of the lake and the ragged peaks of the Karawanken beyond, but didn't feel constrained by the horizon. Nothing Daisy asked her to do, not even cleaning the chronic wards in Emil Kraepelin, seemed to weigh on her. In the whitewashed corridor that led to her room upstairs and in the dark passageways that only the staff would ever see, the air seemed light.

When they were laying the table for drinks before dinner the next day, she wanted to tell Johanna about the revolution in her mind. To care for someone else was not a burden, it was a release. How could she never have guessed that? And the sense of liberation came in waves. But when she looked at Johanna's face, the thought of explaining made her laugh. Could she ever find the words to describe what she was feeling – even to someone who was almost a sister?

'Whisky, for you, Herr Heideck?' she said, handing him a glass into which she'd poured a double measure, hoping ... Hoping for what? That, suddenly intoxicated, he would carry her to his room, tear off her dinner dress and do what he had done with her before? That the jolt of alcohol would clear the blockage in his memory?

'Why are you laughing, Lena?' said Anton.

'I don't know. I think it must be something Johanna said.'

'I'm wearing one of the new shirts. Is it all right?'

'Yes, it's nice.'

'Tomorrow morning, it's the blue one.'

He smiled and turned to talk to Dr Bernthaler, as though he had spoken to Lena for as long as politeness required.

Quelling an urge to kiss him on the cheek, Lena hurried back to the kitchen, where the cook was shouting at the porter, Norbert. Hans was decanting wine with a tremor in his pouring hand.

'Let me help,' said Lena said, giving the kiss to Hans instead, something he never seemed to mind.

'All right. You can leave the white wine in the bottle. Pour the red carefully and leave that last little bit with the dregs in.'

'I will,' said Lena, thinking she might leave a little more than just the sediment for later.

When the church bell clanged half past seven, the dining room began to fill. The circular table held a dozen places, which were taken by the two superintendents, Bernthaler and Andritsch, with Martha and any guests of the Schloss. The remaining places were offered to different people each day. Martha called it the Captain's Table in the hope that people would want to be invited, even if this arrangement placed a burden on the doctors to entertain. The rest of the room was filled with tables holding two, four or six people, drawn from patients who felt well enough. Their conditions varied in severity, from the Viennese of both sexes who enjoyed the hydro and the massage and the large dinners, to those who had suffered severe breakdowns and were being talked and nursed back to health. On good evenings, the atmosphere could be therapeutic, as patients were distracted from their obsessions by wine and laughter.

As a release for her own elation, Lena began to tease Johanna about a young man who sat with his mother in the far corner of the room. Florian was his name, and he had come to the Schloss

Seeblick five weeks earlier, having abandoned his studies as a postgraduate at Vienna University when he fell into a depression that made it impossible for him to work. He was having therapy with Martha as well as an intensive exercise regime of long walks and gymnastic exercises which made him hungry at dinner time – an encouraging sign, it was thought.

Florian had melancholy eyes, a silky brown moustache that made him look older than his age and a brocade waistcoat. He seemed uneasy at the presence of his mother, who had taken the train from Vienna to visit him for a couple of days.

'Don't spill the soup on that waistcoat, will you?' said Lena. 'There'd be hell to pay.'

'No chance,' said Johanna. 'And anyway, that's your table tonight.'

'You're such a cheat, Jo. I know what it means to you. Just the chance of brushing against that lovely moustache. Go on. It's all yours. Here's the soup.'

'But you're the one who's always going on about him.'

'Oh, look, he's dropped his napkin. Quick, you can pick it up and put it in his lap for him.'

Lena wondered whether Johanna really understood it when they spoke like this, but had avoided talking to her about men for fear of giving away the extent of her own experience. Whether she understood or not, Johanna was laughing too much to carry the bowls safely, so Florian and his mother had to wait for Frau Eberl's sorrel soup.

After dinner, when only Norbert was still in the kitchen, taking out bins and sweeping the floor, Lena was able to drink almost half a decanter of red wine that had come back and been saved for cooking.

She made her way out of the main house and down the cloister, through the various courtyards until she came to her staircase. There were no shadows on the wall this time, she noticed, or perhaps she was just too light on her feet for them to reach out for her.

In her small room upstairs, she locked the door and went at once to the space behind the wardrobe. She poured a little wine into the glass on her washstand and opened the window wide onto the hot night. She took off all her clothes and lay on the bed, propped up on the pillows as she drank the wine, feeling a warm south wind come in from the lands that lay beyond the mountains. She closed her eyes and imagined that the breeze was Anton's touch and that she could hear the rasp of his breathing as he kissed her skin.

Lena was polishing the hall floor the next morning when Anton came out of Martha's office at the end of his consultation. She looked up from where she was kneeling, near the fireplace, and caught his eye.

He stopped and pulled back the flaps of his jacket to show the pale blue shirt beneath. 'What do you think?'

Sitting back on her heels, Lena said, 'I think ...' Something checked her from being effusive. 'It's a very good shirt and the colour suits you. But perhaps you should wear a different tie.'

'This one's the wrong colour?'

'Not exactly wrong, but you need more of a contrast.'

'I see what you mean. I rather grabbed the first one that came to hand. I only brought two ties anyway.'

'I see.'

'You know a lot about clothes.'

'I used to work in a clothes shop.' She paused, balanced her options and decided: 'in Vienna.'

'Ah well,' said Anton. 'That explains it. When am I going to see those paintings?'

'I have some time tomorrow before dinner. At about six.'

'Will you bring them to the library?'

'No! I don't want other people to see them. I could take them to the stable yard.'

'You're very modest. But all right. Let's hope it's not raining.'

He turned towards the front door.

'Where are you going?'

Lena had not meant her thought to escape her in words, but Anton seemed to see nothing odd in the question. 'For a walk round the lawns to clear my head of all the stuff I've just been going through in there. Then back to the archive, I expect. And then some more writing.'

'Haven't you finished your article yet?'

'Not quite. I need to make another telephone call or two. To Dr Rebière for one.'

'Will you go down to the lake on your walk?'

'I wasn't expecting to go that far. But I could. Why?'

'Maybe we should meet there tomorrow.'

'By the lake?'

'Yes. Not the stables. The lake. I think that would be ... better.'

'Lake it is.' He smiled at her as he closed the front door behind him.

That afternoon, when she was making her way over to the laundry with Johanna, she heard her name called and turned back to see Martha outside the entrance to the North Hall.

'Could you come to my office for a moment, Lena?' she said.

Lena wiped her hands down the front of her uniform and, after exchanging glances with Johanna, followed Martha to the main house. Although their teatime meetings had continued, she had never been summoned in this way before and she tried to see in Martha's walk whether there was some unusual anger, or bad news on its way.

In the office, she took her place on the chair opposite the desk, behind which Martha was looking at her over the top of her glasses.

'Is everything all right, Lena?'

'Yes, thank you. Very good.'

'You're feeling quite well?'

'I feel very well, Fräulein. Very happy.'

'Good. You're a good worker and you're popular with the others. But there's something I need to talk to you about. Wine.'

Lena felt as though she was falling, even though the chair was hard beneath her. Her palms and inner arms thrummed and there seemed to be a void where her belly had been.

'Do you know what I'm talking about?' said Martha.

Not knowing what to do, Lena lowered her head. She wanted these sensations to be over, even if it meant the end of the life she had made. She would take any punishment to stop this sense of falling.

'Lena?'

'Wine?'

'One of the cleaners discovered some bottles behind the wardrobe in your room.'

'Cleaners?'

'You know we have some men in from a company in town. To do a complete spring clean.'

'Oh.'

'Did you take them from the kitchen?'

'Don't be angry.'

'Not if you tell me the truth.'

'No one wanted them.'

'How long?'

'Perhaps a year. Or two years. I've only taken ...' She trailed off, not wanting to make it seem as if she were justifying the theft.

Martha breathed in deeply. 'I think your mother used to drink a lot of alcohol, didn't she? It was before my time, but that's what I was told.'

'She drank schnapps.'

'Why do you drink wine in your room?'

'It helps me sleep. I don't know. I ...'

Martha turned in her chair and looked out of the window. Lena was motionless as she watched.

'There are two things here, Lena,' said Martha, turning back. 'You know you shouldn't take things that are not yours and—'

'Yes, of course.'

'And there's the question of why you can't sleep. Is something troubling you?'

'It wasn't, no. Not until now, when you called me in. Until then I was feeling happy.'

'And before?'

Raising her eyes from the floor, Lena said, 'There are so many things. My life ...'

She sensed that Martha was not going to tell her to leave, that her job was safe, but she wasn't sure how much to confide.

Standing up and walking round the desk, Martha said, 'What we're going to do is this. I'm going to fine you a week's wages. Then we can consider that matter dealt with. We won't need to talk about it again. But we should probably try to find a way to make you sleep. To make you easier in your mind. If necessary, I can get one of the doctors to prescribe something.'

'I wouldn't want that. I like wine.'

'Why?'

'It makes my edges seem to disappear. And I think it reminds me of my mother.'

'Well,' said Martha. 'It's possible that you've inherited a weakness. We don't really know how these things work. It seems to run in families, but it might just be that people who drink too much tend to live poor lives and then their children do as well. So it's their best escape.'

'I don't think my father drank too much.'

'Who was your father?'

'I think he was a fisherman. In Trieste.'

'But you don't know?'

'Not for sure. But ... Yes, I am sure.'

Martha was still standing next to her. Lena could feel the warmth of her attention and it gave her a moment of confidence.

'Fräulein, you don't know about me ...'

'It's all right, Lena.'

'You don't know who I really am.'

'No one knows who they really are. No one who comes into this room.'

Lena looked up and saw Martha's eyes steady on her face.

'I've done things. In Vienna ... And ...' The words stopped in her throat. She had wanted to unburden herself, but was now afraid.

'Take your time.'

'Not just with wine, but with drugs ... And with men ... And ...'

The words stopped again. Martha waited for her to carry on, but Lena said nothing.

Eventually, Martha said, 'We all have secrets. There is a place in the human animal where shame and joy are ... very close together.'

'What?'

'For instance, I'm an aunt. I'm telling you this in confidence, though I expect most people know already. Charlotte has a three-year-old daughter. In London. The result of an affair with a married man.'

The news stopped Lena for a moment, but it didn't make her feel less alone.

'You don't understand, Fräulein. I've been paid to do things. With men.'

'Stand up, Lena.'

Lifting her head, Lena saw that Martha was holding her arms open to her. To feel the arms of someone else around her was a new experience. And the feeling of Martha's cotton blouse on her cheek and the hard ridge of the collarbone beneath; a vague scent of lily of the valley; Martha's shoulders and the spine between them so solid under her own hands; a sense of the other not as distinct or alien but as almost a part of herself as she was enfolded.

'It's all right, Lena. It's all right.' Martha repeated the words many times as she stroked Lena's hair.

After a few minutes, and with some reluctance, Lena pulled her head away and took a step back.

'Are you all right?' said Martha.

'No one has ever done that to me before,' she said.

'In all your life?'

Lena shook her head.

'Dear God,' said Martha. 'No wonder.'

'No wonder what?'

'Everything.'

4

In the early evening, Anton made his way to the lake and sat on the jetty, smoking a cigar.

The idle days were going by slowly. He had finished his article, but had still not sent it to the magazine on the pretext that there was further research to do; the editor had accepted a delay. He had cut back much of what he had written about the Viennese School. It was clear to him that in any properly administered jurisdiction Dr Freud would have been struck off for misdiagnosing his early patients and discharging them 'cured' of an illness from which they were not suffering. His self-justifying logic, selective recourse to paradox, his plagiarism, opportunism and lack of scientific integrity were appalling. On the other hand, his later writings, the psychological ones, untainted by his obsession with 'hysteria' and tea-leaf dream reading, were not just well-written but persuasive. Anton could imagine that an understanding of them could help someone like Martha in her work.

What the magazine had asked for was an idea of 'where psychological medicine stands today'. Had Austria lost its pre-eminence to America?

He kept the answer brief. To the delight of its European founders, New York had embraced psychoanalysis. Freud had been especially pleased that his teachings had been adopted by American Gentiles and not remained a Jewish concern, as he had feared. But it had gone further. In their enthusiasm, some credulous Americans had built the teachings into a sort of fundamentalist church in which the followers were obliged to swallow the whole canon, including the embarrassments, or risk being excommunicated from the faith. Freud, alas, had not demurred.

The problem came when his theories of dreams and infant desires had been co-opted by doctors treating people with inherited neurological conditions, where they could be of no help. They had in fact intensified the suffering of families by telling the mother that her son's delusions were her fault – as though a father were to blame if his daughter developed Parkinson's disease.

Condensing all this into a couple of paragraphs, even for a magazine with patient readers, had proved difficult. It was with relief that he switched his focus back to the Schloss Seeblick and to the people involved.

By now his continuing visits to the archive were revealing little he could use; they were made to satisfy a personal curiosity about the men who had founded the clinic. Daniel, the son of Jacques and Sonia, also intrigued him, being only a little younger than he was, but having fought in Belgium and Italy – and on the enemy side. How arbitrary these things now appeared. Which men you tried to kill. Borders imposed on prehuman landscapes by men in offices with dividers and a wavering pencil. Chances of birthplace and parentage determining your allegiance. Would he himself have taken dead aim at Daniel's head and tried to kill him?

Yet the slow days accumulated fast as well. The light on the lake had an autumnal burnish these days, less of a whitened blade, something more to do with butter or melting gold ... But as he had told Lena, he was not good with colours. What he liked most about the lake was the freshness of the water and the fact that it was not in constant flux, like the sea. The churn of salt water on sand or rock always filled him with a sense of despair, the waves signalling some kind of futility, the ceaseless search for shape or form, breaking and breaking since the beginning of time. The lake, you could plausibly believe, held the same water, refreshed by the clouds above: no unsubtle symbolism, just a sight that reassured the eyes.

There was a wooden seat on the jetty in which Anton now leaned back. His sessions with Martha were helping him. He felt like a ship in port whose moorings were being freed by an invisible crew: ropes the thickness of two arms loosened from squat capstans driven deep into the dock, chains with ponderous anchors being hauled in by clattering winches. And already he felt a sense of some buoyancy as the water was allowed to bear its due weight – though nothing dramatic, because what was being found was only a natural balance.

He opened his eyes to see a young woman coming down between the birches, carrying a parcel under her right arm. She wore a grey dress, the maids' dinner uniform, and there was a red ribbon trying to keep her hair in order. At the sight of him, she waved, her left hand making high circular motions in the early evening light.

Perhaps this moment of anticipation could last perpetually, he thought. It reminded him of a time he had been in the mountains with Friedrich. They had become lost for hours before stumbling on a remote refuge, which, against all their expectations, was still open. They had sat outside on wooden benches, stretched out their aching legs, laughing at their escape. The owner laid the table with a red cloth and brought beer in china mugs. From inside the refuge came the smell of cooking and the clash of pans. A minute or so later, out of the corner of his eye, Anton saw the edge of a tray being carried out to them. He had wanted time to stop then, at once, because when expectation turned into something you could touch, a shadow fell.

'Have you been waiting?' said Lena.

'No, I came down early to look at the water.'

'I like it here,' said Lena, laying her parcel on the jetty. 'I came down very early on the first morning I arrived. The lake was frozen and I walked all the way out to that floating platform there. I remember looking back at the building, which seemed so big and strange. It was half hidden by snow. I was wondering if I'd done the right thing.'

'And had you?'

'I don't know yet.'

'Well, this place has an ambience, a climate of its own, don't you think?'

'I don't know what you mean.'

'There are so many people here who live in a world of their own torment. And yet somehow it doesn't seem a sad place,' he said, looking for simpler words.

'I think that has a lot to do with the people. With Fräulein Martha.'

'Yes, she's remarkable.'

'And the doctors. And Mary. Even Daisy and Hans.'

'You may be right. Shall we look at these paintings?'

'Most of them are drawings. Of people here at the clinic. And some I've just imagined.'

She pulled a string from a roll of papers and spread them flat.

'This is a man who was here for two years. This one with no teeth used to help in the gardens. This is another patient, a very nervous old lady, but she liked to sit for me because she said it made her feel calm.'

'Is that in Lamp Court?'

'Yes, you can see the edge of the cloister there.' She leaned across and pointed. He could smell the soap on her skin.

The sketches looked enviably good to someone who couldn't draw.

'Where did you learn?' said Anton. 'Or was it just natural?'

'A little at school. Though I left when I was young. And then I did some classes in town. With a man called Tomas.'

'They're very good.'

'They aren't. Compared to most people in the class. But if you look at something carefully, and you know one or two rules, then you can do a drawing like this.'

'What about the paintings?'

'I've only brought two. Here.'

She showed him one of a man's head. 'Is this someone in particular? He looks ... kind.'

'Yes.'

'But a bit remote.'

The image was not realistic in the way the sketches were. Edges were blurred and proportions were out. But there was feeling in it – a sort of commotion at least, given by the whirl of the brush.

'It's my father. Perhaps.'

'I see.'

'Have you lived in Vienna all your life?' said Lena.

'Me? No, I was brought up in Styria. But since university.'

'And are you married?' Lena was looking out over the water.

'No. Never have been.'

'Why not?'

'I don't know. The war, probably. Everything seemed different afterwards.'

'I was too young. I was only eight when it began. School carried on the same. What was it like?'

Anton looked into the far distance. 'It was like nothing. An experience from a different life. The hard thing was coming out alive. Then trying to find a place for it in your head. To keep it apart and not let it flood you with its blood and poison into thinking all life before and after was meaningless and absurd.'

'I understand.'

'Do you really?'

255

'I think so. From what you said.'

'My sense of what life was about had so utterly changed. I saw that the idea of planning and a shape and providing for the future as though some order underlay everything – some providence – was ridiculous. And I didn't want to rope anyone else into my aimless journey. Like asking someone to get into a car with you when there's no steering wheel.'

Lena did not reply, but took out the second painting. 'This is something I've been working at for a long time. I never get it right. It's meant to be the Schloss seen from the middle of the lake. Like the first morning I was here, when it was all frozen. I felt I'd found not just a new place but a new world. And I was like Eve, the first person in it.'

Anton looked at the painting, which had been scratched in places with a knife and worked over. 'That's a difficult feeling to get into paint, I should think.'

'More than difficult.' Lena laughed. 'For me anyway.'

Neither of them spoke for a time as they looked over the lake towards the scattered houses on the far side and the mountains behind them.

Anton felt an unusual serenity, though wasn't sure if it was from the lake view or from what had been transacted in Martha's consulting room.

The presence of Lena did not disturb him. He was coming to accept that she was not Delphine, at least not in any sense that could be made comprehensible. In some way (those words again, he thought) the two of them might be coterminous, or overlapping; they might be spiritually or physically one; but Lena was another woman, a second person, and in that individuality there was life and hope: her life and his hope. He looked closely at her face in the autumn light that reflected from the water.

She turned her head to meet his gaze, and smiled. 'I have to go,' she said. 'I'll get your whisky ready, Herr Heideck.'

*

The next morning, Anton found a blue envelope had been pushed under his door. It contained his weekly bill, which he opened at the desk. He calculated that it was costing him the same as a room at the Imperial. In addition, there were charges for laundry and wine and for a day in the hydro. The pre-dinner drinks were free. A list of optional extras ran in a column down the left-hand side of the page. Only one was circled: 'Private Psychotherapeutic Treatment'; and this accounted for the largest part of the bill after accommodation.

He put the paper down. The Schloss Seeblick had advantages over the Imperial, notably its rambling grounds and its views; he didn't begrudge the payment, which, as he knew, helped subsidise the treatment of the acutely ill. The establishment was clearly struggling, however. The introduction of a new currency, the schilling, a few years back had eventually brought an end to uncontrolled inflation, but it had proved to be only a breathing space before the depression that now gripped the world. He wondered if either Martha or the two superintendents had a proper grasp of the finances. Perhaps that rather charming lawyer, Herr Plischke, had been able to offer some advice. And they badly needed a new young doctor, someone who could take over from the aged superintendents.

He walked in the grounds for half an hour before going to Martha's office and knocking at the door. He was wearing the last of his new shirts with a contrasting tie, as recommended; Martha was in a cotton dress with a damson-coloured cardigan.

When he was settled in the armchair, Martha said, 'Last time you were going to tell me about Delphine. It obviously meant a great deal to you and I wondered if you wanted to continue.'

'Straight into the deep end?'

Martha looked down at her writing pad. 'We can have some small talk if you like. But with only fifty minutes at their disposal, most people prefer to—'

'It's all right. Let me see. I lost the love of my life and I don't even know what became of her. I presume she died, but I have no way of knowing. I wrote to her old employers in Vienna, but they'd had no word. They had an address in Rouen, where I believe her parents lived, but I received no reply to my letter. Many people died, not only the ten million soldiers. And as you remember, more than twice that number of the Spanish influenza. And why should my life be different or special? None of us is spared by history. That's what history is. A leveller. A universal joke whose shape is visible only in retrospect. God laughs when he hears our plans, but history laughs louder.'

There was silence. Martha watched. The church bell sounded. 'She must have been a ... wonderful woman,' she said at last.

'She was. Some of her qualities could be appreciated by anyone. Intelligence, wit, warmth ... Originality, talent ... Spontaneity. But most of what was wonderful about her was visible only to me, I think. And that was what was so hard to deal with. The idea that without me there to observe and appreciate them, those qualities might die. Even if by some chance she herself was still living. That loss. And what flowed from it, the sense that my own life, like hers, was over.'

'What did you do?'

'I went to war for four years and killed other men. Or tried to. I think in an odd way it helped me. To know my life was all but done in any case. On long marches. Lying under the rain in Galicia, hearing the Russian artillery boom. Forcing myself to join some futile dawn attack. It made me indifferent to what happened. Not brave. No one ever called me that. But I felt like one of the walking dead, so it didn't matter if I died again.'

'So it was an advantage.'

'I think so. But when the war was over I then had two large and unresolved experiences to deal with. The only way I could think of managing them was by doing nothing. I worked, I went about my daily business. I hoped that the rhythm of normality would help, that it would wear them away.' Anton shifted in the chair. 'Perhaps five years went by and I kept myself busy writing my book. I poured a lot of undigested things into it, then took them all out again when I revised it. It was published nearly ten years ago.'

'And that was a turning point?'

'Not in the way you might think. Not because it made me a little money and gave me a fraction more standing in my profession. But because it brought to an end what I'd thought about the world before the war. So it freed me to think about what had happened since 1914, since the Caillaux trial and all those closed chapters of another age.'

'So you were in the foothills of a new mountain.'

'After all I'd lived through, that's where I found myself. At the very bottom.'

'What did you do?'

'I went out to find myself a lover.'

'So easily?'

'Not so easily at all. The sisters of old army friends, women glimpsed in bars or introduced at the theatre, the whole connected world of Vienna ... I had a couple of dalliances, but I quite quickly saw that I didn't want to spend weekends at music festivals or visit some family who meant nothing to me. I wanted intimacy. Burning closeness.'

'Not so easy to find, I suppose.'

'I decided to pay for it. Don't be shocked.'

'I'm not. I'm listening.'

'I had this crazed conviction that there was a number, a figure that I could reach and once I was there the memory of Delphine would finally be burned away. Some of the women did nothing for me, but some counted double – when there was something of her about them. When you love someone so much, it's hard to know which bits, which parts of the body, which habits of mind are essential and which ones could be replaced without loss.'

Anton stopped talking and coughed for a few moments. When he had regained his breath, he looked over to see how Martha was responding. If she had been embarrassed, she showed no sign of it.

'In retrospect, I think my plan was to convince myself that Delphine was not unique. By building a new version of her with parts taken from other women. And then it might be that I could also convince myself that what I loved about Delphine was no more than something itself made up of things I'd encountered before – in looks and eyes and voice and touch. Even from women seen in books or dreams. So that she too was in some way a composite – not a unique compound, but a mixture that could be made again.'

'So you wanted to destroy the idea of her as an individual. That was what you couldn't bear.'

'That power, yes. It meant forgoing sentimental memories, but that loss seemed worth it if it rid me of the pain. Before I go on, Fräulein, I expect you know from your reading the sort of things that people do in these circumstances.'

'Do you mean sex? I've read Krafft-Ebing. He's encyclopedic, goodness knows, though to be honest, I learned more from a book called *The Memoirs of Josefine ... Somebody*, I forget, in which a girl becomes a prostitute because she enjoys it all so much. Everything that men and women do to one another was described in that book with a sort of childish glee. And of course my patients here have told me things. So it's all right. You don't need to worry.'

'Thank you,' said Anton. 'It seems odd to me now, portraying myself as this nocturnal creature. I'm not really like that. When I compare it to my first time with Delphine. I was innocent and could hardly control myself. That's much more what I'm really like. But my innocence was taken from me when Delphine vanished. I blamed myself.'

'Why?'

'I was in Paris when the war broke out. I stayed on to finish some work. If I'd hurried home I might have rescued her. I lingered in pursuit of my career.'

'But surely it would have been impossible to get a train back in those first few days.'

'I could have tried harder. Anyway, after the war I had to find a way of living. Some peace of mind. So I prescribed myself these night-time visits.'

'And did the prescription work?'

'In the long run … Yes, I think it did. Surprisingly.'

'Surprisingly?'

'Because I was just guessing. That it might be a cure. There was no guidebook. Sometimes making love to a stranger was difficult. It enhanced my loneliness. At other times their generosity to someone they had never met was thrilling. There was one who kissed me in almost the same way as Delphine, there was another who was different, but in some small detail … even lovelier.'

'Was it all … carnal?'

'It was. We were brought up believing that the physical is low and that the emotional or the spiritual is elevated. But I discovered in those many nights that they're not opposites.'

'It's what my father used to tell us,' said Martha. 'To distrust simple oppositions. The mind is part of the brain, which is a large organ composed mostly of fat. A thought has an existence as physical as a house. The fact that you can't see something doesn't make it any less real or less important. And "psychosomatic" doesn't mean fake. It means doubly real, because it describes an event that has occurred in both mind and body.'

'I see.'

'He was in this very chair when he said that.'

'I wish I'd met him.'

261

'You would have liked him, I think. But we've digressed. I'm sorry. Tell me what went on during these visits of yours.'

'I would often ask them to dress up as Delphine. I had some clothes of hers that I'd take along.'

'Was that helpful?'

'Sometimes. If their attitude was right or the scent they wore, then it worked. They were very sweet most of these women, you know. Very placid and modest. They had quite low expectations of what their lives might be. They were realistic. I tried to be kind to them in return. I believe they enjoyed it. I'd become a little more ...' He trailed off.

'Proficient?' Martha was smiling. 'Over the years?'

'Not for me to say.'

'And what if the "attitude" as you call it was wrong?'

'Yes. Well, on the bad days I just felt how unique Delphine was. How irreplaceable. It was awful. We would lie there naked and I would look at this stuff beside me that was just ... flesh. Matter. Devoid of ... anything. And then I felt appalled by myself. And by life.'

Anton was silent for a while, then stirred himself. 'Some of the better times were when I used to ask them to act out one of the fantasies that Delphine and I had had.'

'Excuse me! You didn't ask these girls to pretend to be your lost lover but to be your lost lover pretending to be someone else?'

'Yes.' Anton looked down. He felt as though he had gone too far. 'Well,' he said eventually, 'I suppose it does sound strange. As though not even the best lover imaginable was enough in herself, but only a gateway to something better, something perhaps archetypal. Or taboo.' He smiled. 'I feel I may have read something like this in my old philosophical studies. Plato, perhaps.'

'You don't have to try to make it respectable for me.'

'I know. I was romantic as a young man. But I think in the end romantics hurt more people than sensualists. I don't think they really understand or adore women in the right way. You need to love each fold of skin.'

'And sensualists are capable of romance?'

'They can be. And love, as well.'

There was another pause, while Anton weighed up how much more he could tell. Martha appeared unflappable, but he didn't want to shock any sensibility that had not been toughened by her training.

'I'd like to tell you something odd,' he said. 'You know Lena? The maid? The first time I caught sight of her outside the building, down by the lake, I thought for a moment she was Delphine. There was something in her walk, her bearing. It was more than just a superficial thing – the tilt of the head or a look in the eye. It was like a spirit reincarnated. I became quite obsessed. I'm sorry to say I followed her and her friend Johanna into town one day.'

'That sounds rather—'

'It's all right. I didn't persevere. They went into a house. I left them there and came back here alone.'

'And do you still think she's a ... reincarnation?'

'No. She's a ... She's a young woman who works here. Who came not from Rouen but from a town in Carinthia. A rather unusual and strong-minded girl. I like her. But I know she is herself.' He coughed again. 'Yet there's still something about her. Something that they share. And it doesn't matter that I can't completely understand it. I think we have to be content sometimes to be in uncertainties, in doubts – not to be irritable about it and reach out for certainty, but to accept and as far as possible luxuriate in the experience of not knowing.'

'And you say you're not romantic!'

Anton smiled. 'I've not made love to a woman for – let me see, three years at least. And I don't mind at all. I still think of skin and touch and scent a little, but I'm not tormented any more. It's quite easy now. I can concentrate on work and other things of a higher – or by the logic we agreed – possibly a lower nature. Work.'

'What about the company of someone? Are you never lonely?'

'Sometimes. Not in this place. I've loved being here. But as I was saying the other day – to Lena, in fact – I couldn't ask someone to join my life now because it would be like asking them to climb into a car with no steering wheel.'

Outside, from the hall, they could hear the sound of patients gathering before lunch.

'And the last time you made love?' said Martha. 'When the cure worked?'

'I remember it only dimly. There was no sense at the time that I had finally cauterised the wound, or reached a magic number. It was just that in the following days I felt well again, as though after a long illness or fever. As I was walking in the Belvedere Gardens, I made a resolution to stop my night-time visits and I never went back on it.'

'And the woman in question?'

'She ... It was rather dark in her room. It was on a top floor, I remember. Of a hotel, perhaps, though I don't think she could have afforded a hotel room, so perhaps I'm wrong about that. But I seem to remember a number on the door. On a little china lozenge. The room was lit by candles, as though she didn't want to be seen too clearly. Perhaps she was modest or quite new to it. She was happy to dress as Delphine, as I recall. Even in her hat. She seemed to enjoy the game. And to enjoy making love as well. I left her some more money. She said I could come back. "You wouldn't have to pay," she said. But I knew I shouldn't. There was no need. And I would only have hurt her.'

5

When Anton had closed the door behind him, Martha turned her chair to look out of the window. This Delphine was clearly an estimable person, with her grasp of languages, her piano playing and her confidence to live in the way she chose – a cottage in Baden, rooms in town ... It made a striking picture. But how had she acquired such confidence? Something in the way that Anton spoke about her made Martha wonder if he himself had fully known or understood this woman, the object of his passion.

Martha wondered what it was like to be desired so intensely. Would it colour your idea of yourself, make you puffed up and vain? Would it make you self-conscious – anxious that you might lose this power, not knowing how you'd acquired it in the first place ... Did you need to cultivate the aspects of your appearance that he worshipped? And suppose it wasn't something that stayed the same, not a breast or a knee, but something that changed, like a look in the eye, a band of glimpsed silk or a trick of the light? Would you after a time consider such fierce desire to be a quirk – the sickness of a singular man? And then what would it be worth? And what price your hold over him?

Taking up her pad, Martha flipped back through the notes of earlier sessions. She still hadn't questioned Anton about his religion. She was inclined to believe that what didn't arise spontaneously could be left to one side; the only exception was that she liked to leave something half-finished, a loose stitch, in the hope that it might develop in the patient's mind and be picked up at the next session.

She had not been able to do that today because time had run out; though when she looked back she saw that Anton had perhaps done the job himself. The last thing he had said was something like: 'She said I could come back and I wouldn't even have to pay. But I knew there was no need and I knew it would only hurt her if I did.' Here was a woman with whom he had at once established an erotic connection and who had clearly liked him very much; so why had he assumed that if he went back he would end up inflicting pain on her? It seemed to be against the idea of male vanity as she had understood it: to be the lover so adept that a line girl would let him do it free ... surely that was the result that most men dreamed of. And even if his ego wasn't touched, how could he resist the bargain?

She smiled. These were the moments of her work that she enjoyed the most: when a flash of humour for a moment lit up the seized paradoxes of the mind. She was still smiling when she arrived at the sideboard in the dining room and helped herself to some of Frau Eberl's goulash. She was late for lunch, where most people were coming to the end of their main course. Some had finished second breakfast only an hour or so earlier; and that in itself was no snack, but a sideboard of ham, with dishes of sweetbreads as well as cheeses, pumpernickel, blackcurrant jam, oatmeal porridge and thick yoghurt with silver pots of tea or coffee and bottles of stout or Madeira to drink. Feeding people seemed an easy way of giving them value for money. Offal, oats and butter were cheap to buy from local farms; it was only Frau Eberl's skill that cost a little, and she in return worked long hours, driving on her young assistants with obscene rebukes delivered in the local dialect, which she wrongly assumed Martha wouldn't understand.

Martha took her plate to a table where Florian sat alone with his newspaper and his soft moustache, his mother having returned to Vienna.

'May I?'

'Of course.' The young man gestured. It was known that at lunchtime the members of staff might move from table to table; the meal was informal and the only rule was that patients wouldn't talk about their health.

'May I fetch you some wine, Fräulein?'

'No, thank you. The water from the spring suits me fine. Wine tonight, though. Ah, Charlotte. Have you two met?'

Florian stood up and shook hands, looking modest but entitled, like a student who has received the top academic prize of his year.

Charlotte sat down with her plate of vegetables from the kitchen garden with a slice of ham and mustard. She put Florian at his ease on the matter of twins, fraternal and monozygotic, mistaken identities and uncanny coincidences. Soon they were on to politics.

'Is it true what I've read in London,' said Charlotte, sipping on her apple juice, 'that there are two private armies in Austria and that they're on the verge of civil war?'

'There were two,' Florian corrected her, 'but the Schutzbund, who support the Social Democrats, have been driven under-ground. They were banned by the chancellor, Herr Dollfuss. So now there is only one private army, the Heimwehr, who support the old Catholic right wing. The provincials in other words.'

'Can he ban the Schutzbund? Just like that?' said Charlotte.

'The question is whether we should have private armies at all.'

'And should we?' said Martha.

'No. It's a result of the terms imposed on us after the war. The reparations we've had to make to the Allies. Parliament is para-lysed and the country is divided. Vienna against the rest. And the pro-Germans against the antis.'

'I understand,' said Charlotte. 'But it doesn't seem fair to ban only one side. And didn't the Heimwehr defend Carinthia against the Slovenes after the war? When there was no Austrian army?'

'Yes, but Dollfuss has banned the Communists and the Nazis as well.'

'So who has he not banned? Who's left?'

'Just his own party,' said Florian, 'the Fatherland Front. He said Parliament had suspended itself.'

'So Parliament's banned, too?'

Florian laughed. 'Yes, since the spring. He's just one big man for banning things. Ban, ban, ban. Though Mussolini supports him.'

'Is that important?' said Charlotte.

'Dollfuss thinks it is.'

'Does anyone else back him?'

'No. Certainly not Herr Hitler. Can I fetch you some dessert, ladies?'

After lunch, the sisters went for a walk in the grounds. 'You should have lunch with Florian every day,' said Martha as they went under the chestnut tree. 'You've done more for his spirits than all Franz's powders and my listening.'

'He doesn't seem very seriously ill,' said Charlotte. 'He probably just needs to see less of his mother.'

'Talking of mothers ...'

'Yes, I spoke to her on the telephone. It was quite a palaver. They had to switch the call through Vienna. Anyway, they're fine. I told her I was coming back on Sunday. Harriet spent a morning at kindergarten and it all passed off without tears.'

'Don't you miss her?'

'I do. But I know she's in good hands. And it's quite a relief to be away for a little while. Mother said she hopes to come out in the week before Christmas for the party.'

'And will you come back then? And bring Harriet perhaps?'

'I'll try. It may be difficult getting more time off work.'

'I thought you could go in when you wanted.'

'I can, but the office really shouldn't be running quite this smoothly without me. I'm meant to be the manager. Also, the train's quite expensive. And as for the sleeping car. What a misnomer. Well, maybe the car does sleep, but not the people in it. I was on the top bunk coming out and there was about a foot between the surface of the bed and the ceiling. I felt like a letter being posted.'

'I remember an awkward dance with a very proper couple I was sharing with once,' said Martha. 'The wife didn't want her husband to take his trousers off in front of a stranger. I tactfully left for ten minutes, but he was still hopping about when I got back. Then the wife stood in front of his bunk so he couldn't see my legs when I climbed up.'

They had come to a bench on the slope that overlooked the lake.

'What did you think of that lawyer?' said Charlotte, sitting down. 'Herr Plischke, was it?'

'He gave us some good advice, I think. About selling some land and leasing it back.'

'And did you like him?'

'Personally? He had charm. And energy. Though ...'

'Though what?'

'I didn't altogether trust him.'

'He was always asking me to go for walks with him. After dinner.'

'And did you?'

'I did once, yes,' said Charlotte.

'Did he try anything?'

'No. He wanted to talk about God and politics.'

'How very disappointing,' said Martha.

'Did he try anything with you?'

'No. Not even a walk.'

269

'I had the feeling someone was watching us, when we were walking down the cloister,' said Charlotte. 'Perhaps he sensed it, too. And that put him off.'

'You could always have said it was me. In the dark.'

'No one would believe that. They know you are above suspicion. Whereas I ... The scarlet woman.'

'What would Father say?' said Martha.

'"I never thought I'd end up the grandfather of a child born the wrong side of the blanket ... and both still unmarried at the age of thirty-six."'

'"But life is long, girls. And you must do what seems right to you. Be true to yourselves and be kind to others. The rest is pure chance."'

'Do you miss him?' said Charlotte.

'Yes. But I hear his voice. In the office. He's never far away. And you?'

'When I put Harriet to sleep at night I give her a kiss from him.'

'Do you ever see Peter?'

'No, he's more married than ever. He sends a cheque occasionally.'

'And are there others?' said Martha.

'There are friends. And occasionally someone asks me to the theatre, but it doesn't seem to develop. I always have to rush back for Harriet. What about you?'

'I never meet anyone here. At least, only patients and that's obviously forbidden.'

'Herr Heideck?'

'I think I know too much about him,' said Martha. 'And he's fixated on someone else. He wants to take responsibility for his actions, morally, but he feels they're beyond his control. I think he fears being just a consciousness, a whirlpool of impersonal energy. A toy of history with no will of his own.'

'Like the man in that book. By Musil, was it?' said Charlotte. 'But I think Lena likes him. I see her when she takes him his drink before dinner and he chats with her for a while. She can hardly tear herself away.'

'Well, maybe he'll turn his attention to her. Though he may be too damaged. Anyway, I imagine he'll be going back to Vienna when we finish our sessions together.'

'Aren't your patients meant to fall in love with you? "Transference" or something?'

'If they have, they do a good job of hiding it.'

'Perhaps it's your steel-rimmed specs.'

'Silver, if you don't mind.'

'So are you going to stay a one-man girl? The dashing Maximilian, the one who got away?'

'Oh, I don't know about that. I'm open to whatever comes along. And it wasn't just Max. There were others.'

'Were there? Really?'

'You don't know everything about me, darling.'

'Well, who then?' said Charlotte.

'That man from the Chelsea Arts Club.'

'Not Tony Tucker!'

'God no. A Hungarian. With lovely hands. I'm not sure you met him.'

'And did you ... sleep with him?'

'Mind your own business! And then there was that young army officer. You did meet him.'

'Philip Someone. Yes. He was beautiful, I admit. And that bedroomy voice.'

They were silent for a time, looking down towards the water.

'You know what it reminds me of sometimes, here?' said Charlotte. 'That place in Cumberland where we were sent to escape the Spanish flu.'

271

'God, I was furious. The only time I was ever cross with our parents, I think. It was not as though we were children. I'd started teaching by then.'

'I know. And I had a job with that printing company.'

'Those long empty days on the farm. Do you remember?' said Martha. 'Trying not to touch anything. Or breathe. I did read a lot, though. The lending library at Keswick.'

'And that silence. I remember walking on the fells one day over Coniston, I think it was. There was no one else there and it was too high even for the birds. It was that funny weather, do you remember? Sunny but with cold air. I stopped by a rough cairn and listened. There was nothing. Less than nothing. It was like hearing the beginning of time.'

They got up from the bench and went down to the lake, where they continued to talk. Martha felt spinsterish in her provincial life, carrying on their father's work; she tended to sound a racy note when talking to her sister, to show she wasn't trapped. Charlotte felt guilty about the latitude she had in London and not sure she had made the right choices; she could never tell if Martha disapproved or envied her for being a mother. Eventually the common memories of girlhood on a mountaintop, the cableway down to school in the valley and the extended family of staff and patients, both sane and delusional, was enough to make differences evaporate. You wouldn't need to be genetically identical, as Charlotte had once pointed out, to find a bond in such beginnings.

The Maximilian that Charlotte had referred to was a distant cousin on their mother's side, a German from Hanover, who had overpowered a twenty-two-year-old Martha with the ardour of his certainty. He had taken her to the Black Forest to walk; he had taken her to see castles in Bavaria; he had taken her to see transsexual cabarets in Berlin, where the performers made a show of degradation, as though defeat and loss of empire, two million

Germans dead and bankruptcy were not enough; and he had ended up by taking her to his hotel bedroom where he had insisted that he could see no similarity at all between her and her sister. Dizzied and drunk on his attention, Martha had managed to keep only a small degree of detachment when she looked up into his dark eyes and heard his words of Prussian endearment. After short spells together over a period of almost two years, Maximilian married a French woman and went to work for a bank in Paris.

Hurt though she had been, Martha found that after a year or so she could smile at the thought of Maximilian's excesses. Eventually she persuaded herself that she had seen him as a curio, an interlude with shuddering excitements, and not much more. She had certainly not believed that he was the other half of her soul. He was too much of a show-off, for one thing; and for another, she had never felt that half her soul was missing.

When she saw the various griefs of her patients, she was pleased not to have carried this feeling of incompleteness in her own life. The search for what was absent made them vulnerable. Perhaps this was one way in which she differed from Charlotte, who was more restless: a minute variation not in gene or upbringing but in an old-fashioned thing called 'temperament'. Or 'pure chance,' as her father might have said.

Martha felt lust for men, their hands and voices and crushing physical certainty, and had experienced what she had seen some-where described as the 'boundless joys of shame' – with the army officer as well as with Maximilian (though not with the Hungarian, for reasons she now regretted and didn't want to confess to Charlotte). She had read widely to understand the physical back-ground of the romantic pain that she was sometimes presented with in her consulting rooms; she knew of everything that women and men did with one another, even if some of it made her shudder or laugh. She sometimes regretted that she had never, so far as she knew, been the object of a fixated desire in the way that Delphine had been to Anton; but not when she saw where the passion had left him.

She believed she had in fact been too much loved when young. She had had an alter ego in her twin; she needed no other. Her uncle, Jacques, had provided her with a youthful object of admiration and love, and perhaps some smoothly sublimated desire. She had been able to find a release for latent maternal feeling early on in the shape of Daniel, her cousin. She had had the playful adoration of her father and the humorous support of her mother.

So, what was missing? What was the grail in pursuit of which she would tear out her heart? Perhaps, she thought, as they began to walk back to the house, I will know it when I see it.

6

One chilly Tuesday evening, Rudolf Plischke left a meeting of Rebirth in an upstairs room near the Café Central, knowing he would never return. The situation was deteriorating too fast.

The next day, in the early evening, he met an organiser from the banned Schutzbund in a tavern on the edge of the university district. The man, who gave his name as Niklas, at first seemed more interested in the beef stew than in the political crisis; it had been his idea to meet in a place known for large helpings and Rudolf could see he had not eaten recently. He pushed his own dish across the table to Niklas and waited until it disappeared.

'Dollfuss is a Nazi in all but name,' said Niklas, wiping a piece of bread round Rudolf's empty bowl. 'But the Germans will have him killed if he becomes too much of a nuisance. They'll come for the rest of us when they're ready.'

Rudolf nodded.

'How many people are in your Rebirth party?'

'About five thousand members,' said Rudolf. 'And many more sympathisers.'

'All in Vienna?'

'Almost.'

'Who are they?'

'Most of them are young. We have a council and we talk a lot, but the members are idealists, people hoping for a better life.'

'Some hope. Our choice is to be crushed by Germany or crushed by the Fatherland Front.'

'I don't want to mislead you,' said Rudolf. 'I'm not offering you guerrillas.'

'I'm not offering you guns.'

Niklas wiped his sleeve across his beard and sat back in the chair.

'What will happen,' he said, 'is a general strike. It's hopeless to think we can make progress through the ballot box. It's too late. This is a fascist country now and the only language it can understand is resistance.'

Rudolf looked down at the grainy wooden table. His hope of spiritual rebirth was almost gone. He could sense it evaporating in the steam of the stuffy room.

'The Heimwehr have access to such arms as this country still owns,' said Niklas. 'Artillery, for instance. A handful of tanks. And they will have the support of the state and the police in searching our houses and arresting us. So we must take control of the factories, of the power stations. Solidarity. Numbers.'

It sounded forlorn to Rudolf, like a speech at a student rally. But he could see no alternative.

'Here's my card,' he said. 'I'll see what I can do. I have your telephone number.'

He paid the bill on the way out and walked back to his apartment. Now that the critical moment of his life had come, he felt only sadness. He had wanted to be elected by people he'd persuaded by the fire of his oratory and the purity of his cause; he had wanted to see a spiritual awakening across the country based on something more than rural superstition. But the Social Democrats in Vienna had stolen his clothes; then they had been neutered in Parliament and their private army declared illegal. His own party, he conceded as he walked past the *Rathaus*, was too small to matter.

If there had to be bloodshed, he would have wanted it to be in a fight against the German Nazi party; failing that, against the British or French empires. Instead, he would be throwing bricks at fellow Austrians. He would tussle with anti-Semitic thugs, though he was not himself Jewish; his blood would be spilled on a factory floor by a Heimwehr volunteer. Even the Great War – in which a million of his compatriots had died in the name of curbing Bosnian separatism, or whatever pretext they had finally agreed on – seemed noble by comparison.

And maybe he would die. In an electricity substation on the far side of the Danube. He would lie unidentified for weeks in a mortuary and would be remembered only as one of 'a number of anti-government protesters'.

He took a piece of paper and wrote a letter to Lena at the Schloss Seeblick.

When Martha handed her the envelope, Lena didn't open it at once. She recognised Rudolf's handwriting and knew that he'd be trying to persuade her to join him. She felt his words ought to be less effective on paper, without the urging of his voice and his bright eyes; but she feared they might be even more compelling, like the sums on Herr Kaufmann's old blackboard: 'facts' she didn't really understand, so couldn't contradict.

It was Wednesday, one of the days she liked, when her afternoons were spent in the kitchen garden with Young Joseph. She cut cabbages and cauliflowers, dug up beetroot and carried in baskets of stored apples for Frau Eberl's speciality, which she called Apple Frost and which no one was allowed to see her make. Egg whites and cream were beaten, apples stewed with cinnamon, lemon peel and a secret liqueur before everything was folded in and made sparkling cold in cut glass. The staff were allowed to eat what was left over.

Working outside, pushing the apple baskets on a barrow to the scullery door, where Norbert was waiting to unload them, Lena was thinking all the time about Anton. Although she was still exhilarated, she had begun to feel anxious. She didn't like the speed with which, when Martha's name came up, Anton had called her 'remarkable'. True, he hadn't actually said, 'She's beautiful' or 'I love her', but he might at least have hesitated.

Naturally, she had no chance of competing with Martha, who was the right age for Anton and a thousand times more educated and more in tune with his world. But was Martha also the kind of woman that men fell for? She was slim and well dressed, but maybe men liked women to be plumper. And did they even notice clothes? Anton seemed not to care about his own at all. Martha had ears like pretty seashells and lots of earrings in different shades to show them off. Would that count? Her hair seemed a lovely colour to Lena, but maybe men preferred a darker shade, like those of the American actresses she'd seen in the cinema.

Inside the house, Lena's daily duties included arranging cut flowers in the vase on the circular table by the stairs. The display was now mostly winter foliage from the grounds, though a few hothouse blooms had been delivered from town. As she struggled to arrange them, she made up her mind. It was no use expecting Anton to remember. She had told him that she used to work in Vienna. She had stood close to him when she showed him her drawings by the lake and looked into his eyes; she had even leaned across in the hope that the scent of her skin might remind him.

The good thing was that since the episode in the clothes shop they had become friends, of a kind. He knew her name. He seemed to like her. And she had learned more about him. He didn't seem to be the sort of man who would fake some indignation because, God bless him, he seemed to live differently from other men. He wouldn't care about the rules and the conventional ways of doing things. Why else had he found himself in a candlelit room with a naked girl he'd never met before?

When his sessions with Martha came to an end and his article was finished, Anton would return to Vienna and she would never see him again. She would therefore need to find one more excuse to be alone with him and then she would simply dare to tell him – tell him that he had made love to her one evening by candlelight and coughed and moaned until she'd thought he might die there in her room. And that years later, hearing him try to be interested in the colour of some shirts in an old-fashioned outfitters, she had fallen so in love with him that she wanted to wrap him in her arms each night for the rest of his life.

In the same post that brought Lena the letter from Rudolf, there was one for Anton that had been forwarded from the offices of the *Neue Freie Presse* to his apartment in Vienna and thence, along with half a dozen others, to the Schloss by the caretaker of his building. Assuming it would be a question or correction from a reader, he put it in an inside jacket pocket, his usual place for things he couldn't quite face, and went down for his final session with Martha.

'Shall I sit here?'

'Wherever feels comfortable.'

'Perhaps today I'll sit opposite you across the desk.'

'That's perfectly all right. Feel free.'

'Is this where you ask the staff to sit when you're telling them off?'

'I don't need to. Daisy does that. Or Hans.'

'Does anything throw you, Fräulein?'

'Oh, yes. Many things. But we're not here to talk about me.'

'Have you ever been married?'

'Good heavens, no!'

'Close to it?'

'Not especially. What about you?'

'I had thought I would when I was young. It was expected.'

'But you were a rebel. Fleeing from the sausages, you told me.'

'True. Then in Vienna I saw so much poverty and degradation it gave me a taste for some aspects of bourgeois life. Comfortable beds. French wine after hard work. But my life was always in some crisis or another. I was travelling, I was writing, I was fighting a war.'

'So you were a bourgeois manqué.'

'In a way. And then Delphine ... She didn't seem to be a wife. She was not that kind of woman. Don't get me wrong, she was a wonderful companion – intellectually rather my superior. But not a wife. Certainly not a mother.'

'She told you that?'

'She said she couldn't have children.'

'Did that alter things between you?'

'Only as far as contraception was concerned. It didn't alter what I felt for her.'

'Do you think it altered things for her, though?'

'What do you mean?'

'The way she saw the future?'

Anton thought for a long time. 'Perhaps.'

'And after Delphine? All these young women in Vienna?'

'Not that many. I may have exaggerated the number.'

'I don't think so.'

'The point is not the number. The point is that I was then not someone you would want to marry. I had nothing to offer.'

'Why?'

With a wheezing sigh, Anton began. 'My unit of the Common Army fought at first in Galicia. Part of Poland now. It was not as bad as I'd expected. We were alongside the Germans. Often our billets were in barns or farm buildings. Or we'd take over whole villages. I was in with other men from Vienna, including Friedrich, my best friend. I think I mentioned him.'

'Many times.'

'We were always hoping to be switched to the Italian front. To be up in the mountains.'

He saw Martha glance towards the photograph of Daniel.

'Asiago, wasn't it?' he said.

She nodded.

'I never got there. In 1916 we had the pleasure of moving to the Ukraine, where we lost half our men. The Brusilov Offensive. You probably remember.'

'They said it was the worst event of the war.'

'I'm not sure how you measure that. Each side lost about a million men. When the Russians left to have their revolution we were sent home on leave. I even went back to see my mother and uncle at the sausage works. We hoped it would soon be over. Unfortunately, our German allies had different ideas and in 1918 they launched their Spring Offensive in France.'

'It failed, didn't it?'

'Eventually. Our leave was cut short and we had to report back to Vienna. Training and manoeuvres. Then we were told we were being moved to the Western Front, where we were going to have new enemies. We might even be fighting the Americans. I was a commissioned officer by this time – not because I was a good soldier, you understand, but because I'd been to university. They thought that meant I'd be good at planning. Because I'd read Plato and Kant. Or some of Kant, at least. Prague, Nuremberg, Saarbrucken, Metz ... That was the route to the Western Front. German railways and roads were good. It was just the numbers that were a problem. So many grumbling Slavs and Magyars. One night in Nuremberg ...' He coughed. 'Do you want to hear all this?'

'I think so.'

'It does have a point. Shall I go on?'

'Please do.'

They had been billeted round the medieval town, with its stone river bridges and half-timbered houses rendered in shades of ochre and pink. Anton and Friedrich had managed to complete their duties by seven on an August evening, when they met outside a bar in a cobbled square.

'We could jump into the river here,' said Friedrich. 'And float downstream.'

'Yes, but where would we end up?'

'It joins the Main, which in turn joins the Rhine.'

'Which ends where?'

'In the canals of Amsterdam, I believe.'

'I've never been to Amsterdam,' said Anton. 'It's worth a try.'

'You'd like it. Rembrandt, herrings, Vermeer.'

'But will they still be there?' said Anton.

'The herrings?'

'I was thinking of the art. I mean, will we still be able to appreciate it? After what we've witnessed. Do you think a painting of a girl reading a letter will seem important?'

'More than ever,' said Friedrich. 'That's the life that we have to believe in.'

'It's like a religion, then. Like believing in a god you can't see. All a matter of blind faith.'

They had left the bar and were sitting on the parapet of the bridge with their legs hanging over the fast waters. Anton had been only half joking. It would have been possible to get into a riverboat and go; there was a little blue-painted skiff moored almost directly beneath them. Their commanding officer would soon be asleep in the Bürgermeister's house; there had been no time to organise any patrols or military police. His own mental fatigue was such that he had no fear of discipline. The rump of the bedraggled army had barely the willpower to pursue and court-martial them, and a bullet at dawn would in any case have been more dignified than being dismembered by a shell.

'And do you think your father will now believe you are a "solid" citizen?' said Anton.

'I think he will. And my mother. Watching millions die and having killed a few myself will earn me some respect. Perhaps even a corner office in the ministry.'

'And will you be able to enjoy that office? And the view?'

'I'm afraid not. It'll seem to belong to a different life. Something promised to me in a plan that got thrown out. A route map drawn up by fools.'

'Yes,' said Anton. 'That's the trouble, isn't it? You won't be able to go back to the ministry, to the concert halls, to your lover's apartment and go through the motions as though any of it mattered. How much can you pretend?'

Friedrich smiled. 'Perhaps in Vermeer's time they thought the same, you know. His life coincided with the Thirty Years War – in which, if I remember from our schooldays, eight million Europeans died.'

'Many Dutchmen?'

'Yes, plenty. They fought alongside Austria.'

'So you're saying that we're watching just another chapter in the bloodlust of Europe? That's too sad for words.'

'Would you rather believe this war's a freak that stands apart from history?'

'I think so,' said Anton. 'I'd rather believe anything that makes it possible for me to live a life again as something resembling a civilised creature. Or a hopeful one.'

'All right,' said Friedrich. 'I understand. But in that case you'd better not believe that Vermeer's girl is reading a letter from her lover on the Bohemian front. Now let's go back to that bar and drink Franconian wine.'

The transport of an entire corps through Germany was achieved without any officers absconding by riverboat; and on arrival, they were instructed to move up through the German reserve lines opposite the French positions at Verdun. Further north, the Allies made a surprise attack at Amiens, advancing seven miles in a single day when their tanks rolled over flat, dry turf. The German generals acknowledged they were beaten at last; in Berlin there was rioting as the public pressed for an armistice. But the politicians in Washington and Paris and London could find no satisfactory way of ending it. The Allied advance out of Amiens stalled; the Germans dug in; and the result was that, while the outcome of the war was no longer in doubt, the killing intensified.

For Anton and Friedrich, the promised fight with the Americans did not materialise. The United States forces had become bogged down in a salient, in conditions unfamiliar to them; and in the second week of August, the enemy they faced was the French. Some were veterans of the mutinies of 1917; many were conscripted young or older men, not the first flower of French manhood, which had died in the 'meat grinder' of Verdun. Still, there was experience among their officers, and their gunners had each blade of enemy grass covered by interlocking cones of fire.

'This should be fun,' said Friedrich, as he went down into the German dugout they were taking over.

'I imagine we won't actually attack,' said Anton. 'I mean, we're just here to occupy the line until Washington and Paris make their minds up.'

Friedrich took a photograph from his tunic pocket and propped it on a shelf. 'Nice carpentry,' he said.

'Who's that?' said Anton.

'My wife.'

'Your what?'

'Ilse. You've met her. We got married in Vienna before I left.'

'Why didn't you tell me?' Anton was appalled.

'It happened in such a hurry.'

'You mean she's pregnant?'

'We would have married anyway. She's one of three sisters. They're all lovely, but she's the best. She has courage. And humour. You'll like her very much.'

'She looks charming.'

Friedrich turned away, as though embarrassed.

Anton smiled at his back. 'I understand. She's your Vermeer girl, isn't she? She's what you believe in.'

'Be quiet, Heideck. Give me a cigarette.'

The routine was as they had expected, with early stand-to, weapons inspections and some occasional shelling from the heavy German artillery behind them, with a sporadic French response. No one mentioned going over the top, even on a raid to pull in a French prisoner. They spent a week in the trench before being moved into reserve, making way for another Austrian unit. Billeted above the bakery in a village, they had time to write letters home and visit the church. Anton knelt in a pew near the front and began with an apology for his long neglect and an explanation of why he didn't really believe. He felt better when he had finished. If the god of his fathers did exist and their paths were to cross in the next few weeks, he would at least be able to look Him in the eye. As he stood up, he was surprised by the concentration he saw on the face of the kneeling Friedrich. He felt a wretched surge of jealousy, but walked as softly as he could to the back of the church to wait for him. He passed the time by reading the inscriptions on the memorial tablets on the wall, hoping that the outline of a face might emerge from the carved lettering.

In the morning they were told they were to move up the line again. After an hour of marching, they left the made-up road and went onto a farm track from which they could see the transport area behind the German trench system. There were no more trees, only blackened trunks; what had been agricultural fields were shell holes with pools of water in the bottom, where flies hung. It was difficult to keep any formation in such terrain and Anton's unit became separated from Friedrich's on his right.

There was an enemy spotter plane high above, Anton noticed. From the French batteries in Verdun they could hear shellfire growing more intense, and coming closer to them. The noise of a shell came whining overhead, then stopped. The more experienced men threw themselves to the ground before the explosion went through the field. Anton was knocked over by the blast, but unhurt. When he stood up, he saw that the main impact had been to their right. With a dozen others, he ran to help.

Horses and men lay dead or wounded round a crater. An arm in blue uniform hung from a splintered tree. In a shell hole they found Friedrich and another man. Both had lost their legs and had been blown against the wall of earth, where they were sitting, as though propped. Friedrich's eyes were open when Anton knelt down and offered him water from his bottle. He tried to make a tourniquet round the thighs with his field dressing, but it was difficult to stop the flow of blood. The thigh bones stuck out white from the stumps. Anton pushed his morphine tablets into Friedrich's mouth and poured more water in, but Friedrich seemed unable to swallow, so the mess ran down his chin. Anton tried to encourage him, saying the stretcher bearers would be with them soon. With his arm round Friedrich's back, he felt something hard in his tunic pocket and pulled out a hip flask, from behind which a photograph fell out. It was the studio portrait of Ilse. He held it up in front of Friedrich's eyes while he poured the contents of the flask into his mouth. Friedrich coughed, but seemed to swallow some of it. He lifted his right hand and held on to Anton's wrist, so the picture stayed in his line of vision. For half an hour Anton talked to him, remembering their after-school walks down the Bahnhofstrasse, the covered windows of the Gymnasium and the grand houses with their pompous owners that they had sworn that they themselves would never become. With his arm round him and with Friedrich's fingers clamped on his wrist, he kept talking until it was over.

'... and that was it,' said Anton. 'That's how Friedrich died.'

286

Martha looked at him levelly and he could sense that she was fighting a desire to speak.

'I suppose it was no worse than the things that happened to millions of others,' Anton said at last.

The rims of Martha's eyes were red, but still she said nothing. Anton stood up and crossed to the armchair, where he sat down, exhausted. He had nothing to say and the silence in the room grew thick.

Sullenly, Anton shook his head. He had spoken for half an hour. Why should he say more? The church bell struck. Martha raised her eyebrows, then looked down at the pad on her knee and tapped it with her pencil.

'That sense,' said Anton, reluctantly, 'of having lived before. That thing I mentioned to you. Reading Jacques's letters from America. The feeling that he himself described of in some way being reincarnated. Remembering that feeling I had in the jungle in Panama ... My awe at human insignificance in the face of nature and of being connected somehow ...'

He trailed off, but looked up to see Martha nodding encouragement.

'Perhaps I would have married Sonia, Jacques's wife. If I'd met her. And if I'd recognised who she was. These choices look fated only in retrospect. Perhaps it didn't matter who married Sonia, as long as life got lived. And Lena, if she was a version of Delphine ... Does it matter? Perhaps I really have lived before as different people. I've married both Lena and Sonia. And time has run in many parallel ways. Or perhaps I have lived in fact different versions of myself. With Friedrich, bleeding to death. With Delphine in Baden. With those girls in Vienna. Here in this place of refuge. I think perhaps the reincarnation is not of other men through me, but of myself at other times. I've been forced by circumstance into many separate lives. If I could reconcile those different selves into one man ...'

287

'Then?'

He looked away, reluctant to come to the conclusion that she wanted. Then he said, 'I believe that we are lost, at the mercy of chance and that history laughs at our attempts to make a pattern or a plan. You end with your legs blown off. Dying of the influenza. Or in a dementia ward, dribbling and alone. That is what life is. But if I can believe that I carry the essence of others who have lived before and that it doesn't threaten me, but in fact enriches me ... And if I can understand that the mystery of these unexplained familiarities I see in other people is that they relate to aspects of my broken self ... Then ...'

'Then?'

'Then that would be at least enough to live with, enough to go on.'

'And?'

'And then I would be whole.'

Martha stood up and crossed to the window, standing with her back to him.

Anton felt too tired to move.

7

Rudolf's letter was not what Lena had expected. He did say how much he missed her and how well he would behave towards her if given a second chance; but much more of it was about private armies and the Nazi threat. The two of them together: a mark in history, whatever might happen to them ...

The less she understood, the more she felt drawn in. To prevent herself from going, she had to find Anton at once and tell him who she was. And who he was.

She knew he usually walked in the gardens after lunch and often went down towards the lake. She could ask Johanna to cover for her while she went to speak to him. She'd take a picture with her, something to start the conversation. A sketch of him, perhaps. It was feeble, it was sad, he had seen her wretched drawings before, but in this emergency it was the best she could manage.

After his session with Martha, Anton had slept late and almost missed breakfast, though it would hardly have mattered since second breakfast started only an hour later. As it was, he was in time to take his coffee and his newspaper to a table in the window while Johanna brought him a boiled egg.

Much of the paper was still concerned with Germany's withdrawal from the League of Nations after Herr Hitler had complained about the humiliating demands made of his country. Feeling in his jacket for a notebook to jot down a politician's comment he wanted to remember, he came across the letter forwarded from the *Neue Freie Presse*.

This was still not the moment to find his accuracy questioned by a pedant or his good faith called into doubt, he thought. He'd read it when he had nothing else to read or to detain him.

The effect of the previous day's appointment with Martha was not immediate. There was no catharsis. There were not even tears for him as there had been for her. He had spent the afternoon reading and planning his return to Vienna; it was his intention to take his finished article with him and hand it over in person because he had no carbon paper at the Schloss and he didn't want to risk the post.

Walking in the garden after lunch, he was aware of a buoyancy, a sense that his ship was ready to set sail. How strange it was, he thought, that you noticed how tightly you had been tethered only when you started to be free.

He strode through the birch trees and made for a bench that overlooked the lake. Birds were singing in the air above him and a small steamer was going over the water, perhaps the last pleasure boat before the snow came.

It was tempting to risk the post with his article and book into the Schloss Seeblick until the new year. For as long as he could remember, he had not felt so at one with the natural world. He was even breathing more easily.

From inside his jacket, he took the letter and made up his mind not to be irritated by it.

Dear Herr Heideck

This is the only way I can get in touch with you. I saw your name in this magazine so I hope they will send on the letter to you.

If you are a different Anton Heideck, please throw away this letter, though I would appreciate a reply. My name is Claudia Hartung and I have recently taken charge of a religious retreat in Lower Austria near the village whose name you will see at the top of the page.

I first came to work here in 1915, when I was thirty-five years old. The retreat was for women only and was well known in Bavaria and Upper Austria as well as here. People came from far and wide. After the outbreak of war, the village was used to house people from enemy countries. I believe that one of them, a French woman, may have been known to you.

Her name was Delphine Jacob and I believe her date of birth to have been the year 1876. The foreigners, of whom there were about two hundred, were not kept behind barbed wire, but their movements were restricted and they were not allowed to correspond with their homes. They were required to do some work in the village, mostly in the farms. Madame Jacob came to work at the retreat, where she helped in the office and gave lessons in French and English and at the piano.

Anton was interrupted by a hand pulling at his sleeve. He looked up to see Lena, her faced flushed and pleading.

'Herr Heideck, I wanted to show you this.'

She held out a drawing of two figures.

'This is not a good moment, Lena, I—'

'Please look. This is you, and this is me.'

The drawing was not well executed.

'I don't know what you mean.'

'In Vienna, when—'

'Please leave me. I can't deal with this now. Tomorrow maybe. Now please go.'

291

'Anton, I beg you. Please.' She leaned down and kissed him on the cheek.

'Not now, Lena! Leave me alone.'

He stood up and walked away from her, his head flaming, towards the water's edge. He began to read again.

In 1916, she entered the retreat herself. You must understand that we are not nuns here. There is no uniform and few rules. There is a chapel and a garden and a workshop. We are a Christian community that observes silence except for one hour each day, when people are encouraged to talk about their lives. It was the habit of my predecessor to keep a note of what was said at these meetings, in broad outline.

While going through the papers I have inherited, I came across half a dozen of my predecessor's notebooks, with records of these conversations, and saw your name mentioned several times. I also discovered a diary kept by Madame Jacob.

I am reluctant to say more in case you are not the Herr Heideck in question or in case you don't wish to revisit the past. Kindly let me know. Our space for storage here is limited, and I am not minded to keep documents for which there is no need.

Lena went back to the main house and reported to Daisy, who sent her to join Johanna in the Emil Kraepelin building, where they were to scrub the corridors. At five o'clock, when their time was up, she went back to the main house for their break before dinner. Going in through the scullery door, Lena passed the wine cellar, where Hans was selecting some bottles for dinner. He declined her offer of help, but while he was facing the bins, she took an open bottle from the table and held it behind her back.

'See you at dinner, Hans.'

'Don't be late.'

'I never am.'

Concealing the bottle under an armful of laundry she took from a basket outside the scullery, Lena went quickly out into the cloister and through two courtyards until she came to her own staircase. Up in her room, she poured some wine into her glass and drank it. Then, when she had washed and changed into her dinner dress, she sat at the table and wrote a letter telling Rudolf she would join him in Vienna.

PART FIVE

1

The train was going through wooded country and there were white churches visible through the forests. After a stop at Hollabrunn, where a tiny farm boy called Engelbert Dollfuss – now the self-appointed ruler of Austria – had once been at high school, they went north through more woods towards the border with Moravia. It felt like going back into a simpler and more devout time.

From his seat at the window, Anton wondered if Delphine had come in a train like this or in some sort of cattle transport. He had replied at once to Claudia Hartung's letter, left the Schloss Seeblick and returned to Vienna, where the first thing he did was to visit the library of *Die Presse* and read the back numbers of 1914 and 1915. The headlines were about fighting and casualties; civilian detail took him longer to find. Austria's biggest problem, it transpired, had been an influx of 300,000 Jewish refugees from the East in the autumn of 1914. The numbers had overwhelmed the government's attempts to deal with individuals stranded by the closing of borders. The luckiest of the French, British and Italians had been sent home or allowed to remain in their houses under curfew; the less fortunate had been taken to camps and kept with the refugees behind barbed wire; others had been sent to villages in Lower Austria.

To Anton, the most urgent mystery was the fact that Claudia Hartung believed Delphine's surname to be Jacob. Since the turn of the century, Jewish families in Vienna had been the object of suspicion and resentment; the outbreak of war had only increased the hostility. In these circumstances Delphine would not have volunteered a Jewish name; so she had either lied to him from the start about her family or had assumed the identity in the course of a marriage she had not felt able to mention.

It was starting to grow dark when the train arrived. Anton, who had expected cattle and mud, was surprised to find himself in a cobbled square, next to a well-kept *Rathaus* and streets laid out in the bend of a river. A taxi took him to the retreat: a pink-washed house, perhaps a hundred years old, that stood on the side of a hill next to a vineyard, where half the rows of vines had been grubbed up. He went through some wrought-iron gates and across a gravelled terrace towards the front door. To his left, at a lower level, was a paddock in which two horses were grazing. Before he could pull the bell, the door opened and a maid beckoned him in.

'Thank you. I've come to—'

The maid lifted her finger to her lips. He followed her upstairs, along a dark corridor, down some steps and eventually into an end room that overlooked the gates. It was like a quarantine, he thought – or perhaps he was the only man in the building.

Speaking quietly, the maid said, 'I'll come for you at seven and take you to meet Fräulein Hartung. There's a bathroom over the way there.'

There was a crucifix above the bed and half a dozen religious texts between bookends on a chest. Otherwise, the room was bare. Anton opened the window onto the terrace and heard one of the horses snorting in the paddock below. He found the bathroom, washed and changed his clothes, then went back and settled down to wait.

The maid arrived promptly and gestured him to follow. On the ground floor, they went along a wood-panelled corridor at the end of which the maid knocked on a closed door. The woman who opened it dismissed the maid and turned to Anton.

'Herr Heideck? We have dinner in half an hour, but we can talk now. I'm Claudia Hartung. Is your room all right?'

'Yes, thank you. It's good of you to see me. This is all a little ... unexpected.'

'I suppose it is. Still, we must try to do the right thing. Do sit down. When did you last see Delphine?'

Claudia Hartung had a bun of orange hair and glasses with smears on the lenses. She sat at a desk with shelves and a metal filing cabinet behind her; there was a sofa beneath the window, which looked over a backyard. Anton took a chair opposite the desk.

'I last saw her in the summer of 1914. Nearly twenty years ago. We had lived together near Vienna. I went to Paris for work. When I finally got back, I could find no trace of her. I assumed she'd gone home to France. Or perhaps she'd met with some accident. It was odd that she left no letter. The trouble was, I couldn't carry on making inquiries because by then I was in the army. I had no time to myself.'

'Shall I tell you the facts as I know them?' Hartung had a metallic voice, pitched rather high, though not tuneless.

'Thank you.'

'Delphine arrived in June 1915, soon after me. She had been arrested and held for about nine months in a Jewish camp called Deutsch-Brod just over the border in Bohemia. Perhaps that explains why she had no time to leave a note. She was under suspicion because of the name in her papers. Eventually she must have persuaded them that she posed no threat or that she was not in fact Jewish. So she was moved here, where there were already almost two hundred foreigners in cottages and rooms all round the village. The important thing was that her status changed when she got here. She was no longer interned, merely "confined". But because of the Jewish question, she was still not allowed to write home and was let out only under supervision.'

Anton found it hard to concentrate. History had taken the shape of a red-haired anchorite. It was as though he had died and the meaning of his life was being explained rather too fast – and not at the gates of eternity, but in the dingy back room of an old vineyard-owner's house.

Delphine arrested ... Dragged from their rooms in Vienna ... Held in a camp with Jews from where – Russia? ... Telling the commander of the camp who she was ... This was the only part he could almost picture – her explanation: *Monsieur le commandant, je peux vous assurer que je suis française de souche, d'une famille catholique* ... He could hear the amused edge to her voice, even in such straits.

'Most of the foreigners worked on the farms, of which there are many, as you can imagine,' Claudia Hartung was saying. 'Some worked in the vineyard here, which was still active, though that was rather seasonal. Delphine came here to work as a cleaner to begin with, but it soon became obvious she had more to offer. The following year she began to give lessons in French and English and to teach the piano. She became attached to us, to the place.'

'I see. But she was still under supervision.'

'Yes. Until the summer of 1917, when there was an agreement between the governments that French nationals could go home.'

'And did she go?'

Fräulein Hartung shook her head silently.

'What happened?'

'She had decided to join us here. In the retreat. She had found faith.'

There was a pause.

'Faith?'

'Yes.'

Silence filled the room. Anton looked at the floor. 'She never seemed particularly ... religious when I knew her.'

'I believe faith came slowly. It had begun in the camp. I told you in my letter about our daily meetings here when people are allowed to speak. In these meetings she did talk about her life before the war. She mentioned a husband in Paris and a man called Anton in Vienna. A journalist. She spoke very warmly of you. But she seemed to feel some guilt as well, as though she was responsible for suffering. She spoke of failure. Of the limits of the flesh, as she called it. And the limits of human love. Eventually, she found a greater love in our Lord.'

'Did she now?'

'Please don't be bitter.'

Dry-eyed, Anton looked round the room, at the faded print of a woman in blue robes with a halo behind her head; at the wooden carving on the mantelpiece of a man with nails through his hands and thorns in his hair.

'What chance did I stand?' he said. 'Against ... this?'

Claudia Hartung said nothing.

'And then what happened?' said Anton. 'She's not still here, I presume. She did eventually go home?'

'I'm sorry, Herr Heideck.'

'Sorry about what?'

'I'm sorry to tell you that she died here. In the November that the war ended. We lost six people to the influenza. All of us were ill. In a way we were fortunate not to lose more in a place like this, with people living so close to one another.'

There was the sound of a door opening down the corridor, and of many footsteps.

'And where was her god then?' said Anton. 'In her hour of need?'

'She is with Him now. That's what matters.'

'I loved her.'

Hartung stood up from the desk. 'I am sorry, Herr Heideck. We all loved her. I believe she was touched by grace.'

Standing up, Anton said, 'No god could love her as much as I did.'

'You mustn't believe that. You must not allow yourself to believe that. The love of God is without limits.'

'She settled for a second best.'

'We must go to—'

'I had thought better of her.'

The next morning, Anton walked back into the village, looking for something to eat. He had not wanted to have dinner or breakfast in the religious house that had stolen Delphine. In the square, he found a café of sorts, where he drank coffee with rolls and apricot jam. As he was finishing, a clock struck nine. Leaving some coins on the table, he went out and walked in the direction of a church spire on a hill above the river.

There was a humpback bridge over the water, after which the road bent round to the right, leaving a track going left up to the church. It was built of white stone, weathered to a yellowish grey, with an open bell tower. A line of untended yews stood along a low wall, on which was a noticeboard giving the times of Mass. It was called St Ulrich's. Anton walked up a gravelled path, between headstones, lichened and leaning out of the hillside.

By the door into the church, he stopped and looked down on the village in the crook of the river's elbow. Delphine in her new religious life would have come to this church; she must have stood where he was standing now and looked down on the view. And at one such moment – while he was fighting in Galicia, for instance – was she thinking about the house in Baden? Or the Döbling apartment where he'd first found her playing the piano? He remembered the steamy little post office in Colón and the elation he'd felt when he came out of it, grasping a letter from her. Did her words have such an uplifting effect on the god she prayed to?

And when she talked to Him, did she call herself 'ta Delphine'?

On the more level ground, there were newer headstones, not yet worn down by rain and wind. Anton began to walk among them, his boots sinking into the wet grass. There were many family names repeated, going back hundreds of years; all that was missing was the names of those who'd been buried where they fell on the Eastern Front.

At last he came to a row of about thirty crosses whose inscribed dates were all in a cluster. The smallest and the simplest were of an Italian man and a French woman, exiles with plain graves. The latter read: 'Delphine Jacob, 1876–1918. Daughter of God.' Beneath the dates was an addition, made by a different mason: 'Née Fourmentier.'

Anton rested his hand on top of the headstone, then knelt and leaned his cheek against it. The pimpled surface was hard against the skin. He ran his fingers into the letters of her name. Then he stood up and went blindly down the hill.

There was a note in his room asking him if he would like to go and speak to Fräulein Hartung again in the evening as she had 'something to show' him.

At the same time as before, he went down the panelled corridor.

'Come in. Please sit down. I understand it was a shock to you last night. I'm very sorry for your loss. And for our loss, too. If it's any consolation to you, Delphine was loved here. By all of us, I think.'

'Thank you. I saw her grave today.'

'I'm glad. Is it in good repair? One of the women goes to St Ulrich's to put flowers on the graves of all of our people once a month.'

'Yes. It was ... all right. It was legible. I'm glad someone put her real name on it.'

'That was her sister.'

'Her sister?'

'Yes. She came about two years after the war. With her husband, an Englishman. She was a charming lady. She had lost two sisters, she said, to the outbreak. They left some money and instructions for the mason.'

'An Englishman? I would never have ...'

'Yes. He was ... Polite. But strange. I felt he was wounded. Perhaps the war.'

Anton nodded. 'Could you show me which room she lived in? I'd like to see it.'

'You already have. You slept in it last night. It was hers for a year.'

'Good God.' Anton was determined not to lose control in front of this strange woman.

'She loved the sound of the horses in the meadow. Different horses then.'

'And did she ... die in it?'

'No, no. She was taken to the hospital. It was a room of happiness, of peace. I would not have put you in it otherwise.'

'You said there was something for me.'

Claudia Hartung opened her desk drawer. 'Yes. It's her diary. There are not many entries, I'm afraid. She was very busy here. And everyone makes their confessions in church or at our evening meetings. So perhaps there was not much left to confide to the diary. But I thought you'd like to see it.'

Anton held out his hand. 'Thank you.'

'Will you join us for dinner tonight?'

'No. No. I'm not hungry.'

'I'll ask the maid to take something to your room later. In case you change your mind.'

*

The diary was the size of an ordinary book with a soft black leather cover and lined paper. Delphine had written the date in blue ink at the top when she'd made an entry, of which there were no more than forty. It was a joy to see her handwriting. It was the first evidence of her that his eyes had had since the day he'd left for the Caillaux trial nearly twenty years before; he could almost hear her voice in the open vowels, see her smile in the swirl of consonants.

He sat on the metal-framed bed and held the diary in his hand, for a moment unwilling to open it, afraid of what he might read.

At least he knew why she hadn't written. She had been held in a camp where letters were forbidden; then she had been watched in the village, still not allowed to write. He had the impression that things had become easier; that there had come a day when she could have posted a letter, even if she had had to ask one of the others to do it for her. But by then she had decided not to reopen communication. Would it help him to understand why she had made that choice? Or was this another box of pain better left closed? He knew what Martha would say. That only he could decide.

The other thing he had established was that Delphine was thirty-seven when they met, eleven years older than he was. He had thought the difference to be nearer seven or eight. But it hardly seemed to matter now.

He drank some schnapps from his travelling flask and opened the diary.

11 September 1915
My room is sordid, it was once used for cattle, and I am running out of money to pay the rent. The village shop charges me more than the locals. Going to the Vineyard is the highlight of my day. Life is in parenthesis. The hours go slowly but the days go fast.

16 December 1915

Christmas is coming and I will spend it in exile. Sometimes I think I am being punished. I am like the woman in the Bible who was stoned for adultery. You can never shake off the idea of sin if you had a religious upbringing like the one we had. But Christ stepped in to save the adulteress. He called her persecutors hypocrites. 'Let him who is without sin cast the first stone.' The Bible has the cruelty <u>and</u> the answers. I need that heroic intervention, that Saviour.

24 February 1916

Magdalena, the woman in charge, has asked me to teach French as well as scrub floors. I have no money left and can't write home for more, but she says she will pay the rent on my room and give me dinner in return for ten hours' work a day. I have no choice. It's better than the camp.

Anything is better than Deutsch-Bod, where I saw that humans are not human after all.

8 May 1916

Had a dream of Georges last night. We were in our old apartment near Pl des Ternes, but it was smaller. Went to escape to bedroom but there was nothing, just air and a drop to the street. Could hear G behind me. 'You are my wife! I demand that you stay!' And so on.

Awoke in a sweat. Remembered Anton's face when I tried to tell him about G that first night in Vienna, but he could only stare at my body. Of course I loved him from that moment, that look of wonder, when I held him in my hand.

Fought to stay awake so as not to fall back into that old nightmare of having failed A. Too late. Woke again with tears on my face.

What a man. What have I done to him.

If I had been able to conceive, it would have been different. Then I would have made him marry me. I know I could have persuaded him.

I wanted him to have children. I still do. There is something in him worth reproducing.

I say that as someone who at one moment in my life, in the camp, thought the world would be improved if all humanity were dead.

31 May 1916

Teaching French four hours this morning. The women in the retreat are casualties of peace, not war. Magda calls them her lost sheep, but they don't act as a flock. Most of them are perverse and difficult.

The siege of Verdun continues, I see from the paper. I wonder how many men I know, friends, acquaintances, have died there.

A beautiful afternoon, nevertheless. Magda has persuaded the local police that the Vineyard can look after the French Jew spy. So I was allowed to go up to the church under the eye of little Andrea. Stood in the doorway and looked back over the village and woods.

I felt His presence.

1 July 1916

A day of great peace. It's sometimes when I'm not trying that I feel Him near. There are moments of feeling at one with the world that nothing else could possibly explain.

Like that day in the camp when I first knew that I'd never go back to the old life. After what I'd seen. And me in the 'easy' block, not with the Russians, as they kept telling us.

The certainty that winter morning that I would need to find a bigger comfort, another way of looking at our short lives.

Before, I tried to make sense of things by love and choice and being with the right people – also by music.

That day on the freezing ground with no shoes I understood that the most sublime moments of Bach or Mozart feel that way because they are at the gateway of the divine. That is why they both thrill us and leave us yearning.

The courage to step through the gateway … I was never sure I had that.

3 November 1916

Have decided to apply to live in the Vineyard. It is the life I want. If I work hard they will feed and house me. I need no more than work and faith. That is what has sustained the best people since the beginning of time. And I have friends among the women here. That is the third part of what makes a life. Or mine from now on, at least.

My life seems divided into the sacred (now) and the profane before the war. I picture the rooms in Vienna, in the shadow of the gasometers. I remember how I tried to make them homely, though not living there myself. And Baden, where at least we were as one, like a married couple, though with an edge of sinful excitement.

Lying on the bed, he'd talk to me of Friedrich, his friend, and about his brother Gerhard and people he'd met, but I knew him so much better than they did. I pointed this out to him one day and he was taken aback. I think he believed that the games we played, the fantasies and imaginings, were a separate part of him, not who he really was – when in fact they were the truest part. Perhaps it was a surprise to him to see how far we'd come together, how much he had revealed.

When he left for Paris, the last time I saw him, I urged him to go. It was not that I was so ambitious for his career, which was in any case quite settled by then. Did I suspect that he would not be able to come back? Was I in some way hoping for an end? And if so, why? Because I was afraid of disappointing him?

I don't think so. I would not have felt so much pain if I had had some unacknowledged motive lying deep beneath my conscious thoughts.

It's when I'm awake, by day, that I feel the grief and the guilt. If he had managed to get back from Paris before they came for me ... I suppose we would have sworn ourselves to one another. We would have written, arranged to meet at some future, unknown time after the war. But then ... I can't say.

The police saved me from a decision. Those two rough men at the door. I thought already he'd be better off without me, though I wasn't sure that I would ever have had the strength to tell him. And then I was spared the need. I do believe he will prosper without me if he survives the war. He will be a father and an example.

I pray for him each night. I pray for the shells and bullets to kill other men, not him.

17 January 1917
I have been accepted into the order and put into a tiny room, which I share with Andrea. A happy day for me. I have quite stopped thinking of home, even of my sisters, though I do pray for them as well.

25 March 1917
At last I have put on some weight. The food here is plain, but there is plenty of it from the farms nearby. I think Anton would approve of me like this, more like the girl he first saw undress in his attic room.

I used to pray that he would stop haunting my dreams. But he is in my blood. Day and night. Looking back at the first

309

few times we spent together ... I think I made myself mysterious on purpose. I even hinted that I had some great secret in the hope that it would make me seem more romantic or attractive to him.

It was easy to do. To give him small glimpses into my past. Half-finished stories. Tantalising. It was something I had done since girlhood, to compete with my sisters. The difference was that by now I had lived enough to have stories to refer to. And Anton seemed to love it – his eyes widened – so where was the harm?

The truth was that my only secrets were mundane. Marriage to a man who changed, and drank too much and ceased to love me. A wretched inability to have children. A longing for love and excitement and transcendence. Restlessness. And indifference to what other people thought of me.

And then to be loved so extremely by A. I believed he had found something wonderful in me, some glorious essence that was mine alone – yet also perhaps purer than I could ever be. Purer than I really was.

Oh, my darling ... That first night, when he was ashamed of himself and I reassured him that we had time. He told me later that he was afraid of not being what he was supposed to be. Then he smiled and said, 'But which of us really is?' And I felt my soul touch his.

Later, there were times when I felt the weight of his love almost unbearable. His scrutiny. I felt his eyes burn my flesh. They were unblinking when he touched my thigh, examining the marks on my skin as though they were some rune or hieroglyph he had to understand ...

I could write a letter now and somehow it would reach him in Vienna, even if it's not until the war is over. The temptation is so strong that I sometimes feel my hand twitching above the paper.

But I will never leave this house, so what is the point of making him unhappy, of stirring up feelings that by now he must have sealed off, shut down ... When I find the temptation winning, I go out into the old vineyard and walk down the rows of vines, stumbling on the dry clay of the overturned soil. I feel like someone in the Bible, though I can never think quite who.

The seed fell on stony ground ... Ruth and Boaz ...

The woman with an issue of blood. Yes, probably her.

11 December 1917

I have moved into a lovely room that overlooks the gates. I will be happy here, on my own. There is an oil painting in the corridor outside of the Blessed Virgin. She is the opposite of me, I suppose, a virgin yet a mother.

I am 41 today. Even if I had been fertile, I'm getting too old to be a mother now. I have no regrets. It was not my destiny, not my task.

Mary's lot was to bear the child and to lose Him. To cradle Him once as a baby and then as a man at the foot of the cross. I feel with her. I ache with her in every breath she took.

One day after death perhaps I will be united with my A in heaven, as it's promised. If not – if it's to be the dark, and existence was all along a joke at the expense of our human-kind – then Amen.

8 April 1918

Movement in the war. Perhaps an end in sight before the year is over. It doesn't matter who is 'victorious'. All is already lost.

24 October 1918

Awoke feverish again. Went down for morning prayer but was too weak and had to come back to my room.

*

There was a knock at the door and Anton made a noise in answer.

The maid came in, carrying a tray with food and drink. She put it on the table.

Still sitting on the bed, Anton swung his feet to the floor. He could not speak, but held out both hands to the maid.

She stopped and looked at him, her eyes wide.

Then she crossed herself and went out of the room.

2

'Because I want to go back to Vienna.'

'But why? I thought you were happy here,' said Martha.

'I was happy,' said Lena. 'But not any longer. There's a ... new life for me. In Vienna.'

'You tried it before. And it was hard, wasn't it?'

'It'll be different this time. I'll have someone to look after me.'

'Can I ask who?'

'I don't want to say.'

Martha stood up from her desk. 'Lena, I want you to think very hard about this. We're friends, aren't we? You can trust me. Although I had to be strict that one time about the wine. You've told me about yourself. Not in detail, but enough to give me a picture of your life.'

'I know.'

'We like you here. And you're so much more confident than the frightened girl who first arrived.'

'I know.'

'There'll always be a place for you. It's your home. And if you're bored with the work, I wouldn't blame you.'

'No. I like the work.'

'Would you like to train as a nurse? We could help with that, perhaps. If you went to Klagenfurt, for instance, we might be able to pay for your lodgings. Or Graz has a good hospital. If you promised to come back.'

'I don't think so.'

'Daisy will retire any day. We'll need someone to take her place. Someone young would be marvellous for us. A real tonic.'

'That's kind of you, Fräulein, but I've made up my mind.'

'I'm worried about you, Lena. I'm anxious that you're going to come to grief. Who is this man anyway?'

'I told you. I can't say.'

'But it is a man, is it?'

'Yes.'

'It's not that lawyer, Rudolf, is it?'

'No,' said Lena. She wasn't lying. It wasn't Rudolf who had made her go. It was Anton.

'Is there anything I can do to make you change your mind?'

'No.'

'Although times are very hard, as you know, we could probably pay you a bit more. Or I could open a savings account for you and put something into that each month.'

'It's not money.' She was thinking of Rudolf's apartment. She'd hardly need money there.

'Suppose we move you to a nicer room. There's a bigger one in Clock Court – with window boxes. I could have it redecorated. What's your favourite colour?'

Lena shook her head and looked down at the rug on which she was standing. 'My room's nice. I like it in the summer when the breeze comes in through the window. I like to lie there and feel it on my skin.'

Returning to her chair, Martha said, 'I never tell people what to do. They come in here and talk and talk, and all I can do is help them ask the right questions, then let them decide for themselves. But it's different with you, Lena. I have a responsibility for you. In a way you're a child of this place as much as I am. Mary remembers looking after you when you were a baby.'

No one had spoken to Lena like this before. A pressure was building up behind her eyes and she had to force herself not to weaken.

'Thank you, but I have to go.'

Martha sighed. 'All right. You can work out your notice, which I think is two weeks. We'll be having our big party on the sixteenth and we'll need all the help we can get. My mother's coming. And Charlotte is hoping to bring little Harriet. At least stay for the party, Lena, then you can leave at the beginning of the new year.'

On her way back to her room, Lena went into the office in Lamp Court, where she found Hans bent over some paperwork on the desk.

'Sorry to disturb you.'

'It's only the rota for next week. It always gives me a headache.'

'I need an address to send on something to Herr Heideck. You remember? The journalist. He left about ten days ago. But I found a tie in his room. It had fallen down behind the armchair.'

Glad to be disturbed, Hans pulled out a file and opened it. 'He's paid his bill, anyway. Here you are.' He handed the account to Lena, who copied the Vienna address onto an envelope from the wastepaper basket.

'Thank you, Hans.'

'Is it true you're leaving us?'

'Yes. In two weeks,' said Lena, deciding in the moment not to accept Martha's compromise.

'We'll miss you. You're a good team, you and Johanna.'

'Maybe I'll come back one day. As a nurse.'

'Or a patient, more like.'

'Very funny.'

Lena thought she should flirt a little more with Hans, so he'd forget her odd request for a visitor's address.

She perched on the edge of his desk and said, 'I'm going to miss you, too, Hans. Our little glasses of wine.'

'I don't know what you mean.'

'It takes one to know one.'

'Dr Midwinter – Thomas – he used to give me a glass every night if I was working. Said it was good for my blood.'

'So you're just continuing an old tradition.'

'Yes, and what's your excuse?'

'It's a family failing. Inherited. That's what Martha says. You remember my mother?'

'I do. Carina. She was a ... a strange lady, if you don't mind me saying.'

'She was a drunk.'

'That's putting it strongly.'

'It's true. I don't know how she ever managed a day's work here.'

'She wasn't the best we've had.'

Lena laughed. 'I should think not. But I still loved her.'

'Of course you did.'

'When are you going to retire? You and Daisy?'

'We can't all leave at once. We'll go back to England. We've got a little house there, you know. It's let out. Martha says we can't go till we've got a new superintendent. That should be next year.'

'And will you take Mary with you?'

'Mary has a room in our house if she wants it. She knows that. But I think her home is here. She knows each cobble, every blade of grass. This is where her life began, you see.'

'She could come to you for a holiday each year.'

'It's a long way for a blind lady to travel.'

'Maybe I'd go with her.'

'Well, we'd put you up, too. We're not far from the sea. Lincolnshire, it's called. It's where Daisy grew up.'

'I'll look forward to it. I'd better get back to work now.'

In her room, she wrote: 'Dear Rudolf, I will come to Vienna as I said, in two weeks from now.'

Then she began a second letter, to Anton. When she had finished, she put it in the envelope and wrote Anton's address on the front. She would know when the moment came to send it.

3

Anton was surprised to receive an invitation from the Schloss Seeblick to its Christmas party in ten days' time. 'Do come – M.M.' was scrawled across the bottom right-hand corner. He looked at Martha's initials and wondered. It was hard to tell. Did she want him to come because she felt something for him? He had, after all, seen her weep into her handkerchief at the end of their last session. Or had she sent the same message across the bottom of dozens of cards?

It didn't matter. The woman he loved was dead, having long ago decided not to see him again. He believed he had, over a period of years and using his own peculiar methods, inured himself against the pain of that loss. But now a visit to her place of exile had made him uncertain; an equanimity, a balance he believed was settled, had begun to look precarious.

Still, this was no reason to decline the invitation. He felt at home at the Schloss; he liked the people there; and in those spreading grounds he had come to understand something about himself. So, yes, he would be delighted to accept, he wrote. He also asked if he might stay in his old room for a couple of nights afterwards, paying his way, to make the journey worthwhile.

A week later, he was on the train. His suitcase on the rack above his head was packed with books, his new shirts and small gifts for Martha, Lena and Johanna. There was no one else in the compartment, so he took off his brown walking boots and put his feet up on the plush seat opposite, lighting a cigar. It had begun to snow in fat, settling flakes.

When the words in his book became hard to follow, he gazed out through the window. The roofs of the shepherds' huts and wooden chalets were already white; the castle on its crag was almost lost in cloud with only the turret showing through, the topmast of a ship in fog. A flight of ducks was squawking low across the river as the train entered a tunnel with a bang of air.

At Kapfenberg, they stopped to take on water. Anton opened the window, letting the cold pour in. It had grown dark. On the platform was an old man with a lantern, walking slowly. Flakes of snow were caught by the furred glow of the platform light. No one boarded the train and no one got off. The railwayman disappeared into the darkness, his boots printing the white ground black. The train heaved and jerked backwards, then began to move. Anton dragged his sleeve down the window and touched the cold glass with his finger as the snowfields began again.

There was a coal fire burning in his room and he had time to wash and pour the schnapps from his travelling flask into a glass in the bathroom and drain it before going downstairs. The hall was covered in red-berried holly with thin trails of ivy; a bunch of mistletoe hung from the main chandelier. Thick candles on the mantelpiece and on the side tables sent shadows up the walls. In addition to the staff and patients, there were many guests that Anton didn't recognise. One was a man, perhaps in his seventies, with a white beard and windswept hair down to the collar of his black coat. He looked like a prophet, standing with his back to the main fireplace, talking to Martha, who seemed rapt.

She shook Anton's hand when he went up to them. 'How nice to see you, Herr Heideck. How was your journey? Not too cold on the train, I hope. May I introduce Jacques Rebière?'

'What a pleasure,' said Anton. 'More than a pleasure. A delight. I've spent many hours reading about you and your work.'

'Poor you,' said Jacques.

'No, no, it was very interesting,' said Anton. 'We also corresponded briefly about the article I was writing. Martha gave me your address.'

'I remember.'

Jacques's tone suggested he wanted no more questions about his former work, so Anton asked him instead about Paris. Jacques described his life there, explaining that he did occasional consultations at the Salpêtrière. 'It's funny, I suppose. I went back to my early specialities in neurology. But I do feel quite at home there. It's where I did my thesis years ago.'

All the time Jacques spoke, Anton was imagining him as a thirty-six-year-old, burning with rage and frustrated ambition as he travelled across the plains of America, feeling himself to be the re-embodiment of a storm-battered pioneer.

'And your wife,' said Anton. 'I understand she was an important part of the clinic.'

'Yes, she was a cornerstone. She's not well enough to travel, unfortunately. Not this far, at any rate.'

'Do you come back every year?'

'If I can,' said Jacques. 'I'm hoping Sonia will be well enough to come next time. She made this place what it is.'

'I envy you living in Paris. I spent a few weeks there before the war.'

'It's a wonderful place to work. Though I don't think a boy from the provinces will ever fully understand the Parisians themselves.'

As Jacques went on to describe his apartment near the Jardin des Plantes, Anton remembered Martha telling him that Jacques had come from a poor village on the coast of Brittany. His elder brother, Olivier, suffering from delusions, had been kept chained up with the horse in a stable. It was Jacques's outrage at this treatment that had fired his career.

'I've brought you some whisky, Herr Heideck,' said Johanna, appearing out of nowhere at his elbow. 'Is that right?'

'Well ... Thank you, Johanna. How are you?'

'I'm fine. It's nice to see you again, so soon.'

'And how's Lena? Is she not working tonight?'

'No, Lena left. She's gone back to live in Vienna.'

Anton held the glass tight in his hand. He didn't know what to say.

'You look as though you'd seen a ghost, Herr Heideck,' said Johanna, laughing.

'Do I? How odd.'

'A nice one.'

Rallying, Anton said, 'I've seen many ghosts. Perhaps too many.'

'I'll tell her you asked after her,' said Johanna, moving off to fill another tray.

When he turned back, he found that Jacques had been moved on by Martha. In the hope of having a different drink, Anton decided to drain the whisky glass, trying not to flinch as he did so. Johanna had made it even stronger than Lena used to and it struggled briefly with the schnapps in his stomach before easing its way into his bloodstream.

Meanwhile, the band had started to assemble its music stands and unpack its instruments. The grand piano couldn't be moved, but there was enough room on the half-landing of the main staircase for the accordion, fiddles and flute. The musicians wore lederhosen and silver-buttoned velvet waistcoats decorated with what looked like heraldic motifs.

For a moment, Anton regretted coming. There would be more small talk and dinner would go on for hours with windy speeches to follow. He'd have to pretend that he minded where people he had never met would spend a holiday he didn't care about – a little house in Alpbach, how lovely; to Salzburg, nowhere better; in Vienna, so charming at this time of year. A festival for children, above all, he would agree – though having none himself, nor having ever planned to plant another soul, unasking, on this woebegotten earth. Children! Children to be indulged and made happy by scarlet paper and the fragrant brilliance of the decorated tree – when he had at best mixed memories of his own childhood in a town where the only light had been his laughter with Friedrich as they wandered home from school …

He brought his mind back to the hall, and to an elderly woman who was telling him about her festive plans. He touched Johanna's elbow as she went past and asked if she would bring him a glass of the hot punch the others seemed to be enjoying. Near the front door, her red dress helpfully different from Martha's green, stood Charlotte, holding the hand of a small child.

Emboldened by the punch, Anton went to reintroduce himself.

'This is my daughter, Harriet,' said Charlotte.

'Delighted to meet her. Will she be joining us for dinner?'

'No, she's eaten already. She wanted to see all the party dresses.'

'Well, she can't see much down there. Would she like to be carried round?'

There was a muttered consultation and the child was suddenly on his shoulders, rather heavier than he'd expected, clinging to his forehead with sticky hands and kicking him in the chest with her heels. Already regretting his offer, Anton toured the hall, then went up to the half-landing so that Harriet could see the musical instruments. Gripping her tightly by the ankles, he made one more circuit before delivering her back to her mother.

'That was a great success, Herr Heideck. Thank you. She doesn't get much rough and tumble at home. Just the two of us and I'm not very good at that sort of thing. I'd better put her to bed now.'

'I'll keep you a place at dinner.'

Johanna, with a sprig of holly in her hairband, was urging the guests into the dining room. People seemed unwilling to move in front of another or to break off conversations in which they shared their triumphs in having arrived safely despite the snow.

For a moment, Anton considered abandoning the festivities and going up to his room to read a book instead.

To give himself time, he stepped outside the front door and walked a few paces in the frosty air. He stopped to listen. The church bell for once was still and no night birds had ventured out. He could see three or four points of light from houses along the distant road; everything else was extinguished by the night. He put his head back and breathed in hard, swallowing some of the darkness that stretched to the mountains. There was this elemental quiet that went back almost to the beginning of time; and there was the hot rage and confusion of his tiny brain, striving with its billion synapses, somewhat overheated by the alcohol he'd drunk indoors.

Either reality would do, presumably. Yet he felt shaken to his core. He had a desire to lash out or break something.

More wine would help to calm this urge, he thought, as he turned towards the house, his boots crunching for a moment on the gravel, before he pushed open the heavy door and was engulfed by noise. He elbowed his way through the hesitant crush and took a place at the 'Captain's Table' in the dining room, throwing his arm round the back of the neighbouring chair.

'I'm afraid it's taken,' he told the melancholy Florian when he tried to sit there.

'Are you all right?' said Martha, taking her place on the other side of the table.

'Very well, thank you. I'm keeping a place for your sister. She's putting the child to bed.'

'How very thoughtful. Thank you,' said Martha with her unreadable smile.

Johanna put a decanter of red wine down beside him. 'Hans says you're to pour it for the others, not drink it all yourself.' Her hair brushed his cheek as she whispered her instruction.

'In that case, you'd better bring a second decanter at once,' he said.

What a nice girl she was, he thought, as she laughed and disappeared. Quite guileless. Perhaps she would lose her way back to the servants' quarters at midnight and knock on his door instead. Then they would have such fun together, keeping warm under the heavy winter duvet with its starched cover. It would be like the old days of the night-time excursions. He had been alive then. Unhappy, desperate, but at least alive.

'Thank you for keeping my place,' said Charlotte, sitting down. 'This room is always such a lottery. I've had the best and the most boring evenings here. On consecutive nights.'

'How's the little girl?'

'Asleep. She was tired from travelling. Mary's going to sit with her.'

'Poor Mary, missing the party.'

'I'm going to take her some cakes and wine afterwards.'

'Does she ever join in?'

'She'll come down later. And she'll dance. It's a tradition.'

'Who's her partner?'

'It used to be my father. Now it's Dr Bernthaler.'

'Does she enjoy it?'

'Not at all. She only did it to please my father. She could tell it made him happy.'

'Would you like some wine? It's rather good, isn't it?'

'Jacques built up a cellar when the clinic first opened. When it was doing well and they could afford it.'

Charlotte was easy to talk to, he found. Reassured by the fact that his article about the Schloss was at the printers', too late to change, she felt free to tell him stories of life on the Wilhelmskogel, where she and Martha had grown up, and then about their move to London.

Anton wondered, as she spoke, if she had lovers or if men were deterred by the child. Perhaps Charlotte, not Johanna, would come and knock at his door. That was more likely. Yes. She'd marched with the suffragettes, she told him. As well as being such good company, she'd be athletic and commanding. And would he think of Martha when he made love to her? Would it count as having slept with both of them? Would they make the same sounds, kiss him in the same way? Perhaps, for reasons of research, he'd also need to sleep with Martha, to be sure that . . .

'More wine?' Johanna was pouring it into his glass.

'Thank you. So, by this time your father had retired, I suppose.'

'He was unable to carry on working,' said Charlotte. 'He was too ill. Tell me, Herr Heideck, are you going to write another book one day?'

'There are too many books already, don't you think? What do we have left to tell each other?'

'But you should. There may be too many books, but not enough good ones.'

'How do you know mine would be good?'

'The first one was. Martha told me.'

'I didn't know she'd read it.'

'It was quite well known, wasn't it? She said there was a particularly fascinating chapter on Chinese cookery.'

Anton laughed so much that he began coughing. He felt Charlotte's hand on his arm. 'Are you all right?'

'Yes, yes . . . I . . .' He drained his glass. 'I haven't laughed so much for years. It took me by surprise.'

He looked down at the table where the cutlery caught the light among the shining glasses. He wanted to take Charlotte by the arm, forget about Christmas, enact something delightful and true

— the thing that Vienna had never found a proper place for. He knew that she'd enjoy it. So why . . .

'If we'd read other books, by chance, then we'd be different people. Wouldn't we?'

Anton collected himself. 'I imagine so.' He drank some more wine.

'Suppose I'd read only Jules Verne, for instance.'

Recovering further, Anton said, 'Or Sherlock Holmes. You'd think every suburban villa had a body.'

'And I wouldn't want to live in Carshalton Beeches.'

'Or Freud. You'd think every mental anguish could be solved by a set formula. Or by its opposite. Or both, selectively.'

'Who made the most impression on you?' said Charlotte.

'Journalists, I suppose. Foreign correspondents.'

'You're teasing me.'

'Not really. I tried to ignore all those sex writers in Vienna before the war. Weininger and people. They saw humans as animals. Even the fiction writers. Schnitzler. Musil, too. That story about the military academy where they do awful things to that young man.'

'Well,' said Charlotte, 'I do think if I hadn't read Balzac or Jane Austen I would have a different understanding of what goes on in people's heads. And my own.'

'And Shakespeare?'

'He's a case apart, isn't he? My father had a theory that by having characters explain their thoughts and desires he made people aware for the first time in history that they all had minds of their own. Before that, they appeared to one another as two-dimensional. That woman was often angry. That man was often sad. He kept sheep, she made shoes. They gave each other names to signify these things.'

'Are you saying he invented human nature?'

326

'It's what my father thought.'

'So every play-goer standing in the mud thought himself a Hamlet?'

'Once you're awake to the possibility, it's hard to forget. It's a thought you can't un-think. Like the moment the first man or woman achieved self-awareness. There was no going back, no return to what our ancestors might have been.'

'Oh, God. There's going to be a speech.'

'Don't worry,' said Charlotte. 'It's Franz. He keeps it short.'

Bernthaler's speech was little more than words of welcome and an outline of events the next day. He hoped as many guests as possible would go skating on the lake if it was frozen hard enough. Martha would be the master of ceremonies and certain rituals would be followed; these included the famous late buffet lunch. He seemed to be on the point of sitting down, when a thought detained him.

'I won't be here next year, of course. By then we shall have appointed a new superintendent. My friend and colleague Peter Andritsch will stay for a year to oversee the change, then he too will retire. I don't know if we can afford to replace him as well. We are living in difficult times, as you all know. We have very little money in reserve and the depression shows no signs of easing up. As for what is happening in the political world ... I suppose one day our children will be able to make sense of it. I certainly can't. To see democracy suspended – and the country in the hands of private armies ...'

Franz resettled his rimless glasses. 'I came here forty years ago. It was in another century, when we believed that science was our servant and that between us we could cure all the ills of humanity. I had studied under Dr Alzheimer. And I was grateful to come to this place and find in Dr Midwinter and Dr Rebière two men who shared the great optimism of the age. So before we confront whatever challenges await us, I would like you to raise a glass to them both – and to a better time. Our founders and our benefactors, Thomas and Jacques.'

There was applause and earnest assent – 'Jacques and Thomas' – from those who remembered and from those who had never heard of either man.

'How nice for you,' said Anton.

'Thank you,' said Charlotte, her eyes shining.

Anton was not so drunk that he couldn't see the effect of the mention of her father's name.

This must be what a child's love is, he thought, seeing the flush beneath her skin. A current that electrifies a living person after you yourself are dead. An energy as powerful as the one that made Galvani's frog fly from the dissecting table ...

'... outside for a moment. Once I've checked on Harriet,' Charlotte was saying. 'Would you mind passing that saucer of chocolates so I can take them up to Mary?'

'Of course ...' The reflexive courtesy of some old Styrian rule book made him stand and pull back the chair for her, swaying for a moment as he did so. He watched her leave, finished his glass of wine, then, after a moment's hesitation, Charlotte's glass as well. She'd hardly touched it anyway.

Outside in the hall, in the press of bodies, he found himself next to a woman who looked as if she might be the twins' mother.

'Excuse me, may I introduce myself?' he said.

'Of course. My name is Kitty.'

'I thought so. Though in the archives of the clinic you are better known as Fräulein Katharina von A.'

Kitty blinked. 'You must be the journalist.'

'I am. Anton Heideck. The most remarkable thing is that you look so much like Martha and so little like Charlotte. Yet they are indistinguishable.'

'Well, that would be remarkable. Almost impossible, some would say.'

'No, no,' said Anton. It seemed suddenly important to him to underline his point. 'Genetically, of course, they are identical. Dizygotic.'

'Monozygotic, I think you mean.'

'Indeed, indeed. Half of you in each. And half your husband. But then they're also different, aren't they? One wears glasses.' He felt he made an important point and leaned back to watch it register.

'Oh, they're quite different once you get to know them, believe me,' said Kitty with a laugh. 'Do you have brothers and sisters, Herr Heideck?'

'One brother, much older. But what I mean is that although they may be identical there is something else ... And if we could discover what that was, that thing that is both familiar and elusive, the ghost beneath the skin, then I feel sure the world would be a better place.'

Kitty looked deep into his eyes and said, 'I think you've put that very well.'

Anton wasn't sure what it was that he had put so well, but felt a surging wave of warmth towards this woman for having told him so.

'Would you like another glass of wine?' he said. It was the only way that he could think of to register his gratitude.

Shaking her head, Kitty said, 'The only other person who really understood, I think, was Daniel. The girls' cousin.'

To be compared to the young man in the photograph in Martha's consulting room ... This was too great an honour, Anton felt. The man he might have killed on the battlefield ... Tears were stinging his eyes. And then they were on his cheeks.

Perhaps it should be neither Johanna nor Charlotte who knocked on his door, but Kitty, this older woman of such resounding intelligence ... In her arms he would find his deepest conflicts reconciled.

'Would you excuse me for one moment?' said Kitty, her hand on his sleeve. 'I need to ask Martha something.'

His saviour gone, Anton took another glass of punch from the tray on a side table.

There seemed to be music, of a local kind. Some sort of hand drum was beating a rhythm and he was being shepherded to one side while the floor was cleared.

Blind Mary in a blue dress with a white flower in her hair was being manoeuvred slowly down the hall by Dr Bernthaler, while everybody stamped their feet and applauded.

Some of the people from the Emil Kraepelin building were coming in through the servants' door behind the stairs, their anxious nurses following. Since dinner had ended, the staff had set out trestles with lemonade and beer, hot chocolate, meat pies and cakes for the new arrivals.

To begin with, they hung back against the walls, but, encouraged by Daisy and Johanna, some of them took to the dance floor. An elderly man who, it was well known, believed his thoughts to be controlled by French spies living in the grounds, had taken Martha by the hand and was now pushing her slowly and with intense concentration, like a gardener with a barrow full of fragile pots. By the fireplace, an old woman danced alone, her arms held out in front of her, as though rocking an invisible child. Cot death, thought Anton; husband lost to shellfire in Galicia. Or merely a chance arrangement of the limbs.

Draining another glass of punch, he turned to the nearest woman – Florian's mother, it transpired – and invited her to join him. He had never had dancing lessons, but felt sure he could be doing no worse than the others. Florian's mother was soon claimed by her son, smiling for once, and Anton was dancing with a stout patient who held him tight. The music

330

changed to a polka, and he found himself being rushed up and down the hall between the flaming candles and swirling red of the holly berries and the orange flames where Hans fed more wood into the fire.

An instinct told him to leave the room. He pushed open the front doors and went outside, where he leaned against a pillar of the porch and took in lungfuls of the icy night. Hearing the music still, he saw that in his hurry he had left the door open behind him. He closed it carefully and began to walk, feeling the sweat dry cold at once on his forehead.

He went down the side of the house, leaving the stables on his left, up three stone steps, and stumbled onto a lawn. To his right was South Court; and upstairs were many lights in what he knew had originally been Thomas and Kitty's rooms. He wondered if Kitty had been allowed to stay there tonight for sentimental reasons. How strange it must be for her, to return to somewhere she had thought finished when they moved to the Wilhelmskogel – like a false memory, or a slippage of time.

By now he was nearing the chestnut tree, with the main court-yard building to his right. He saw that the double gates were open into the cloister, above which, Daisy had told him, the young Katharina von A had once had her room, the infamous number twenty-three.

His hands were beginning to freeze, as he thrust them into his pockets and went through the gates into the colonnade.

The cold air had sobered him a little, but still he felt an urge to break, to make a stand. He wondered what had so unsettled him, what news, what change, as he strode ahead, seeing his shadow loom and overtake him on the wall. For a moment he asked himself what Friedrich would do. He seemed to hear his school friend's footsteps beside his own, the usual half a pace ahead.

'Are you all right?' It was a woman's voice, quiet in the darkness.

'Yes, I'm very well.'

'I was just coming back from checking on Harriet. Are you quite sure you're all right?'

He could see it was Charlotte, as she stepped towards him, out of the darkness.

'Would you like to see my room?' he said.

'No, thank you. I have to go back to the party. I have to dance with Franz and Peter.'

'It's a very nice room. It's where I stayed while I was researching my article.'

'Well, we should get a memorial plaque to stick on the wall. If it's a friendly article.'

'You don't need to see the room itself. You could just close your eyes and I would look after you.'

'I'm sure you would, Herr Heideck. But I have other plans I must stick to. And I think you've had too much to drink.'

'Too much for what?'

'Too much to know what you're saying.'

'But not too much to know what I'd like. Or to be able to make it happen.'

Charlotte laughed. 'You are a very nice man, Anton, if I can call you that. And who knows, in another life ... With no Harriet, no Martha, no party ...'

'My dear Charlotte, what use is another life to me? There is only one life.'

'And it is therefore perfect.'

'Come to my room, you dear, kind woman. I have wine, I have schnapps. I have a soft bed and a wonderfully warm, clean duvet. I have experience.'

'I'm sure you do. And your experience must tell you that it would end badly.'

'Why?'

'Because we can't have such simple pleasures in life. It's not allowed.'

'By whom?'

'By God. By anyone. By life. It's the nature of things. There's always a price to pay. And the punishment must always exceed the crime.'

'But that's unbearable.'

'It's a law of nature. It's like gravity. As you know.'

Anton looked down. 'I know.' He kicked at a cobble. 'I do know.'

The north wind was bringing more snow; it came in a gust through the open gates behind them.

'Walk with me to the end of the cloister there,' said Charlotte. 'Then you should go up to your room. If anyone asks, I'll say you said goodnight.'

'No one will ask.'

Charlotte put her arm through his and helped him walk.

'We can skate tomorrow on the lake,' said Charlotte. 'Can you feel that freezing wind?'

'It makes me want to die.'

They walked a few steps further in silence. 'Why do you feel like that tonight?' said Charlotte. 'On such a happy occasion. Think of all those faces in the hall. Even the poor people from the Kraepelin wards. Even they were smiling.'

'Something broke in me.'

They walked a few more steps, then Charlotte said, 'Maybe it didn't break. Perhaps something merely altered. Shifted. Maybe you don't understand that yet.'

'Please come and—'

'This is where I'm going to leave you. You know how to find your room.'

Anton nodded, as he used to nod when rebuked by the Gymnasium teacher.

'You'll be all right,' said Charlotte. 'The lake will freeze hard. We can all go skating tomorrow. The sun will burn bright. I know this country. I was born here.'

Her voice had grown quite loud. 'You will be all right,' she said again, then kissed him on the cheek and hurried off towards the main house, back to the music.

4

Lena's room in Rudolf's apartment was larger than she'd expected and she wished she'd had more things to put in it. The sailing boat from Trieste sat over the fireplace and she bought a frame for her attempted portrait of Stefan, which she hung on a wall between two windows. Even though Martha had allowed her to take her dinner dress when she left and had given her a couple of old things of her own, Lena's clothes took up only half the wardrobe in her new room.

Until such time as she found a job, Rudolf was giving her a weekly allowance, out of which she had bought an easel and some paints with a view to one day completing her picture of the Schloss Seeblick under snow. He also gave her money to buy and cook food, though they were seldom at home for dinner. She missed the laughter of Johanna at drinks time in the hall.

She looked for work in a half-hearted manner, stopping often for coffee to escape the January streets. One day, she found herself near Frau Haas's shop and on a whim decided to go in and see her. The new assistant at the till was suspicious, but agreed to go to the office and ask. A minute later, he came back and showed Lena through, watching her as though she might steal something on her way.

Everything was the same as the last time she had been there.

'I have something for you, Frau Haas,' Lena said. 'A train fare and the price of my lunch that day. I managed to get to my mother's funeral in time. I've added a little interest as well.' She held out her hand.

'Thank you, Lena. You look well. I like your dress and coat. Are you married now?'

'No.'

'Your clothes. And ...'

'I'm a kept woman.'

Frau Haas coughed. 'I don't quite understand.'

Lena smiled. 'A man I love.' She gazed up at the blank wall above her former employer's head.

'Well, of course—'

'But he's not the man who keeps me.'

'I'm sorry, I—'

'That's a different man.'

Frau Haas said, 'You've ... certainly grown up since I last saw you. You are quite ... transformed.'

'Time has passed.'

'I thought perhaps you wanted to come and work here again.'

'Is there a vacancy?'

'Not at the moment. But if you leave your address. Perhaps you could manage the ladies' floor. I'd want you to wear a wedding ring, though.'

Lena smiled. 'All things are possible. Thank you for lending me that money.'

'I didn't think I'd see it again.'

'Well, I told you. All things are possible.'

She smiled as she left the shop and began walking. The old hotel where she had her top-floor room had still not been renovated, she noticed as she went past. It was now more run-down, as were all the buildings in the district. The lack of money everywhere was obvious. It was not only amputees and war-wounded men who asked for coins, but the young and able-bodied of both sexes. To be able to return to Rudolf's apartment, with its hot pipes and velvet curtains, felt like an unearned comfort.

Rudolf was at work all day in his lawyers' office and at political meetings in the evening, where Lena sometimes joined him. The council of Rebirth voted to suspend its search for parliamentary candidates; there seemed little point in drawing up a list when there was no prospect of the Fatherland Front ever calling another election.

'The time for talk is over,' said Rudolf, though he still seemed to spend most of his evenings talking – often to Niklas, who came round to the apartment at night. They deplored the weak leadership of the Social Democrats and someone called Otto Bauer in particular. Again and again these people had missed the chance to take strong action.

Lena would often go back to her room and drink some wine on her own until Niklas had gone home. Sometimes Rudolf then called her to his bedroom. It was something she felt she had to do. Once, she pretended to herself that it was Anton inside her, hoping this might make it more bearable. Instead, it made her cry and Rudolf wanted to know why. After that, she stopped imagining.

More often by the time Niklas left, Rudolf was too tired; so Lena slept alone and didn't see him till she took him coffee in the morning. In some ways she preferred not having to pretend, but it also made her feel unwanted, in her back room, with her model boat and her wine bottles.

One Sunday evening in February, Rudolf took her to a concert by the Workers Symphony Orchestra. In the foyer, Niklas introduced them to a young man from Carinthia who had come to persuade the party leaders to give him the arms he needed to fight off the fascist Heimwehr. At the end of the concert, everyone stood and joined in 'The Solidarity Song'.

Lena saw the tears in Rudolf's eyes as he sang. Afterwards, in a crowded tavern, Niklas told them that their last hopes were dying.

Even the Left's own private army, the Schutzbund, was selling out and telling the Government in advance of their plans. To Lena, it seemed that the struggle was therefore almost over. But to Niklas and to Rudolf, it was about to start.

Two days later, the police raided the headquarters of the Social Democrats in Linz, searching for weapons. The workers inside the building responded with machine-gun fire.

Rudolf came home from his office in the middle of the day, his face flushed.

'Come on, little girl, this is it,' he said, taking Lena by the hand.

'What?'

'There's a general strike. The electricity workers have shut down the grid. We're going to occupy the Karl Marx-Hof.'

'Wait a minute. I need to pack.'

In her room, Lena put some warm clothes in a bag, then went to the bottom drawer of the chest and took out the letter to Anton. She added her new address, at Rudolf's flat, placed a small package inside it and put a stamp on the envelope.

The time had come. Her only fear was that she'd left it too late.

In the hall, she took Rudolf's hand. 'Let's go.'

At the same time, only a few minutes' walk away, Anton was buying a box of chocolates from a shop he knew in Schellinggasse. He had wanted flowers, but nothing in the February window of the florists seemed cheering. He asked for their best chocolates and insisted that they wrap the box with their prettiest ribbons; then he took a cab to Döbling, where he left the package with the porter in a large block, not far from Erich's family's apartment.

It had always seemed more tactful to remember Friedrich's birthday than the day of his death. In the first years after the War, Anton had often called to see Ilse and sometimes taken her out to dinner. He brought presents for his godson, young Friedrich, as well. There had even been a time when he thought he might close

338

some circle by marrying his best friend's widow; she had seemed well disposed towards him. But as the shock of the War receded and he started to confront the loss of Delphine, mourning her in his way, in candlelit maids' rooms, the idea of Ilse began to seem absurd. And whenever he saw her smile, it brought back the studio portrait — and the memory of Friedrich's hand clamped round his wrist to keep it visible.

With a million Austrian men dead, it was not easy, even for charming Ilse, to find a second husband; but eventually she married a man who had been too old to fight. An electrical engineer, previously wedded only to his work, he was delighted to join forces with a younger woman. He had his large apartment in Döbling and money for them all; Ilse was happy to play housekeeper and was flattered by her husband's daily delight at the unexpected turn his life had taken.

Anton wondered if, while he was doing his yearly duty to Friedrich, he should telephone Gerhard to arrange their annual dinner. Gerhard had been thirty-four when the War broke out and had not been required to enlist at once. Although he had later played his part in treating the wounded from the Eastern Front, he had passed the entire war in Vienna and this had caused a coolness between them. It was unreasonable, Anton knew, and Gerhard had served his country better in the hospital than by trudging into the Russian guns; but Anton found it hard to communicate with someone who had not seen what he had seen.

Back in his own apartment, he lifted the telephone receiver, then let it drop. Gerhard could wait. There was something more urgent. He poured himself a glass of the whisky that had been presented to him when he left the Schloss, grimaced, put his feet up on the desk and looked out of the window over the lights and motor traffic of the Ringstrasse. The taste of the whisky took him back to the hall before dinner. 'Where on earth is she?' he heard himself say out loud.

*

With the trams on strike, Rudolf and Lena were starting to walk – through the middle of town, past the Café Central and the spiky Votive church. Rudolf led the way down Berggasse, where Lena posted her letter to Anton.

As she let the paper slip from her hand and heard it land inside the box, she felt a sense of power. She had thought she might feel relief or anxiety, but not this sense of having taken control. She pictured Anton opening the envelope and his breath coming hard as he read it.

When she and Rudolf had completed whatever it was they were setting off to do, she would move out of his apartment. And then her life would either be with Anton or she would live alone, as she had done before, but knowing better this time.

They were walking by the canal and her footsteps were light. The wind was funnelled down the path between the railway track and the water, through the leafless birch trees, and Lena had to wrap her coat tight across her as they pressed on through half-rural suburbs, before they came into the southern parts of Döbling.

When they arrived, after an hour and a half's fast walking, they found the Karl Marx-Hof like a town of its own within the outer limits of the city, its walls the length of several streets, painted in dusty apricot, pitted with identical windows.

'How on earth are we going to find Niklas?' said Lena.

'Follow me.'

They went beneath an arch into a courtyard the size of a village and Rudolf found an office where he began his search. Lena watched in awe. It was as if this moment, which to her was nothing but a cold and rather fearful void, was all that Rudolf had ever wanted from his life. It took them until late in the evening to find the building and the staircase, though Rudolf's belief never flagged.

The corridor, lit by candles in the absence of electric light, was full of people, some of whom Lena recognised from Rebirth meetings. The tenants and their families had shared their rooms with hundreds of the Schutzbund and its supporters. In the small kitchens, teams of people worked to provide soup or sausages, while the ground-floor bakeries were emptied of their supplies.

They'd found Niklas in an end apartment that faced out over the main road. He was surrounded by young men drinking and smoking. One of them was playing an accordion, which, with the candles, gave it the feeling of an amateur nightclub.

Lena found herself fascinated by the apartments, comparing them to the rooms she had lived in as a child, where the basin was behind a curtain in the corner. But here there were water closets and separate kitchens and downstairs all kinds of shops. On the other hand, there was no wharf to watch and no sound of a river-boat's deep engine.

No one seemed to be in charge. Niklas and three or four others tried to exert control, standing on chairs and shouting. Rudolf managed to gather most of the Rebirth people down to his end of the corridor and organise a food supply.

Looking through a small back window onto the expanse of courtyard, Lena could see that many other buildings of the Karl Marx-Hof were occupied and those who had not been able to find space were lighting bonfires outside to keep warm, singing workers' songs. Their efforts looked fragile, and Lena found a sadness passing over her.

The talk inside was about arms, and who had them. It seemed there were some rifles in another building, rescued from a Schutzbund headquarters. There were rumours of grenades and machine guns as well, but no one seemed to know where they were.

'Who is it we're going to attack?' said Lena.

'It's for self-defence,' said Rudolf. 'In case they come after us.'

'They will,' said Niklas. 'Have no doubt. The government will send in what's left of the infantry to clear us out.'

The woman whose apartment they were in gave Lena some pea soup and said she could share her bed with three others. 'I've asked the men to let us have this room to ourselves. There's not many of us.'

Lena pulled out all the warm clothes she had brought in her bag and put them on. She used the water closet while the door was guarded by her new friend, then lay down with the other women.

It was impossible to sleep in the cold, in the noise. Lena closed her eyes and thought of the night she had spent with Carina in Stefan's warm bed in Trieste, while he had taken the couch. She thought of her maid's room in Vienna and of Anton holding her, and whispering in her ear. Somehow, it was enough to take her away from the world in which she found herself, and she slept, on and off.

In the morning, she went stiffly to wash and to search for Rudolf. She found him eventually, outside, where he had gone to look for a telephone.

'I've spoken to a friend in town,' he said. 'They've sent troops to attack the Schlingerhof. They'll be coming here, too. If you want to leave, Lena, you should go now.'

Before she could answer, Niklas ran towards them. 'Come upstairs,' he said. 'It's not safe down here.'

The mood in the crowded corridor was not as jubilant as the night before. Few people had slept. There was not enough coffee to revive them and even cigarettes were running short. Towards the end of the morning, a panic went through the building. Men were running in from the main road outside, shouting and waving their arms. Lena pressed her face to the window. She could hear a low rumbling, coming closer. Then she saw the long barrel of a gun on a mounted carriage being pulled by a motor lorry. It was like something she'd seen only in newspaper reports of war – a gun that would knock down buildings.

She felt Niklas push her to one side. He swore in her ear.

On the main road, more lorries and gun carriages were appearing.

In the corridor behind her Niklas was shouting. 'Artillery. They've sent the artillery.'

As word went round the building, there was a crush of people trying to escape.

She heard Rudolf's voice. 'It'll take them time to set up. We mustn't panic. Stay where you are!'

There were other voices shouting in the confusion.

'We can bargain with them. Make a deal.'

'They said the infantry would take too long.'

'They won't just open fire!'

'Move to the back of the building. Everybody to the back!'

Lena did as she was told and went into the women's room where she had spent the night. For perhaps an hour, they waited, hearing the rumble of heavy traffic from the front.

Then there was an explosion and the windows trembled. They could hear crying and shouting, but the shell had gone into another building, not theirs. There came another blast, louder than the first, and this time the windows of the bedroom shattered.

Thinking she should help, Lena went through the apartment and out into the corridor, which was filled with smoke and dust. There was a man lying, bleeding, at the far end. She saw Rudolf and Niklas running towards him. Then there was no floor beneath them, and they were gone.

Rudolf had been wrong about how he might die, and he was wrong about what happened to him afterwards. The fighting lasted less than a day and the Government allowed friends and family to collect the bodies of the dead.

A funeral was arranged by Rudolf's family in Klagenfurt and Lena took the train from Vienna. She managed to offer some consolation to his father without admitting that she had shared an apartment and sometimes a bed with Rudolf. While the coffin was lowered into the ground she could think only of the jolly young man who had waved to her on his crutches in the hospital. She imagined the crutches in there with him ... his bright blue eyes ... and the floor of the corridor disappearing beneath him.

Afterwards, she read everything in the papers. They named many of the dead, including Rudolf, a 'promising young lawyer', though estimates of their number varied from two hundred to six hundred. More than a thousand, it was agreed, had been wounded. The leader of the Social Democrats was forced into exile; the Government began legislation to outlaw the party and all the trade unions. Red Vienna was dead, and only the Fatherland Front remained; it was, said one newspaper, the final triumph of the old Catholicism. Lena found it hard to believe that the corridor with the flimsy doors, the women-only bedroom, the pea soup and the wheezing accordion had been part of something that was going to be called history.

She had believed that Rudolf loved her, but was too diffident to make his feelings clear. Her desire to help him, and to ease her loneliness, had led to misunderstandings and dismay, to confusions lasting years. Yet when she thought of him now, buried in the Catholic cemetery of his home town, she felt resigned. The country he had loved seemed set on some twisted course that, for all she knew, could entangle the rest of Europe. Dead Rudolf had at least been true to his beliefs. What she chose to remember of him was not any marginal deceit or unacknowledged self-interest, but his high spirits and his spontaneous kindness to a fifteen-year-old girl.

Two days after the funeral, she took the train for Vienna.

5

Anton Heideck was sitting in his apartment, smoking a cigar and staring out of the window with his boots up on the desk, when he received a telephone call from the editor of the magazine for which he had written his article about the Schloss Seeblick.

'We've had a good response,' said the editor. 'I know we're not your natural home, so we're grateful for the trouble you took. I hope you thought it came out all right?'

'Yes. Thank you. I liked the photographs. And the little inset of the Schiele painting.' He coughed. 'I'm afraid I got a bit carried away with the Freud stuff.'

'No, you made it very clear. And he needed to be in it. He's our own local man, after all.'

'You didn't think I was too rude?'

'We'll have letters, but we don't mind that. And you acknowledged his influence, at least. And his later work.'

'I'm sorry there was no room for a picture of the maids. Johanna and Lena. They rather embodied the spirit of the place.'

'Yes. Now could I interest you in another piece for us, Herr Heideck? It would mean travelling to Germany. There's a political rally due to take place in a medieval town called Nuremberg. Have you heard of it?'

'Oh, yes. I've heard of it. I almost deserted there once. There was a little blue-painted skiff ...'

'It's a lovely place, I've heard. Worth a visit.'

'Yes, it's charming. Pastel-painted houses. A swift river. The Pegnitz. It eventually joins the sea in Amsterdam ... So I was told.'

'So, would you—'

'I'm afraid I have other projects. A book, perhaps.'

'Perhaps you'd let me know if you're free again one day.'

'I will.'

For lunch, Anton went to the restaurant Delphine had mentioned in one of her letters to Panama ... *That place at the top of Schottengasse that you like, with boiled beef and horseradish and the spinach purée with so much nutmeg and salt. It made me think of you when you wolf it down.*

He drank some Grüner Veltliner to take the edge off the salt, then walked up to the Café Landtmann, which served the strongest black coffee he knew, with a tall glass of iced water and a side plate that held a few squares of chocolate with splinters of roasted almond inside.

As he walked home, he thought of Charlotte's words to him in the snow. 'You will be all right.' There had been so much conviction in her voice, so much warmth and womanly wisdom, that he had almost believed her.

Nearly two months had passed since the party and he had stopped feeling embarrassed about how drunk he had become. He had apologised to Martha and she had assured him that no one had noticed. His dancing had helped put everyone in the mood, she said, and after that ... He'd vanished. He didn't tell her he had invited her sister up to his room. There was no need to complicate the matter.

It can't have been a simple misjudgement or a fear of being bored that had made him drink so much. There was something else. Someone had told him something that had wounded him, made him self-destructive in his desire to erase the knowledge of it. An absence, a departure.

He bought an evening paper from a news-stand. In Bruck an der Mur, in Styria, near his birthplace, the metal workers had taken over the town and were fighting Government forces.

As he let himself into his apartment building, he saw a letter for him on the hall table, written in a hand unknown to him.

He took it upstairs and opened it in his sitting room. The address of the Schloss had been crossed out and replaced by that of a street not far from the Imperial Hotel.

Dear Anton

This is Lena, the girl at the Schloss, the one with the drawings, the one who chose your shirts for you. I'm writing because I have something to tell you.

You know me from before. Can't you remember?

When you came here to do your article I recognised you at once. I don't want to describe how we met because I feel ashamed.

What I remember is the white scar on your back, on your ribs, and how you found it difficult to breathe. The thing is what I want to say is that I am in love with you. It's hard for someone like me to know exactly what these words mean but I know what I feel.

To begin with when you came I was just scared that you'd tell on me and I would lose my job. I liked working here but I had so many secrets about what I'd done before, and if Fräulein M found out she would get rid of me.

But I know different now because I've talked to her and she says she understands. In any case I don't feel so bad now about what I was and what I did.

When we were in the clothes shop and I heard you talk to the man about the shirts and I knew your heart was not in it – it was somewhere else. I know how to find your heart because mine is lost too.

347

The time we met before was on the top floor of an old hotel and there were candles round the room because I was shy and that's all I can tell you to remind you. I want to hold you in my arms and stroke the scar on your back.

You can reply to me if you want but you don't have to. It doesn't matter because I will always love you anyway.

From Lena

At the bottom of the envelope was a small package wrapped in tissue paper. Inside was a long, pearl-headed hat pin.

Lena walked up from the station and let herself into Rudolf's apartment. She dropped her suitcase on the floor.

Anton must have had the letter for a few days now. She should ask the porter if there had been any callers.

She would be all right in any case. She was not the girl who had first come to Vienna; she knew how to survive. Presumably she would have to leave the apartment when Rudolf's affairs were sorted out and the lease was sold. Until then, she had her own room. She was not afraid of what might happen to her. She preferred not to revisit the past because it felt like giving up on the future, but Martha had made it plain that she would be welcome at the Schloss Seeblick; and perhaps if she trained as a nurse, it would seem less of a backward step.

There was a ring at the doorbell. The only visitor that Rudolf had ever had was Niklas. Perhaps it was the caretaker come to take away the rubbish – or a lawyer from Rudolf's family telling her to pack up and leave. She heard her own footsteps on the parquet of the hall and the clank of the bolt as she pulled open the front door. It was Anton, holding a small bunch of freesia, mixed with lily of the valley, wrapped in newspaper.

They stood, looking at each other.

'Not a good time of year for flowers,' Anton said at last.

Lena stepped back to let him in. They stood in the hallway, neither willing to move.

'I've been coming every day since I had your letter,' said Anton. 'More than once a day. I telephoned the Schloss. I've been frantic. Shall I put these on the table here?'

Lena nodded.

'Can I?' He gestured the taking off of his coat and Lena nodded again. He threw it on a chair.

He smiled at her. Lena held his gaze.

Eventually, he spoke. 'You are Lena.'

She unfroze a little. 'I am.'

'What is your second name?'

'My father's surname was Fontana.'

'Italian?'

'On his father's side. His mother was from Villach.'

'Then you are not Delphine Jacob.'

'No.'

'You are Lena Fontana.'

'I am.'

'And, Lena, I love you.'

She swayed a little where she stood and he ran the short distance between them to catch her, as though she were dying.

He took her hand and held it between his. 'I love you for what you are. And all that you are. And nothing else. I admire you and love you from the bottom of my soul.'

Lena looked down at the floor.

Dry-eyed, she said, 'Will you let me love you, too?'

'If you're sure.'

'I am. But are you ready to let me hold you and stroke that scar each night until it disappears?'

'The scar?'

'Some butcher in a field hospital.'

'Yes.' He swallowed. 'Yes, if you want to.'

She reached out and gripped his arm. 'You can't hold on to it. It's not a part of who you are. Not any more.'

'I think I can do that,' said Anton.

'And,' said Lena, 'you have to have my whole ... exploding heart. That moment I heard you in the shop ... Pretending to be interested in shirts ...' She began to laugh. 'You have to take all of what I'm ... what I'm giving you.'

Anton breathed in, trying not to cough. Moments of his life's denial flickered through his mind. The dead fly on the windowsill in Baden, Friedrich's white thigh bones, the papered-over windows of the schoolroom ... Madame Caillaux fainting in the witness box ... The snow swirling through the open gates.

'Yes. I'll let you do all those things.' He had to cough. 'And I will change. I will become a man who's worthy of you.'

'But you already are.'

He held her in both arms and squeezed her against his chest.

Lena pushed him away so she could see his eyes. 'And I want a child. You must have children, Anton. It's your duty.'

'Someone else said that once.'

'And do you want to?'

'We can have a child, Lena. More than one if you like. Poor things ...'

She took him by the hand and led him into the main room, where she sat down and he stood in front of the fireplace, testing how long he could be apart from her.

'Thank you for the letter,' he said.

'I tried to tell you before. At the Schloss. But you wouldn't listen.'

'There was something I was reading when you came to tell me. It took all my attention. I couldn't take in what you were saying.'

'Well, you'll have to listen now, won't you?' said Lena.

'I know.'

'And the letter you were reading then?'

'It's finished,' said Anton. 'It's a closed book at last.'

Giving in, he went and sat beside her on the sofa. 'Will you come and live with me?' he said. 'My apartment's not as big as this, but we can get rid of some of the books.'

'I'll come today.'

'There's a second bedroom which—'

'No, I need to be in your room.'

'I'll help you carry your things.'

'I only have two bags,' Lena said. 'And tomorrow I'll go and find some work. Frau Haas said there might be something in her shop.'

Anton stood up again and walked over to the window. He looked down the street towards the Belvedere Gardens, where a group of armed policemen was moving purposefully along the pavement. He felt Lena's hand on his sleeve and her lips against his ear.

'Will we be together now?' she said. 'Even after death?'

'I ... believe so.'

'You do know I'm just a little girl from the wrong side of the bridge.'

'I do. And I know that you are more than that as well.'

'And if it turns out that it was all a joke?' said Lena. 'The whole thing of being alive at all. There was no love that lasted, no life afterwards ... And I die in a back ward of Emil Kraepelin, not even knowing my own name ... Or I lose you to a gun ...'

'Then Amen.'

Acknowledgements

In 1935, the Japanese novelist Yasunari Kawabata wrote a novel called 雪国, or *Yukiguni*. An English translation by Edward Seidensticker appeared in 1956 as *Snow Country*. I acknowledge the inspiration of this translated title, and the book itself, with gratitude. Kawabata received the Nobel Prize in 1968 and died in 1972.

My thanks to the Civitella Ranieri Foundation (https://civitella.org/), in whose retreat in Italy this book was started in October 2018.

The Slaughter Man

ALSO BY TONY PARSONS
FROM CLIPPER LARGE PRINT

The Murder Bag